PROFESSOR MARTENS' DEPARTURE

PROFESSOR MARTENS' DEPARTURE

Jaan Kross

Translated by Anselm Hollo

THE NEW PRESS

Published in the United States by The New Press, New York
Distributed by W. W. Norton & Company, Inc.,
500 Fifth Avenue, New York, NY 10110

Published in the United Kingdom in 1994 by Harvill, an imprint of
HarperCollins Publishers, London. Originally published in Estonia
as *Professor Martensi Ärasõit* by Eesti Raamat, Tallinn, Estonia, in 1984.

ISBN 1-56584-111-5
LC 93-83812

Established in 1990 as a major alternative to the large, commercial
publishing houses, The New Press is the first full-scale nonprofit
American book publisher outside of the university presses. The
Press is operated editorially in the public interest, rather than
for private gain; it is committed to publishing in innovative ways
works of educational, cultural, and community value that, despite
their intellectual merits, might not normally be "commercially"
viable. The New Press's editorial offices are located at the City
University of New York.

Printed in the United States of America.
94 95 96 97   9 8 7 6 5 4 3 2 1

Publisher's Note

In this English translation from the Estonian
original, the translator has also taken account of the
Finnish and French versions of this work.

As the author studiedly leaves a number of words
and phrases in the language in which they were
originally recorded in the narrative, the reader will
find English translations, keyed to the relevant
page number, along with a few other notes, at the
back of the book.

1

It is a lovely Sunday morning in June, with a fresh and gentle northwesterly breeze blowing from the river and the sea. The sky is as blue as I used to imagine it was in Madeira when I read my brother August's letters from there. If the weather we are having here in Pärnu extends northeast, across land and sea, and all the way to the Strait of Björkö, then those two – Nicholas and Wilhelm – have picked an ideal day for their momentous meeting. At least as far as the weather's concerned.

I stop by the gate, and turn to look back at my pretty little house in its fresh coat of yellow paint. The windows, blinds drawn, reflect the morning sun that shines on the dewy and well-trimmed lawn in front of them. I really don't feel like going anywhere, especially since I don't even know when I'll be able to return. Probably not before the end of August. Of course, over there with Kati, in the pine woods of Sestroretsk – beyond St Petersburg, with its din, and dust, and coal-stench, and forty new cholera victims every day – things will be just as nice as here . . . Strange, how people try to improve things by simply insisting that they are, or will be, better than they really are. I am guilty of that myself; no doubt about it. One might say that it is a professional habit of mine . . . Not in this case, though. But I remember how at my retirement celebration at the university, last year, I had some difficulty keeping a straight face when that pleasant young Taube said to me that I would now be able to – how did he put it – to spend more time at my "enviable estate in Livonia". I have never owned an "estate" in my life. True, there was Villa Waldensee near Volmar, but it was no estate, merely a summer residence, and I signed it over to my son Nikolai the year before last, so that he could have a place of his own. All I have now is this yellow house. But a Privy Councillor without an *estate* is, of course, unthinkable. Taube could not imagine that this is all I own: a thousand square fathoms of apple trees and pines on the outskirts of tiny Pärnu, and those seven rooms plus a porch. It was my father's house. He bought it after he lost his position as parish clerk at Audru and moved to Pärnu to eke out a livelihood as a tailor. After he died, the house was sold twice, and it fell into a state of disrepair. Until I bought it back – when was it? Ages ago. Thirty years . . . After I had taken my first trips abroad, and had some funds. Kati's dowry, to begin with. So I bought it, and had it restored, and built an addition to it.

Gartenstrasse 10.

The address is still the same.

I lock the garden gate and pocket the key. Kati disapproves of keys in my pockets. She says they pull my suits out of shape, especially lightweight summer suits like this one made out of natural silk. I don't give a damn. I don't wear this suit to audiences with emperors or kings. It's exactly the right thing for a trip from Gartenstrasse to Sestroretsk.

I pocket the key and get going. I have made all the arrangements with Kaarel who will use the rear gate when he comes to cut the grass, water the flowers, and pick up the fallen apples, if I don't get back before then.

I start walking down vacant Gartenstrasse in the dappled sunlight. Last night, Kaarel wanted to order a hackney coach, but I told him that was quite unnecessary for these few hundred paces to the railway station. I'm travelling light, as always.

"But – Your Excellency, what about your ratchets –?"

"Rackets, my dear man. My tennis rackets. When have you ever seen me lugging those around? I have another set in St Petersburg, and a third one at Sestroretsk. All I'm taking is my briefcase. So, no coach tomorrow."

And that's all I'm carrying now. Nightclothes, a toothbrush, a cake of soap. A couple of books. Yes, books. Including that particular one, damn it to hell. But the briefcase is really quite light.

I am walking briskly, not in that circumspect shuffle people in these parts tend to expect from sixty-four-year-old Privy Councillors. More in the style I've admired in younger gentlemen in Western Europe: not showing off, but still – considering my years – with the light and bouncy step of a seasoned tennis player. Long-legged, determined, fast-paced strides. The way my Aunt Krööt told me my father used to walk. The way my mother probably moved when she

8

walked out to the well and back with a full laundry tub balanced on her hip, the beater in her other hand, and me toddling at her heels. I assume that her legs were similar to mine, long and straight; my memories are none too clear – I had lost both her and my father by the time I was nine. In the same epidemic – Asian cholera, I was told. Miraculously enough, the four of us survived: August, Ludvig, Heinrich and me. August and Ludvig weren't even affected by the disease; Heinrich and I were, but by the grace of God we recovered. Those weeks or months are nothing but a grey, flickering blur in my memory. But I do remember Aunt Krööt telling me later, when she sent Heinrich to apprentice with a shoemaker, and took me to St Petersburg, that Heinrich was so slow and simple because of the illness we had when we were young. It had made Heinrich apathetic, but I, she said, even in the throes of that fever, had kept trying to get up to run off somewhere. So it was family lore that my perennial restlessness dated from that time . . . Last year I was told by Doctor Fischer, the Empress's private physician, that my sudden onset of cardiac arrhythmia may also be an after-effect of that illness, compounded by the intervening years of strain and stress in my life. So much for one's imperturbable façade . . .

At first, those sudden palpitations – they're over now, thank God – felt so ominous that I decided to resign from all my teaching duties at the University, at the Alexander Lycée, and at the Imperial Academy of Law. I heard that Nicky hadn't wanted to accept my resignation until he received assurances that I would still retain my seat in the collegium of the Ministry of Foreign Affairs. I found it hard to believe that His Imperial Chicken Brain even remembered my existence . . .

Before I know it, I've reached the intersection with Alexanderstrasse and the corner bakery, its door wide open under the golden pretzel sign. In this weather, one can smell the freshly baked rolls from ten fathoms away. And here comes Mrs Christiansen, stepping out of the bakery door: a pretty, youthful, slender woman, dressed all in white down to her ankles, the most accomplished tennis player among the ladies of Pärnu – closely followed by her husband, that paunchy overdressed fortyish dolt, the managing director of the Waldhof cellulose factory and its three thousand employees. After my nephew Johannes, Heinrich's firstborn, had

9

refused the assistance I had offered him, he had been one of those three thousand for a while.

I raise my light yellow Panama (four francs at the market in Brussels, the year before last), and the lady nods and smiles, and her spouse, behind her, returns my greeting by raising his own light-grey velour (fifty francs at Putor's in Paris, two months ago).

"Oh, Fyodor Fyodorovich – how nice to see you, although I know you're leaving us," says Mrs Maria, and her husband gives me a white-toothed grin. To his wife he says:

"But Mary, my dear, at such a time – with the emperors meeting, and all – *of course* the Privy Councillor *has to* go to the capital! Perhaps even to *join* their majesties. I'm surprised he isn't there already –"

"Oh no, no, my trip has nothing to do with that," I reply, and look at them in a calm and friendly manner, the way I have always looked at everybody, at least I hope so – at wise persons and fools, at the mighty and the weak, at friend and foe. Yesterday I spent all afternoon playing tennis with Mr Christiansen, his lady watching us, and beat him 6–4, 6–3. Later last night I could feel the exertion. But the distinct heartache I felt was not only physical; true, I had been the winner, in the presence of his wife (good Lord, what a vain old man), but that still hadn't seemed quite enough (obviously, I don't ever come up to my own expectations) . . . So now I say, with an amiable smile and a glance at the rounded corners of Mr Christiansen's grey waistcoat:

"*Quelle noblesse* – yours is the first weskit I've seen here in Pärnu that is *tout à fait à la* Edward VII!" But I don't go on to tell him the history of that particular touch of fashion. The day before yesterday I told Mrs Mary that King Edward was an incredible fop: when he noticed that his massive stomach caused traditionally cut waistcoat corners to stick out, he told his tailor to cut and round them off, so that the garment would conform to the curve of his portly figure. That, I had told her, was the origin of the waistcoat à la Edward VII – prudently refraining from adding that I, of course, had no *need* to camouflage my own midriff in this manner. Hence, I am sure that pretty Mrs Mary will understand the drift of my remark – without, I fervently hope, considering it malicious. Well, she smiles with a touch of embarrassment, blushes, glances at her husband who stands there all aglow with what he perceives as flattery; then she looks down at the pavement. I doff my four-franc Panama and kiss the back of the lady's narrow hand, inhaling its lavender scent. Then I exchange a hurried handshake with the gentleman. His grip is firm and sweaty.

"*Alors, mes amis* – Happy midsummer! And till we meet again! When? Oh, I'm afraid not before the end of August. But that'll give us plenty of time for a few more games. Just don't forget to practise in the meantime."

With a sense of regret I look deeply into Mrs Mary's sparkling brown eyes and feel a little embarrassed by the intensity of my own gaze (it is, after all, a pointless game). I grant her husband a final smile of forgiveness and continue my walk to the station, thinking: *why* did I have to humiliate that portly and energetic business man? Was it because of Mrs Mary's youth and charm, or her wit, which is perhaps rather superficial but nevertheless seems wasted on her husband? Or was it because of himself, his paunch, his self-importance? Or, perhaps, because of Johannes? Because of the winter mornings Johannes had spent in the draughty sawmill shed wielding a blowtorch to thaw out the frozen spark plug of the old Wiegand engine, to make the machine explode into life and the transmission belts hum . . . Johannes had told me, here at Gartenstrasse 10, standing in front of my desk in a greatcoat stained by machine oil, his narrow face vehement and flushed: "Uncle Fyodor, sir, we don't need any handouts from Privy Councillors!" With that, he had turned on his heel and left. So, was it because of him? Or because of the humiliation I had felt when he turned his back to me? Or – was it because Mr Christiansen had – only yesterday – pointed out a certain book to me . . . ?

I enter the brownish station building that always seems to be either freshly painted or covered in soot. The waiting room is far from crowded, only six or seven people stand in line by the ticket window with their baskets or plywood suitcases bought at Luther's shop. Third-class passengers. At this time of the year, very few people travel from here to Valga. Stationmaster Huik, jovial, short-legged and barrel-shaped in his white summer uniform, a red cap on his head, notices me immediately and comes waddling diagonally across the black and white tiles.

"*Mayo pachtiénye!*" He stops right next to me. "The Privy

11

Councillor wishes to travel? To Valga and St Petersburg? Just a moment, please."

Oozing eagerness to serve, he pilots me to the ticket window and personally pushes aside three or four people in order to honk at a pimply face behind the grille:

"For the Privy Councillor – to St Petersburg via Valga – *one ticket, first class!*"

Here comes my ticket. I pay, smile apologetically at the people in line, and motion them to return to the window. Had Huik's high-handed behaviour been merely obsequious, I would have prevented him from shoving those folks aside; but his eagerness to serve me is also based on genuine respect for a *self-made man*. That is how he sees me (and himself – after all, he is now the stationmaster). Both our fathers were humble servants of the church . . .

Huik stays by my side:

"Your Excellency's train leaves in ten minutes. Would Your Excellency like some refreshment at the buffet –?"

He tries to steer me to the door of the station restaurant.

"No, no thanks. But I would like to send a telegram."

"Ah, just a moment."

He is already at the door of the telegraph office. He swings it open and announces:

"The Privy Councillor wishes to send a telegram!"

The spindly telegraph operator springs to his feet. Among the passengers from St Petersburg, who come here for a few days at the beach, there surely are some who command considerably greater respect than some old Privy Councillor, but they don't very often appear in person at the telegraph office, and even if they did, the stationmaster would not announce them with such fanfare.

I use a corner of the desk to write my message. I can tell that the stationmaster is reading it over my shoulder:

Yekaterina Nikolayevna Martens
Care of Senator Thur
Sestroretsk, Government of St Petersburg
Arrive Baltic Station on the eighth at eleven a.m.
   Kisses
Fred

I pass it to the operator who adds up the words, five kopecks a word, and I add them up, too, and ask myself a number of unanswerable questions: five kopecks for the word *Senator* . . . Why did I write *Care of Senator Thur*? Out of old habit? I haven't been including that in the address for quite a while – my father-in-law passed away a long time ago. Or did I write it to remind the stationmaster standing behind my shoulder of something he knows anyway – the exalted circles to which I have ascended . . . ? If so, I have to admit that it was rather silly.

I pay for the telegram. The stationmaster wants to escort me to the train.

"One moment, Mr Huik. Let me get the papers."

He escorts me to the newspaper stand. The most recent papers I can find are yesterday's *Revaler Beobachter* and *Päevaleht*; then there is a *Novoye Vremya* of the day before yesterday, and a week-old London *Times*. I buy the lot.

The stationmaster follows me to the platform, ready to escort me all the way to my seat.

"Thank you, Mr Huik. This is fine." The platform is practically vacant. In typical country-folk fashion, the other passengers have already taken their seats and are now watching us through the carriage windows. To rid myself of my recent twinge of embarrassment, I shake hands with the stationmaster.

"I thank you for taking such good care of me, Mr Huik. Goodbye."

"*Rad staratsa*, Privy Councillor!" He snaps to attention, clicks his boot-heels with pitiful enthusiasm. "I wish you success . . . in your great . . . in the affairs of state" – his ruddy face is dewy with delight at his own eloquence – "and I wish you a happy return . . . to our dear town of Pärnu!"

2

Now that he's gone, I can turn my back to the little train for a moment. Face the sun, close my eyes, and listen.

Behind me, a couple of travellers are approaching their third-class carriage at such a fast clip that they're out of breath:

"Come on, Jaak, hurry up –"

"Stop fussing, Liisu – what's the rush! Look at that gentleman, he's still out here, enjoying the sunshine . . ."

A hackney coach drives past the station, rubber tyres bouncing over the cobblestones, and with the wind that smells of tarred railway sleepers comes the sound of rustling aspen leaves from the small park in front of the station.

I am amazed at the attraction this little backwater has for me. I've been coming here every year, if only for a short visit, ever since I bought the house back. The first years, I would take the train to Tartu, then proceed to Pärnu by mailcoach – that trip took two and a half days, which was a bore, and yet . . . Later on, I could take the train to Valga, then the old coach again, but the last ten summers or so, it has been this little choo-choo. Yet every single time I arrive here I feel a weight lifting off my shoulders – right here, as soon as I step out of the station. And when I walk through the gate at Gartenstrasse, with or without Kati, I feel completely – well, almost completely untrammelled, as if I had returned to the carefree days of early childhood. A silly sentiment, of course . . . Leaving here, I have always felt exactly the opposite.

I open my eyes, and at that moment stationmaster Huik comes through the glass doors in his red cap and white summer garb and strides onto the platform, holding the semaphore stick with the round disc that is white on one side, red on the other. He has come to send off my train in person, a thing he does on rare occasions to honour his most distinguished passengers. I turn and get on the train.

Ding-ding-ding-ding: under the awning above the platform, Huik himself rings the departure bell for the third time. In the narrow corridor inside the carriage the sound strikes me as excessively loud and makes me wince.

So this is our proud first-class carriage, a fairly recent addition to the others pulled by the hissing and puffing locomotive. It is just as tacky as those of the second and third class: five tiny compartments, and the seats are so narrow that none but a very short person could stretch out on them. Nevertheless, the light-brown wood is varnished, and the seats are upholstered in mauve plush, and there are mirror-backed lanterns in every compartment. The flat, angular tops of the lanterns remind me of the headgear I was given when I received my honorary doctorate at Cambridge . . . I smile at the thought. This little carriage tries, in its cheap, crude, tasteless, and intensely obvious way, to compete with the tall, pretentious coaches and ministerial automobiles in which I've been driven through the streets of the world's capitals . . .

All five compartments are empty, and I pick the one in the middle for the smoothest ride. As soon as I sit down, the train starts with a jerk, and the ochre station building with its dark-brown trim starts sliding past. Then comes a stretch of platform, and a couple of people who happen to be standing there, then pear-shaped Mr Huik in his white summer uniform. His ruddy face and bushy whiskers under the red cap. Then, a long stretch of yellow board fence, with nettles growing out of the gravel down below.

We crawl past low buildings and the trees in the park, blow puffs of coal smoke into the treetops, and rumble on alongside the Riga road, spreading soot over the red tile roofs. We approach the river: on the left, beyond the sparse buildings, sheds, and fences on the outskirts of town, it flashes into view, an expanse of water glittering in the morning sun, a quarter of a verst wide. I stare at the dazzling blue-grey stretch of river extending all the way across to Rääma until I have to close my eyes. They feel gritty from lack of sleep. I dozed off at four in the morning, even then only thanks to sleeping pills, and my fatigue is now animating my imagination in an abnormal way that I recognize with a start – as I always do, when *it* starts happening . . .

What happens is that something I'm looking at suddenly changes into something else, something usually quite similar yet different;

around that perception, the whole world suddenly changes, both temporally and spatially. I have described the phenomenon as a *turn* executed by the world, a turn of eighty-nine degrees – and years . . . Thus, the river, whose dazzle just forced me to close my eyes, is no longer the Pärnu river . . . And the boy – glimpsed standing there with his fishing rod, in the reeds by the water's edge – he is not I – or rather, he *is* I, of course he is, but *another* I, by *another* river . . . I'm not sure whether it is the Elbe or the Alster or the Bille, whichever one it was, there at Hamburg's Sand Gate Harbour . . .

Where, on a narrow old-town street (for Heaven's sake, am I simply making all this up?), in an old, proud, mildly pretentious building belonging to a lawyer (no, I am not making this up, so help me God), I was born, eighty-nine years before my own birth. In 1756 . . . I was born, I existed, I grew up to be a man: I, Friedrich Martens. *Georg* Friedrich, that time around. And as I roamed round that city, I feasted my eyes – even before I was old enough to go to the *lycée* – on the ships, faces, languages and flags gathered at the piers of the harbour. From the *lycée* I went on, with my father's blessing (but I have to strain to remember his face: it was thin, somewhat sallow, dignified, grey-browed, and always sombre – very much, in fact, like my father Friedrich's, as I remember or imagine him, long, long ago in the sacristy of Audru Church), to Georgia Augusta University at Göttingen, to study and to find out, in 1776, *exactly how* all those languages, ships, flags, and nations participated in the great game of the world . . . Since no one in the German-speaking countries had been able to create more than a dim over-view of that game, I had my research cut out for me. And so, when I rediscovered those ships and languages and flags, or at least some of them, eighty-nine years later in the river harbour at Pärnu, it was all revived within me – at first, quite unconsciously . . .

A jolt, and my eyes open wide – ah, yes, I see: I am Friedrich Martens, professor emeritus, Privy Councillor for life, attached to the Ministry of Foreign Affairs of the Russian Empire, born eighty-nine years after the birth of the first Friedrich Martens imprinted on my memory – and we are making a three-minute stop at Waldhof station.

The massive long buildings, and smokestacks, and water towers over on the right, behind a screen of grey willows and a cluster of one-storey houses, are the Waldhof factories. Yes, we stopped here back when . . .

It was less than four years ago. Our strenuous chess game with the Japanese had lasted a whole month, over there in faraway New Hampshire where Roosevelt had summoned us, almost peremptorily. On the twenty-third of August, we signed the Portsmouth peace treaty. More precisely, Witte and Rosen signed it for our side, Komura and Takahira for theirs. Three weeks later we arrived back in St Petersburg, via New York and Cherbourg. We had been playing with the black pieces, and it had been a game we were predestined to lose; and yet, we had managed to turn it into what amounted to a draw. That is to say, Witte knew all along what he wanted: no war reparations to Japan. Not a single warship that had fled to neutral ports. No territorial concessions, or if push came to shove, half of Sakhalin Island. In his bull-headed way, Witte stood firm on those conditions, but he did not have the faintest idea how to reach them, how to justify them, what precedents to apply, and how to formulate those precedents. It was up to me to act as his crammer and prompter every night as we sat in his hotel room and analysed the day's progress. Sergei Yuliyevich was so egocentric that he avoided taking me along to the actual negotiations whenever he could – even though he had no idea what his next move should be . . . Japan had won the war, in a scandalously total manner, and was, of course, bent on gaining maximal advantage from it. If there was anything that could restrain Japan in that desire, it was Japan's other ambition: to be recognized as an equal, as a full-fledged member of the international community of nations. Our only hope lay in exploiting that ambition and using it to persuade and dazzle Komura and his delegation. We had to impress on them that they were inexperienced in diplomacy; that they could easily lose their way in the maze of European and American foreign policy; that they had not been trained in these traditions. That the only international treaty they had negotiated, the Simonoseki agreement, was still only a half-civilized effort – between them and the Chinese. But that Russia *could* make them, by means of this peace treaty, her own equal among civilized nations – as long as they showed themselves to be flexible and trustworthy.

17

Although it took Witte quite a while to understand this strategy – the way it took him quite a while to understand anything at all – he managed to implement it, in his own ham-fisted way, and we wrestled the Japanese to a draw. When we returned, St Petersburg, *official* St Petersburg, gave us a splendid welcome; it seemed as if the Portsmouth Treaty had not sealed Russia's defeat, but had allowed her to emerge victorious. Witte was not slow to put himself into the limelight of all the acclaim – just what one would expect from a man with a banker's conscience and an engine driver's intelligence . . . Unofficial St Petersburg was a very different place, in early October 1905. The Liberals were more vociferous than ever before, and so were the Black Hundred. Mobs began to storm and ransack arsenals . . . But that was none of my business. It was Witte's job to deal with it, now that the Emperor had made him a count and appointed him Chairman of the Council of Ministers. It was his task to compose the October Manifesto.

As soon as all the audiences and debriefings and official visits were over, I left the city for a short vacation in Pärnu. I don't remember the exact date, but I know that the trains were not yet affected by the strike, at least not all of them, and we were able to make our way to Tartu and on to Valga. On our journey, Kati kept fretting that we had made the wrong decision; she felt that it might have been safer to stay in St Petersburg, where the authorities would surely uphold law and order – while in the more rebellious provinces, the Baltic lands, anything might happen . . . I remember a group of students – some, I assumed, from the university, others from the veterinary school – patrolling the rainy platform at Tartu station. They wore red carnations on their lapels. They told us classes had been suspended a long time ago, and the lecture halls were now used for day-long political meetings. This did not surprise us; similar things were happening in St Petersburg. Nevertheless, it increased Kati's anxiety, and I remember keeping my arm round her still-so-girlish waist all the way from Tartu to Valga, in the privacy of our first-class compartment. We watched muddy fields, grey buildings, dark spruce forests and yellow shrubs slide past the wet compartment window, and I remember murmuring into Kati's ear – it smelled of eau de Cologne – : "Believe me, darling, I know my Estonians better than anybody. They're the most law-abiding and least threatening people on earth. Now, in St Petersburg, among those Russians, you never can tell what might happen in times like these. But not among my Estonians . . ."

At Valga, we changed to the same little train in which I'm sitting right now. At Möisaküla, after dark, the train made a longer stop than the schedule warranted, and we were told that a political meeting was about to begin at the train depot. Nevertheless, after a half-hour delay, we were allowed to proceed to Pärnu. But at this very station – Waldhof – our journey came to a halt. When we arrived here around midnight, forty or fifty men surrounded the train. Forty or fifty strikers, rebels, freedom fighters, tramps, hooligans – call them what you will. They drove the train onto a siding and let the steam out of the engine. Then a few of them walked through the train and announced that the personnel had joined the strike. This train was not going anywhere. The "citizen travellers" – they made a point of calling us that – would have to walk the remaining three versts to Pärnu.

The man who came to inform us of this was holding a lantern, and in its light I recognized him. Since I was sitting in a corner of the dark compartment, he did not recognize me at first. I squeezed Kati's fingers and said:

"If that is the case, the revolutionary gentlemen will have to help us procure a hackney coach for our baggage. Or will the revolutionary gentlemen themselves help us carry our suitcases to Pärnu? Either way – who among you can make a decision in this matter? Or is it you, Johannes, who decides?"

I thought I saw the lantern tremble a little in his hand.

Then my nephew, the worker from Waldhof's sawmill, raised the lantern up to our faces.

"Oh, it's you, Uncle . . . And you, Mrs Martens . . ."

I said, not maliciously but nevertheless as ironically as the situation seemed to warrant:

"That's right. Well, you must have read about it in the papers: we've made peace. We have done what your party has been demanding so loudly and so long. Now I'm on my way home, all the way from America, where we signed that treaty. And this is how you welcome me back? I think that's a little odd – don't you?"

The boy had regained his composure. I thought of him as "the boy", but he was twenty-five years old at the time. If, indeed, the cholera epidemic of our childhood had affected Heinrich's mind, there certainly was nothing wrong with the wits of his son. Johannes said, matching my irony word for word:

"Well, I'm sure that a man as wise as I've been told you are can see that if a whole trainload of people manages to solve this problem, you, too, will be able to work out what to do. Good luck."

"Thank you. I'll go and look for a hackney."

"No hackneys here, in the middle of the night. Even if there was one, we wouldn't let him take you."

"Goodness me. Why not?"

"He would have to join the strike."

"I see . . . But what if I can produce a certificate that says I have a weak heart and *need* a hackney coach?"

Back then, I had no such problems at all. I merely wanted to trip him up on his own naïve logic. But the damned boy just stood there in the doorway of the compartment, his pink lantern shining on his pale face with its small blond moustache, and smiled:

"We couldn't make any allowance for that. What if the government came up with a certificate – oh, it could have done so a long time ago! – a certificate saying that *it* suffers from atrophy of the brain – and then used *that* as an excuse to ask the people to stop their revolution?"

I was dumbfounded. I laughed. I, the old fox of conferences at Brussels, The Hague, Berne, and so forth – the cleverest of them all – was at a loss for words . . . Not for long, of course. No more than five seconds or so. But that was long enough for the boy to say "Goodbye" and slam the compartment door shut behind him.

"*Qu'est-ce qu'il t'a dit? Qu'est-ce qu'il t'a dit?*" Kati kept asking me in the dark, taking hold of my hand and pulling me towards her.

In thirty years, she hasn't managed to learn enough Estonian to understand what Johannes said. Oh, I've teased her about that: "Listen, Kati, you're not even a Russian! You're a tad Russian, a tad French, a tad German, probably even a tad Jewish . . . You're not the daughter of a Pobedonostsev, you are Catherine de Thur! One would expect some tolerance from you, even towards the unimportant languages . . . If, indeed, you consider your husband's native tongue unimportant." Nonetheless, she has never managed to study it, and I have never *seriously* insisted that she do so. If the truth be told, I myself regard that language – no, not as something to be despised, but – well, I never have had time to really consider that question. And so, Kati kept saying:

"*Fred, je te demande: qu'est-ce qu'il t'a dit, ton neveu?*"

I translated and explained it to her, with a cruel precision that left a bitter almond taste on my tongue.

I explained to her that there was no hackney coach to be found here at this time of the night, and that even if there were one, they wouldn't let him take us to Pärnu, but would compel him to join the strike. Even if I showed them a certificate that said I had a weak heart and needed a ride, they wouldn't consider it.

"*Mais pourquoi?*"

"Because, if that were possible, then the government – the imperial government – could have given them, the people, a certificate, a long time ago, that said it was suffering from atrophy of the brain. And if they accepted *that*, then they would have to stop their revolution."

Kati laughed like little silver bells. I could feel her black tresses tickling my cheek.

"*C'est ça, ce qu'il t'a dit? Les révolutionnaires estoniens est-ce qu'ils ont tous tant d'esprit?*"

"Hardly," I said. "They're not all Martenses."

And Kati laughed again. To this day, she has no command of Estonian, although she does have an instinct for small impertinent jokes – she can hear them coming . . .

How did we get to Pärnu? It wasn't hard at all. Right there, near Waldhof station, I found a house whose inhabitants had been woken up by the stopping train and the rushing noise of the escaping steam, and a man sold me his garden wheelbarrow for two roubles. Apart from a few manure stains it was a perfectly good wheelbarrow. I put the bright yellow leather suitcases I had bought in New York into the wheelbarrow and pushed it all the way to town, walking along and chatting with Kati. It took us an hour to get to Gartenstrasse. But the horrors of the autumn of that notorious year, 1905, and of the months to come – they still lay ahead of us, then.

21

3

We're on our way again.

Choo-choo – choo-choo . . . That word *"choukhna"* – it would be interesting to know its derivation. *Choo-choo-choo* – slowly, awkwardly, comically in its self-importance, the train proceeds through the pine barrens between Waldhof and Surju.

It really is a lovely Sunday morning with a clear blue sky. The seventh of June, 1909. Today, the Emperors are meeting in the Viipuri archipelago. With the same pomp, on their royal yachts, and in the same place where they met four years ago, while I was in America with Witte. Right next to the same island of Koivisto (or Björkö) where Willy bullied Nicky into signing a treaty that would have turned the whole world upside down if Witte, upon his return, hadn't managed to bully Nicky into rescinding it . . . In the cabin of the *Standart*, in private, Willy presented to Nicky the prepared text he had written out in French in his own hand: *Leurs Majestés les Empereurs de toutes les Russies et d'Allemagne, afin d'assurer le maintien de la paix en Europe, ont arrêté les Articles suivants d'un Traité d'Alliance défensif* . . . To the effect that Germany and Russia would enter into a defensive alliance and agree to defend each other with all their might if any third party attacked either one. Our autocratic Emperor must have had an orgasm at the thought that his formidable kinsman was suddenly taking him seriously . . . In any case, our imperial chicken-brain had completely overlooked the fact that the "third party" Wilhelm had in mind was, of course, France; that from the German point of view, such a treaty could only serve as an alliance against France. The only problem was that Russia had entered into precisely such an alliance with France, twelve years prior to that time (the foundation of the balance of power in all of Europe!), in which the third party was, of course, Germany . . . Nicky forgot all about that and stupidly signed the thing. Rumour had it that he even shed a tear on Wilhelm's whiskers. Afterwards, the ministers were obliged to deliver long lectures in order to get his signature nullified.

Is he about to commit a similar blunder today?

But, no – if there is a touch of malice in that question, it is not because they haven't deigned to invite me to this meeting. No, thank God for that – and besides, I'm sure no slight has been intended. In our dealings with the Germans, we avail ourselves of the services of other persons. For a long time, my duties have been restricted only to the most general affairs, except for our relations with France, and recently, our relations with England.

Choo-choo – choo-choo – choo-choo.

Typically, the press has proclaimed this meeting of Emperors a purely private affair. Merely a cordial visit between kinsmen sans any political significance. That is what they always say, and it is always a lie. Almost always; there may be a few very rare exceptions. Let us hope that today is one of them.

I have no difficulty conjuring up images of that meeting. Blue water, pink rocky shores. Dark spruce forests, light-green birch trees. Two white vessels outlined against the hills of the island, the *Hohenzollern* and the *Standart*, no more than half a verst apart. In the foreground, out to sea, two imperial escort cruisers, theirs and ours. Further away, sheltered by the island, our watchful gunboats: if any outsider approaches those yachts, he'll be in trouble . . . But they'll have to take care not to open fire on some stray merchant ship – as they did the time Rozhdestvenski, crossing the North Sea on his way to Tsushima, turned his guns on English fishing boats, mistaking them for Japanese mine vessels . . . What a feast that was for the world press: see – you can't trust Russian officers with guns! The Russian government paid England sixty-five thousand pounds sterling in reparations. And now the cruisers fire their salutes – nothing like the thunder of cannons to celebrate peace . . . Then the *Standart* lowers a white motor launch and a rope ladder, and Nicky, decked out in his striped sash and his decorations, descends the swaying and clanking ladder into the launch and putt-putts across half a verst of blue water in the mild summer breeze. Then he is alongside the *Hohenzollern* and ascends another swaying ladder, after which the shiny German brass explodes into blares and drumbeats as they play "*Bozhe Tsarya khranii*" so loud their

23

eyes bulge, immediately followed by *"Heil Dir im Siegerkranz"* . . .
Here and there, on the nearby vessels and on the *Hohenzollern*, on
the various decks, bridges, and turrets, men frozen into rigid lines
roar "One – two – hurrah – hurrah – hurrah!" Then the Emperors
approach one another: one, a forty-year-old milksop with a pointy
beard, the other a cunning, slightly mad, goggle-eyed fifty-year-old
buffoon with upside-down whiskers and an arm and a half . . . The
Emperors step forward – Willy is wearing a striped sash similar to
Nicky's; indeed, in order to show that he is "one of us", he is wearing
the uniform of the Viipuri regiment named after him. The Emperors
step forward, embrace and kiss each other three times . . . How many
kinds of kisses are there again? Kisses of greeting, kisses of peace
(*osculus paci*, if I remember correctly), kisses of holy vows, kisses of
fidelity, Judas kisses, uxorious kisses . . . Funny, isn't it, but I don't
have to worry about that any more: international law does not concern
itself with the classification of kisses.

According to protocol, a visit like this should last exactly thirty
minutes. Review of the honour guard. Introductions of entourage
and officers. After twenty-nine minutes, Nicky returns to his launch.
Both Emperors are no wiser than before. The launch departs to the
thunderous strains of the band. Ten minutes later, Wilhelm gets
into his launch and rides over to the *Standart* where they go through
the same rigmarole; this time, however, it lasts forty minutes. At
one o'clock, which seems like a long way off, luncheon is served on
the *Standart* to the Emperors, Empresses, ministers, and a few
generals and admirals. Nothing noteworthy happens. Each Emperor
delivers a three-minute speech in French for the benefit of the
world press: "Our old wisdom . . . our fraternal love . . . our eternal
desire for peace." After that, absolutely nothing. The company
settles down to cold lobster and champagne. If anything has happened at all, it has happened during the hour or half-hour *before*
the luncheon while the Emperors retired to Nicky's cabin: that is
the only time when something *might* occur . . . You can never tell
what Willy might come up with, and the only thing that's certain
about Nicky is that he never knows what he is doing. Most probably,
though, Wilhelm remembers the fiasco of his previous Koivisto
scheme . . . As far as our side's concerned, we don't need to take
any kind of initiative. All we need is the fact that Wilhelm has come

to visit – please, God, no more, no less. We do need that, in order to make him understand what we are telling him: "Dear cousin, now the whole world sees that we do not only invite the King of England (who visited us last year in Tallinn), or the President of France (who came to Tallinn a little later), but that we have also invited you, dear friend, you who are our kinsman just like that paunchy Edward. But of course the two of us, being *emperors*, really are the *closest* kin, in terms of our souls, or our fate, or who cares what else . . ." Or something along those lines, because such noncommittal compliments to Wilhelm are precisely what we need to exhibit at this point. Let's see what Menshikov says in *Novoye Vremya* – I pick up the paper from the stack on top of my briefcase and read:

> . . . *A great event* . . . *Historical moment* . . . (It always is, isn't it.) . . . *Possibly decisive for an improvement in inter-national relations* . . . *Subterranean rumblings have been heard for a long time* . . . *Where will the next eruption take place* . . . ?
> . . . *In any case, it will be far from Russia. Probably at sea, between England and Germany. Is it not a fact that England is presently engaged in the heaviest rearmament effort?* (England is the scapegoat we are offering up to Wilhelm.) . . . *Russia must sustain its strict neutrality in the case of an Anglo-German conflict* . . . *Why would Germany want to go to war against Russia? Only Russia's enemies in Germany are talking about such a possibility. Would Emperor Wilhelm even consider it? Not at all. If that were his desire, why did he not launch an attack on us four years ago, when our forces were tied up in the East? He is a chivalrous man* . . . (True, Wilhelm loves to play the blameless knight, but Mr Menshikov ought to watch his own logic a little more closely: since our forces are no longer tied up in the East, Wilhelm shouldn't feel the least bit restrained by his sense of chivalry. But you can't expect Menshikov to notice such things; he simply babbles on.) *That neutral stance assumed by the German Emperor marked one of the most glorious pages of German history, because that neutrality was not only just, it was also benevolent – more*

benevolent, in any case, than the neutrality exercised by France . . .

So much for that. It is mere empty blather, and Wilhelm's visit really has no substantive significance. Whereas Edward's visit to Tallinn, last year, in which I had the honour to participate to some degree . . .

Now we're clattering across a bridge over the Reiu river, a blue ribbon of water between sandy, gravelly, rocky banks. Among the reeds on the bank to my right, the township's red cattle have gathered to drink from the river. A cowherd, wearing a coarse shirt and a battered grey hat, raises his face with its grey stubbly beard to the sun and yawns – in the same spot, exactly the same spot, where those cattle were watered fifty-three years ago. And that is Peeter Pustuski: I remember him. Fifty-three years ago, he was one of the two boys helping the township's cowherd; they were paid one rouble for the whole summer. It was their job to use their switches to chase frisky calves back to the herd. So – he must have stayed on, after his companion was sent off to the orphans' school in St Petersburg . . .

I have a vivid and detailed memory of Edward VII's visit to Tallinn.

Public opinion in England is very different from German public opinion. I won't even consider our own – although, since 1905, we have witnessed some incredible things in terms of the public expression of ideas . . . But it was public opinion in England that came close to aborting Edward's visit to Tallinn, even though Izvolski, Benckendorff, and myself had made careful preparations for it in London. As soon as news of the planned visit became public knowledge (London is utterly irresponsible in that respect – any political move becomes instant news), the left wing of the Labour party made an issue of it – in a vociferous, ridiculous, and ultimately dangerous manner. O'Grady demanded that Parliament cut Grey's – the Foreign Secretary's – salary by a hundred pounds a year, because his foreign policy had led to such improprieties as the King's visit to Tallinn . . . That, of course, was a Labour joke at the Liberals' expense; but what that former Scottish fisherman with aspirations to international statesmanship, I mean Mr MacDonald, wrote in his *Labour Leader* – that had to be taken quite seriously. I remember it fairly well: *Does our country really intend to put up with this insult, with the King's trip to Russia? Where hundreds of people are being executed every single day? And the sand dunes behind the city of Riga are reddened by the blood of the very best, the blood of freedom fighters, the blood of martyrs for a sacred cause? While the prisons of Russia are crowded with people whose only guilt lies in their love for their friends and for freedom* . . . (As a member of the collegium of the Ministry of Foreign Affairs, one is permitted to read the *Labour Leader*.) I also read that Summerbell had questioned Grey in Parliament about Russia's political sentences, punishments, and banishments to Siberia, but Grey had refused to answer (he did not have much choice in the matter) on the grounds that such a question smacked of interference in Russia's internal affairs . . . In his paper, MacDonald called upon Labour Party members to organize nationwide protest meetings to adopt resolutions condemning the King's visit to Tallinn. I don't know how many such meetings were held, probably quite a few, but not enough to make a difference. The *common sense* of the English – or was it something like the German *Staatsräson?* – prevailed, which is to say that the will of the lobbies that proved most decisive in the matter, the Vickerses and Armstrongs, the industrialists and shipping company owners, prevailed, and Edward was able to go to Tallinn.

In anticipation of his visit, our newspapers wrote: *The event that will take place in the roads of Tallinn will further strengthen peace in Europe . . . The monarchs, connected by kinship, will reaffirm that bond and put an end to the discord of centuries . . . What only recently seemed impossible to realize, will now achieve definite forms: England and Russia may now relate to Tibet, Afghanistan, and Persia in a peaceful manner, no longer dissipating their strength in political delusions* . . . This was a reference to the treaties signed by Russia and England in 1907 regarding their spheres of interest in Asia; treaties I had authored, for the most part . . . *Birzhevoye Vedomosti* wrote, I remember it verbatim: *The Anglo-Russian Treaty* (the one signed at Tallinn) *marks the beginning of a new chapter* (journalists like these "new chapters" – but once in a while they're right) *in the history of peaceful competition between civilized nations* . . .

27

On the morning of May twenty-seventh, the imperial train brought Nicky, the Empress, their children, and their retinue to Tallinn. At the Baltic Station, they immediately changed trains and proceeded to the harbour. From there, they strode past ministers, governors, a guard of honour, and neat rows of schoolchildren to a launch that took them out to the *Standart*.

I witnessed the imperial family's arrival, or at least some of it, from a considerable distance. I stood on the port-side deck of the cruiser *Almaz*, a hundred and fifty fathoms from the *Standart* in the direction of Pirita, in the company of Stolypin, our new Prime Minister. He was observing the scene through binoculars. I had not brought mine, nor did I think to ask to borrow his. He, for his part, only remembered to offer them to me after the imperial personages had already disappeared into the forward saloon. By the way: I don't believe that the nation can expect anything positive from a prime minister of his ilk, a man whom even Witte has called a "Junker of the Bayonet" – never mind how far-reaching his agricultural reform plan may look . . .

Ten minutes later, Stolypin ran a comb through his short black moustache and took a launch over to the *Standart* in order to be on board before the King's arrival. Izvolski and the others were already there. He did not deign to invite me to come along . . . But that was simply business as usual, and in the course of years and decades, I had become used to it. Nevertheless, I can't say I have quite managed to rid myself of resentment – over the fact that if you're not the bastard son of a grand duke, or a duke yourself, or a millionaire, or some charlatan people believe to be a miracle worker – if you are merely the world's best specialist in your field, you're still a nobody in this Russian Empire of ours. Less than nobody. But they do need me. Well, I have no childish illusions about that. Once I slough this mortal coil, Russian diplomacy will go on without me, if a little more carelessly, slowly, and in a less civilized fashion than today. However, there is some truth to my sense of indispensability, because all they know, at best, is what they *want*: mostly they have only a dim notion of what that is, and set out to grope for it in the dark. They lack the ability to express their desires in a way and in a language found acceptable and under-stood by the rest of the world without tripping themselves up or

28

arousing suspicion in their counterparts. I have found it astonishing, for many decades, how *incredibly* helpless they really are when called upon to express their political objectives in an adequate fashion. They regard that skill, the skill to give verbal expression to goals for which both sides are striving, as a secondary matter – the way amateur musicians tend to regard their scores as secondary; it is the same contempt with which this empire generally treats any genuine expertise. I've been told that even Witte (once in a while such remarks reach my ears) has expressed his deep amazement over the fact that "such a limited person" as myself has received an incredible amount of acclaim as an authority in his field . . . I know he considers me particularly "limited" because of those treaties with England we signed in 1907. In Witte's opinion, we gave away Persia. He believes that because of those treaties, whose main designer I was, Persia is slipping out of our grasp and into the sphere of influence of England and perhaps even Germany . . . To which I say that it may indeed slip away – but then I ask Mr Witte and his followers: Tell me, would it be better to hang on to our hegemony in Persia and then confront Germany, Austria, and Italy without an ally? Or is it better to relinquish that influence now, since one can't do much else, and then face a war, let us say, ten years hence, against the countries of that Triple Alliance with England and France on our side? Tell me, which do you prefer? For my part, I can't conceive of a third possibility. As we were standing there waiting for Edward's arrival, I felt convinced that he had come to visit us only because we had managed to create those treaties.

At nine o'clock, our ship and the coastal batteries west of Tallinn started firing their salutes. At half-past nine, the *Victoria and Albert* sailed into the roads, escorted by two cruisers and four mine vessels.

After the deafening homage to peace faded away, the imperial couple took their launch to the king's ship where they were greeted with anthems, fanfares, and further salutes. Half an hour later, they brought the king and queen back to the *Standart* to a similarly clamorous reception. Then, I believe, the king returned to the *Victoria and Albert* to receive a steamer-load of representatives of the local nobility, and the urban, and (yes, amazingly enough) even the rural population. Whatever the case may have been with the nobility's and perhaps even the city's delegations, it was obvious that the rural delegation had been thoroughly vetted by Governor Korostovets' underlings. An hour later, all the representatives of the people returned to their own vessel and steamed over to visit the *Standart*. After which the Englishmen took their launch to the *Standart* and settled down to luncheon: *Potages Pierre le Grand et Marie Louise, Petits pâtés, Sterlet au champagne, Chevreuil grand veneur*, and so on.

After hosts and guests had washed down their *Glace à la Parisienne* with coffee and spent a moment digesting their food, two large motor launches left the *Standart* and came alongside the *Almaz*, bringing Stolypin, Izvolski, and the English party to the ship.

Since I had not been invited to be present at their reception, I made no haste to greet them. While they discussed matters in Stolypin's cabin, I sat in the stateroom reserved for my use and looked through the open porthole at the Kadriorg shore. I had borrowed a pair of binoculars from the Second Mate, and now I observed how people – or ants, depending upon whether I used the binoculars or not – were planting scores of tall poles – or little sticks the size of pine needles – into the ground beside the seaside promenade. Barrels (or little smidgens) of tar were fastened to the tops of the poles or sticks, and these would be lit at dusk to create a festive atmosphere for the monarchs . . . Then there was a knock on the door: the Chairman of the Council of Ministers was summoning me.

I stepped into Stolypin's cabin, which was, in fact, the officers' mess. Around a baize-covered table with stacks of papers sat Stolypin, Izvolski, and two Englishmen. The former, of course, remained seated, but the latter rose and greeted me almost exuberantly: "*Dear me* – my dear Professor Martens, you've been on board and haven't come to our aid? And we've been labouring here for over an hour!" This was Sir Charles Hardinge, former ambassador to St Petersburg, and then as now assistant secretary of state under Grey. A tall redhead, the type that plays golf with great precision. A little too slow for me at tennis, as I had found out on several occasions. Now I hear he will soon ascend to the throne of viceroy of India. The other man was the head of Grey's department of Eastern affairs, Sir Arthur Nicolson, a lively fellow with a black moustache – also a former ambassador to St Petersburg. I had become better acquainted with him during the preparations for our treaty on Persia.

I remember how Stolypin, with his bald yellowish pate and dark eyebrows, watched us morosely and impassively, his usual attitude when he isn't resorting to his notorious theatrical gestures. Izvolski greeted me with a slack and weary smile. He must have known already (I didn't) that intrigues were afoot against him, that he would have to leave his ministerial post – and not for London, his city of choice, but for Paris, which he considered second-rate. He told me later that it was he who had suggested to Stolypin to ask me to join the negotiations – instead of merely sending the text they had produced to my stateroom, for me to provide the finishing touches . . . It was also Izvolski who defused the Englishmen's excessive flattery by some well-turned phrase: in Stolypin's presence, their respect and friendliness could have proved damaging to me. Not that it wasn't understandable. After all – well, I don't know if Stolypin was aware of this (if he was, it did not endear me to him), but Izvolski certainly knew, as did the Englishmen: I had been a candidate for the Nobel Prize . . . (As embarrassing as it is to think about it, but in 1902 I had come *even* closer to receiving it than, let us say, Tolstoy.) And so, Izvolski ameliorated the effect of the Englishmen's exceeding politeness towards me with considerable skill, and I sat down with them. In half an hour, we arrived at a final version of the monarchs' agreement, with a couple of emendations I made to render it more precise, initially in French, according to custom, and then in mutually approved Russian and English translations. The text was brief and dealt in generalities, the way such agreements always do. In order to make it sound a little more concrete, the monarchs had included a subject unlikely to upset any third party: their shared positive attitude towards the development of Turkey. I won't bother to remember it in any further detail, the Tallinn Agreement between the Emperor of Russia and the King of England, signed on the twenty-seventh of May, 1908; it can or certainly will be found in any history book. In the more detailed ones, it will be called the true beginning of the Entente Cordiale.

Back at my porthole, I saw how the ants ashore at Kadriorg lit their festive torches in the gathering dusk. I remember that I was trying to see it as a bittersweet Watteau scene, but against the clear

31

vernal evening sky, the reddish flames and black smoke of the tar barrels looked rather ominous. I could not help being reminded of an oppressive painting of Rome burning, by some Polish painter whose name I cannot recall, but in whose St Petersburg atelier I had seen it, a dozen or so years earlier. Old Köler had insisted that I go with him to view it. Feeling curiously perturbed, I closed the porthole and went on deck to see what was going on in the roads.

The evening banquet for the monarchs, ministers, and military and naval dignitaries (the English party also included General French and Admiral Fisher) was held on the Empress Dowager's pleasure yacht, the *Polyarnaya Zvezda*. When I reached the deck of the *Almaz*, three small steamers had just left the port, wreathing the violet sky above the towers of the city with black smoke and heading for the *Polyarnaya Zvezda*. After a few minutes, they dropped anchor, a quarter of a cable length from the yacht. Then the concert began. The *Polyarnaya Zvezda* and the vessels ranged next to it stood a cable length from the bows of the *Almaz*. "God Save the King" followed by "*Bozhe Tsarya*", sung by choirs on all three steamers, rang out across the calm purplish-grey water. By the way: to my reasonably musical ear, those anthems have always sounded ridiculously similar . . . Searchlights from surrounding vessels were trained onto the Empress Dowager's yacht, lighting up the gunwale decorated with gilded ropes. Fresh from their banquet, a large group of ants appeared at the rail. Through the binoculars I was able to recognize Nicky, in his scarlet British uniform, and Edward, in a Russian cavalry uniform with white braids. They were surrounded by ladies and gentlemen whose identities I was unable to establish.

A gentleman who had appeared beside me at the rail explained to me that the steamboat to the right belonged to a Russian choir, the *Gusli*, which was active in Tallinn under the auspices of the Russian Club and the direction of a Mr Diakonov. The one in the middle carried the German *Männergesangverein* and *Liedertafel*, conducted by Mr Türnpu, and the one to the left was an Estonian choir whose conductors, so my informant told me, were Mr Topman and Mr Bergmann. However, the anthems were sung in unison by all the choirs, conducted by Mr Türnpu, which was why that gentleman was standing on top of the roof of the German boat's compass-bridge, starkly illuminated by searchlights. After the anthems and subsequent imperial and royal applause, Russians, Germans and Estonians sang three more songs each, in their respective languages. In my ignorance, I did not recognize the first two Estonian songs, but it seemed to me that the third one was Miina Hermann's "*Tuljak*". The stranger next to me at the rail said: "Very moving, this trilingual concert – don't you think? They planned it this way, so King Edward can hear for himself how *untrue* all that Socialist talk is – about the oppression of the Baltic peoples. Just listen to them: all of them have the right – in the presence of the Emperor himself – to praise their emperor and their fatherland *in their own language*."

I remember turning my head and looking at the man. There were no searchlights trained on us; in the half-dark, I made out the face of a sturdy forty-year-old fellow adorned by a brown moustache and framed by the brim of a black bowler and a black overcoat collar turned up against the cold. It was a perfectly nondescript face. I thought: he is either an official of the Estonian government who has managed to get himself invited aboard to witness this ceremony, and is now affecting this stupid loyalty to the Russian crown – or else he *is* stupidly loyal, which may well be the safest position these days, as long as one doesn't mind laying oneself open to ridicule. Or, a third possibility: he's one of Stolypin's spies and wants to find out what I think of his master.

He turned his calm round face towards me and returned my gaze with steady grey eyes. I realized, with a physical sense of shock, that his thoughts were exactly the same as mine: "Some civil servant of the empire – who knows what department? Or else one of Stolypin's snoopers. In either case, I better watch my tongue." He didn't say anything, but it suddenly seemed to me that there was – in his face, and type, and in the Russian sentences he had just uttered – something indefinably strange: that is to say, something *familiar* . . . So I asked him, in Estonian:

"Do you happen to know the names of the Estonian choirs?"

He stared at me for a moment. Then he replied, without the least trace of surprise in his voice:

"*Estonia. And Hope.*"

33

4

Those peoples and languages, flags and nations were present and waiting for me in my innermost consciousness long before I encountered them in the river harbour at Pärnu. Because I had seen them all, and many more, eighty-nine years before that time, in the harbours along the Elbe. And the dark, blue-green pine forest of Vaskrääma gliding past my compartment window – it isn't a forest at all, no, it is the blue-green water of the Elbe, its waves drawn with a child's eye . . . And a boy, seven years old, in a neat tunic and clean trousers, descends the steps from the pier to play with a toy ship that flies the red flag of Hamburg . . .

Somewhere behind his back – yes, indeed: *Gartenstrasse Nummer neun* (I have not made this up, dear God – it *was* there – it *is*), a tall yellow building whose narrow stuccoed front faces the street . . . For some reason, the windows on the top floor are oval . . . possibly a French influence . . . I *have* seen that building. I was born in it. Not literally, not with these eyes. When I went abroad on my first mission, I travelled first to Hamburg (where else? it was where I was born eighty-nine years ago), and found that all the buildings behind the former Sand Gate were quite new. In 1842, a great fire devastated the city, including the house where I was born, and at the time of my visit, a very different building stood in its place. But in antiquarian bookshops I found old engravings to refresh my memory . . . Gripped by the same obsession, I went from Hamburg to Göttingen, and there too I found traces of my previous life, or the life *before* my previous life.

There, near the foot of the hill they call something like Barrow Hill, I had once roomed in a pleasant pink house by the bank of the river Leine. By the time I got there and looked for it in 1869, as *Friedrich* Martens, it too was gone . . . Up under the black slate roof, a student's garret, rented from the widow of a justice of the Land Court . . . My father, the Hamburg attorney Jakob Nikolaus Martens, must have known that judge in his professional life. In the autumn of 1776, I moved into the chirpy widow's garret room that smelled of saffron; I was twenty years old . . . Or have I been making this up? But I can clearly, very clearly remember the lectures on constitutional law given by the venerable Professor Pütter . . . And the professor himself: the small, reddish, pimply nose, the watery eyes, the curly wig, the slightly wrinkled frilly shirt front, the slightly soiled cuffs – for God's sake, I can't have made all that up! Why would I have done that? After all, Pütter regarded me as one of his favourite students, perhaps even the best . . . Later, everybody said that Pütter had exercised a particularly strong influence on the direction Martens' scholarship was to take, even though Martens must have brought his keen interest in international law with him, from his background in Hamburg. In any case, one of Pütter's favourite students . . .

But what was I *really* like, then? Probably the same as later, with some slight differences. Most probably a touch inferior from a moral standpoint – just so that the present incarnation could prove himself a touch superior . . . Even by birth, a much more polished and fluent version than the present son of Pärnu and St Petersburg. More superficial, it seems, but also more energetic, daring, enterprising, even while pretending to be modest, as was the fashion a hundred years ago. A merry student nevertheless, whose mastery of the minuet was, at first, much greater than his mastery of the pen. Popular, of course, in social gatherings in professorial homes and among fellow students. Obviously gregarious – yet, to an attentive observer, curiously – what is the expression – *unbeteiligt*. An outsider, and understandably so, because back then he was born in the latter half of February, a Pisces. Not at all like the clumsy lion cub who appeared in August, eighty-nine years later . . . So, *unbeteiligt*. I'm still not sure whether that was to my advantage or to my detriment. To my advantage, perhaps, if my outsider's stance arose out of an inner desire to attain the serious goals I hadn't yet discovered for myself. To my detriment, if it only underscored a coolly egotistical ambition in the game of success . . . (As if that game were so utterly alien to me in my present life –!) In any case, an agile, alert, peppery young man who seemed to make friends with just about everybody who was anybody, including the Poets' Circle at Göttingen – Boie, Hölty, the Counts von Stolberg, and so

35

on, whoever else was then still in town. They were my dear friends, even though all they did was labour over their verses, a pursuit I considered frivolous; even though they revered Klopstock, for whom I did not care; and even though they detested the spirit of France and its language, the language in which I was soon to deliver my first lectures . . . Well, my studies took a while, because, as I've said, I was a rather superficial young fellow and even had to rewrite my doctoral dissertation (in 1778) before it was accepted. My present incarnation has not been subjected to such humiliations.

Then I became a professor of international law at St Petersburg – no, no, Göttingen, in 1784, at the age of twenty-eight, and not long after I was appointed to tutor the princes of Hanover in constitutional law. But in between those tutorials, lectures, diplomatic assignments, dinners, and dances I managed to write a book that made me famous: *Précis du droit des gens moderne de l'Europe.* After that, I invented a task for myself that would immortalize my name: my *Recueil des Traités*, of which seven volumes would appear in my lifetime. Later volumes were compiled by my cousin Karl, and under the aegis of Geffken and others, the work is being continued to this day. It is a compendium of the world's most important international treaties from 1761 onward. The *Précis* gained me the reputation of having laid the foundation for the theory of the positivist school of international law; the *Recueil* made me the greatest systematizer of the same school's practice . . . Thus, it is no wonder that I was still a subject of study in law schools fifty years after my death. And that I was to find out – again – about my previous existence . . .

In 1855, during the terrible January frosts of that year, I was sent off to St Petersburg. That is I – Friedrich Martens – little Priit . . . First I spent a week with my brother Julius who had already been working for two years as an apprentice in a pharmacy on Moika Street. Unable to keep me for very long in his tiny lodgings, he enrolled me in the paupers' boarding school at St Peter's Church. It was an old, dank, permanently cold stone building painted institutional blue, between Malaya Konyushennaya and Shvedskaya, behind the church. I had been there a little less than two months, among a hundred St Petersburg orphans of the Lutheran faith, when the church bells suddenly rang out, and we were herded into the church for a service, then back to the school for a memorial assembly: Czar Nicholas I had died . . . This led to two events that had a decisive influence on my later life. The first was an assignment given to us by Inspector Zeiger: every child was told to compose a poem to mourn the Emperor's death. Inspector Zeiger was a lively, prematurely bald, ruddy-faced man; his brother owned a clothes shop, and his uncle was a general. In the hallways of the school, I had often seen the brother who paid frequent visits to the Inspector. I had never set eyes on the general who was the Emperor's personal physician, Doctor Mandt.

So, the assignment was a poem on the death of Nicholas I. I don't know if it was Mr Zeiger's lack of experience as a pedagogue or his desire to curry favour with the authorities that led him to give us this task; surely, he could not have expected noteworthy results from the likes of us. True, the assignment was mainly addressed to older, thirteen- or fourteen-year-old students. Nevertheless, then as ever, I felt compelled to have a go at it. I know that I am not the only one who has noticed this eagerness in me, which my adversaries have interpreted as excessive vanity, while my admirers have seen it as a highly developed sense of duty. Not for me to say which group is right . . . Frankly, that was a hypocritical remark. To be honest – of course I believe that my admirers are right. But in order to be considered a magnanimous person who sees all sides of every question, I will say this: there are times when the former, and other times when the latter, are correct in their opinion. To seem even wiser, I may add that I do, of course, believe the latter are right more often than the former . . . Oh, what a silly game with mirrors this ends up being, like that of a child trying to catch a reflection of sunlight scudding across a wall. To get on with my story: ten years old, I settled down to the task of composing a poem on the death of the Czar. The language of instruction in our school was German, of which I had acquired a good command on the street-corners of Pärnu, both from the surrounding air and in two years at Mr Krüger's German elementary school. Following my father around, I'd had ample opportunity to study both Estonian and German hymnals and had some idea of meter and rhyme. The eulogies I had just heard gave me sufficient inspiration, and the first stanza flowed from my pen with an ease that surprised even myself:

Wir, Waisen, hier im stillen Hafen,
Wir wissen doch nicht, was uns wird,
Da Gott uns nahm, den armen Schafen,
Den, der uns Vater war und Hirt.

The first line of the next stanza was no problem at all – I borrowed it from our principal's eulogy:

Dank dem illustren Herrscherhause

But then I was stuck, hopelessly stuck, for three days. I was still stuck when Zeiger asked us to show our results to him. Most of the students hadn't managed to write a word; a couple of boys had produced a certain amount of text, but Mr Zeiger didn't spend much time on them. After glancing at my lines, he looked straight at me through his glinting spectacles:

"Martens, did you write this *yourself?*"

"Yes, sir."

"Ahem. Come and see me at the end of the day."

He pocketed my unfinished poem, and when classes were over for the day, I walked down the corridor past our dormitory rooms and knocked on his door.

"*Herein!*"

I entered. Mr Zeiger stood firmly planted on his feet in the middle of the room. I had the impression that he had been pacing back and forth on the braided rug, arms crossed over his chest, holding a goose quill with a steel nib. My poem lay on the desk.

"Well, then. So – you wrote this yourself?"

"Yes, sir."

"Do you have it memorized?"

I rattled off my five lines.

"Uh-huh. Do you know what this means: *Le roi est mort, vive le roi?*"

"The king is dead, long live the king."

"Ah, you know that? What a clever little beetle you are . . . Well. What a pity there's no rhyme for *roi* in German."

The solution came to me in a flash. I said:

"Well, sir, we couldn't very well use *roi* anyway. What if we said *Der Zar ist tot, es leb' der Zar –*"

"Listen –"

He looked at me with an expression of surprise that soon became misty and remote. "That's it!" He handed me the quill. "Sit down at the desk and write." He dictated the rest of the poem to me.

Dank dem illustren Herrscherhause
Sind wir doch aller Sorgen bar
Und können rufen ohne Pause:
  Der Zar ist tot, es leb' der Zar!

At the next morning's assembly in the school auditorium, Mr Zeiger made yet another speech on the Emperor's death. He used the same themes that had already been expressed in our collaborative poem. He spoke about us poor little orphans who had found a safe haven here at the orphans' school. About our natural grief upon losing our beloved fathers and shepherds. About how our most illustrious dynasty helped us overcome that grief by giving us a new emperor. It strains credulity, but after ruddy-faced Mr Zeiger was done with the dear shepherd idea, he went on to say that our late emperor had been the great model for all of Europe's rulers, and as his voice cracked with emotion, two or three small glistening drops rolled, quickly and as it were furtively, out from under his round spectacles and down his rosy cheeks . . . I remember thinking that it looked as if his spectacles had just produced puppies. But then he declared that I, little Friedrich Martens, *tertianus*, had written a beautiful and laudable poem about all this, and he invited me to come up and read it to the whole school.

It was my first public performance. I was no more nervous than I would be later, at least until I turned forty and finally lost my stage fright. But I was no less nervous, either. My mouth felt dry, my voice sounded hoarse, and I had to force myself to retain my composure in front of a hundred childish faces that became simply a blur, but I don't think this was more noticeable to others, that first time, than it was later at all the conferences in Brussels and The Hague and Geneva.

Standing on a small podium below a portrait of the late Czar in his white uniform, I recited the poem. The portrait, not yet replaced by one of Alexander II, had been garlanded with black crêpe paper. Zeiger brought the morning prayers to a close, beckoned me over, sent the other children to their classrooms, and said to me:

"Martens – until now, the *tertiani* have taken turns to bring me my teapot from the kitchen every night at seven o'clock. They've taken turns, and they haven't been paid. From now on, this will be your task. Every day, at seven sharp. I'll even pay you. Twenty kopecks a month."

Inevitably, my promotion to this job also earned me envy and ill-will; at the time, I didn't know how inevitable that was. At first, I wasn't aware of the expressions it took. But I don't want to dwell on childish envy. My second crucial memory of that time concerns something far more adult and frightening. (And it is interesting that it still bothers me enough to make me feel like reviewing it.)

I had been bringing Zeiger his tea every night for a couple of weeks. I was supposed to carry the teapot to his room and place it on a tray next to the cups on a small table behind a tall bookcase, and Zeiger, who would be sitting in his armchair next to the window, would always make some small-talk or comment on the books that lay on the table beside the tea tray:

"Take a look at that. It's an interesting book. *Gulliver's Travels* – you should read it."

I set the teapot down on the tray and picked up the book. Its pages were amazingly light, thick, and white.

"I can't read English . . ."

"You'll learn, you will," Zeiger said, beaming benignly. I turned the pages of the book and found some surprising, finely drawn, fantastic pictures: dwarves, and humans, and giants, fettered and unfettered . . . Well, I don't think that my sense of the universal relativity of things was born entirely in those moments behind Zeiger's bookcase – or at least, not only from those pictures in *Gulliver* . . .

Then, one evening, it must have been April, I appeared once again at Zeiger's door with his piping hot teapot at exactly seven o'clock. I knocked, but he did not ask me to come in. I didn't relish the thought of having to carry the teapot all the way back to the kitchen, up and down stairs and down long corridors. I tried the door. It was open. I entered and closed the door behind me. I walked around the bookcase, put the teapot on the table, and noticed that *Gulliver's Travels* which hadn't been there the day before, nor the day before that, but probably next to its owner's bed on the floor, had been returned to the table. I opened the book and studied a picture to find out how those Lilliputians had managed to tie Gulliver down . . . At that moment, Zeiger and his brother came in. I couldn't see them from behind the bookcase, but I recognized their footsteps and the sound of their breathing. I stood there and suddenly felt a little frightened. I know that I should have stepped out from my corner, apologized, explained that I had brought the tea, and so on. In my childish awkwardness, I hesitated, but not out of curiosity, not expecting to hear something unexpected . . .

The two men walked past the bookcase and sat down in their armchairs.

"So, what is it you want to tell me?" Zeiger's brother asked.

"Did you see Uncle Michael before he went to Germany?"

"No, I didn't. He left so suddenly that I –"

Zeiger said, in a whisper:

"The Emperor did not die of a neural fever."

"Then what did he die of?"

"Poison," Zeiger whispered.

"What are you saying? Who would have given him poison . . . ?"

"Who else but . . . But I couldn't tell, from what he said to me, if he administered it himself, or if it was his colleague Doctor Karell who did it."

"Good God! You can't be serious?"

"And it wasn't a crime. It was done on the old man's orders! Do you understand? It was done *on the Emperor's own orders* . . ."

"But why on earth –?"

"Because he had steered the empire into the ditch that it's in now. And he didn't know how to get it back on the right track. His pride no longer allowed –"

"He did the right thing, by God. Yes, he did the right thing," Zeiger's brother said.

"But of course," Zeiger agreed. "He sent half a million men to their graves in the Crimea. Twice as many as all our enemies lost, put together. And what a brutal regime it was. And the economy in ruins . . ."

I don't remember what else they said. I just stood there – not because I was prudent, but because I was frightened and unable to comprehend what they were saying – for two, three, four minutes, without making a move or a sound. Then I tiptoed back to the door – they were sitting by the window and couldn't see me behind the bookcase – opened the door quietly, slipped into the hallway, and closed the door again as quietly as I was able. Then I rushed down the hall and into the toilet.

I don't know if they heard or didn't hear me leave. The following day the Inspector asked me:

"Martens, at what time did you bring me my tea last night?"

"At seven o'clock, sir."

"Why didn't you knock?"

"I did, sir. But you didn't hear me. You were conversing with your brother."

"Oh, I see . . . What were we talking about?"

"I didn't hear that, sir."

"What do you mean, you didn't hear? You have ears, don't you?"

"Well – if one doesn't listen, one does not hear, sir."

"I see . . ."

I stared at his spectacles as innocently as I knew how, but it seemed to me that he didn't believe me, that he was still suspicious. He did not demote me from my duties as the bringer of the teapot, but it seems to me now, looking back, that he began to be a little afraid of me. A year later, when he gave me his enthusiastic support in my efforts to get myself admitted to the *gymnasium*, he did it not only because he was convinced that I was good academic material, but also because he wanted to get rid of me as quickly as possible.

5

And so, I truly don't know what it really is, this window I've been gazing at for a while, with the green pine trees gliding past behind it . . . Is it still the window of this tiny train compartment? In which that still fairly spry old fellow, Privy Councillor Friedrich Fromhold Martens, is travelling from Pärnu to St Petersburg, urgently summoned to a consultation with the empire's Foreign Minister: they can't do without him – without Privy Councillor Friedrich von Martens, who will soon be sixty-four years old. Or is it a window in a horse-drawn carriage proceeding down a highway through the pine forests between Kassel and Frankfurt, eighty-nine years ago? Whatever all those villages were called, Ober- or Nieder-Ohmen . . . And in that carriage rides Court Councillor Georg Friedrich von Martens on his way to the Diet in Frankfurt where he has a seat on four or five different commissions, and they simply cannot do without him . . . The Court Councillor is still an amazingly agile and clear-headed fellow, even though he'll soon celebrate his sixty-fifth birthday.

And why shouldn't he be in a grouchy mood? Why, indeed, should he not be gloomy? Why should I not feel anxious?

God knows, it is true what I've been saying all my life: the princes of this world may be our well-disposed friends, but scholarship is our most benign mistress! Which is not to say that I've refrained, or been able to refrain, from giving the princes their due. Rumour has it that I have even been excessively eager to do so, and in regard to the wrong princes. But that's easy to say, now that the French have left, and there no longer is a king or kingdom of Westphalia, and I have returned, after many difficulties, to the service of good old Hanover; and yet, there are many who say (not to my face, of course not, but behind my back): Yes, yes, his *Recueil* and his *Précis* and so forth, and the services he rendered to the Congress of Vienna, those were fine achievements. But when the French had conquered these lands, who went to Paris to kowtow to Napoleon? *He* did.

Now, of course, he says it was the city council of Göttingen that told him to do so. No matter: did the council exercise such powers over him that he couldn't have sidestepped the order? And despite his hesitations and tergiversations, was he not, in his own mind, all too eager to hasten to the Emperor's court? He claims that he undertook the journey for the sake of the University of Göttingen, and that he gained the Emperor's protection for the university. But in addition to that, he also gained the Emperor's personal favour! Now, of course, he says that this favour was a very relative matter, very ephemeral, but that is what all opportunists say! All traitors! Because that's what he was. He gained such favour with Napoleon that our – that is to say, Westphalia's – King Jérôme, the Usurper's own brother, granted him countless audiences and even summoned him to the court at Kassel, where he appointed him to the Council of State of Westphalia: *Membre du Conseil supérieur de l'Etat de Congo* – but what am I saying? I think I'm confusing things . . .

A jolt, and I return to my senses, although I don't know for sure whether I'm still asleep or awake. I feel worse than before. We've stopped somewhere in the middle of the woods. There is a narrow station platform bordered by weeds. Queen Victoria (God, she's been dead for eight years) comes trundling down the platform with the heavy tread of an old matron, a grey shawl on her head and a small milk canister in her hand, and disappears from sight in the direction of the third-class carriages. So, here I am. We've stopped at Surju station and will continue our journey in a minute: but I have written what I have written, *and what I am*. No doubt about it. I won't recant one syllable. I – Frédéric de Martens, *Membre du Conseil supérieur de l'Etat de Congo*, appointed by Léopold II, King of Belgium, with the personal permission of Alexander III, Emperor of Russia. I won't take any of it back. The only thing I need to push away from me is this damned briefcase which the infernal jolting of the train has slowly, millimetre upon millimetre, moved right up against me so that it seems to interfere with my breathing. I push the briefcase aside, and with it, that miserable book I decided to bring: the Jefron-Brockhaus Encyclopedia, Supplementary Volume Number Two. No need to erase anything I've written, because it is true, every word of it. Everything I said about the matter. I remember every word of those two pages, as I remember almost all of the thousands I have written: two pages in my book *Vostotshnaya Voyna*, published in 1879:

By means of the circular issued from the Imperial Chancellery on the eleventh of April, and the Supreme Proclamation dated the twelfth of April, Russia solemnly declared war against the Ottoman Empire. The Russian Government found it necessary to issue a separate note, also dated April twelfth, to the Turkish chargé d'affaires in St Petersburg, Tevfik Bey, who was also told to leave the country. "As for Turkish subjects in Russia," the note continues, "those among them who wish to leave the country are free to do so, while those who prefer to remain may rest assured of the full protection of the law."

On the previous day, April eleventh, the Russian chargé d'affaires in Constantinople, Mr Nelidov, had on behalf of his government informed the Sublime Porte that, first of all, diplomatic relations between Russia and Turkey had been severed, and secondly, that the Consuls of Germany had agreed to protect the interests of Russian subjects in Turkey . . . That same day, Mr Nelidov and the entire staff of the Russian Embassy and Consulate left Constantinople.

In the light of all these exchanges, it appears truly incredible that the Turkish government decided to accuse Russia of opening hostilities without a declaration of war!

What changes would I make in this text? I would not change a word, even though it was written thirty years ago. Indeed, time only makes the truth more manifest. And I do not hesitate to say the same about the page that follows:

Considering the documentary evidence presented here, such an accusation is bound to seem completely nonsensical. Nevertheless, the Turkish government made it in a telegram dated the thirteenth (twenty-fifth) of April addressed to the Turkish representative in London. The proclamation given to Tevfik Bey in St Petersburg was declared "abnormal and contrary to customs always observed by civilized nations". "Guided by humanitarian sentiment" the Sublime Porte asked the Great

Powers to intervene, in accordance with Point Eight of the
Treaty of Paris of 1856, because Russia was allegedly "in viol-
ation of all its international obligations". Furthermore, the
Sultan personally complained to the aforementioned English
ambassador Liard that Russia had begun hostilities "without
previous declaration of war".

In regard to these pronouncements of the Turkish govern-
ment, it is hard to decide whether to marvel at their malici-
ousness or at their naïveté. In view of all the Russian
proclamations cited above, the Turkish government's accusa-
tions can only be seen as an utterly shameless calumny, one
that in itself demonstrates to what lengths Turkey went in the
last war to spread the most appalling fabrications in Europe
about Russia, and her honour, and the defenders of her rights.

No one could argue with the truthfulness of this passage, either –
especially when one considers that it was addressed to *informed*
readers, not to novice nuns who might interpret it as a claim for
Russia's boundless moral superiority over Turkey . . . The informed
reader knows that no absolute judgments on moral standards can
be made in the political sphere. And *if* I were to rephrase something
on that page – well, maybe I wouldn't put quotation marks round
"humanitarian sentiment": not because I no longer consider the
Turks' use of those words manipulative, but because . . . Well, I
don't really know why. Let me say this: *if* there were anything I
would like to change, it would not be a matter of correcting any
factual error; I might change a few words because I am thirty years
older than I was when I wrote them. But just look at what those
scoundrelly editors of the Jefron-Brockhaus have done . . .

With a feeling of disgust, I push the old yellow briefcase away
from me on the dark purple upholstered seat. Disgust for the beastly
tome I decided to bring after all. In my mind, I apologize to my
dear old briefcase for that gesture. Don't get me wrong: until now,
I've mostly found the Jefron-Brockhaus a useful encyclopedia, even
though there are instances (especially in the more recent editions)
of impertinent liberalism, one might even say, revolutionism, in
some of its articles. Nevertheless, it has been a serviceable reference
book; while using it frequently in my work, I've never made a

detailed study of it. I have the complete set in my bookcase, forty-three volumes in green boards and black spines with gold tooling. I like their solid feel in my hands. In spite of my reservations. Until now, ha-ha. I've had no objections to speak of in regard to the entry on myself in the eighteenth volume . . . I know this may seem ridiculous, but it is a sensitive matter: now, in their second supplementary volume, they are *slandering* me. That volume must have come out a year ago, but I hadn't had a chance to peruse it because someone had taken it from St Petersburg to Pärnu – probably Nikolai, last autumn. He has a habit of moving books around. So I found it on my shelf at Gartenstrasse where it must have stood, unnoticed, all winter long. Until yesterday, when Mr Christiansen, after our game of tennis –

Although Mrs Mary had been freezing while watching our game, she had not wanted to retire to the clubhouse to watch from a window, but remained outside, on a bench next to the court. The weather was springlike, with a brisk northwesterly wind. While maintaining an implacable serve and volleying the gentleman's rather stupid returns, I asked myself: This is interesting – *why* does Mrs Mary insist on sitting out here when she is obviously suffering from the cold? Is it simply to avoid boredom? Or is she really enjoying something about this? If so, what? My relatively elegant, slow, but inevitably victorious game? Or the clumsy struggle her husband is putting up – the fact that this overweight fellow is still doing his best against me . . . ? I tended to doubt that. There was no aesthetic pleasure in that, especially not for a woman . . . So, I said to myself, it must simply be that she wants to watch me beating her husband.

After we had showered and dressed and rejoined her, I noticed that her shoulders were shivering, and invited both of them to come to Gartenstrasse to warm up with some tea and rum. Kaarel's wife Frieda served us hot tea, and I opened a bottle of Jamaican. In an instant, the whole room was filled with the powerful, sweet, incredibly reassuring fragrance that brings to mind the smell of old lumber . . . I poured generous splashes of it into our cups of fiery Popov tea, and that, of course, intensified the fragrance tenfold as we sipped the tea and let the warmth flow into our bodies. We talked about my impending trip to St Petersburg. We talked about this and that, until I started – I don't exactly remember how it came about, but it must have been in response to some small hint of Mrs Mary's – telling her about the ladies of Brussels and The Hague and London; and while I did not do so overtly, my description nevertheless implied a comparison between those ladies and herself that was perceptibly *favourable* to her – until her husband got up and said it was time for them to go. And at that point, as all three of us were standing there, the (as it turned out, not really all that docile) director turned to my bookcase and fired a devastating parting shot:

"I see that you have the supplementary volume to the Jefron. Not too long ago – don't really know why – I ordered the whole set from St Petersburg. Have you had a chance to look at the last volume? There's a very detailed article about you. It's worth a look . . . Well, *au revoir* –"

I returned to my wicker chair, took a sip of lukewarm rum-flavoured tea, and opened the book.

I read the entry on Friedrich Martens, and I have to confess that it dumbfounded me for quite a while. I sat there, motionless, depressed and paralysed, as if by a physical blow. I stared at the wallpaper pattern with unseeing eyes until it got too dark to see its blue braids and golden flowers . . . What had I done to deserve such treatment?

I thought: Of course, I know I have adversaries. Anyone who has reached my level *is bound to have them*. But surely, I thought, I don't have any *enemies*. There are only people who disagree with me. Certain retired octogenarians have always regarded me as a smooth-talking upstart, but over the years they've been compelled to admit that I have been a capable servant of the state. There are contemporaries who simply envy me, but now that all of us are rapidly approaching retirement, their envy is no longer as vitriolic as it used to be thirty or forty years ago when we made our collective mark as a generation, with varying individual degrees of success. Among them there are some who can't stand me on, as it were, principle – revolutionaries with whom I've never been in sufficiently close contact to engage in serious conflict, and a few liberals à la let's say Koni, canonized in their own circles; also the right-wingers of varied persuasions, from the Black Hundred to traditional courtiers, who detest my superiority, my education, and the acclaim I have received abroad, because those things make them dimly conscious of their own suspicion that they are boneheads. And then, well, there are of course many among the young – whether they call themselves Monarchists, supporters of the Constitutional Democratic Party, or Socialists – youngsters in any case, who see me as just another more or less decorative but tedious dinosaur . . . But enemies, persons who would want to destroy me as an ethical being – surely I don't have any of those? Or do I? Who are they? And why?

This Vodovozov: a man who looks like the director of a church choir. A mediocre talent. Took his examination in international law in the spring of 1891. I remember it well – I passed him with honours. So, why –? Am I to be held responsible for his chequered career? Is it my fault that he had been exiled to Arkhangelsk and had to petition the Governor for permission to take his exam, and was then obliged to go back there, and so on?

Here, in this rattletrap train chugging through the marshy woods round Surju and Sirgaste, I take the book out of my briefcase in order to read Mr Vodovozov's article one more time – to turn the knife in the wound, as it were. Here it is. After I had fallen asleep with the help of a pill, around four in the morning, I kept pondering it in my dreams. When I woke up at seven, I thought for a moment that it only existed there, in the realm of dream. But here it is:

Martens, Fyodor Fyodorovich – Russian jurist. All right. Not a German or English or Estonian jurist. That's for sure. *Was one of Russia's representatives at the Peace Conference at The Hague in 1899.* Yes, undeniably; even though there isn't a word here about the role I played among those representatives . . . *Frequently served on tribunals of arbitration dealing with international conflicts. In May, 1895, Great Britain and Holland mutually agreed to resolve a dispute arising out of the imprisonment, by Dutch authorities, of a British subject named Carpenter at Macassar, by submitting it to international arbitration. In order to do so, the governments in question decided to ask Emperor Nicholas II to appoint a judge to the court of arbitration. The Emperor appointed Martens.*

49

On the twenty-fifth of February, 1897, Martens decided in favour of England and sentenced the government of Holland to pay 8,500 pounds sterling with interest in reparations and 250 pounds sterling for court costs. To this day, I feel justified in saying that this was the first of a long series of cases I dealt with in which England was, indeed, in the right. Although the case was complicated and took a long time, the verdict was indisputably correct. It showed that Russia's representatives were not always predictably hostile to England, but quite capable of reaching just decisions. *In 1897, England and Venezuela reached an agreement whereby an arbitration tribunal was created to establish the border between British Guyana and Venezuela. The four members of the tribunal selected by the two governments appointed Martens their chairman. The tribunal was in session from June until September, 1899.* An incredibly hot summer in a city, even a city as charming as The Hague. The sessions alternated with those of the peace conference. Kati came to join me at the end of June, and once in a while, after lunch, we had time to take the train to the North Sea, walk along the damp grey beach at ebb-tide, and listen to the tide coming in at night . . .

Martens proposed a judicial procedure of his own devising which was accepted by the tribunal. Under his direction, the tribunal performed the enormous task of examining 2,650 documents and came up with a unanimous verdict. I remember it well: "Extending from the island of Corocoro up the Cuyuni River all the way to the Roraima Mountains" – places none of the judges had ever seen . . . The border dispute was inflamed by the fact that gold had recently been found somewhere in the hinterlands of the Orinoco, and that, of course, was of interest to both poor Venezuela and wealthy England. The case required levels of diplomacy no layman could ever dream of. *In February, 1904* – ah, here it comes: *In February, 1904, Martens wrote an article for* Novoye Vremya *concerning the hostile actions taken by Japan against Russia. In this article, he claimed that Japan had violated international law by opening hostilities without a declaration of war. The press commented on Martens' inconsistency in this matter: in his own book on*

50

the Turkish war, he had ridiculed as antiquated the protest lodged by the Sublime Porte after Russia opened hostilities in 1877 without a declaration of war, and had claimed, in the book and in his lectures on international law, that obligatory formal declarations of war were pointless and had become obsolete.

Fussy language, to be sure; as for the content, it is sheer effrontery. I can't say it comes as a total surprise. When he says *the press commented,* that is certainly true: one of the principal "commentators" was Vodovozov himself. But, I ask you – surely such casual remarks in the daily newspapers don't deserve canonization in an encyclopedia! Ill-informed and ill-intentioned, those journalistic pinpricks had made me lose some sleep and given rise to several tiresome discussions when well-meaning persons came to offer helpful arguments against the hacks, just as if I hadn't known those arguments better than anyone else. With a smile, I had to pretend (God, why do we always have to *pretend* in those situations) that this journalistic mud didn't even stick to my shoes, even though I actually felt immersed in it for a couple of days . . . I got over that business fairly quickly, and completely, since the press kept providing so many examples of gutter mentality that I soon forgot their *comments on inconsistency.* In recent times, the press has started taking unprecedented liberties: *Päevaleht* informs me that during a session of the Douma Mr Purishkev-ich has called Mr Tsheidze and others *a bunch of Caucasian apes,* and that they, in turn, have called Mr Purishkevich *a damned psychopath* . . . This is regarded as fit to print, and these days we see so much of this kind of stuff in the papers that the slur on my integrity disappears like a needle in a haystack. But an *encyclopedia* is something else: what appears in an encyclopedia is more or less permanent. The article on Purishkevich doesn't refer to him as a psychopath (justified as that might be in his case). But Mr Vodovozov is given a free hand, and he proceeds to slander me in this authoritative encyclopedia. Why do they trust someone like him? And in order to make absolutely sure that I'll feel like one who has been dragged through the mud and won't ever be able to wipe it off, he adds a final flourish: *It was also pointed out that Martens could not have been unaware of the note issued by the government of Japan on the twenty-fourth of January, 1904, which, although it had not been officially published in Russia, clearly amounted to a declaration of war . . .*

As I watch, the green forest with its brown tree-trunks gradually dissolves and fades to grey, until it becomes a wall of mist . . . I know that the mechanism that causes bothersome things to evaporate is a self-protective one I hadn't mastered when I was younger; now, when I need it, it comes to my aid, as does Kati . . .

6

Kati – Lord, it is wonderful to see you here . . . But how did you get on this train? You just *showed up* . . . Of course, you've always been good at that, at just showing up. So you got on at Surju? With Queen Victoria? Yes, I did notice her, but I didn't see you, forgive me . . . And you came all the way to find me here? You're right, I have spent too much time away from you, all these years. I may have been paying more attention to queens than to yourself. But now I'm here. And you're here. Now we're travelling together. Where? No, no, not to that other life, the one when you were Mrs von Martens at Göttingen and Vienna – but also the widowed Mrs von Born, née Magdalène Bennelle, daughter of a French wine merchant, purveyor to the Auerbachs . . . We have talked about that, imagined, even lived that life. But were we happier then than we were later? No. So, let's not travel there. Let's try to manage with only our later life. Will you help me? Thank you. I know, you've always helped me. Now I need your help more than ever, because, you know – now I want to be completely candid with you. Have I not been candid with you until now? Oh, don't ask. Show a little human kindness. I'm sure you understand . . . But why now, all of a sudden? *Complete candour – why?* I'll tell you why: *because of my fear of death.*

No, don't get upset. Why should one get upset about such a natural occurrence? Yes, I am afraid of dying. Why? I don't know. If I knew the reason, the fear probably wouldn't exist. No, no, don't be afraid, it's not all that oppressive, it doesn't paralyse me. It is merely *ordinary* fear of death. The only unusual thing about it is that I haven't been aware of it so clearly until now . . . Oh, and anyway . . . Candour – fear of death. Candour of death, fear of candour, candour of fear, death of candour – they all make sense, don't they . . . Oh, Kati, I'm babbling; forgive me. Because, to tell you the truth, we don't have all that much time. I want to begin at the beginning. To create candour, you have to go back to the source.

Do you remember when you still were the way you are now, sitting here, facing me in this compartment . . . ? Do you remember when I first came to your father's, Nikolai Andreyevich's house? He needed someone to help him review documents of the commercial court. The amount of these had grown to unmanageable proportions, and he was showing the first signs of the fatigue that precedes sclerosis. This, by the way, was at the very beginning of those symptoms. He had asked Ivanovski to find someone, and Ivanovski had recommended me. I had recently returned from my first study trip to Switzerland, Belgium, and Germany, and had just delivered my first lectures at the university as a newly appointed assistant professor.

This was in the autumn of 1871. I came to visit you. Vanda Avramovna, your mother, was away at Sestroretsk. Nikolay Andreyevich received me, and we talked. At that time, his beard was so imperial that I found it hard to detect what he thought of me. But then he invited me to stay for tea – and I understood that his personal impression of me had confirmed Ivanovski's recommendation. And who joined us for tea in that long blue dining room? You, Kati . . . For forty years, I've been telling you that it was love at first sight. Now I want to appease death, if only a little, by confessing: I have been lying to you for forty years. I had no illusions about my background, and I was already wise enough – but no, once again, for the sake of our new, our complete candour: not wise enough, but clever and sophisticated enough – to check instantly any impulse to fall in love with a Senator's daughter. I looked at you. You were exactly the same as you are now, sitting in this compartment. I said to myself: Yes, she's eighteen years old, pretty, and even intelligent. She has a fascinating face, and such a straight neck: a half-open black tulip, supported by a white stem. A small, straight nose with lightly flared nostrils that give her profile an exotic touch. And under the high arch of her brows, these dark grey, ever so slightly bulbous eyes, full of curiosity, proud, sensual – I really can't describe them . . . But now, as she gets up from the table to fetch a spoon for the currant jelly from the sideboard, my watchful gaze notices a certain disproportion (and, at the same time, finds an argument against falling in love): she has girlish shoulders, small, firm breasts, a waspish waist – and then, under the fashionably shimmering grey skirt of her gown, these almost indecently wide hips and powerful buttocks . . . Her shape, it occurs to me, resembles that of the jam-spoon she's bringing to the table.

Surely you understand that one who had no social standing, who felt like a *homunculus novus*, could not risk falling in love with a Senator's daughter? Which was why the wretch came up with that spoon metaphor, in order to make the girl appear ridiculous in his eyes . . . Can you understand that, Kati? Can you forgive me for persuading myself to see in those dear if abundantly feminine hips of yours something a little comical, a little vulgar – to keep the poor boy from falling in love with a Senator's daughter? Even when, in 1873, I was promoted to associate professor, which might have given me a little more of a right to look at you with amorous eyes; and even later, God help me, when I received my imperial appointment, and did so well from the very beginning, and suddenly found myself a respectable person – even then, I resisted, although there was a new playful element in that resistance that had to do with testing and raising my own opinion of myself . . .

Kati, why are you getting up, so suddenly? Now you're standing right in front of me, in the narrow space between the seats, so that my knees ought to be touching yours. But now my whole body is permeated by that – you know what I mean – that heaviness that overwhelms one in dreams and keeps one from feeling anything else. I would like to encircle your perennially girlish waist with my hands, but my hands are petrified, glued to my knees. Kati, I implore you, don't leave! You alone protect me from the fear of death. No one else can help me any more . . . But you're leaving, no matter what I say. With a smile, you pass through the wall of the carriage . . . You've always known how to do that, how to simply leave . . . But surely not with that Mr Vodovozov, Kati . . .

7

Such delirium . . .

Ah, now I see where we are: between Pändi and Vallimäe, on our way past the first large cultivated fields to be seen on this route, and heading towards the township of Kilingi-Nõmme. As always, as always when we've travelled on this train. But then, as I was saying, in '73, I received my first full professorial appointment. That autumn I had turned twenty-eight. Well, that was when I *had to* receive my appointment – because it was on my schedule. The Martens schedule. Göttingen in 1784, St Petersburg in 1873. As for my discovery of that schedule: I had become aware of it quite a few years before that time.

Let's see: I first came across the name Georg Friedrich Martens in 1865. In the curriculum, lecture classes on international law were required only in the fourth year of study, but I had the habit of reading the essential texts on subjects to come well before we had to attend classes on them, in order to be well informed when the time came. I no longer remember the source in which I first found his name – *my* name, in a certain sense. Naturally, it aroused my interest, and the following day his *Précis* lay in front of me on my study desk in the library. The impression it made on me could be described as both monumental and – I would still say so today – absolutely *masterful*. So I hastened to look up the obituaries published in Germany after his death, in what copies of German newspapers from the year 1821 I was able to find in St Petersburg. I already knew that obituaries provide primary source material for biographical facts. And I remember: although I found only a few personal references, in two or three of these obituaries, some of the facts I discovered gave me hot shivers of astonishment . . .

His name was Georg Friedrich, and I was Friedrich Fromhold. So both of us were at least fifty per cent "Friedrich". He was from Hamburg. Throughout my childhood, due to my familiarity with foreign ships, and flags, and seafarers speaking many different languages, I imagined the word "Hamburg" to mean a city very much like Pärnu, only much, much larger – it was almost impossible to imagine how large – a city of many more ships and flags . . . Pärnu was the Hamburg of Livonia, Hamburg was the Pärnu of Germany. Only the cardinal directions and dimensions were different . . .

He, Georg Friedrich, the son of a Hamburg lawyer, hadn't been born in a tailor's cottage. The wealthy young gentleman had not been a cowherd, nor had he been sent to a school for orphans. But he had been a brilliant student, from elementary school through the *gymnasium*: this was still noted in his obituaries. So that we *differed* mainly in that it had been my fate to start on a lower rung. As long as I hadn't been aware of his existence, I had been unable to surmise the differences and similarities between myself and my predecessor and double. Instinctively, I must have compensated for my low birth by throwing myself into my studies with such fanaticism that I matriculated at the law school of the University of St Petersburg when I was one year younger than he had been at Göttingen. And it was during my second year of studies that I found out about his existence, and began to reflect upon it, and to discover, inevitably, one similarity after another. For instance: by the time he became a law student, he knew six languages – by my third or fourth year, I had mastered German, Russian, French, English, Swedish, and Italian. And, of course, Estonian: that made seven. I too found international law the discipline that attracted me the most, in its range, diversity, and what one might call its elegance – and thus, remoteness from a boy of my background who found himself competing with the offspring of the sons of noble families, all of whom had foreign service traditions. Only diligence could aid me in that competition, a diligence matching that of my predecessor and double, perhaps even surpassing it. Then, there was the most disturbing similarity – or perhaps dissimilarity: still in the first flush of my enthusiasm for Martens I read – I can't remember where – that despite his diligence, his wit, his versatility, Georg Friedrich, after all, had been only an outstanding systematizer, not a truly *creative* spirit . . . The more I pondered my rather magical connection to him, the more I felt either encouraged or depressed by the thought that I was bound to reach a stage where I would have to deal with my discipline in a *creative* way – or the thought that I,

57

his double, was forever doomed to labour within the limitations of a mere systematizer.

In the spring of 1867, I left the university with the degree of *magistr*. I was twenty-one. A *magistr* degree from St Petersburg was the exact equivalent of a doctoral degree from Georg Friedrich's Göttingen. I remember that when I pocketed my diploma in the dean's office, I was both elated and depressed by the notion that Georg Friedrich, like me, had received his doctorate before he turned twenty-two.

Yes, I suppose it was all a matter of alternating elation and depression. I was elated because I had managed, in spite of a considerable social handicap, to keep pace with a young man who had grown into a great scholar. Yet even that thought could be depressing when it occurred to me – as it was bound to occur to me at one time or another – that I just might be, in some esoteric, mystical, unscientific way, merely a shadowy variant of my predecessor . . .

The image of the future conjured up by this magical parallelism was similarly divided. Was I destined to become a great scholar and diplomat, in spite of my poor and pitiful background – or would I languish on a dull sytematizer's Procrustean bed?

Not that my curious double existence worried me every day and night, but it occurred to me with sufficient frequency – at least once a day – to make me toy with the idea of declaring my independence and going to Alaska to hunt whales. Unfortunately, we had just sold Alaska to the United States. I read the deed of sale and amused myself by trying to figure out ways to declare it invalid and preserve Russia's sovereignty over that territory. I also thought about heading for the South African diamond fields I had read about in the papers, but I didn't go there, either. Perhaps this proved that I really was not capable of *creative* decisions. I decided it would be madness to walk away from all the time and energy I had spent on my law studies. I also decided that the only factor that could make me competitive in my field was the quality of my efforts, and that the only place where that quality counted was precisely there – within the walls of the university. It was time, furthermore, to rid myself of the spell cast by my previous incarnation. I went to see the Dean.

"Well, Fyodor Fyodorovich – what can I do for you? Please have a seat."

Old Ivanovski seems to be feeling the effects of an unseasonably warm spring morning. He beams at me while wiping his ruddy face with a handkerchief.

"Ignati Yakinfovich – I have come to ask if you think the University could see its way to retaining me on the faculty."

"Hmmm . . . I assume that you're thinking of – eventually – becoming a full professor?"

"Yes, exactly."

"And what chair would you prefer?"

Here it is, the moment of decision. This is my chance to rid myself of the spell under which I've been labouring the last two years. It is true that my thesis deals with matters of international law – wartime law, to be precise: "On Private Property in Time of War". Ivanovski knows that. He also knows that the only two examinations I passed with a grade below "excellent" were those in economics and Roman law, but that, on the other hand, I received honours for my performance in seminars on criminal law. I say:

"Ignati Yakinfovich, I have decided that I would like to aim for the chair of criminal law."

I think: Why shouldn't he accept that? Especially now that there is an opening . . . I gaze insistently at his friendly rosy old face, and then, to avoid an impression of rudeness, I look past him and out the window at the tops of chestnut trees in which small pale green candle-stubs are already sprouting, and past those at the sky where a rain shower is rapidly moving across the city and obscuring the view of Alexander's statue and palace, of the bridges and the river, and then splatters the windows of the Dean's office. I know that if the old man says "All right, then" (and why shouldn't he – he has to say it, he has to!), the Martens spell will be broken . . . There won't be anything particularly noteworthy about someone named Martens embarking on a career in Russian criminal law. But Ivanovski raises his droopy eyelids, opens his eyes wide, purses his moist lips into a disparaging grimace:

"*Criminal* law? But why? No, I don't agree with that. It's true that we have lost Spassovich, but we'll appoint Tagantsev his successor. So that takes care of the future of that chair. But – you see, I chose international law. Without, at first, giving it much thought, but then it became a vocation. All my life, I have held the highest regard for my discipline. And have recommended it to those I have held in high regard, if they have shown even the least talent for it. You're an ideal candidate. You were born for a career in international law."

"But, Ignati Yakinfovich, it's precisely because of the circumstances of my birth that I'm *not* suited for such a career –"

"Listen to me, Fyodor Fyodorovich. It is true that you'll never become Minister of Foreign Affairs. Ambassador? Well, probably not. But all *those* people do is engage in *politics* – not *law*! What I mean is a serious, scholarly, academic career. And who is capable of that, and upon whom our good Lord has bestowed gifts like your own, he'll find the doors of diplomacy open to him, never mind – and I beg your pardon – how *lowly* the circumstances of his birth may have been."

One last try:

"But, Ignati Yakinfovich –"

"No more buts, Fyodor Fyodorovich. Go for the chair in international law. Any other choice would indicate such a lack of self-knowledge on your part that I wouldn't be able to support you. But in *my own department* I'll support you with all my heart. What's more, I predict *that if you choose international law, Russia will gain its own Martens, and the world will once again have a Martens – this time, a Russian!*"

He falls silent and looks straight at me with an intensely benevolent expression. I close my eyes for a moment and listen to the raindrops rattling against the windowpane.

"Well, Fyodor Fyodorovich, do you accept my recommendation?"

I did. I acquiesced and followed his advice, because it dawned on me that if such forces came into play at such a moment of decision, there was simply no way I could even dream of escaping my curious destiny – the destiny of a double.

8

To my left, behind the compartment window, the great pine forest of Kikepera goes on and on. We've been chugging through it for a while. But on the right, it suddenly turns sparse, and then, as I can see through the glass door and the corridor window, we are already crossing open meadows and approaching the low grey buildings of Kilingi-Nõmme township.

Behind the houses I can glimpse the green tops of the tall birch trees in the cemetery. As always. Further away, the solitary church steeple of Saarde. As always. And somewhere behind all those grey houses lies the blackened site of one that was burned down a little more than three years ago. Some rebel's house. The "pacifiers" reduced it to a pile of ashes. Around Christmastime, 1905. One of the thousand houses that were burned down in retaliation for attacks on a hundred estates.

Our train doesn't stop here. Why should it? Who in this country cares about a paltry town of a couple of thousand people such as cobblers and millers and shopkeepers? Twelve years ago, when the railway was built, Mr Stryck of Voltveti estate insisted that the station be built in the middle of his pasture, five versts east of the township. And there it still stands, as always. Just like everything else, "as always" – after an interlude of some curiously short months, terrifying months, proud months, God alone knows what one should call them; here in Livonia, all of it, stations and trains and everything else, is precisely as it always has been. Or could it be that it is no longer *quite* the same? In the opinion of some people, things have changed from bad to worse . . .

I am told that in St Petersburg, Mr Bulatsell, that Moldavian adventurer formerly of Tallinn, the most expensive and unscrupulous member of our Bar, has let it be known that the Prime Minister will soon order the courts to drop all unfinished proceedings against "true Russians" and to refuse to hear any new cases brought against them. In Tallinn, however, they're beginning the third week of a trial against the Tallinn Committee of Social Democrats. Did I say trial? It is nothing but a court martial, with almost thirty accused. A dozen or two will be sentenced to hard labour and deportation to Siberia. Further court martials are being prepared . . .

Good Lord, yes, the day before yesterday, Friday evening, I walked into Pärnu station on my way home to pick up my newspapers. I had been at the winter marina, cleaning and testing the engine of my boat. I always do this myself. It's sheer indulgence, of course, that boat and its little Priestman engine. Where have I ever taken it? To the dam at Sindi. A short stretch up the Reiu and Sauga rivers, where you can't go in a larger vessel. A couple of times to Kihnu, to show visitors from St Petersburg the picturesque garb of our island women. I have owned the boat for five, six years now, and the fuel pump needs to be cleaned and adjusted from time to time, a task I won't leave to Kaarel, even though he'd probably do a better job than myself. Just another little eccentricity of mine. But on Friday evening I stop at the station, stuff the papers on top of the tools I'm carrying in my old briefcase, then suddenly notice a curious atmosphere of suppressed agitation in the station hall. A number of sombre-faced men and pale weepy women emerge from the stationmaster's office into the waiting room, go to the buffet, and return to the office with small parcels wrapped in paper. The office door opens for a moment, I can see inside, and it gives me a start: I see a dozen men in handcuffs, guarded by a few soldiers with rifles and fixed bayonets, and realize that these men are prisoners waiting to be transferred to the Tallinn train. From time to time, rebels captured in Livonia are returned to be tried in Estonian courts. To avoid undue public attention to these handcuffed prisoners at the station – in such matters, we tend to be disproportionately cautious – Huik has been given orders to keep them in his office until they can be taken to the train. Nevertheless, their next of kin have found out about the transport and bribed the guards (God be praised, you can still bribe guards here in Russia), so that these, out of the kindness of their hearts, will allow the relatives to say goodbye to the prisoners. Some of the relatives buy a little bread and sausage for their shackled brothers or sons or husbands.

The grey door of the stationmaster's office has closed again. He himself is not in there. He doesn't seem to be in the station at all. For a moment I stand in the middle of the waiting room, in that state of vague unease that the proximity of prisoners, especially shackled prisoners, always generates, and that one has come to feel so often here in recent years – an unease composed of emotions, questions, assertions . . . *Those poor people – But I'm sure some of them are guilty – They may even be murderers, who knows – There but for the grace of God – None of my business – But perhaps it should be – Nonsense, I'm not that young any more – Nor have I ever been that crazy – Or maybe I was, once – No, no, not that way, not for such a cause – But what do you think their cause really is? – In any case, it is none of my doing –*

I stand there, and just as I'm about to turn and walk outside and go home to the supper Kaarel's Frieda will have ready for me, the door to Huik's office opens again, and one of the prisoners comes out with an armed guard behind him. He approaches, comes closer. He is being taken to the lavatory, under guard. We recognize each other instantly.

I'm aware that if I don't acknowledge him, he'll walk past me in silence. But that would be an insult to him, even if he wanted to spare me. I don't want to insult him, I want to show my courage, and I suspect that I also feel as if I owe him something, although I can't tell what it might be. I say:

"Johannes . . . How come you're *here*? I thought you were in Riga –"

He doesn't break stride, but says, under his breath:

"I've been in detention in Riga, for two years. Awaiting trial. Then here, for a week. And now they're taking me to Tallinn."

"Two years . . . I knew you weren't here in Pärnu – but I didn't know . . ."

Automatically, I fall into step beside him. The guard stays three paces behind and pretends not to notice me. He must have received his bribe.

"Why didn't you let me know?"

"Why should I have?"

"Is there anything I can do for you?"

"No."

We stop in the half-dark hallway, in front of the lavatory door.

Now the guard stands right next to us. Behind my back, I pass a crackly blue five-rouble note to him:

"Just a word or two. With my kinsman. You understand?"

The guard stays outside the door.

The lavatory, its walls covered with a thick coat of brown oil paint, is empty. Johannes and I face the urinal drain and relieve our bladders. Because of the cholera epidemic in St Petersburg, all the lavatories, even here, have been liberally sprinkled with chlorinated lime. The smell of chlorine makes me nauseous. In my experience, all Russian lavatories stink, except for those in castles. I consider the thirty or forty roubles in my pocket. Would he accept them now? But I won't offer them to him. No, I won't, because of the way he snubbed me two and a half years ago. Nevertheless, I repeat my question:

"What can I do for you?"

He shrugs, goes on urinating. He is pale and gaunt, and his clothes are rumpled. He has no woman to take care of him now, nor did he have one before he was jailed. He is wearing a wrinkled grey scarf around his neck. His bushy blond hair has grown long, but his cheeks are clean-shaven. With his cuffed hands, he shakes off the last drop and buttons his fly. Then he looks straight at me. His eyes are grey, the colour of water, and their expression is a little disdainful.

"If you had a file, in there . . ." He points, with his chin, at the briefcase which I've put on the windowsill to keep it off the dirty stone floor. "But you wouldn't be carrying one around. *That's* just for your international treaties."

"What if I *did* have a file?"

"Then I would ask you for it."

I do have a file in my briefcase. I don't ask him what he wants it for. It goes without saying: he needs it to get rid of the handcuffs. But I don't want him to tell me that, I want to pretend I don't know. I say:

"I do have a file."

I button my fly, open the briefcase, and dig out a small file from under the newspapers. It is high-grade steel and belongs to the tool kit that came with the boat engine; its red lacquered handle bears the legend "Priestman" in gold letters. I give it to Johannes. He grabs it with both hands, how else, and makes it disappear with a conjurer's or – I think – criminal's dexterity, so quickly that I can't tell whether it has gone into his sleeve, or into his boot, or under his shirt.

"Thank you. I wouldn't have thought that a Privy Councillor –"

"If someone asks you where you got it?"

"From my uncle. The Privy Councillor. In the smallest room at Pärnu station."

Now the damned boy is pulling my leg. Ha-ha. But then he says, seriously:

"I just found it. In the station lavatory. But in Riga. Is that all right?"

"That's fine. What are the charges against you?"

He shrugs sarcastically. "The seven deadly sins."

"And what do you think your sentence will be?"

"Three or four years of hard labour."

Now I feel a ridiculous and dangerous urge to provoke him into really wanting something from me:

"Do you need a lawyer?"

"Would you come and defend me?"

I laugh, then say: "No, I'd be disqualified. But I could arrange –"

He looks straight at me:

"I don't need a lawyer. Now that I have a file."

What can I say to that? I tell him:

"Send word when you know where you'll be. Either to Pärnu – they forward my mail – or to St Petersburg. Panteleimonovskaya number twelve."

"All right. We'll see. And thank you for your help."

He leaves the lavatory, and when I walk across the waiting room and out of the station, he is already on the other side of the grey door to Huik's office.

And now, as we leave Voltvet station with a jolt, I am jolted out of that memory and think: Two nights ago, in the train to Tallinn, he had six or seven hours in the dark narrow-gauge "Stolypin" carriage. That's what the people have decided to call the prison cars with barred windows and locked compartments you now see hitched to every other train – they've named them after our prime minister. So, by the time Johannes gets to Tallinn, he may well have filed through his handcuffs, perhaps even someone else's. Once a train arrives at the station, I don't think they keep prisoners on it until daylight. I'm unfamiliar with the exact locations of prisons in Tallinn, but I suspect they take the prisoners off the train and through the city at night. If his luck has held, Johannes may well be God knows where now . . . For some reason, I suddenly see him sitting on the red doormat, leaning against the door of our apartment at Panteleimonovskaya number twelve, awaiting my arrival . . . And for a moment, I am glad that I don't intend to go to the city apartment but directly to Sestroretsk with Kati. She'll meet me tomorrow at the Baltic station, with our chauffeur and the landaulet.

But on Tuesday morning I have to be ready for my meeting with the Minister.

9

And so it was that my university career began, in 1867. In the autumn of 1869, my *magistr* diploma in my pocket (for that completed thesis on "Private Property in Time of War"), twenty-four years old, I embarked on my first study trip to the West – to Berlin, Amsterdam, and Brussels, the same three cities where, eighty-nine years earlier (almost to the month), twenty-four-year-old Georg Friedrich had journeyed from Göttingen . . . In 1782, a year and a half later, Georg Friedrich became Assistant Professor of International Law. I assumed the same position in St Petersburg in 1871. In broad daylight, in the midst of people and events, in the flow of everyday life, I naturally told myself that those were mere *coincidences*. But at night, in the dark, and by myself, when I looked up from my desk to glance at the three portraits that stood on top of a bookcase – Grotius, Vattel, Martens – and met the eyes of the third, my double's ironic and knowing gaze told me that none of this was accidental.

During my student days I had lived in an attic room of my old school, the Peterschule, and paid my rent by tutoring students who needed help. When I became an assistant professor, I moved to the island of St Vasili, behind the university. There, in the Fourth District, I had a three-room bachelor apartment: a living room, a bedroom, a study that was also my library, and next to the kitchen, a small servant's room for "Auntie" Alviine, my sixty-year-old housekeeper. Years ago, she had moved from Pärnu to St Petersburg to live with her daughter. After her daughter died, she had fallen on hard times, until I happened to find her at the clubhouse of The Estonian Society, where she was scrubbing floors. Meeting her was the only practical benefit I ever received from my membership in that society – even though many people told me, over the years, that my attendance at its functions was an almost patriotic obligation . . . The first person who took me there was, I think, Janson, who had recently received his doctorate in statistics . . .

Gone to meet his maker twenty years ago; and so has "Auntie" Alviine.

In those bachelor quarters, I would look up from my dissertation manuscript (on consular matters in Turkey, Persia, and Japan) and stare at my double. There really is no physical resemblance, at least not as far as facial features are concerned: that much I was able to establish from a photograph of an old engraving I found in Weber's *Dictionary of Scholars*. My face had nothing in common with Georg Friedrich's foxy visage and its side whiskers. But this made our connection all the more internal and fateful, and I was aware of that whenever I looked him in the eye, whenever it occurred to me that I was his double.

In 1873, I became a professor in St Petersburg, just as he had achieved that rank in Göttingen in 1784. True, I started out as an "associate" while he had been appointed a "full" professor from the start – at that time, associate professorships did not exist in Germany, or at least not at Göttingen. Hence, that "difference" was merely an illusion. And then, that same year, came the first link in the chain that I was to wear forever . . .

I don't know whose idea it was. As they say here in Russia, all good things flow from our little father, the Emperor. Whether *he* had received his inspiration from Ivanovski or the Imperial Chancellor, our Minister of Foreign Affairs, I do not know. One day (as I recall, a nasty November day, cold and dark, but too early for snow) I was summoned directly from my lecture to the university president's office. With a radiant smile, the president told me that I was invited to an audience with the Imperial Chancellor, Prince Alexander Mikhailovich Gorchakov, at two in the afternoon the following day. When I asked if His Excellency had given any hints about the reason for the audience, the president shook his head.

I thanked him for the important invitation and asked if it would be all right for me to give my morning lecture, but cancel the seminar that began at one o'clock. "But of course, Fyodor Fyodorovich – of course you're excused. It is such an honour, to have an audience with His Excellency . . ." I don't suppose our professors were granted such audiences with any frequency; come to think of it, I had never heard of anyone on the faculty being invited to one. I remember walking back to the lecture hall, apologizing for the interruption without any explanations, and continuing my lecture on the special status of civilized nations in the international community. In the realm of general theory, this had long been my favourite subject, and I feel justified in saying that it is one to which I have made a contribution.

I finished what I had to say, and then, in a state of boyish enthusiasm engendered by the prospect of my audience with the Chancellor, proceeded to digress and embark on another theme: how one of the criteria for judging the ethical standard of any state was the degree of self-realization it allowed its citizens. As I was speaking, I glanced round the lecture hall to spot the shabbiest student uniforms, the most emaciated faces (and there were some), the most critical pairs of eyes (of which there always are more than enough, thank God). I launched an example that I told them was *closest to my own physical existence*:

"Dear friends, let me tell you something. I have two brothers, sons of a tailor from the Livonian town of Pärnu, like myself. One of them has stayed in Livonia and is a shoemaker in Riga. Mostly he just mends people's old shoes. That is my brother Heinrich Martens. My other brother, August, the same father's son, is a physician with a university doctorate. In the town of Funchal, on the Portuguese island of Madeira, the grateful citizens have erected a statue of him – in his lifetime – to honour his selfless services to the people: an honour usually reserved for good monarchs."

And I concluded:

"So, gentlemen – in spite of all the hardships you may encounter while striving to realize your potential, I beg you to remember this: what matters is not where you *come from*, but what you *bring with you*, and where you *take it*, and *with what care.*"

I went home, told Alviine to press my evening dress trousers, and pondered, over my afternoon coffee and cigar, what it might be His Excellency wanted to see me about. Ivanovski had taken to his bed in the grip of a fever and lumbago, so I couldn't ask him what he might know about this; besides, he had not given me any warning of it. I had the general impression that it was a matter of some urgent theoretical consultation. I realized that it probably wouldn't be a question of, let us say, the Entente of Three Emperors, which His Excellency had recently signed in Berlin with

69

Bismarck and Andrássy, more to his own satisfaction than to that of the Russian populace at large. What seemed more likely (especially in view of Ivanovski's emphatic recommendation) was that His Excellency needed me to consider the conflicts between Russia and the Emir of Bokhara; at that time, I was becoming a budding specialist in Eastern affairs.

The next day I came home from my lecture, put on my white tie, called a hackney carriage and rode through dismal sleety weather, yet in a state of mild festive excitement, to the Foreign Minister's office. One minute before two o'clock, I let my presence be announced to His Excellency.

This was my first personal encounter with the old man. Two years earlier, when I had been given some tasks by the Ministry of Foreign Affairs, I had only visited his deputy for five minutes. Pushkin, whose friend Alexander Mikhailovich had been during their schooldays at the *lycée* at Tsarskoye Selo, had written a poem about him, fifty years before this audience:

> Scion of the great world, so skilled in its ways,
> You tell me it is time to leave my happy clan,
> To cease from leisured worship of the Muses
> And join the tumult of our days –

something in that vein. I can see myself sitting on the silk-covered sofa in the Chancellor's antechamber, trying to piece together what I could remember of Pushkin's *Epistle to Prince Gorchakov* which I must have read in a manuscript copy circulating in my school before it appeared in print:

> So dear to me, I must confess, the happy crowd
> Of carefree friends whose arguments are loud,
> Feelings run high, wit flashes, great ideas soar,
> A gathering where no one is a bore
> Unlike those soulless, sombre meetings
> That numb the mind and chill the heart
> Where droning lectures ignorant Buturlin,
> Schöpping is king, and boredom reigns.
>   . . .

70

No shopworn jokes are tolerated here
Nor stuffy politicians, fools and sycophants:
    So, leave that court and all its blandishments,
Wild worshipper of beauty, join your brothers true,
Bless us with wit that spares no one, not even God,
O come, you rogue divine –

I had to suppress a chuckle and thanked the Creator for not blessing the liveried lackey standing by the door with the gift of telepathy; had he been able to read my thoughts, he would have turned blue and succumbed to a heart attack . . . Then I was invited in – to meet the old man who had managed to be a close friend of both the *enfant terrible* of Russian poetry and three successive emperors.

I wasn't able to ascertain to what extent Pushkin's vision of him, from half a century ago, was still accurate, but Köler's painting from six or seven years ago had certainly caught the present essentials: this was a haughty, calm, seventy-five-year-old gentleman of the old school, a little old-womanish, but far from senile. Probably still quite a rogue, to judge from the glint in the bespectacled eyes. Certainly wise and experienced. Experienced in everything. Even in doubt, and even in doubting his own wisdom. But never in doubt of his own superiority. Egocentric but capable of kindness, if a little petulant and easily offended.

But I haven't come here to offend him. I've come to hear what he has to say, and to do what he wants me to do. There is an air of weariness and resignation about him – we are, after all, living in the year 1873, and since Prussia's frightening ascendancy after the Franco-Prussian War two years ago, the old gentleman's friendship with Bismarck has begun to cause him some grief . . . Nevertheless, at this moment, he seems alert and determined and greets me jovially and amiably from behind his enormous desk:

"Professor Martens? Fyodor Fyodorovich?"

A silky, almost negligently relaxed hand reaches across the bronze desk set. *"Prenez place, prenez place . . ."*

For ten minutes, we converse about this and that, in French, Russian, and German, feeling each other out, establishing common ground. We talk about our shared Livonian background ("You know, I was born at Haapsalu . . . and on my mother's side, the family is

71

Estonian – she was a von Fersen"). He doesn't seem to feel a need to explain that he is a descendant of Rurik, the ancient founder of Russia, on his father's side. Then he wants to know what my interests are, outside of my immediate *branche* of scholarship: Tennis? Boating? Excellent! Those are fine youthful pursuits. But what do I think of the proclamation of a republic in Spain? That the followers of Bakunin will destroy the republic, and the Royalists will return to power? I see. (Does this mean that I've been asked here to discuss *Western* politics, after all?) But then: Have I read Bakunin's new book *The State and Anarchy*? (I have, indeed, but I keep that to myself, because if I didn't, I would have to explain where I obtained it. Of course His Excellency has a right to ask me that. Not to spy on me, just out of sheer curiosity. But I can't say that I don't remember, or that I would rather not answer that question.)

"No, Your Excellency. I haven't."

"Oh, I'm sorry to hear that. You should read it. You should know what the man is saying."

"I'll keep that in mind, Your Excellency." (I don't go so far as to ask him if he would be kind enough to lend me his copy.)

"But what about literature? What do you like to read? Have you read that new novel by, oh, the name escapes me now, that Frenchman – about this marvellous Englishman who travels round the world in eighty days, with a police agent in hot pursuit? You have? Really? Very good. I think it is an excellent depiction of the way the world has been shrinking in our time. And yet, there is so much in this world that we don't know, or hardly know at all. All the more reason for us to consider it our duty to expand our knowledge of it. And that is why I have asked you here today."

He has lost me, for the moment. I wait for him to continue.

"Fyodor Fyodorovich – the Emperor has come up with an idea that matches the dimensions of his intelligence . . . You see, international law – it consists mostly of agreements and treaties, doesn't it?"

"Yes, Your Excellency – as a matter of fact, *all* it is, is treaties – nothing but –"

"Right. Now, then: even those treaties, even the treaties into which Russia has entered over the years, are practically unknown territory. They are a world unto themselves. The Emperor has decided that we should learn to know that world. Do you understand?"

"I think I do, Your Excellency."

I feel a little vertiginous, because I have a premonition of what he is going to tell me next, what is beginning to unfold before my eyes. It is vertigo with a touch of anxiety. But I still can't be certain.

"So, Fyodor Fyodorovich, it's like this. The Emperor wants to see all the treaties Russia has made with foreign powers over the years in an easily accessible, synoptic, and systematic form. I see this as a series of many volumes of Russian and foreign language texts, arranged chronologically and by country, and provided with commentaries. It would be the first work of its kind in Russian. Not, of course, the first of its kind in the world. That famous namesake of yours –"

So, that is where we *are* headed . . .

"Yes, your famous namesake already made that attempt once. In his *Recueil des Traités*, right? Now, on behalf of the Emperor, I suggest that you compose your own *Recueil*. A Russian one. If you agree in principle, I'll ask you to submit a written outline, a proposal, within a week. Then I can present it to the Emperor, with your candidacy for the job."

Lord, what a prospect! What labours – what fateful recurrence . . . I can feel the pull this realization is exercising on me – as if something were pulling me into the void. My own voice sounds strange to me as I reply:

". . . So, an editorial plan, an outline, a schedule . . . Does this mean that I'll have access to all the archives of the Ministry of Foreign Affairs?"

"Yes, of course."

I refrain from adding: But it won't give me the right to read Bakunin's *The State and Anarchy* . . .

"Well, then," Alexander Mikhailovich concludes with a smile, "I'll expect you here next Tuesday, at two o'clock. Tell the President that I wish him to relieve you from your academic obligations for a week."

I shake hands with the old man and go home. I ask Alviine to make twice as much coffee as usual, change into a smoking jacket, and start striding back and forth in my study. Now and again, I stop

73

by the desk to jot down notes. I keep doing this all evening and night, and by four o'clock in the morning I have it all mapped out. Lord, to be *young*! I'm still only twenty-eight.

Yes, indeed, by four o'clock in the morning I had a complete outline of the project. It would consist of twenty volumes of approximately five hundred pages each. The contents would be organized by states, and chronologically. Publication would begin with the most readily available and finished material. Thus, the first volumes would consist of our treaties with Austria, in Russian, German, and French. Latin texts would be included wherever that language had been used in former times. The texts would be printed in two parallel columns. Then, of course, there would be commentaries. *Materialia, personalia.* It also would be absolutely necessary to discuss the developments that had led to the treaties in question, to observe the facts and the processes. But aren't those "facts" always distorted, by definition, in ways considered advantageous at the time? And won't the truth, which we claim to be preserving, be lost in any case? But is it really the truth that we want to preserve? Scholarship strives for a record of the truth. The powers-that-be want to see their own point of view confirmed. In the end, it doesn't really matter who wins: as far as I can see, the truth survives distortion. Our temporal distortions will be secondary truths in the future, and an informed reader always will be able to see through them. Besides, there is nothing one can do about past distortions. So: every treaty has to be annotated in regard to the developments that led up to it. These have to be described as truthfully as possible, or as expediently as possible, should expediency demand it. The first four volumes will consist of our treaties with Austria since 1675. Followed by (probably) three volumes of treaties with England since 1710. Then all the rest. The first volume will be published in the autumn of 1874. Oh yes, that should be possible. And the rest at the rate of one or two volumes a year. I'll manage. Now, to the practicalities of the compilation of the Austrian volumes: I'll begin by researching the historians – Solovyov, Springer, Mailáth, Rogge, Gervinus. Then I'll proceed to the correspondence preserved in the archives of the Ministry of Foreign Affairs. Later, of course, people will grumble. Some will find my commentaries too long, others will say they're too short, a third group will find them too drily official, a fourth will consider them too anecdotal. In the end, posterity will find them – *if* it does find them – the most interesting part of the whole compendium . . . But will I really manage to do this? Of course I will!

I open the window to cool my feverish brow . . . What's to manage, anyway – it won't even be difficult. It is quite feasible, natural, even simple, as long as the Emperor and the chancellor open doors for me. *Recueil des Traités et Conventions conclus par la Russie avec les Puissances Etrangères, publié d'ordre du Ministère des Affaires Etrangères par F. Martens* – PRINTED WITH THE PERMISSION OF HIS IMPERIAL MAJESTY.

Then I go to my bookcase and take down the first of a row of leather-backed folio volumes, open it, and read: *Recueil des Traités d'Alliance, de Paix* and so forth, *Tome premier, par Georges Frédéric de Martens, Göttingen 1785* . . .

I return Georg Friedrich to his shelf, stand in the middle of the room, shut my eyes tight and ask myself: is this not, all of it, merely a hallucination?

I go to the window and stick my head out into the cold wind of a November night. The street is empty, cold, and dark except for three gaslights. An icy northeasterly blows along Stredi Prospekt. I can hear its angry whine. My forehead gets chilled, and I turn my face back to the room and feel how the wind is trying to grab hold of this exposed corner building, to grab hold of my neck and push me back into my study – to work, to work, to work . . . And I think, I'll manage to do it – as long as the chancellor, and the Emperor, and the wind stay behind me, and the shade of my double and predecessor leads me on. I'll manage to complete that enormous, mind-boggling task with a sleepwalker's ease and certainty. It will be irreproachable, magnificent, world-class. And yet, the prospect is frightening . . .

10

Kati, my love! I'm so glad you're back! I knew you would come
back. You always do. Don't you? It would be terrible if you didn't,
if you hadn't come back *now*. If you had been offended by my
candour – you're not used to that. Candour, I mean. Life with me
has not been conducive to it. And your life before me provided you
with even fewer opportunities to get used to it, because you were
extremely well-bred. Candour does not agree with good breeding.
Not in the family, nor in the state, nor in international relations.
I'm sure you remember what they say Bülow once said about me:
that I was a man of such extreme natural integrity that he had never
heard me utter a single *original* lie – whenever I was forced to lie,
I resorted, on principle, only to official platitudes! Well, Kati, that
was a sharp observation. That is what I do. Not only at conferences,
but even in the company of my family, and perhaps even with
myself? That is difficult for anyone to judge, but it may well be the
case: even with myself. Until now. Please note: *until now*. Until we
passed this village – three houses on the right, four on the left, a
few apple trees, small fields, woods all around – it's gone . . . What
village was that? You don't know? Well, yes, for you this is, after
all, a foreign land. Merely a moving picture behind a train window
on summer holidays. Sadly enough, it has become foreign to me as
well. On the other hand, the names of these villages have remained
in my memory for decades, they're still there, even though I sometimes surprise myself by forgetting important matters. Or maybe I
have just begun to notice the insignificance of important matters,
and the importance of insignificant ones? Who knows if that's true.
It does seem like a handy way to excuse senile memory lapses by
elevating them to symptoms of wisdom . . . Anyway, Kati – that
was the village of Punaparg, "red park". I don't know why they
called it that. What use would it be if I did? I still would not know
the why of the why, would I? Maybe it was named after a stand of
red maples, whose leaves turned early . . . But you do know why

I want to be completely candid with you, and with myself, from this moment on. I explained it to you once, do you remember, one winter when we took the mail coach from Kassel to Frankfurt, around the time when there were rumours that Napoleon had escaped from St Helena and gone to America . . . Forgive me, I'm getting delirious. Yes, now I understand, I'm dreaming within my dreams . . . But you know why I want to change. I told you: because I am afraid. But let us not repeat what it is I fear . . .

Oh, how wonderful, to have you sit here next to me. Quite close. I would like to put my arm round your waist, but my hands have gone numb, I told you that already. But your scent is strong in my nostrils. It is still the same perfume of violets that has surrounded you ever since Nikolai Andreyevich invited me to tea that first time. And ever since Vanda Avramovna started inviting me over for lunch, once in a while, after Nikolai Andreyevich had told her that I really was a great help with those commercial law papers. He also told his wife that I enjoyed the patronage of the Imperial Chancellor and seemed be on my way to a spectacular career. He had heard that the first volume of my *Compendium of Treaties* had attracted a great deal of attention, even abroad. Whenever we met, *you* were always attentive, friendly, kind to me in a well-bred way. Once in a while, you rewarded one of my intentionally dry little jokes with a little peal of laughter. I didn't have the faintest idea what you thought of me, and I took care not to ask myself that, nor to analyse the details of your behaviour with that in mind. *Because I had decided to abstain from any sentimental feelings about you.* You were the daughter of an esteemed older colleague of mine. Quite pretty. Neutral. Physically, well, a bit comical. And that was it, all those years. Until Vanda Avramovna asked me to spend a weekend with the family at Sestroretsk, and I understood that I had been found acceptable to your circle.

Do you remember, Kati? I went there with you, on a beautiful cool Saturday in June, in '76. We played a few desultory sets of tennis, walked by the seaside, ate lunch on the verandah in sunlight filtered through a young stand of pines. It was blustery, the pine branches waved, and the whole verandah, the table, the dishes, the chairs, and your light brown-striped gown were all astir with flitting dots of light. I took great care to act irreproachably, to avoid any

77

impression of fawning on the senator or his wife, or of pressing my attentions on their daughter, even though I was well on my way to becoming a Councillor of State and should have felt quite worthy of a senator's daughter. But you know this trait of my character: once I have decided to regard something as beyond myself, it remains *ausgeschlossen*. It seems that I needed reassurance to such a high degree that I couldn't make a move until your parents asked me to marry you. Obviously, I was still so unsure of myself that I needed some such radical gesture to help me lose my fear of not being taken seriously. Well, they did begin to give me the encouragement I needed, at least your mother did. With all due respect, Vanda Avramovna does like to *corriger la fortune*, as the French say, even at cards . . . In the pursuit of her familial plans, she proved, if not more, at least as enterprising as is customary. Soon after my visit to Sestroretsk, she started poking fun at my modesty. She would look at me with her round brown eyes and say: "Fyodor Fyodorovich – I look at you and I ask myself: Aren't you going a little too far with those – how should I put it – those *gentlemanly* ideals of yours that are so incredibly alien to Russian society?"

I remember that I felt extremely hurt, offended, unmasked, the way a young defenceless man feels in front of an older woman when the latter has seen through his secret armour and has expressed her findings with friendly but unsparing irony. I considered my response for a fraction of a second. Then I said, with a smile:

"Let us see, Vanda Avramovna. The findings of a court of arbitration are always more convincing when there is more than one judge . . ." You were playing the piano in the next room. I called out: "Yekaterina Nikolayevna – can you spare a moment?"

At that point, I didn't even know what to say next. I must have been quite beside myself to act in such a precipitate manner, propelled onward by a desire to leap into the unknown that I have almost always managed to curb. You came into the room. I had already risen to my feet and met you halfway. You gave me a questioning look. I said:

"Yekaterina Nikolayevna, your mother thinks that I may be going too far in my own, as she puts it, gentlemanliness. Tell me, do you think so too? If you do, I will have to mend my ways."

Kati – do you remember what you did? I stood there and waited, afraid that you would blush, be embarrassed, shuffle your feet, especially after I heard your mother say:

"Oh, Fyodor Fyodorovich, why make such an issue of it . . ."

But you didn't blush. You turned a little pale, and looked straight at me, and your pretty, slightly pouty lower lip trembled a little, but then you said, in a perfectly normal voice:

"Yes. You could mend your ways. But I would still consider you a gentleman."

Oh, Kati. After such an embarrassing moment nine men out of ten would have beaten a hasty retreat – would have taken advantage of the freedom they had gained by keeping their distance for years on end. But I decided that at a moment of such deep candour (you see, Kati – candour *has* played an important role in our destiny!), at a moment of such openness, one climbing up from the cellar really doesn't have to step aside to let another descending from the tower pass, but may hold his ground and take a good look at who this other really is. I stayed put and gave myself permission to take a good look at you. And then, only then, Kati, I fell in love with you. With your lively intelligence, your forthright practical temper, and your physical being. That too. With the surprising way that you are both sturdy and slender. I had realized, ages ago, that you wore almost no horse-hair padding in the *tournures* of your dresses: you didn't need it, you had your own. Now, I found that fact amusing; it seemed like a secret bonus. Of course it was also a joy to hear what you told me after you became candid with me: you said you had fallen in love with me at first sight . . . But listen, Kati – dear God, tell me (look, I would like to put my hand on your knee but I can't, my hand, my whole body feels as if made out of clay and iron nails), tell me: *perhaps you, too, have been lying to me for thirty-five years, the way I have* – by telling you the same thing? No, no, no. Besides, what difference would it make? Now that we're telling the truth, ever since that village of Punaparg.

You see, I want to tell you the truth even about matters that really don't concern you, that have never been of any interest to you. Matters of my profession and my work. Although it is true that you have, on occasion, given me good plain practical advice even in some of those. In its own elemental astuteness, that advice has sometimes been truly inspiring. But from now on, I want to tell

79

you everything. and by that I mean everything that is necessary for the sake of complete candour. You see, in that book of mine on the war with Turkey, the one I dashed off in '79, I wrote certain things that I would not care to repeat . . . Oh, did you see the lovely road through the woods we just passed – it's gone now, but it leads north, to the village of Riitsaare. I've never been on that road, I know these parts only from studying the map. But it looked like a fine road through young pine woods, and it would be a pleasure to walk it with you, just the two of us, instead of . . . But we can't . . . In that book of mine on the war with Turkey, I wrote:

The behaviour of the Turkish government seems even less excusable when one considers the following points. First of all, solemn declarations of war disappeared from international practice after the treaty of Paris of 1763, and secondly, all of the more authoritative writers of our day regard such a declaration as a superfluous formality, on the simple grounds that it is hard to imagine, in the present era, any sudden, surprising, deus ex machina *outbreak of war between nations.* And I remember quoting some famous Englishman at this point: *"In modern times the practice of a solemn declaration made to the enemy has fallen into disuse,"* and so forth. Then I continued: *Thanks to progress in international relations and communications, even the most trivial misunderstandings between governments immediately become common knowledge, and stock exchanges use them to their advantage, one way or another. Even at the beginning of the eighteenth century, noted law scholars argued that declarations of war were completely unnecessary due to the undeniable fact that no war begins without cause, without an increased tension in international relations and diplomatic negotiations. It is true –* I wrote – *that in the middle of the seventeenth century Hugo Grotius, the "father of international law", insisted on solemn declarations of war, but the Sublime Porte should not have overlooked that we are now living at the end of the nineteenth century when genuinely civilized nations have developed different ways of dealing with "international obligations and customs"* . . . Then I finished by saying: *As for the "humanitarian sentiment" that*

*Russia has supposedly violated by allegedly neglecting to
declare war in the desired manner, it hardly seems proper
for a government that ordered the extermination of the entire
population of Bulgaria to lecture others on matters of "humanity and philanthropy".*

Kati – in some part of my consciousness, at some deep level of
my conscience, I have always felt rather uncomfortable with these
assertions and quotation marks – even a little ashamed. Whenever
I've thought about them, I have felt a slight twinge and – and then
smiled a thin smile, and said to myself, all right, well and good,
they may be assailable from an ethical point of view, but in terms
of forceful polemical writing, they seem entirely appropriate . . .
Still, I've regretted them, because I have understood, or perhaps
merely felt, that the assertions I made express contempt for a more
childlike, more truthful world, while defending one that is more
mechanical, and in fact, more horrifying. Kati, look! Look – I *can*
move my hand! Look, I put my hand on your shoulder . . . But
why do you seem so bored, even pained? Listen to me! Those
quotation marks in my text – round "customs", "responsibilities",
"philanthropy" – I know that they are really nothing but crude
sarcasm. And my assertion that we did not have to pay any attention
to Turkey's accusations simply because Turkey was an even more
barbarous state than Russia – from a strictly ethical standpoint, it is
simply vile.

But listen, Kati, couldn't you look at me while I'm talking to you,
telling you about my anxieties? Please, look at me. You won't?
You're looking at the forest flowing past us – all right. Your *ear* is
turned towards me, so you're able to hear me. And judge me as
best you can.

You must remember, and understand, that – to some extent –
my perhaps excessive eagerness to pick up the pen had something
to do with my careerist enthusiasm. There seemed to be a need for
such a book, and I had all the necessary information at my disposal.
It was my fate to write it, my fate in both the objective and the
subjective sense. There was a decisive moment when those two
aspects coincided . . . Try to remember my situation in 1878. The
first four volumes of my *Compendium* had been published and had

gained me entry to the front rank of *scholarly* internationalists. This, of course, increased the antagonism of our hereditary clique of nobly-born diplomats. Who was I, anyway? Where had I come from, and how and *with whose permission* had I arrived here? In Russia, no one can even be *born* without somebody else's permission . . . You were soon to become my wife, and you lived through all the turbulence in and around me with the same marvellous empathy that you've always had. You were aware of the force-field I had entered. No one could doubt my loyalty. But was I ready to strike a blow for the Empire? Had I, while concerning myself with political history on a grand scale, been able to shake off my petit-bourgeois, small-town, "Pärnuesque" morality? That question, too, was raised, and hung in the air for a while, six months before our wedding. Our predestined wedding . . . Göttingen in 1789, St Petersburg in 1878 . . . Thus, I was sorely tempted to prove my mettle to the circles that considered themselves statesmanlike.

Yes, yes, I know that there are great variations in the ethical standards of the upper classes. They range from, shall we say, Stolypin, all the way to Tolstoy. Although I must admit I don't find the latter altogether credible. I gather that he has recently published his latest pamphlet – "I Cannot Remain Silent", or something to that effect. I ask you: *Why* can't he remain silent when everybody else seems to be able to do so? I am able to remain silent. You are, too. That is how we get by. You and I, Kati, we understand that if we spoke up, we might create a minor sensation, but it would do no one any good. So we keep our mouths shut. From time to time, when we come across some particularly repulsive instance of brutality or misery (as we do, on occasion), we do get a feeling of – well, suffocation . . . Then I write a little note to some bureaucrat at the penal administration, some former student, and beg him to permit the transfer of a prisoner, let us say a student who has been agitating among the workers and whose ignorant family has turned to me for help, from a damp and cold prison to a slightly drier and warmer one. Or – and this is as brave as we've managed to be – we write a polite collective letter, as we did, for instance, when Professor Famintsyn was imprisoned for allegedly supporting and defending a few boys who had participated in student riots.

At that time, fourteen of us professors, Berketov, Kosovich,

Tagantsev, myself and others, wrote a letter to the Chief Procurator. Of course, it was I who composed the letter, but not because I was particularly enthusiastic about the case. I remember being afraid, but I felt compelled to do it, by both exterior and interior forces. Yes, interior ones too. The other thirteen took it for granted that I was the man to do the actual writing, even though Tagantsev was the specialist in criminal law. So, we begged most humbly (as the form required) for the release of our esteemed academic and bureaucratic colleague. We even asked for his *immediate* release, because we were convinced (or so we said in the letter, even though we weren't) that he had not taken any part in any kind of agitation against the government. We suggested that he be released on either our or the university president's recognizance, and pledged to come up with whatever bail was deemed necessary. After a couple of weeks, Famintsyn was released, and charges against him were dropped.

Fortunately —*and* regrettably – such occasions are rare. Occasions on which we actually *do* something, and feel redeemed by our doing. Mostly, when that feeling of suffocation attacks us, we simply open the window, if it isn't raining or blowing too hard, or take a walk, if it isn't too cold outside. If the suffocating feeling turns into nausea, we run to the toilet and throw up. Then we proceed to drink ourselves into a stupor. I don't mean the two of us, Kati; we merely exercise our light sarcastic wit on the Emperor, his ministers, his court, the secret police, the rascals favoured by the state, Rasputin, the empress's brides – but always within limits, and metaphorically, even when there's no one else around. In the presence of outsiders, we hold our tongue. And we manage to do that! But this Tolstoy, he sits down and writes another pamphlet! In which he claims that he *can't* remain silent! I ask: Why not? And I answer: Because he is just a vain and spoiled old man!

Oh, Kati, forgive me – it wasn't my intention to start ranting about Tolstoy. What do I care about him? Besides, in a certain sense, I have proved myself the better man. That occurs to me sometimes, although it is a sore point. I have come closer to receiving the Nobel Peace Prize than he has come to the Literature Prize during the years that have passed since Nobel created the foundation. But instead of talking about him, I would like to talk about us, and about myself, to reach complete candour with you at last. To do without the condom of upbringing and caution and hypocrisy . . .

Goodness, that one unseemly word has made you vanish from my side. But Kati – you've been the ideal reader of my thoughts these past thirty years, in your own quiet feminine way. I know that. And today, in this carriage whose walls cannot keep you from coming and going, you can read my thoughts just as well.

So, at the risk of offending you again, I'll start over by considering the word that chased you off, made you vanish through the compartment wall like a ghost . . . Condoms. Or preservatives, as we used to call them, symbolically enough. We have preserved ourselves, from each other, and from the world. For thirty years, we have used condoms during almost all our intimate moments. I won't try to remember all the reasons, but there were the times when you wanted to travel with me; there was the time you didn't want to give up your tennis lessons; the time we were worried about your lungs. Besides, you wanted to keep the house quiet, to prevent the noise of children from interfering with my work for the state, with my research. And I agreed. Later, we kept saying, later, later. Often I was the one who was most emphatic about it. So that, frankly, our Nicol – don't be afraid, I'm merely telling the truth – he is simply a mistake, a fruit of our negligence. I know that is a terrible thing to say about a person – what's more, one's own child. I know. *Listen, son, the fact that you exist, that you are alive, and breathe, and think, is simply due to your parents' negligence* . . . Well, that may be the more appalling one of two possibilities. The other is . . . I don't even know, and you, Kati, don't know either, *which* possibility led to his conception. We had been using my brother Julius' product for years . . . After Julius had fulfilled his military service as pharmacist to the Semyonov Regiment, he started his own little factory. At Chornaya Rechka, the black river. "Julius Martens & Co. Hygienic Supplies." So – the other possibility is that Nicol was the result of poor quality control at his uncle's factory. It's hard to say which possibility is more disturbing. And it's hard to tell how many of the human beings alive today are the results of either their parents' negligence or poor quality control at Julius' factory. A fairly large percentage, I'm afraid; which includes our son, sadly enough.

Of course, as soon as a child is on the way and has been granted an entry visa, so to speak, one tends to forget the initial circumstance, that taste of dull depression we got when we first found out. But somewhere, deep down, the knowledge remains, and eventually makes itself known to the child, if only as a surmise. And then the child starts taking revenge on his parents for not having been, from the very beginning, the longed-for fruit of their love; for having been, at least for some time, a completely unwelcome and repulsive frog, even though the parents later got used to him. A child wants more than belated affection. Please, Kati, don't tell me that this is sheer pedantry. True, there's no way I can prove any of this, but intuitively I am convinced of it. True, too, that as soon as one looks at things with complete candour, surprising undercurrents come to light. The fact is that a child demands *everything* from its parents. You know what I mean. And if it has any reason to believe that this demand has not been satisfied, it starts taking revenge on the parents, without even being aware of it. *Subconsciously*, as Doctor Freud puts it. I have experienced this in regard to our Nicol, our Nikolai, and I know that I'm providing him with more reasons for revenge every day. He is not insensitive to my dissatisfaction, and yours, too, Kati. Both of us ask ourselves: Who and what is he to us, this son of ours?

All right, he has managed to learn three, four languages; he's had home tutors ever since he was an infant, so he was bound to learn something, refractory as he was. Then we sent him to Heidelberg and Oxford. Thanks to his father's reputation, he was given a post in the foreign service, and now he seems to be doing all right there in Stockholm. When he comes to visit Pärnu, he looks pleased when the drunkards at Rääma's call him *a university man*, and rewards their flattery by buying them drinks . . . And we think, well, when all is said and done, and sad to say, this son of ours is nothing but a privileged mediocrity . . . And because we conceived them intentionally, we favour Katarina and Edit over him. Do they really deserve it . . . ?

11

So we passed Voltveti already? And are almost in Möisaküla? There it is, with the two red brick smokestacks. The one on the left belongs to the railway machine shop, the one on the right to the textile mill. Pine trees, low grey houses. The train will stop here for fifteen minutes, and I'll spend ten of those on a walk, get some fresh air. I will, of course, attract more attention in the streets of this little town than I would like, but that's the kind of thing one must take in one's stride. Simply pretend not to notice that one is being noticed. *If* one is, for that matter.

The first-class carriage stops right in front of the station, a long low-slung tile-roofed building painted brown and darkened by soot like all these stations. There are a couple of dozen people milling about on the platform. Some Möisaküla dignitaries are getting off, returning from their trip to Pärnu. Here's a foreman or engineer hired to help run the new textile mill; here's a shopkeeper who has risen to his present estate from years as a pedlar or itinerant potter; here's the owner of one of the region's large estates. Spouses, house-keepers, servants have come to meet them. Then there are the people getting on the train with their wicker suitcases – a few young moustachioed blades in stovepipe trousers and starched collars, a few young ladies under floppy wide-brimmed hats, over there by the steps of the second-class carriage, in the fresh morning wind, dappled by the almost dazzling sunlight. That wind may also be blowing in the straits of Koivisto at the Emperors' rendezvous – who knows, the seas may be getting choppy there . . .

I step down from the carriage and walk quickly through the breeze and across the flickering puddles of sunlight, into the station building and the slightly nauseating smell of sauerkraut generated by its restaurant. Then out again, on the town side, in the cool breeze and bright sun, onto a recently if somewhat carelessly clipped circular lawn with a well-pump in the middle and four gnarled lime trees to one side.

I follow the gravel path across the lawn and pass by the well, so close that I get a whiff of the moist gravel under the pump tap. If there hadn't been so much talk lately about Mechnikov and bacilli and cholera, I would tip out what's left in the bottom of the bucket, then pump it full to the brim with fresh water and raise it to my lips for a few hearty gulps . . . Then I'm seized by an irresistible urge to do something I *can* do in spite of the cholera scare – even though it involves a moment of activity that might attract some attention. But who says I can't do what I please? I pick up the chained tin bucket, pour out the water left in it, then pump it half full of fresh water. That's all I need. I take out my handkerchief. As I shake it out, then wad it up again, the breeze carries a whiff of the lavender water I use as my cologne – Kati's choice. I lean the bucket on the well-cover, tilt it to splash cold water on the wadded handkerchief. I tilt it a little too far, and the water runs over my feet, completely soaking the sock on my right foot. Surprised, I raise that foot into the air; then I think, What a scene: here we see the man who presided over eleven delegations representing His Imperial Majesty the Absolute Ruler of All Russians and so forth and so on, standing in front of Mõisaküla railway station on one foot and shaking the other – just like a dog that has pissed on its own paw . . . Or do dogs ever make those kinds of mistakes? I lower my foot to the ground again, let my chin jut a little in order to avoid wetting the front of my coat, and wipe my forehead and eyes and whole face with that marvellously ice-cold, amazingly pure and refreshing damp cloth. I feel how the shock and hesitation and refreshment change and renew my face. I open my eyes and notice – yes, I do! – how the whole world acquires another face when we ourselves look at it with new eyes . . .

I take care to wring out the handkerchief to keep it from soaking my pocket, and glance at my watch. I still have at least ten minutes. So I walk, quickly but without effort, down the street into the little town whose vistas appear amazingly crisp to my refreshed eyes. Here are the shops, Röigas', Kull's, and so on. Since it is Sunday, none of them are open. Here's the pharmacy, and here is Lilienthal's restaurant, open although it isn't quite eleven o'clock. As I pass, the doorman on its steps stifles a yawn, just in case, and greets me with a bow, just in case. Here's the new bank building, the

87

township's pride, three recently completed storeys. And here's the clean-swept market square, empty as always on Sundays. Below the closed shutters, a small whirlwind stirs up fine sand that smells of dust, hay, salt herring brine, and horse piss. I won't have time to cross the market square to take a look at the red brick buildings of the new textile mill, so I turn right on Pärnu Street which will take me back to the station in seven or eight minutes. There, almost in front of the school, I run into a freckled twelve-year-old girl. She is carrying a large (a couple of feet in diameter), round basket woven out of white pine-roots. She stops, holds the basket up to me, and says in a birdlike voice:

"Would you like to buy this basket, sir? It's really pretty, isn't it. Your missus can use it to keep things in, like yarn, and knitting wool. And it's cheap, too. Only one rouble and fifty kopecks!"

Coming from such a slip of a girl, her brown hair in braids, the gypsy-like intensity of her sales talk is both strange and charming. God knows, perhaps I am reminded, however fleetingly, of what some people said about *me* in St Petersburg, fifty years ago (loudly enough for it to reach my ears): "That country bumpkin – he's such an energetic busybody it doesn't seem like he's from Pärnu, he acts more like someone from Bessarabia, or even Jerusalem" . . . I also remember that lovely Mrs Mary Christiansen does not only enjoy tennis but also likes knitting things, using yarn of five or six different colours; two weeks ago, her husband brought her a lilac-coloured doeskin bag for her knitting supplies, from Paris, and this bird's nest woven out of the pine-roots of Pässaste might, in some absurd sense, compete with that elegant bag . . . I don't even know what else occurs to me, but the upshot is that I buy the basket. I give the girl two roubles and tell her to keep the change before she has a chance to tell me that she doesn't have fifty kopecks.

Only after I have trotted down Alexander Street and arrived back at the station, a little out of breath, and see to my relief that the train hasn't left, I suddenly realize which way that train is pointed – at which end the small locomotive is puffing smoke – and *who* it is I am travelling to see.

Good Lord, you're really getting absent-minded, I tell myself as I get back on the train. But I take the basket with me anyway, I can't very well leave it on the platform, even though I can't and won't make a present of it to Kati (who doesn't count knitting among her hobbies), since I did buy it for Mary . . .

Strangely absent-minded, I say to myself as I sit down next to my briefcase and the train starts steaming towards Ipiku – *choo-choo – choo-choo-choo* . . . God knows what that Doctor Freud, for instance, would make of this odd miscalculation. The thought makes me chuckle. As far as I understand the good doctor, he hangs everything in the universe onto one nail, in a completely irresponsible yet charming manner, then gives a tug to the bottom of the bundle so it spreads out like a peacock's tail, and *voilà*, there is his system! What a philosopher, what a philosophy. Well, I don't know, maybe his system deserves to be taken more seriously than that; I do know, however, that anyone trained in theoretical thinking will find it easy enough to improvise at least two of those all-encompassing systems on a good day. No problem . . . Oh, I'm boasting, am I? Well, let's see. Let us make an experiment. I have systematized the matter of international law. My critics claim that it is not a perfect system. What does "perfect" mean? It is a *living* system. The same critics also admit that my system is the best we have. It is used in universities all over the world, from Germany and Austria all the way to Japan. But it is *not* the result of years of work, as people tend to assume. Not at all. It does, indeed, take years to write five hundred pages, to edit them, to fill in gaps, to make emendations. But the kernel of the thing, the idea that makes it all fall into place – that is the *invention of one happy moment*. It is, of course, easier to capture that moment if one has spent a lot of time and energy on the materials. But if a Viennese medical researcher can come and hang the entire psychology of the human race on the nail he has happened to choose, the *libido* nail – why, then, couldn't a certain jurist from St Petersburg, with sixty years of experience in the observation of human behaviour, come along and hang mind and psyche, creativity, history, and culture onto *another* nail? Well – which one? Let's see . . .

Choo-choo – choo-choo – choo-choo – choo-choo . . .

Hereabouts, one begins to notice the way the railway tracks divide up the countryside. On the left, among the pine woods and small fields, the houses are Estonian – on the right, Latvian. And even though my kinship with the Estonians may be rather diffuse

– what I mean to say is that it is undeniable, in terms of my blood-lines, but diffuse in terms of my consciousness – when I pass through this borderland, I always react the same way. As long as it stays light enough, I look to the right, look to the left – and *compare* things. Houses. Roofs. Windows. Backyards. Gardens. Fields. Woods. And it strikes me every time how difficult I find it to make these comparisons, despite or perhaps precisely *because* of the fact that so many people regard me as the world's calmest, most objective, most impartial arbitrator – at least, in my two decades on international tribunals. What makes this task so difficult is that no matter how vague my sense of Estonian identity may be, I tend to interpret my findings in favour of the Estonian settlements. So much for being the world's most impartial arbitrator. When, on the left-hand side of the tracks, I see a garden that is not as well-kept as a garden on the right, I hasten to notice that the roofs on the left have been shingled more neatly and recently . . . And while I have to admit that some of the houses on the right are more imposing than those on the left, I feel that one must take into account the poorer and sandier quality of the soil of the Estonian side; and so, the houses on the left are really quite nice, perhaps even more attractive . . . When I happen to notice something on the left that is indefensibly pitiful, like that shack over there – roofbeams poking through the straw, broken windows stuffed with rags, a big mud puddle in front of the door, a state of desolation that can't be attributed to poverty brought on by misfortune but is clearly a result of disgusting indolence and alcoholism – I realize, although from a distance and aware that I won't do anything about it, that my heart starts pounding against my ribs and I feel the urge to rush over there and drag those sad stupid loafers off their flea-ridden cots and pummel them until they wake up . . . When I see something similar on the Latvian side, it depresses me, but I don't feel *personally* enraged, personally offended . . . Now then, if the world's most impartial arbitrator can be swayed by a little trace of solidarity, a shred of tribal identity – what will be left of my impartiality in a case where I happen to identify *completely* with one of the two parties I am supposed to compare? That is, when I try to compare someone else with myself?

Choo-choo – choo-choo – choo-choo – choo-choo . . .

Small clouds of smoke, all shades of grey, float past the carriage windows on both sides of the train, so that there are times when the young bright-green pine forest seems to be standing behind a stage set of cotton puffs. The sun flashes through the interstices of those puffs, into the windows and into my eyes. Now I have it! Once again, I can feel my heart pounding, not with rage but with the joy of discovery: I've found it – my own central image, around which I can improvise an explanation of the world! Of course, I have no idea what that explanation will ultimately look like – but I know what I'm going to base it on. I have found the *nail* from which I'll hang the world. For the hell of it. For fun. To see what happens. It is the nail of *comparison*. Comparison between the observer's image of himself, and anyone else. *I and s/he* – that's what the world hinges on. As Aristotle's *zoon politikon*, the human being exists in an inescapable web of social relationships, and the way matter consists of atoms, that web consist of niches. At one end of every niche sits an observing "I", at the other end a "he" or "she". The latter changes constantly, endlessly, yet it is always there. I and – I and Director Christiansen. I and Professor Taube. I and the Emperor. I and Kati. I and Nikolai. I and Mary. I and Johannes. I and Mr Vodovozov, that criminal idiot. I and the Möisaküla girl who sold me a basket woven out of pine-roots that now sits beside me on the purple velvet seat. Now, what's important is this: in every relationship of that sort – openly or obliquely, in the foreground or background – arises the question: *Who is better – I or s/he?* This turns every relationship into a comparison, makes it comparative – and there we have it. I have just presented to you my theory of *comparative*, or perhaps, *comparativist psychology*! I'll have to think about the name; I may come up with a better one. But let us proceed.

The comparison of any "I" with any "other" inevitably leads to one of three results: the I is either better, or worse, or equal to the other. By creating a constantly increasing sum of innumerable self-comparisons, the I tries to establish and maintain a balance between the world and itself. Yet every I has its own model for that balance, and it will therefore be necessary to create a corresponding typology of I's. No problem. First of all we have, let us say, the *superior* or perhaps *supremacist* type. (We'll work on the terminology.) This seems to be the most common one – or am I expressing a bias here? In any case, that type tries to prove that he is better than the largest possible number of others. His sense of balance with the world becomes more perfect as the world affirms and reaffirms his superiority. Then, of course, there has to be (if for no other than purely systematical reasons) an *inferiorist* type. We could also call him the *subordinate* type. Whenever he compares himself to others, he looks for, and finds in himself, some kind of inferiority. (When our system has been fleshed out, we may also want to compare these two types with e.g. the sadistic and the masochistic type, or the masculine and feminine, etc.) The third type would then seem to be the, let us say, *egalitarian* type. The more others he finds with whom he feels himself to be on an equal footing, the more comfortable he is in the world. As always, and in all things, these types rarely appear in a pure or even approximately pure form. The research material presents hybrids in which elements of the first or second or third type are dominant.

Choo-choo – choo-choo – choo-choo – choo-choo . . .

So, there we are. My introduction to comparativist psychology. *Introduction dans une psychologie comparativiste.* I have just sketched the outline of two or three really solid chapter headings for my theory. It is not as sensational as Doctor Freud's, nor, perhaps, as universal, but it makes up for that by great clarity and concreteness. Chuckle, chuckle! Then, let's see, in the fourth chapter we get to the most interesting part – the question of universal world falsification. Everyone, according to his type, falsifies the results of his self-comparisons to make them look more favourable to himself than they really are. The most widespread mode of falsification (so widespread that one should perhaps not even call it that) consists in comparing ourselves to others *only in regard to aspects we have chosen ourselves because they show us in a favourable light.* For instance: I compare myself to Director Christiansen. I restrict the comparison to our standing in society, and the outcome is favourable to me. I am who I am, but he is only the manager of a provincial factory, never mind that it's the largest of its kind in the Russian Empire. I compare myself to him in terms of education and life experience – because I know that I am better-educated and more experienced. The same method works for our physiques. I am in better shape, whether we take or don't take into account our age

92

difference. But I do not compare our relative ages, per se. Nor our wives. That is to say: Mary's youthful bloom to Kati's signs of age. The only aspect I might be willing to compare would be Mary's infidelity to Kati's fidelity . . . And of course I don't compare our respective wealth. Compared to me, Mr Christiansen is an immensely wealthy man. Next to him, I'm merely a pauper, with my five or six thousand roubles a year. I won't compare our family backgrounds – he is, after all, the descendant of respectable burghers from Denmark and junkers from Schleswig.

Yet again, when I compare myself to Tolstoy, I wouldn't think of comparing his station as a count to my own knighthood. Or if I did compare them, I would do it only to question the worth of his family title compared to a distinction achieved against all odds by dint of great energy and hard work. A comparison between Tolstoy and myself that springs instantly to mind, a purely arithmetical one, is the one between my (comparative!) youth and his great old age. I am seventeen years younger – which means, among other things, that I stand a far greater chance of winning a Nobel Prize during the next ten to fifteen years than does he, since the prizes are awarded only to the living. On the other hand, I refrain from comparing my international reputation to his. It occurs to me that it may not be such an advantage to be known by millions, as he is, instead of only a couple of hundred, as I am. For decades, he has addressed himself only to simpletons who enjoy reading legends, while I discourse with rulers and diplomats and leading academic brains . . . I'll gladly compare his regrettable (not to say ridiculous) bondage to religion to my complete freedom in that regard.

And so, it is obvious that all of us, at least all the supremacist types, tend to be like that fellow – his name escapes me now – who boasted that he had beaten both Lurich and Lasker* – the former in chess, the latter in wrestling . . . Thus, no matter how supremacist his temper, a tailor has no need to envy the emperor, because he knows he can cut a much smarter pair of trousers than the emperor ever could if he tried. And if it pleases him, he can always invent the tale about the emperor's new clothes . . . But what if that tailor is a subordinate type (goodness, how easy it is to apply

* (See Notes – Translator)

93

our new terminology in our new system!)? Well, then he won't even dream of comparing himself to the emperor. He'll compare himself to another, more successful tailor, who has a shop in a better part of town, and realize that he's nothing but a miserable failure compared to that colleague with a capital C. Depending on the ratio between his supremacist and subordinate tendencies, there are many different ways in which he can deal with that realization. If he has a strong supremacist streak, he'll admit to failure only in minor matters and attribute his relative lack of success to sheer injustice, saying that the colleague's success depends on attributes quite irrelevant to serious tailordom – his obsequiousness, his slippery tongue, perhaps even the pretty face of his wife. If, however, he is a more or less true subordinate, or inferiorist, he'll readily admit his failure even in more important and concrete things. If he is such a pure type, he'll bore and alienate people by confessing to them that he really is all thumbs as far as the tailor's métier is concerned. Some cases may even gain pleasure from such self-abasement; the mechanism of this perversion needs further examination.

Well. Our fifth or sixth chapter, then, should begin with an analysis of our system of political and social habits and go on to prove that these habits are, in fact, accurate reflections of comparativist psychology. Our entire career system with its rungs on the bureaucratic ladder, our academic degrees (yes, those too), our estates, titles, decorations (those worthless baubles) – all of these exist only because people lust for them, and they lust for them because they recognize them as means for improving their self-comparisons. "Ivan Ivanovich is still only the head of a department, but I was appointed Councillor!" Or we experience both superiority and inferiority as a spur to achieve more favourable self-comparisons: "Pyotr Petrovich is already a Minister, while I am only a miserable Councillor – I really have to make an effort to catch up with him . . ." Or: "Good God, why doesn't Sasha have the Cross of St Vladimir, Third Class? He still only has the Fourth Class . . . I must do my best to get him the Third Class, now that Pavel Pavlovich has managed to get it for all *his* protégés." Only for the sake of the pleasure gained, or still to be gained, from more favourable self-comparisons do we go on to shoulder the required burdens: the kow-towing, the self-sacrifice, the strain, the perennial game of pretence in which the one and only prize is the opportunity for a more favourable self-comparison. All of this applies only within our relationship to the state, to society, to *him* or *her*, whoever that may be. What use would a Knighthood of the Garter be to Robinson Crusoe? He might spread some glue on the ribbon and wait for a quail to land on it.

So much for that. Now to the problem of the inferiorist types. It occurs to me that Christianity, with all its sub-categories, denominations, sects, and cults, has really been designed mostly for them. All those holy beggars, lesser brethren, God's dogs and so forth, all the way to the *skoptshy*. It should be noted that the ultimate objective of all this self-abasement is self-elevation – St Matthew makes no bones about it: *And he that shall humble himself shall be exalted . . .* Although it is true that St Paul, not much later, already managed to deflate that balloon by asking (in the second Epistle to the Corinthians, if memory serves): *Have I committed an offence in abasing myself that ye might be exalted?*

I think I deserve a little catnap. No matter how playful that train of thought was, it seems to have worn me out. The compartment is gliding along, sliding away. One of those puffs of smoke – big and soft and light and rose-tinted by the sun – is suddenly here, and I'm inside of it . . . I'll finish my system later. I would like to give more thought to the type I called the egalitarian. The general attitude it describes might be particularly congenial to me, after all, since I've been congratulated so often on my arbitration skills. There is some sort of a connection there, but now I have to rest a while – Kati, you followed my thoughts all along, didn't you? Of course you did, I know. Tell me: I *was* completely candid, wasn't I? And I deserve to get you back, to have you protect me? Time to close my eyes for a moment . . .

12

Now those grey puffs of smoke have joined together and become so dense that one can't see the sun any more. The sky is completely overcast, so overcast that the rest of the world looks completely grey, as well. Dark, grey, and chilly. Cold, even. But what on earth keeps making that *creaking* noise, quite close by? I strain my ears to determine that – in vain, at first, but then I recognize it: it is the rhythmical creak of oarlocks.

I'm in a boat; with that realization comes the knowledge of what is happening, where it is we are rowing. This huge grey expanse of water is the Elbe that has flooded its banks. This is the Great Flood of Hamburg, June 1770. I know, I know . . . We are rowing against the tide, in the direction of Moorfleet, and I know why. Father has sent me to see about our summer house, the Villa Martens – to see if it's still there or if it has been swept off its foundation. I also know that this is a fool's errand. I don't need to tell the oarsmen that; they know it too. They are men with faces that look like they were carved out of wood, capable and proud, the kind that a Livonian, Merkel Garlieb, will write about at the turn of the century: "Your typical citizen of Hamburg is a broad-shouldered, raw-boned, sturdy fellow who looks even a senator straight in the eye and does not so much as dream of stepping aside or doffing his hat . . ."

These men are not wearing hats, and in this boat they couldn't "step aside" even if they wanted to. Besides, I am no senator, I'm just the fifteen-year-old grandson of a senator who was also a poet. I've never met him in the flesh, but I have studied the copper engraving that hangs on a wall in our town house: it shows a well-fed man with an arrogant smile who is wearing an *allongé* wig in the style of Louis XIV and a colourful velvet cloak wrapped round his shoulders. Without the wig and cloak, this Bartold Brockes, my grandfather, would look very much like one of these oarsmen whose brawn is propelling the boat across the flood waters. I've been encouraged to read his poems, and being an obedient son with a sense of curiosity, I have read a few. Their wooden piety is not to my liking; altogether, he makes me feel ill at ease. At the moment, I am quite apprehensive – the whole island of Billwerder seems to be under water, and all of Moorfleet as well. My blasphemous opinion of my grandfather's verses makes the bottom of the boat seem very thin. I look down over the side and into the grey yet transparent water and see the tops of the roofs of drowned summer houses. I shout to the oarsmen: "Let's turn back! We've seen what happened here!" But they pretend not to hear me and keep on rowing into ever deeper waters, and I get the feeling that the further out we go, the more likely it is that we'll perish. Then I understand – we are rowing towards the church steeple of Moorfleet, and I know why, even though I haven't heard anyone say anything to me, even though I can't hear anything at all except for the creaking of the oarlocks, and even that has become faint. We are rowing towards the steeple because a child is crying there. I know this even though I can't hear it. We reach the steeple, it looks exactly like the one of the church at Audru: I have seen this steeple before, but from below, in the summers of my childhood. And again when I came to Hamburg on my first assignment abroad and walked and looked at all the places of my former life. Now I see it from above. The church roof is deep down under water, and waves are splashing across the belfry floor. The oarsmen manoeuvre the boat up to the balustrade of the belfry, scull to keep it in place, and tell me (although I can't really hear their voices): "Master, that is the bell-ringer's four-year-old boy, crying – there, behind that pillar. Master, your hands are free. Pick him up and put him in the boat." I get to my feet, step onto the gunwale, feel it sink under my feet. Mortally afraid, I climb up onto the balustrade. I perform a balancing act in the dizzying void, walk all round the tower, look behind every pillar. The bell-ringer's son is nowhere to be seen. And now the boat is no longer there, just the wide expanse of water, and the steps descending down from the belfry. I manage to reach those steps and start walking down. As I descend, I begin to wonder: I should be under water now – way under – and then my forehead strikes a cold pane of glass . . .

13

It is the compartment window. As I wake up with a start, I realize that we've made our stop at Ruhja and are on our way again. Yes, I still have the habit of waking up and getting my bearings without a moment's delay . . . I reach into my waistcoat pocket and take out my watch. It is a Fabergé, with ruby bearings and a golden case; before I push the catch to see what time it is, I look at the shiny cover of the case with the capital letter "L" inlaid in brilliants, and think about the strange twists and turns of fate. This watch was a personal gift from King Léopold of Belgium, almost twenty years ago, when our little father Alexander III had sent me to Brussels to attend a congress on the abolition of the slave trade. Léopold had convened that congress, and I managed to define the fundamental points of the abolition treaty to the satisfaction of all the participants. The Belgian monarch gave me something else as well, I can't remember what it was – I already had the Grand Cross of the Order of Léopold, so it must have been a different one. In any case, he gave me this watch. As the old white-bearded fox handed it to me, he told me that it was a token of his personal gratitude as well as the unanimous gratitude of all the participants, for my magnificent contribution. Ho-hum. He added that I should remember, every time I looked at this watch, that times had changed for the better, that humanity had managed to erase one of its stains of shame . . . Well . . . Perhaps we did clean up one little blot. But by and large . . . Anyway – was it Lefèvre who said about me: *Martens is a man who does not disdain any benefit, no matter how small . . .* ? But the twist of fate I was referring to was simply the fact that the King of Belgium gave a man from Pärnu a watch made by another man from Pärnu. Fabergé, that is.

Let's see: we left Pärnu at nine o'clock, and now it's sixteen minutes past one. Exactly. In forty-five minutes we'll reach Pikksaare, in another forty-five, Härgmäe, and in yet another forty-five, Valga. And on Monday, at eleven o'clock, St Petersburg.

Look at that basket. How evenly and handsomely woven it is. These country folk still know their crafts. A piece of jewellery made out of pine-roots. I still don't know what to do with it. Well, what about my decision to exercise complete candour? I'm afraid it may apply more to the world of dreams than to the one we live in . . . In any case, on Monday afternoon there will be time to relax under the pines of Sestroretsk, by the sea, on a white spindle-backed bench, Kati's hand in my own . . . I still don't know what to do with the basket . . . And on Tuesday morning, at ten, I have to attend that session of the Council of the Ministry of Foreign Affairs. It will be a regular working session, so we won't have to wear our Foreign Ministry uniform with its striped trousers, just our own civilian clothes. But Izvolski himself will be chairing the meeting, and we will discuss our renewed negotiations with Japan. Who will be included in the Russian delegation? What points will be raised (if any)? What is our position on these points? What wishes have Nicky's advisers – down to the last little fawning wretch – whispered into his ear? In what form has he deigned to pass these on to Izvolski? And what should we conclude from all this? And how should we act on these conclusions? To be honest, all this makes me curiously tired . . .

"Tired": I didn't know that word when I was young. In my early teens I cast off my childish indolence and began to follow the schedule of a thinking person, a schedule to which I have adhered ever since, by and large. At five in the morning, an alarm clock I had borrowed from Julius woke me up in my poorhouse garret. Out into the hallway for quick ablutions with ice-cold water, by candlelight, in the otherwise still dormant building. A chunk of bread from the cupboard, and then, to the quiet hiss of the kerosene lamp, an hour or an hour and a half, no more no less, of absolute concentration on the day's homework. This was more than sufficient to keep me at the head of my class for my last four years in school. Classes began at seven. At one in the afternoon, cabbage soup in the dining hall. At half-past one I was on my way into town. My first tutorial began at two. I gave tutorials in many different houses, mostly those of merchants and civil servants, some to children of German families to whom the school's principal Steinman had recommended me, some in the homes of Russians on the recommendation of those

Germans. In both cases my students were either indolent or dim-witted *lycée* boys. I taught Russian to the Germans, German to the Russians, French to some in both groups, mathematics, Russian history, world geography. From two in the afternoon until seven in the evening I trudged around St Petersburg, from one house to the next. At the end of the day's last tutorial I accepted tea and a sandwich instead of cash. At half-past seven I was back in my garret, where I hung my uniform jacket on a nail and plunged into self-designed studies, both of subjects I was tutoring and of others that might come in handy later. The walls of my tiny room were covered with old blackboards borrowed from the school's junk room. I read my books until midnight, noting new facts on the blackboards and erasing them when I had memorized them: vocabulary from Dal's standard dictionary, Italian prepositions, generals of the Great Northern War, the religions and populations of Europe, Asia, and America. And all kinds of other things. At eleven, but often only at midnight, I crawled into bed and slept like a log. At five I was back on my feet. This went on for years, practically until the end of my university studies. But I was never tired.

That was four decades ago. And since then – I received my bachelor's degree in '67, the *magistr* in '69, the doctorate in '73, all the while working as an assistant professor, associate professor, distinguished professor. Became a corresponding member of the Academy; an adviser to the Ministry of Foreign Affairs in '69. Lectured at the Alexander *lycée* and the Law School of the Imperial College. From '73 on, I worked on my imperial assignment, the *Compendium*: eleven volumes in the course of twenty-two years. And wrote tens of thousands of pages of other material. Then there were all my foreign missions, practically one a year starting in '69. The first mission lasted eighteen months; subsequent ones, from the beginning of June to the fifteenth of September. My many other official trips at other times of the year: Brussels, The Hague, Paris, Berlin, Copenhagen, Geneva, Rome, Venice. All kinds of conferences. The conference on the codification of martial law. The International Red Cross. The peace conference at The Hague. The annual meetings of the Institute of International Law. The Congo conferences. Sessions of tribunals of which I was a member, dozens, hundreds of sessions. My special missions to London. Our journey to Ports-

100

mouth. Then the other delegations of which I was a member, either as an academic or as a personal representative of the Emperor, to various festivities at major foreign universities. Edinburgh, Dublin, Yale. A cavalcade of places, people, discussions, speeches. And then, behind this foreground with all its hustle and bustle, my true forum these forty years – ten thousand pairs of young eyes, the ten thousand students whose eyes met mine in lectures, seminars, colloquia, examinations . . . But did I ever feel tired? Not for a moment, until just recently. It was all a pleasure, the pleasure taken in playing the game, in the ability to see through the rules of the game, in being able to teach those rules to others . . . Finally, the most intoxicating, most secret pleasure: the pleasure of breaking the rules of the game. Not a trace of fatigue. Now and again, a few days of despair – but that was different. I have never felt tired until just recently; not, in fact, until last night . . .

Kati! Kati! Where did you go? You know what I told you before. So, come back, for God's sake, and listen to what I want to tell you now. Where are you? Oh, I hope you weren't offended by that stupid crack about Vodovozov – you know I have never seriously – oh, Kati, I know you'll come, straight through the steel walls and purple velvet of this carriage. And you'll forgive me that I dared compare you to Mary, Mrs Christiansen, in an unfavourable way – although it was the truth, if we are to stick to our decision to be completely candid. You are old, she is young. But that's all. To me, you are still beyond compare. You are wise; she is really quite childish. She is, in fact, an unknown quantity. You, your palms, your waist, the shape of your ears, the locks of your hair, all the "verses and stanzas and caesuras of your body", as Heine puts it – all these are full of memories of the life we've shared. And if I sometimes spend time with Mary . . . But I'll tell you about that later, in another context, because that is a purely personal matter. Now I have other things to tell you. Thank you for not flying away, thank you for staying. Come close, come right next to me. Oh, I still can't feel your warm presence, but I know you're here. Listen to me. The article that Vodovozov refers to, the one he uses to slander me and to make me look ridiculous in that miserable book – it does exist. I did write it, in February of 1904, a week after the outbreak of our war with Japan. In it, I said that the Japanese had

attacked us without declaring war. And so they had. The whole
world was reporting what they did in January, 1904, at Port Arthur,
and condemning their action. But now Mr Vodovozov, that vicious
milksop, claims that it was wrong for *me* to condemn it – just
because, in something I wrote *a quarter of a century before that
time*, I had declared formal declarations of war a silly anachronism.
Help me, Kati. Tell me: would a wiser and more objective colleague,
an *honest* colleague, not have tried to *understand*, instead of merely
jeering at me? I don't claim that my conduct was heroic. Before my
decision in favour of complete candour I might have tried to make
such a claim; I might have said that I made a conscious decision to
eat my words for the good of the fatherland – that I made that
sacrifice to Russia. In 1879, Russia needed arguments against
Turkey's accusations. I gave Russia those arguments. In 1904,
Russia needed arguments against Japan. I gave Russia those too
and deliberately suffered the shame I felt because of the contradic-
tory nature of those arguments, before those fellow humans – few,
I thought – who notice and remember such things. I did it to serve
the fatherland . . . But no, no, Kati, we are now in the post-
Punaparg era, and I must tell you the truth. Self-sacrifice never
even entered my mind. I simply couldn't refuse when that butterball
Lamsdorf, our Minister of Foreign Affairs, summoned me and told
me, in his oily obsequious way:
"Fyodor Fyodorovich – an hour ago, the Emperor said to me:
Martens is the authority we need to condemn the Japanese attack
in *Novoye Vremya* – their attack on our ships without a declaration
of war. And the Ministry of Foreign Affairs has to make sure that
the London *Times* and *Le Temps* in Paris reprint his article. These,
Fyodor Fyodorovich, were the Emperor's exact words: '*Martens is
the one spokesman Europe reads with the greatest sympathy.¿*'"
And I thought – believe me, Kati – I thought it was astounding
that our chicken in a colonel's uniform could come up with something like that; then I thought, I can't possibly write what he wants
me to write, it conflicts with what I wrote on the subject twenty-five
years ago . . . Let someone else write it. At the same time, I realized
it was impossible to refuse the Emperor's direct and personal wish,
never mind the fact that he's just a chicken-brain. No, Kati – to tell
you the truth, I *could have refused.* It would have been unpleasant,

102

but it was possible. I could have asked Lamsdorf to explain the situation to Nicky. Lamsdorf would have understood. He could have justified my refusal by saying that such an article would not only make Martens a laughing-stock (who cares about the ridicule heaped on some imperial subject called Martens, as long as it is the Emperor's wish?), but that it would also have a similar adverse effect on Russia's credibility. I'm sure he could have managed it, but I did not ask Lamsdorf to go back to the Emperor with such a message. And I'm sure you would like to know: *why didn't I?*

I'll explain. Post-Punaparg, I am able to do so. I didn't do it because I was *too flattered* by the Emperor's approval – by his personal choice of me as the man for the job. Chicken-brain or not, his flattery tasted good to me at that fateful moment. I must, after all, be too much of an *upstart* to retain my independence, my freedom in such situations. Think about it. How deeply ingrained is the tradition of freedom in someone like me? I'm a second-generation freedman – if you can call poor people free. If you *can't*, then I have enjoyed the state of freedom only half of my life. As you know, my grandparents were peasants in Audru parish, Pärnu province. They were partially franchised, but that didn't prevent the estate owner from exercising his power over them. They knew they were the lowest of the low. I, myself, only rose above the beggar caste a few decades ago, and I'm still too intoxicated by that to retain my independence in regard to an emperor's wishes – at least as long as those wishes are not patently criminal: *that* modest statement I believe I can honestly make. Besides, Kati – how many of our illustrious hereditary aristocrats, do you think, would have refused the imperial request in my position? Let me tell you, nine out of ten would not have refused it under *any* circumstances! Nine out of ten would have complied and felt tickled by the honour. It's the same sensation I remember observing, if not in myself, in the sheepdogs of Pärnu when I was one of the town's two young cowherds – the sensation that makes the dogs wag their behinds when you scratch their bellies . . . Kati, I've shocked you, I can tell – I didn't mean to; and besides, when I complied with the Emperor's request, I still had this thought at the back, or if you wish, at the *front* of my mind: I was convinced that Professor Martens had attained sufficient stature to permit himself such a contradiction without perceptibly damaging his ethical reputation. In a way, that was true, because his readiness to contradict himself at an emperor's behest was just a trifle compared to the liberties he had taken in regard to the empire under the eyes of the whole world.

Kati – you're no longer here beside me? You're not here at all. I can't even see an impression on the velvet seat . . . Does this mean you don't believe me?

Oh, dear God, I'm raving again . . . But look, the sun has come out. The smell of coal-smoke seeps in through the windowframe. We are clattering across the pretty Gulbene, a Latvian river. The time is – according to my royal watch, it is five minutes to two, and we'll soon be in Pikksaare. Now, the Fabergé whose atelier produced this watch – not too long ago, I heard a rather revealing anecdote about him. I can't say I really know the present Fabergé – Karl, that is – but his father I remember very well. Gustav Fabergé was the son of a carpenter from Pärnu. He had known my father, and that acquaintance stood me in good stead during my early St Petersburg days. Back then, in the late Fifties and early Sixties, he was only a fair-to-middling goldsmith on Sadovaya Street. His shop was in a good location, but no one considered his skills particularly remarkable. Thanks to somebody's initiative, I can't remember exactly how, I showed up on Gustav's doorstep one day, a gawky boy as perennially hungry as all of us always were at the orphans' school, and received a standing invitation to Sunday dinner at his table. I enjoyed his kind hospitality for many years. And I'll say this (in the spirit of Punaparg) for Karl, whom I first encountered at those dinners: he became a gentleman even sooner than I did. Now, of course, he is a Purveyor to the Crown, the owner of the most famous jewellery shop in Russia, with branches in Moscow and London and Paris and a clientele consisting of royalty and their courts. He is a Russian in Russia, a German in Germany, a Frenchman in France. So – I heard this amusing story about him; I think you won't have any trouble staying with me for this one. It's the kind you've always enjoyed.

About three weeks ago, on my most recent visit to the Estonian Society in St Petersburg, I met a young man whose name I can't recall at the moment – some kind of fish: *Haug? Siik? Latikas?* Hmm. A short name. A young clergyman with a red shock of hair and the face of a cunning peasant. He was doing his internship with Rudolf Kallas. We chatted over a cup of tea. He was a well-spoken fellow who shared my interest in languages and etymologies. We happened to start talking about pejorative family names, particularly among Estonians, names like Lammas, Oinas, Härg, Karusitt.* There are plenty of those, and it is easy to understand why. Then, with a smile that made his little red moustache twitch, he told me this story:

One day, a couple of months ago, he is sitting in the office of St John's parish when this stranger shows up, sporting a sable coat and a cane and a pair of gloves that look like they've been bought at Barthold's *Magasin Etranger* if not at some even fancier place. The man says to him: "Give me my papers! I'm leaving this congregation of peasants. I'm joining the German congregation." The young clergyman says: "Excuse me, sir, but could you tell me your name – I regret that I don't have the honour . . . ?" "I can tell you don't," the gentleman says. "I am Karl Fabergé, goldsmith to the Imperial Court, and I have decided to transfer to the German congregation at St Peter's." But the young carrot-top with the name of a fish asks him to take a seat and gives him a little lecture:

"Dear Mr Fabergé, sir – even though I don't know you personally, your name is, of course, very well known to me. Please tell me, why do you want to abandon our congregation? Have you really thought this over carefully? Please, allow me to go on for just a moment. I am sure that you, Mr Fabergé, are the kind of gentleman who doesn't much care for the old adage that it is better to be a big fish in a small pond than a small one in a big pond. Nevertheless, you are, among the souls in *our* congregation, the bearer of one of its most illustrious names. A *jewel* of a name, if I may say so. Let me assure you that we're aware of that. If you were to join St Peter's, your name would, of course, also be considered worthy of respect. But – it would be just one of many, and, begging your pardon, perhaps not even one of the *most* illustrious, when you consider how many members of that congregation are nobly born and prominent at the court. Our congregation here at St John's is, if I may say so, much more varied and multilingual. True, most of our members are

* (See Notes – Translator)

105

humble folk. Estonians. Civil servants, merchants, artisans. Even servants. But among them there also are quite a few holders of higher office. Prominent citizens. Hereditary prominent citizens, such as yourself. Even hereditary noblemen. Scholars. Generals. Oh yes. Germans, Swedes, Dutchmen. Not too many of those, but a few. So . . . Your father was a faithful member of our congregation all his life. And you've been a member, let's see, for how long? Almost sixty years? Considering that, our congregation, if I may say so, should have become a kind of obligation – a kind of *home* to you, Mr Fabergé, especially since you, as one of its sons, have achieved such a glorious position in –"

At this point, Mr Fabergé bangs the desk with a fist sporting three gold rings and shouts: "That's enough, pastor, or secretary, or whatever the hell you are. Tell me, what have those damn Estonians ever given us? I'll tell you what: nothing but our impossible names. *Do you know* what our family's name was, in Estonian? It was *Vanaperse*. What goddamn obligation should I owe them for that?"

And Mr Fabergé withdrew his documents from St John's and made the transfer to the predominantly German congregation of St Peter's.

Then, Kati, that young minister looked at me with his light-grey country boy's eyes, still smiling, and said, in a half-questioning tone: "But in your case, of course, there could never be such a dilemma . . ."

I understood that he was feeling me out, testing me, a little ironically – so I replied, in an entirely noncommittal, one might say, transparently opaque manner:

"In my case – no, fortunately not. Back in Pärnu, I belonged to the congregation of my almost-namesake Pastor Märtens, if that name means anything to you. But here in St Petersburg I've been on the books of St Peter's from 1855 on – ever since I became a student at their school for orphans."

Then I took my leave, amicably and jovially, and left him sitting there at the table of the tiny club buffet. He looked a little nonplussed, obviously unable to determine whether his irony had reached its mark. I almost felt a little sorry for him.

As for his irony, well – I don't know if it affected me or not.

106

14

We're passing a station with no scheduled stop. A platform. A siding. On the siding stand three small round tank wagons bearing a yellow legend on their black bellies: RUSSKI NOBEL – RUSSKI NOBEL – RUSSKI NOBEL.

This means we're running half an hour late; it also means that the river we crossed a while ago wasn't the Gulbene, as I thought in my half-conscious state, but the one before it, whose name I can't remember for some reason. The station we just passed was Nausküla.

If an outsider could see into my brain, he might find it strange that the Nobel Prize question puts in such frequent appearances in my thoughts. This time around, its appearance isn't due to personal vanity but to mere coincidence. There were three brothers named Nobel, all of them ill-fated and long dead. The two petroleum magnates whose logo flashed at me from those tank wagons don't concern me in the least – but I have been reminded of the third, and of my interest in his legacy.

I find it difficult to assess objectively how much I've coveted or still covet the Peace Prize instituted by that third Nobel, the dynamite king. If I consider the matter in the light of my "comparativist" system, it seems obvious that I would be very pleased to receive it. Funnily enough, I can't think of anyone more deserving; I have no more than a dozen equals in that field. During the eight years since the inception of the Nobel Prize, there has been much debate about its supposed impartiality. At the same time, these awards have gained fame and prestige. I must say that whatever the case may be in medicine, and physics, and all the other fields, the Peace Prize, by its very nature, is not so much a matter of merit as of sympathies. No matter how honest the award committee may consider its decision, there is some dishonesty in it from the very beginning. Mark my words. Take what Mr Berner said, nine years ago, when they first decided to award a Peace Prize: he claimed that it was the Norwegian people's staunch pacifism that had caused Mr Alfred Nobel to entrust the Norwegian parliament with the task of awarding the Peace Prize. Was Mr Berner, the speaker of that parliament, really such a poor psychologist, or such a short-sighted politician, that he didn't know the truth? Of course not. Of course he knew, but he covered it up with a political lie. With a political lie, he covered up for a liar who never reached a Punaparg in his life.

The political background of the matter was quite different; the decision, entirely pragmatic, had nothing to do with the blue eyes of the Norwegian people or their pacifism. It was the *hatred* in those blue eyes that Mr Nobel tried to placate in his will. At the time he was drawing up that will, popular Norwegian resistance against Sweden was growing stronger because of the demeaning role of poor cousin that Norway had been assigned in the country's "personal union" with Sweden. The historical record shows . . . and so on, but in any case: by entrusting the Peace Prize to the Norwegian parliament, Mr Nobel simply wanted to appease the Norwegians' natural anti-Swedish sentiment. It was a classic example of the "divide and conquer" principle. But from a human standpoint – well, maybe the inventor of nitroglycerin and dynamite did not believe in God (or came to believe, who knows, in his final struggle with death at San Remo), but he must have believed in *sin*. The grounds for such a belief were all too evident in our era of industry, our era of explosions, our era of terror – whose Berthold Schwarz, or Faust, or Mephisto, Alfred Nobel was. Even though his inventions decreased the number of accidents during the transportation of explosives by, let us say, $\propto$ times, the number of possibilities for the use of these explosives to deliberately kill people rose to ten times $\propto$. One may of course ask whether the use to which his inventions were put was his fault, and one may answer: probably not, since true idealists never anticipate the baseness of the world. Or one might say that he simply didn't want to know. True inventors never do.

Be that as it may, it is obvious that Mr Nobel was too intelligent to be completely tone-deaf to the music of ethics. His decision to institute a *peace* prize is clear evidence of that. Who can tell, or care, how much it reassured him in regard to his own conscience?

In the eyes of the world, the prize worked extremely well. The dust of oblivion covers the patents once granted to Nobel for his dynamite and smokeless gunpowder, but the Nobel Peace Prize is still coveted and awarded every year. At present, I don't feel inclined to sacrifice time or imaginative effort on an overly active concern with that prize. Whether I'll receive it or not depends on too many imponderables beyond my power. To become a serious candidate for it in the year $\propto$, one would have to synchronize, during the year $\propto - 1$, and several years before that, a whole group of factors. Arbitration tribunals chaired by me would have to achieve results of the kind that receive favourable notice in the world's major newspapers. If not in all, which is practically impossible, then at least in some of them. Furthermore, if, let us say, *The Times* reports favourably on my work, *Le Temps* should not criticize it, but at the very least remain silent. Or vice versa. Et cetera. I must not be a judge on any tribunal considering matters in which Norway is involved. Also, during the year $\propto$ or $\propto - 1$, some of my books have to appear in the West, issued by reliable publishers, and inspire confidence rather than sensational interest. If they are too sensational, this makes them suspect to the rather academically oriented prize committee, never mind how pleasing such explosive and widespread interest might be to their author – as it was, for instance, in the case of my little book *Russia and England in Central Asia* (St Petersburg, 1880). It bore a provocative epigraph from de Tocqueville: *Il faut une science politique nouvelle à un monde tout nouveau* . . . I wrote the book in French, and Russian, German, and English translations appeared within a few months. It generated so much interest in the United States that the American publisher didn't wait for the ship that was to bring him a copy of the English translation, but insisted – it still makes me smile when I think about it – that the text be *telegraphed* to him from London. And so it was; imagine the cost of a one-hundred-page telegram! They produced the book in less than a week, which meant that it was on sale two weeks sooner than it would have been without the use of the telegraph. It was one of those works of mine that pedants now consider "mere pamphleteering". They are entitled to their opinion.

But to get back to the Nobel Prize: thirdly (and at present this is the most essential factor, and one completely beyond my power), during any crisis year, and for at least a few years before any crisis, Russia's international behaviour must be acceptable to the West – to England, France, and the United States. And, of course, Norway. And at least tolerable from the German and Austrian point of view. If Russia has, during this critical period, taken any militaristic or aggressive steps, a Russian internationalist becomes immediately unacceptable – not only if he has publicly defended his government's actions, but also if he has remained silent about them. His chances in Kristiania would, of course, improve immediately if he spoke out against peace-threatening actions taken by his government – not just in any old way, but moderately and academically. Anything else would scare the Norwegians off. However, in my country and in my position, such anti-government utterances are completely unthinkable. I can only hope for years of harmony without a cloud on the horizon of international politics. But when I consider the dark thunderclouds I see gathering – the Balkan controversy between Russia and Austria; our desire to be "the protector of all Slavs"; our policy changes between one foreign leader's visit to the next; our designs on the Bosporus; the revolution in Turkey – my chances seem rather slim, at least in the near future. And to think that they were really good, in 1902 . . .

The first prize, awarded in 1901, could not have gone to a Russian under any circumstances, in spite of the fact that my chances were extremely good: after all, I had been the head of the first subcommittee of the first peace conference at The Hague in 1899 – the committee that clearly achieved the most tangible results. But there was no Literature Prize for Tolstoy, no Peace Prize for me. The Peace Prize was shared by Dunant and Passy, and I must admit that I've always found the former the most interesting person among all who have received the Prize so far – both interesting and irritating, an extraordinary character. Born to a wealthy bourgeois family in Geneva, active in the Young Men's Christian Association, a dabbler in literature; then, suddenly, an enterprising businessman in Algeria, a colonial, almost, if you wish, a colonial overlord, and certainly a millionaire. The working capital of his agricultural concern is said to have been one hundred million francs. Then he makes a business trip to secure water rights for his grand enterprise and seeks an audience with Emperor Napoleon III. The Emperor is on a military campaign in Italy. This does not deter Dunant who sets out to join him, impervious to the hazards of war, spurred on by his entrepreneurial vision. In late June, 1859, he catches up with the French army, somewhere south of Lake Garda – and finds himself in the middle of the Battle of Solferino. And discovers what such a battle, the bloodiest of the century, really feels like when one is in the midst of it, and also what it looks like when it is over: a field of chaos and desperation that reverberates with the screaming agony of the wounded and dying, whose distress no one has made any plans for relieving. In 1862, Dunant publishes a small pamphlet in which he sets forth the idea of an International Red Cross. He proceeds to turn this personal idea, born from a personal experience, into a powerful international organization. On the twenty-second of August, 1864, after Dunant has spent many millions lobbying for it, representatives of twelve nations meet to sign the Geneva Convention and the charter of the International Red Cross.

But his imagination did not stop there. He wrote a book titled *On a Universal and International Union to Enlighten the Orient*, and another titled *On an International Universal Library*. In 1872, he convened an international conference in Geneva charged with the creation of a Universal Union for Order and Civilization. At this meeting, two subjects were raised that became central to my subsequent work: the need for international agreements on the treatment of prisoners of war, and the resolution of conflicts between nations by means of international arbitration tribunals. I had the good fortune to be present at that conference. During the eight years of its existence, M. Dunant's Red Cross had become a prominent institution. Our Ministry of Foreign Affairs had sent me on a mission to Paris. There I heard about Dunant's conference and decided to attend it. I saw Dunant and heard two of his speeches. He was a handsome, tousle-headed man with sparkling eyes, an enthusiastic and absent-minded Don Quixote. In the hallways of the convention chambers I heard, however, that opinion on him was sharply divided. Idealists like himself sang his praises, but business and political circles regarded him as a lost cause. He had ruined himself financially, and a few years later, in 1875 if I remember correctly, he was ostracized by Geneva society. He left town, and for fifteen years he lived God knows where and on God knows what, while a few others, I among them, went on pursuing and propagating his ideas for international arbitration, and for a convention on prisoners of war. He seems to have led the life of an itinerant beggar. According to his own account (who knows how credible it is), he would use ink on his coat, to blacken the worn spots, and chalk on his dirty collars, to make them look white, and spend his nights under the open sky.

In 1890, he reappeared at Heiden, a tiny Swiss village, where the local schoolmaster recognized him and told the world that the founder of the International Red Cross was still alive. There wasn't much the world could do for him any more, because he was ill – with a mental illness . . . He was put in the hospital at Heiden, room number twelve, and he has not left it since. Not even nine years ago, when he was told that he was being celebrated as the foremost champion of peace on the whole planet. Not even when it was explained to him that he was once again, if not a millionaire, a man of some means. He stayed in his room, and there he remains, as far as I know, until this day. It is said that he has drawn up a will in which he stipulates that his Peace Prize be divided equally between Swiss and Norwegian charitable organizations, and that he himself be buried in the village cemetery at Heiden *sans aucune cérémonie, comme un simple chien.*

Frédéric Passy is an entirely different type of person. Extremely reliable, extremely logical, extremely industrious. A true scholar, a member of the *Institut de France*. To that extent, somewhat similar to me. But also a thunderous orator, which I am not, and a member of the Inter-Parliamentary Union – an organizer, which I am to an even lesser degree. In the spirit of our comparativist psychology, I might also add that while Passy may be a more eloquent spirit, I am a more original one. Nevertheless, the Scandinavians consider the French peace movement more real and more credible than its Russian counterpart. Never mind what they might say in public, I'm sure they more or less agree that serious pacifism is impossible in an autocratic state. That can't be helped. So the prize went to Dunant and Passy. Then came 1902.

I can't say that I have a complete picture of what exactly happened, but I won't deny that the whole affair turned out to be the most ridiculous disappointment of my life. I don't think there is anyone alive who has experienced a disappointment quite like it. I had known about my nomination for quite a while. Then I received a telegram, and not from just anybody, not from some circle of well-meaning gossips, but from Emmanuil Yuliyevich Nolde. My most reliable friend. An experienced politician, one of the most critical and well-informed men I know. It came from The Hague, where he happened to be at the time, and where one is informed about everything sooner than anywhere else in the world.

I had gone to Pärnu, although it was quite late in the year, to think things over and spend a little time by myself in the old house on Gartenstrasse. Nicol considered a telegram from The Hague sufficiently important to forward it to me.

As I recall, it was an overcast November afternoon; outside, the ground was still bare, but greyish snowflakes were already drifting down from low clouds. I received the telegram in the same room with the blue wallpaper where I sat yesterday reading Vodovozov's slanderous article. I stood by the old, rather battered, round-legged desk that had belonged to my father. According to family tradition, he had bought it in Audru for the first pay he received working as a teacher in the parish school – before he lost his position, for reasons unknown to me. Aunt Krööt had not been able to part with it, despite her general tendency to turn things into cash, and I had bought it back from her for ten roubles not long before her death. I stood by that desk and opened the telegram:

Most esteemed Fyodor Fyodorovich Stop Congratulate you with all my heart on award of Nobel Peace Prize Stop One hundred thousand roubles but a pittance compared to your merits Stop Nevertheless this supreme recognition has found its most deserving recipient Stop Sincerely yours Emmanuil Yuliyevich Nolde

I stood by the desk. I remember putting the telegram down, closing my eyes, and feeling – Kati, I'm no longer ashamed to confess this to you, as I have been for seven years – feeling weak at the knees, so that I had to lean on the desktop to keep from sinking to the floor. I stood there for a minute and let the triumphal moment pass. Then I sat down and gave vent to my feelings in a note to Emmanuil:

113

Dear Emmanuil Yuliyevich!

My heartfelt thanks for your congratulations on the award of the Nobel Peace Prize. I still have not received official confirmation of it from Kristiania, but I was aware that some foreign friends and persons who value my work had proposed my candidacy. In any case, let me assure you that I regard this Peace Prize as the final achievement and "crown" of my career. I have no further ambitions.

Then I felt a little embarrassed by the excessively solemn and confessional tone of this, and added, with the matter-of-factness that reminds me of the flavour of the lees at the bottom of a tankard of Audru ale, and that once in a while rises up in me through the otherwise benign Martens disposition:

The monetary amount of the prize is, indeed, impressive, even though it is not a hundred thousand. If it has been granted to me in its entirety, it is more like seventy thousand, as far as I know.
Cordially yours,
F. M.

I sent Kaarel to mail the letter as soon as I had finished it, but even before he had had time to reach the letter box at the railway station, I began to feel bothered by one of its sentences. Even though I wrote a great number of notes and letters, I had begun to regard them as *historical* to some degree. That is to say, historical to the extent that I could imagine strangers reading them at some future date; and this was an incentive to pay close attention to what I wrote. Due to its content, this little note was more "historical" than many others. Suddenly I felt annoyed with myself for having written *I have no further ambitions* – as if this personal award had been the ultimate goal of all my endeavours! I did not, however, run after Kaarel. Emmanuil Yuliyevich was a wise old man; he would understand what I meant. So I stayed put. I pondered things for a while, managed to overcome a certain sense of vanity, and rejected the idea of returning to St Petersburg on the morning train. What use would that be? I decided to await the arrival of the official

114

telegram in Pärnu. I was certain that my nearest and dearest would forward it immediately.

Then there were those three or four days . . .

In November, the town was amazingly quiet, almost as if it didn't exist. In the mornings I could hear a few distant train whistles from the station. Like the voices of young deer . . . As if I knew what those sound like. I had plenty of work piled up on my desk in preparation for the tribunal on Venezuela, in response to Theodore Roosevelt's recent request that I serve on it as an arbitrator. Once in a while, I could hear footsteps on the frozen gravel of the path. They would pass, and I would think, no, it wasn't the man with the telegram . . . It was so peaceful all around me, and inside me there was a rare feeling of joyous anticipation, like a wide, warm, slow river. I had no doubts at all. Well, I don't know about "at all" – an experienced person always has doubts about everything. Let's say that I had *practically* no doubts. Even while perusing the documents from British Guyana and Venezuela, I was hatching plans in the playroom of my imagination. I'll resign from all my professorial obligations, once and for all. Taube, my pleasant colleague (oh, I mustn't forget – *Baron* von Taube), is well qualified to take them on, and so is young Nolde, Boris Emmanuilevich – who, by the way, is a baron as well, but one needn't be so careful about remembering that in his case. So, no more teaching. My pension will amount to seven thousand roubles or so, and the Nobel will be the equivalent of ten annuities. I'll be a free man, at last. Completely free. As for my seat on the collegium of the Ministry of Foreign Affairs – I have to think that over, to decide what will best serve the cause to which I have dedicated myself: international arbitration. Practical work at the international court at The Hague, where my authority will be enhanced by the Peace Prize. And theoretical work, a large monograph on the function of international arbitration tribunals: A) The theoretical foundations. B) A historical overview. C) An analysis of the most important cases. D) Generalizations, conclusions, perspectives. Two volumes, at least. No, one is better. It's time for me to learn the concision of age. But – who is fumbling with the latch of the garden gate and coming down the path towards the verandah? – no, it's Frieda, Kaarel's wife. I recognize her footsteps.

It goes without saying that I read the newspapers every day. There was nothing in them about the Nobel Prizes until the fourth or fifth day when I took my customary walk to the station, picked up the papers they saved for me, and on the walk home, at the corner of Karja Street, opened *Novoye Vremya* and read the names of that year's Peace Prize laureates: *Ducommun and Gobat*.

I felt as if someone had suddenly pulled a chair out from under me. I was falling into the void, turning somersaults, destined to keep on falling forever.

I'll spare myself the details of my feelings at that moment. But it was a good thing, Kati, that I had read the papers before you arrived in Pärnu that evening.

You had forwarded Emmanuil's telegram without opening it, but Emmanuil had sent another telegram announcing my Nobel to his own family. Nothing odd about that: he merely wanted to share the good news. Boris, his son, had hurried over from their house to ours, just around the corner, from Mohovaya to Panteleimonovskaya Street. And after that, Kati, you had been waiting too, and reading the papers until you saw those names, a day and a half sooner than I did in Pärnu: Ducommun and Gobat. Without a moment's delay, you got on the train to bring me word of that blow and to soften it by being with me. But I had already received the blow, many hours, half a day before your arrival. So I affected a stiff upper lip and welcomed you with a laugh:

"Oh Kati – how sweet of you to come! To come and sweep that crown of straw off your old man's head, and to help him hold his head high, nevertheless – but look, Kati, I've taken that crown off already, and tossed it into the fire . . ."

Kaarel had made a fire in my study, and the flames were licking the scorched bark of the logs.

"So you know?" you asked in a whisper.

"I know, my darling, I know."

"That it was some terrible mistake?"

"I know, Katyenka. And I have already *forgotten* all about it. Come here –"

You came into my arms, still in your winter coat. I took off your fur hat which was covered in droplets of melted snow and looked into your large, sad eyes; eyes that were trying to smile, to find out

116

how I was dealing with what had happened, ready to join in whatever reaction they found, ready to declare Emmanuil's telegram a
fatal mistake, an irresponsible act, almost a homicide, a swinish
prank, a bagatelle – and to agree with me that the situation was
either a tragedy or a farce or simply not worth another thought.
There was no condescension in that readiness – I knew that it arose
out of a woman's steely resolve to support her husband when he
has suffered a setback. I looked into your eyes, then buried my
nose in the coquettishly grey strands of hair beside your ear and
whispered:

"Thank you, dear. Take off your coat, and we'll share a bottle of
Mignal. And tell me, have you really got rid of that cough?"

I have never found out what exactly happened to my Nobel Prize.
Deeply embarrassed, Emmanuil explained later that he had acted
on premature information. He looked positively ill when he told me
that, and I never asked him for details. My curiosity has, of course,
provoked me to investigate the matter, while pride has held me
back. In the course of the last seven years, I have been able to piece
together a general sort of picture.

At the end of October, the Norwegian parliament's Peace Prize
committee had met to consider the four or five strongest candidates:
Ducommun and Gobat, both from Switzerland; Cremer of England;
the Danes' or Norwegians' own Bajer; and me. Ducommun and
Gobat were eliminated for the simple reason that half of last year's
prize had gone to Switzerland, and the committee didn't want to
let that country monopolize the prize. Sir Randal Cremer, a former
carpenter who had risen through the ranks of the Labour movement,
may have struck some of the gentlemen as too radical. Since Bajer
was one of their own, they probably had too many arguments against
him to sustain his candidacy. Then they discussed me. They must
have remembered the favourable impression I had made at the first
peace conference at The Hague, only three years ago. They also
must have remembered the many arbitration tribunals on which I
had served in the past, sailing between Scylla and Charybdis, putting out many small incendiary fires between nations. Then again,
some of the gentlemen may have voiced the traditional doubts as
to whether Russia was indeed a country fit to receive a Peace Prize.
At that point, they postponed the decision and left my name hanging

in mid-air, so to speak. I don't know how formal or informal those people are in their procedures, but I imagine that they are rather free and easy compared to the committees of our Senate or Douma. However, I don't think they invite the press to their meetings. It may well be that the five of them decided to walk across the square in front of the parliament building to have lunch at a restaurant. Or, God knows, maybe their meeting was *held* at a restaurant. Once bottles of beer had been brought to the table, they may have been joined by, let us say, the editor of *Aftenposten*. I don't doubt that they only mentioned me as one of the candidates, but journalists have a reputation for being impatient folk, especially in countries where they needn't feel any burden of responsibility. And so, I was hailed the next day in some Kristiania papers – not as a candidate, but as the *recipient* of the Peace Prize. That news item may or may not have been corrected the following day; the committee must have read the premature news, and may have demanded a correction. At its next meeting, either because they were flustered by this canard, or to prove that they were able to make exceptions, the committee announced that two Swiss gentlemen, Ducommun and Gobat, were the winners of the prize. However, that first erroneous press report entered the files of all the major libraries of the world. Some time later, I encountered it on the other side of the globe, clothed in very respectable garb . . .

When our delegation arrived in Portsmouth, New Hampshire, in August 1905, this was a semi-official state visit. The Mayor of the town gave a dinner in our honour, and he invited the Japanese delegation to a similar occasion a couple of days later. At this dinner, at the local officers' club, a gentleman from the State Department said a few words of welcome, no doubt prepared from whatever source material he had been able to find on Witte, Rosen, and myself. He introduced Witte as the most distinguished reformer of Russia's economy (well, I didn't have too much of a problem with that). He said that Rosen was a rising star of Russian diplomacy and Russia's newly appointed Ambassador to the United States (the first half of that statement was, of course, absurd, the second, correct). Then he welcomed me with these words: "In this room, Mr Martens does not need an introduction – as we know, he is one of the three men to whom Europe has awarded its famous Nobel Peace Prize."

Once again, the fatal mistake caused me embarrassment. I couldn't very well interrupt the representative of the State Department by shouting "Sorry, sir – there seems to be some confusion here!" – especially since he said no more about me, but went on to speak about the Russian government's deep desire for peace. Any protest on my part would have seemed to cast aspersions on the veracity of *that* assertion as well. In any case, the company at table, both Americans and Russians, cast surprised glances in my direction, and I have to admit that I, too, was momentarily stunned. I asked myself: What does this mean? Have they announced this year's prize this early, in August, instead of at the end of the year, as usual? Was there some reason for an early announcement, and did they really give it to me – and was I the last one to know?

The gentleman went on to praise President Roosevelt's laudable role in the realization of the inspiring endeavour on which we were now embarking, and Witte picked up his champagne glass and whispered to me ironically:

"There you are, Fyodor Fyodorovich – you really are luckier abroad than ever at home. Here, you already have the Nobel Prize. If it were up to the Americans . . ."

After the speeches were over, I had to explain things to several Russians, and fend off congratulations offered by some Americans. "Gentlemen, this must simply be a mistake. Until now, I have only heard of my *candidacy*." But when I pointed out the error to the State Department man (which I had to do, of course), that red-headed Irish rogue looked at me with his mocking green eyes and said:

"Sir, I've never met any Russians before, and I'm unfamiliar with your ways, so I can't be sure what you're trying to tell me: is this some kind of European modesty – or are you acting the inscrutable Asian?"

"I beg your pardon?"

"Well, it seems that you're trying to hide your achievements . . ."

He summoned one of his underlings and gave him an order. Three minutes later, the young man returned with a hefty tome. I don't remember its name, but it was the volume for the letter M of the previous year's edition of a major encyclopedia published in New York. A slip of paper had been inserted at the relevant page.

The State Department man opened the volume and held it under my nose, for me to read with my own eyes:

MARTENS, Frédéric Fromhold de (Russ. Fyodor Fyodorovich Martens), Russian jurist and diplomat: b. Pärnu, Estonia, Aug. 27, 1845. He was educated at the University of St Petersburg, where from 1873 he has been professor of international law. Entering the Russian ministry of foreign affairs in 1868, he became legal adviser to the foreign office and represented the government at many international conferences, including the Le Hague peace conference 1899. A recognized authority on international law and a skilled arbitrator, he was awarded the Nobel Peace Prize in 1902. His best known published works are . . .

And another four or five lines I didn't bother to read.

The fellow looked at me triumphantly. What was I to tell him? How should I respond to his remark about European modesty and Asian inscrutability? Perhaps by pointing out, first of all, that I am not a Russian? Nor a German? That my ancestors have inhabited Europe for at least two thousand years, even though my modesty is not European, but – what? – the modesty of the great forests, perhaps? There have been times when I have gone into such detail, but only a few. Anyway – what now, I mean, then – why should I? What could I say about the strange mistake in his encyclopedia? I said, with a smile:

"I regret to tell you, but it's still a mistake. But let us hope that it is a prophetic mistake. One that will make your kind words of tonight come true in the future."

He shook his head, laughed. "God, you Russians really are something else!"

I was left with the impression that he didn't believe me at all, but held on to his conviction that I was being secretive about my prize due to some Russian spirit of contrariness and hypocrisy that was simply incomprehensible to the Irish-American mind.

At least until now, his words have not proved prophetic.

In 1903, they gave the prize to Cremer. In 1904, the outbreak of war damaged the chances of a Russian candidate. Besides – and I don't deny it at all, which is why I don't need Mr Vodovozov to

120

point this out – I did some further damage myself, with that article of mine which received some Vodovozovian comments in London and Paris. Still, that does not give him the right to . . .

Well. The 1904 prize went to the Institute of International Law of whose executive committee I had been a member for a decade. I've been told that the prize committee's reasoning went something like this: "Since, for obvious reasons, we cannot give this year's prize to Martens, we'll give it to his Institute. He is, after all, one of its most influential members." I don't know if anyone really spoke these words. But they would have been the truth.

In 1905, my participation in the creation of the Treaty of Portsmouth (scandalous as some of its circumstances were) should have improved my chances considerably. At the same time, that year's events in Russia obliterated them, so the prize went to Mrs von Suttner and her novel *Die Waffen nieder!*. A mediocre piece of writing, if you ask me. Well, she didn't get the *Literature* Prize for it. Besides, it had been published in 1889, if I remember correctly, so it took the world sixteen years to take sufficient notice . . . And in 1906, they gave the Peace Prize to – Theodore Roosevelt. For what? For our Treaty of Portsmouth. *My* Treaty of Portsmouth. For hosting the conference at which it was created. Now, it may well be that articles in up-to-date encyclopedias claim (I just demonstrated their reliability) that he received it for "various energetic peace initiatives". They can't very well say that he received a Peace Prize for his frenetic build-up of the United States Navy, or for his escapades in the Spanish-American War at the head of a squadron he financed and equipped out of his own pocket. No, no; what they'll say in future editions will be that Roosevelt received the Nobel Peace Prize because he invited the creators of the treaty to Portsmouth – in other words, the Japanese, Witte, and me . . . While not even the *initiative* to act as a mediator was his own: it was Komura who asked him to do it.

Generally speaking, there seem to be three categories of Nobel Peace Prize laureates. First, there are the quixotic idealists à la Dunant: awkward, strange, even comical, but genuinely dedicated to their cause. Secondly, successful politicians like Roosevelt. They advocate peace only as long as it suits their pan-Americanism or whatever their "ism" may be. As soon as that "ism" demands it, they'll go to war with great gusto. To them, peace is a concern of the second or third rank of importance, and they're ready to sacrifice peace at any moment to their own primary political objectives – which they may well describe as "defending the peace". Then, there is a third, perhaps intermediate category: it consists of theoreticians connected to official institutions, people like myself. Serving two masters – their governments, and their own ideals – they are torn between the two. The more selfish those governments, the more intense will be the interior conflicts these people inevitably suffer. (When the government even *calls itself* an autocracy, the term speaks for itself.) Hence, they devote most of their energies to the concealment of their own dichotomies from the eyes of the world, and from themselves . . .

In 1907, they gave the prize to Moneta and Rénault. The former is a little crazy. When he leaves his house in Milan in order to go to a restaurant on the other side of the street, he gets on the tram at a stop not far from his front door and rides it for a three-verst-long loop to get off in front of the restaurant – all this to avoid crossing the street . . . But he seems to be a popular journalist in Italy, and I gather that the fervour of his Italian patriotism matches that of our own Black Hundred. Rénault, however, is no buffoon; one might say that Rénault is the Martens of France.

However, last year's awards really disappointed me. Rénault received his share of the prize for his work at the second peace conference at The Hague – serious work, but no more serious than mine. All right, the Nobel Prize is a Western European institution, and Rénault deserved to get his prize before a so-called Russian. But once they had honoured him, why did they not grant it to me? The fourth commission, which I chaired, completely codified the laws on modern maritime warfare; everybody knows – and knew then – that this was to a very high degree my personal achievement. God knows, I felt it then, and I can still feel it: the twentieth of September, 1907, was, and still is, one of the high points of my life. That was when I summed up our work at the commission's plenary session in these words:

Si de l'Antiquité à nos jours on a répété l'adage romain Inter arma silent leges *nous avons proclamé hautement* Inter arma vivant leges. *C'est le plus grand triomphe du droit et de la justice sur la force brutale et sur les nécessités de la guerre* . . .

But last year they neglected me again and gave the prize to that Bajer and a Swede no one knows anything about. They think that I can still wait. And I can wait! They can't *ignore* me! But, Kati – it's all just a game. You know that as well as I do. And I am strangely tired of that game . . . I'm reminded of my own student days. When was it? In St Petersburg? During my first year at the university, 1863? Or in Göttingen, in 1774? St Petersburg or Göttingen? St Pettingen or Göttersburg? But this is silly . . .

15

Choo-choo – choo-choo – choo-choo – choo-choo . . .

Once again, the smoke has started seeping in through the compartment window. It is hurting my eyes and making me dizzy . . .

Smoke. And where there's smoke . . . I can't remember exactly *where*: in 1863 in St Petersburg, or in 1774 in Göttingen . . . No, no – if it was Göttingen, it was a little later, in any case. Lord, surely not *everything* in our lives has taken place exactly according to that same interval? Because if the interval between the two Martenses were so rigidly fixed, then – I say this out loud, into the clatter of the train – then I would have to die next year, 1910! Fortunately, the intervals between our lives are in many respects quite variable, and there have been events that don't match up at all. This matter of *fires* is an excellent example. If anything like what I'm about to relate ever truly happened to Georg Friedrich – if I, as Friedrich Fromhold, haven't just dreamed or imagined it – it happened to him considerably later than 1774. It happened to me during my first year as a university student. To him, it couldn't have happened before 1786, after he'd been asked to become the tutor of three English princes . . .

Yes, he is – or we are, or I am, as you wish – a professor at Göttingen. I have held that position for almost three years. And the sons of King George III of England, of the House of Hanover – sons of a king who is mad and sane by turns – are my students. I am a professor at the university, but I am also an *Oberhofmeister* appointed by the Royal Court of England. The boys do not, as yet, attend my lectures on international law, at least not with any regularity. But in addition to my lectures, and seminars, and academic council meetings, and to my participation in the round of festive and social occasions the princes' move to Göttingen has generated, I am also running my own school for young diplomats. I feel justified in saying that it isn't so much the reputation of our venerable Georgia Augusta University as the fame of my own school of

diplomacy that has brought the princes here. Despite their tender
age, they have been deemed ready to learn the arts of diplomacy.
Clearly, this is a little ridiculous, but I have, of course, declared it
to be a very great honour to my humble self . . . *Mundus vult
decipi*, as the old saying goes, and I don't have any problem with
that. All you need to master is that little bow, in the right direction,
at the right moment – and executed in such a manner that only you
yourself will notice the little ironic smile reflected on the floor,
provided that the floor is sufficiently polished . . . The princes have
been here since last summer: Edward, Duke of Kent, aged sixteen;
Ernest, Duke of Cumberland, fifteen; and August, Duke of Sussex,
thirteen. The second will become – as I already know, by some
strange premonition – a king of Hanover notorious for his despotism,
and later my tutorship will stand me in good stead. But Edward –
I know this, too – will be the father of a certain Victoria who'll
ascend to the throne and will, in her ripe old age, grant me, Fyodor
Fyodorovich, a benign smile of thanks for my services . . .

But now I'm riding in the princes' carriage, past the recently
dismantled Grone Gate, back into Göttingen from a walking excursion at Hoher Hain. Halfway back, we ran into rainy weather and
are now proceeding at top speed down the narrow street behind
the Hospital of the Holy Spirit. Our first stop will be the princes'
domicile at Weender Street; we are expected at the Town Hall at
eight o'clock, at a ball given in honour of Georgia Augusta University's fiftieth anniversary – a grand event, since the princes will
grace it by their presence. Five hundred people have been invited
to the ball and banquet. Later in the evening there'll be a firework
display in the town square. But now, all of a sudden, our carriage
is surrounded by a crowd of people rushing down the narrow street
– there are cries and shouts, and the walls of buildings are lit by
flickering yellow light, just as if the fireworks had already begun.
Then our carriage reaches the burning house. People grab the reins
of our horses and bring us to a halt. Big flames are shooting out of
the third floor windows. The fire seems to be raging inside the
building, and I see only a few men with buckets rushing in and out.
It looks like the fire brigade and the water carriers haven't arrived
yet. In the middle of the street, a half-naked man staggers towards
our carriage, supported by two other men. His shirt is in burnt

tatters, his face is black with soot, his hair looks scorched. Now the carriage door opens:

"Please, gentlemen! Take this man to the hospital! See how badly burned his hands are? He was making rockets. For tonight's fireworks. The powder caught on fire . . . Please, can you take him?"

They start helping him onto the running board of the carriage, but I raise my hand:

"Dear friends, I can see that his hands need attention" – they do, indeed, they're covered in purple burns – "but don't you see *whose* carriage you've stopped? My dear people, their Royal Highnesses deeply regret the misfortune this man has suffered. But surely you don't think he can be taken to the hospital in *their* carriage? Please find some other vehicle, and let us pass. Their Royal Highnesses are on their way to an urgent appointment."

I notice that behind me the Duke of Kent is trying to say something, but his command of German is still rather poor. I motion to him to hold his tongue, and he does. Looking contrite and apologetic, my faithful and understanding Göttingenians retreat. They let go of the horses' reins and make way for us, bowing and muttering apologies.

My skilful natural authority, the submissiveness of the common folk in that quarter behind the hospital (I can still see them bowing), the light from the fire reflected on their bent shoulders – despite my triumphant self-confidence, these images bother me; not a great deal, but still perceptibly. And, it seems, keep bothering me through both my lives . . .

In the autumn of 1863, I am a freshman at the University of St Petersburg. My excellent reputation as a tutor has followed me from the *gymnasium* to the university. Thanks to recommendations from the Dean and old Köler, I have been appointed the tutor of the three sons of Admiral Krabbe, Russia's Minister of War. I've been working with them for two weeks, and on a stifling hot Sunday afternoon in late summer, I'm riding with the admiral's sons towards his residence on the English Quay, coming from the Okhta side. The admiral's coachman is an Estonian, a former sailor named Juhan from Töstamaa, and we've been on friendly terms from the very first day of my appointment. Now he decides to take a short cut, and in a moment or two we find ourselves on a narrow street between the

Neva river and Suvorov Prospekt. The houses on both sides of the street are humble log cabins, and I realize, the way one realizes things in nightmares, that this is exactly the kind of street – with Russian country-style dwellings, windowframes decorated with carvings, tall board fences, mean little backyards in which dry birch and aspen logs have been stacked high against the walls of sheds and barns, and the barn lofts are filled to the rafters with dry hay – where there have been fires every single day during this uncommonly hot and sunny summer. Riding on the new horse-drawn trams down Nevski Prospekt, and even in the university library, I've heard people whispering about *Polish arsonists* . . . The rumour is that some Polish insurgents have managed to escape the imperial crime tribunals, made their way to St Petersburg, and are now trying to burn down the city. Suddenly, there are excited people running and keeping up with our open barouche, and then there's such a throng behind us that it's impossible for us to turn back. Then, right next to us, tall crackling flames leap up to devour three of the log houses facing the street, and we barely avoid getting scorched.

So help me God, I'm positive I hadn't read anything yet about Georg Friedrich's ride with the King of England's sons . . . If, indeed, I have *ever* read anything about it: what source would I have consulted? I don't think I even knew about Georg Friedrich's existence, at least not by any of the ordinary means we use to gather information and knowledge . . . With great difficulty, we make our way through the shouting, staring, undulating crowd and past the fire. We manage to turn right, into another street where people immediately rush up to the barouche, grab the horses' reins, and bring us to a halt. Two men in tattered shirts, with red burn marks on their faces and arms, jump onto the running boards:

"Please, gentlemen! Take us to the hospital! We have terrible burns – look . . ."

I look. I'm only two years older than the admiral's eldest, but I am also a university student and their tutor. It is up to me to make a decision. I have to do *something* for these tousle-headed, sweaty, common men, although I really don't know what, and even feel a little frightened by them. I say to the boys: "Let's get out!" Then I tell the men to get in the barouche and instruct the coachman: "Go to Dyegtyarnaya Street. It'll take you straight to the military hospital. Then come back home. We'll find another carriage."

The coachman drives off with the men. The boys and I start walking in the direction of Znamenskaya Square. We have to walk three-quarters of a verst before we find a hackney coach for hire; while we're walking, I tell them about the significance of philanthropic actions and about the great fire hazards these miserable wooden suburbs represent. The following evening, Juhan the coachman comes to see me in my old attic room at the paupers' school:

"Mr Martens, I wonder what we should do . . ."

"About what, Juhan?"

"About . . . Mr Martens, yesterday, when you told me to take those men to the military hospital –"

"Yes?"

"Well, I took them there. But when I was just about to turn into the hospital drive, I looked over my shoulder, merely to see if they were sitting or lying down or still alive at all –"

"Yes, and?"

"The barouche was empty."

"Empty? Uh-oh . . . What do you think that means?"

Of course, Juhan had drawn the right conclusion. In his opinion, the disappearance of the men, their falling or most likely jumping out of the barouche, could only mean that they didn't want to go to the hospital at all – that they weren't victims of the fire, but most probably were the arsonists who had started it. They may have received burns while setting the fire, but their main concern was to make a getaway. What better conveyance for that purpose than the barouche of the Minister of War, its roof raised up against the hot sun, its side flaps down, with a bearded veteran wearing his silver stripes in the coachman's seat . . . ?

What should we do? Was it even possible, or necessary, to do anything? I made a rapid assessment of the situation. The boys must have told their father about our adventure, or if they hadn't, they surely would do so tomorrow. The Minister was considered a liberal; he even wanted to abolish corporal punishment in the Navy. Thus, it was unlikely that he'd scold us for our philanthropic impulse. Juhan had made sure that no traces of blood or dirt remained on the upholstery of the barouche. The Minister's humanism would hardly extend to making inquiries about the victims of Sunday's fire at the military hospital. No, he was too busy to do that, he was far too absorbed by his grand plan to armour-plate our battleships. Fortunately, it was also unlikely that newspaper reports on the fire would renew the Minister's interest. It went without saying that Poles had nothing to do with the St Petersburg fires; those kinds of rumours were spread by the same types whose descendants would call themselves the Black Hundred and engage in all kinds of mayhem. No, these fires were caused by our own Russian drunkards and the hot weather, or perhaps, in isolated instances, by some of our own terrorists. In any case, the press was under strict orders from the authorities not to publish detailed reports on the fires. And so, all we had to do was to keep our mouths shut. To ponder how easy it can be to mistake a culprit for a victim. And to hold our peace.

That is what I have done, in regard to that event, until this day. God knows, it isn't hard to remain silent about such a trivial incident, when one of the very foundations of one's existence consists of knowing when to hold one's tongue . . .

16

But I don't want to remain silent any longer. Do you hear me, Kati? *No more silence.* Well, maybe in regard to the world at large, but at least no longer in regard to you. It's time to lay our cards on the table. What chance of winning do we have any more? Why not show our hands? Because we're not in the habit of doing that. Yet it is tempting; it might even be enjoyable. But that's not important. The important thing would be the feeling of *liberation*.

Kati, you're here again, aren't you? I can't really see you, but I know you're back. As always. You know, my body has become curiously absent and disobedient. I give myself an order to turn my head to see where you are – but my body simply ignores it. Yet I can sense that you're here again. Come a little closer to me. Even closer. Don't let that yellow briefcase bother you. Listen to me, Kati: I've been amusing myself with imagining what they'll say in my obituaries . . . Believe me, I know exactly what they'll say. I don't mean our *own* papers. With them, everything depends on chance and that morning's phone calls. In the case of *particularly* favourable circumstances, it might not be impossible . . . What do they care? They won't have to let go of the least little shred of their power. It won't be the same as having to recognize the importance of a living person. Merely a drop of honey on a dead man's tongue . . . *Ivan Ivanovich? The editor, himself? What a pleasure! Have you heard? Martens just died, Fyodor Fyodorovich. Sad? Of course it's sad. Very sad. A great loss to the nation. Well. So – we have to come up with something. Honour his memory, recognize his achievements, remind people. Very great merits. Over many decades. Imperial assignments. Confidential missions. Yes, yes. On a grand scale. List all his honours and decorations* . . . What a farce! Or, in the case of a very bad day: *Ivan Ivanovich – about Martens' death. Your standard obit. All right. What was he, really? Merely a specialist. Not too well-defined a character. But we do have to mention it. Just keep it short. All right.* And finally, in a normal, everyday sort of mood: *Ivan Ivanovich, you've heard that Martens has died – Fyodor Fyodorovich? Oh, you hadn't heard. Well, we got the news, so – we need a piece. Of course. Yes, yes. That's right. But let's not overdo it. A man of merits, long years of service, universal respect. Keep it low-key. Abroad? What about it? That's their business. We stick to the facts, we're reliable. And moderate. That's right.*

Further away, where I'm not one of their own but a more or less exotic specimen with whom they've had some dealings, things will be less complicated. Let's say, in England. Let's say, in *The Times*. They'll run a proper little essay about me. I'd be willing to bet on it. *A great peacemaker*, or something in that vein. But I don't think they'll discuss Portsmouth or The Hague or Geneva or Brussels. Those concerns will seem too remote, not sufficiently important to England – at least they'll pretend that's the case. Nor will they mention the Anglo-Russian agreements that are, indeed, important to them – only too important. Never mind their freedom of the press. They'll expend most of their enthusiasm on my work as an arbitrator. They'll consider that my most important achievement. Again, not in all of its aspects, only in those that concerned England and turned out in her favour. Referring to those cases, within those limits, the English will say that I was (in their eyes – but they'll generalize that to "universal acclaim") one of the most intelligent, most cultured, most reliable, most fair-minded arbitrators on earth . . . Ridiculous, isn't it. I feel ironic about them in advance – and they'll be ironic about me in retrospect. Inevitably. They'll be ironic about me, about Russia, and about both, because they won't be able to comment on my loyalty without irony. But in general, their little obituary treatise will be positive. First of all, they'll be pleased to note that I wasn't really a Russian. Nor a German, either. They'll be aware of that, but they won't bother to find out what I *really* was: Estonian, Latvian, Livonian, Lapp – "*What the hell is that?*". Then, of course, they'll note the great volume of my writings and admit its impressiveness. They'll probably qualify the admission by remarking that, when all is said and done, the percentage of truly original material may be rather low. After which they'll proceed to examine the central idea of my theory of international law . . .

Kati, did you ever ask me what that central idea really is? You didn't? Well, you've never asked me very many questions along those lines. Theoretical questions. You've always been very interested in the people with whom I've been dealing, and you've often given me excellent advice on how to proceed with them. But since I am fantasizing that you are here, next to me, listening, I'll unfold that central idea once more, for your benefit, and for my own. I'm sure you find my motives for doing this quite transparent, but that no longer bothers me. I want you to see me plain.

I no longer remember the precise moment when that central idea began to dawn on me, the way ideas do before they crystallize, or when I first expressed it in words, or what I thought or felt at that moment. I'm sure I felt the joy of discovery, but also certain misgivings due to the ambiguities of the matter; of those, I must have been aware from the very beginning. I first presented my idea to the public in lectures during the spring term of '76. The same spring, it occurs to me now, when our little father Alexander Nikolayevich suffered that tragicomical – or really just tragic, even horrendous – misapprehension in regard to a captain of his guard. Anyone who has followed these matters at close range and is old enough to remember will know the event to which I'm referring.

After three assassination attempts and a conspiracy that the *okhrana*, his secret police, had partly uncovered, partly invented, the Emperor was in a state of extreme nervous agitation that sometimes reached the level of sheer panic, possibly even mania, and expressed itself in orders like the one to dig a ditch one fathom deep round the entire Winter Palace. The task was accomplished under the pretext of repairs to the palace sewers; the real purpose of the operation was to find a secret subterranean tunnel supposedly dug under the palace by conspirators so that they could smuggle in a bomb. By that time, the Emperor's personal routine had become quite erratic, and his irritability was explosive. God help anyone who dared to smoke in his presence during those months. Indeed, that was how it happened. After coming off duty, the aforementioned captain was chatting with his fellow officers in the Winter Palace guardroom and had just lit a cigarette when boot-heels could be heard rapidly clacking through the adjoining room. The officers stood to attention, and the Emperor stormed into the room. The captain, who found himself in the way of the Emperor's progress, jumped to one side, tossed his burning cigarette under a table and was about to stand to attention – but the Emperor, who evidently no longer went anywhere, even in his own palace, without a pistol under his coat and his finger on the trigger, didn't give the captain a chance to assume the appropriate position. He had seen the officer's sudden move and something burning flying through the air – it had to be a bomb. He pulled the trigger, and the imperial bullet killed the captain instantly. Fear turned the autocrat into a murderer. It goes without saying that the matter was hushed up. Officially, the captain had lost his life in active service, and his family received some compensation. Rumours about the incident began to circulate. Ashamed and furious, the Emperor drank himself into a stupor. Or let us assume he did – assuming also that he understood how revealing and symbolic his reflex action was: of the dead end reached by the state, the society, and the psyche of Russia . . .

It was, indeed, soon after this that I presented my own ideas in my introduction to a series of lectures on international law. It is this introduction many authorities have later called the core of my theory. I formulated it in context, with a light touch, tactfully, elegantly. At the time, it attracted no particular attention. If agents of the *okhrana* were present in the auditorium (and of course they were, and of course they took notes with customary zeal), they must have concluded that it was merely innocent scholarly speculation. In the course of the next couple of years, I edited and reviewed it and used its main points in other parts of my system, making it an integral part of my course on theory. Then, in the year 1882, in the era of Alexander III, Loris-Melikov, Ignatyev, Pobedonostsev, and Bogolepov, in an atmosphere of increasingly severe censorship, Russification, pogroms, and police terror, I published it, in my book *The International Law Among Civilized Nations*, which was soon translated into nine languages. I published it like a *clef*, in among all the rest, with a light touch, tactfully, elegantly.

The purpose of our examination of the development of inter-national relations and international law should not be restric-ted to facts or phenomena of international life as such. It is not our intention to simply review the sequences of wars, diplo-matic negotiations, and treaties that have taken place between states from antiquity to our time. No, we wish to examine the ideas that prevailed during a given era and determined the forms of international relations, and the laws that governed these at the time. Events are by their very nature ephemeral and impermanent, often arbitrary or accidental. On the other hand, the ideas that permeate a certain historical epoch and provide the ground for all the events that occur in it, permit us to orient ourselves in the enormous mass of particular conditions and circumstances in which proceed both the lives of individual nations as well as the life of the community of nations that belongs to the political system of Europe. Seen this way, the ideas of different epochs play a similar role in international relations, acting as motive forces and levers of the law, as do Montesquieu's principles in the forms and structures of the life of the State. The interior conditions and political structure of a State exercise a profound influence on its international relations. Only through a knowledge of the interior life of a country and its official institutions can one gain an understanding of the principles and rules it obeys in its relationships with other nations. The present treatise assumes familiarity with those institutions and that life, even though we will endeavour not to lose sight of those institutions on the one hand, and the relationships between nations on the other, during all the known periods of their history.

In the end, the fundamental principle evident in the history of international law whose general outline will be given in what follows, is the principle of a progressive evolution of international relations. This enables us to combine, and understand as a whole, phenomena encountered in different periods of the lives of nations, as well as those periods themselves. The closest and most immediate expression of the principle of progressive evolution proves to be an element that in one way or another seems to impregnate the entire historical life of nations – the element of respect shown to the individual person. The degree of acknowledgment given to the person as such is a good indicator of the evolutionary status of international relations and international law. When that respect is great, when the epoch regards the human individual as the source of

*the people's civic and political rights, then the life of nations
also proceeds on a higher level of justice and order. The reverse
also applies. Where nations in their internal lives do not grant
citizens their inalienable rights, we shall find neither juridical
order nor respect for the law in international affairs. The per-
manence of this truth is reflected in the history of international
relations from antiquity to the most recent times.*

My critics may well say – have, indeed, not refrained from saying
– that I didn't express my idea forcefully enough, nor in sufficient
detail . . . Some of those critics know, others, of course don't (critics
mostly don't know even a tenth of the things they discuss), that
there have been times when I have been much more explicit – in
my oral presentations, my lectures. So explicit that if one combines
and organizes the thoughts that I have both spoken and published
on this question, the indisputable outcome is as follows:

*A State can be a member state of a community of civilized
nations only if (and to the extent in which) it theoretically
acknowledges, and actually defends, the inalienable rights of
the individual.*

*A State may morally and juridically be a member of the
community of civilized nations governed by international law,
or it may remain outside that community and practise its own
local selfish government.*

*Its moral and legal status is not determined by the perfection
of its parades, the reach of its cannon, or the thickness of the
armour plate on its battleships.*

*The only true criteria for a State's international credibility
and reliability reside in the extent, the actuality, and the inviol-
ability of the possibilities offered to the human being to realize
his or her potential within it.*

Allow me to ask you, all of you, including Mr Vodovozov – is it such
an insignificant act to propose such criteria in our country, in our
situation, in our epoch? I admit that there were times, in earlier
years, when I was afraid even to think about them – to remind
myself that I had managed to insinuate such an enormous heresy

135

into the discourse of our time without anyone, not even myself, really noticing . . . And I was perturbed every time people hinted or told me outright that they *had* noticed it. The first of these were certain talented students. Taube, for instance. And also that choirmaster, Vodovozov. He was, in fact, a rather interesting young fellow. Rough, unshaven, loudmouthed, to be sure, but not a dimwit. His clothes smelled of the tarry forests of Arkhangelsk. After I had conversed with him for an hour – about international bills of exchange, if I remember correctly – and marked his student card "very good", he put it in his pocket and said to me:

"Professor Martens, allow me to tell you that I think the way you place Russia in the company of the Sultanates of Sarawak and Zanzibar is truly a stroke of genius!"

When I raised my eyebrows and looked sternly at him, he saw fit to add:

"What I mean is – that is what you *do*, when you declare respect, or lack of respect, for human rights the ultimate touchstone. I'm sure you understand."

I looked at him and smiled. I was both flattered and disturbed, gratified and annoyed, as one always is at such times. I said:

"Mr Vodovozov, I regret that I don't have time to explain to you how arbitrary your interpretation really is. But I believe that the difficulties in which you have already managed to embroil yourself will point you in the direction of reason."

By my reference to his *difficulties* I wanted to remind him that he had been sent into exile and had needed special permission to come to St Petersburg for his exams. He was under orders to report to the police, to get his passport stamped by them, and to return to Arkhangelsk in ten days' time. But he pretended not to have heard, or at least not to have understood me, and marched off with a confident smile.

Mikhail Alexandrovich Taube was more tactful when he indicated to me that he *could see the possibility* of an interpretive comparison between Russia and, let's say, Zanzibar. I think this was when I first decided I liked him. But my students weren't the only ones who let me know that they had heard what I said – although there weren't that many mature contemporaries who noticed, and only very few in Russia. That is to say, of course there *were* such people, there just had to be, but their voices seldom reached my ears. They either belonged to fairly revolutionary circles, where one's own criticism of society might be reinforced "even by the lectures of a Martens", or else they were drunken adherents of the Black Hundred who would grumble: "Do you really *believe* that this damned upstart Martens doesn't *know* what he's said and written? Of course he does!"

My most qualified readers in Russia, my own colleagues foremost among them, acted unanimously according to the principle suggested by the tale of the emperor's new clothes. None of them had seen that I had stripped – at least in those two or three pages – both the Emperor and the empire. Vershinin declared to me, apropos of those pages: "Magnificently put, Fyodor Fyodorovich! And with such courage! Without any dubious hesitation or fear of possible . . . well . . . you know what I mean! Besides, how *true* it is, especially now, don't you agree, since the reforms of the late Alexander II have been guaranteed by his noble son in such a far-sighted manner." This, at a time when even the most timid liberals deplored the systematic attrition of those reforms . . .

In any case, I found more candour among foreign colleagues who approached me in the hallways of various international congresses, or in the relaxed and almost jocular atmosphere of farewell banquets, and confessed, sometimes in private, sometimes among a crowd of guests: "*Cher* Monsieur Martens, allow me to express my purely personal admiration for the consistency with which you defend your government's points of view. It is remarkable, as is your ability to achieve compromises. But neither one of those two skills would be so impressive if it weren't combined with your equally remarkable and surprising *doctrine of respect for human rights . . .*"

Well . . . yes. But to get back to *The Times* and its imaginary obituary, I'm afraid I can foresee what those English ironists will say. It may well be something like this: ". . . Mr Martens confirmed the truth – or paradox – that the more consistent governments are in their respect for their subjects' rights, the more stable and pacific they are likely to be in their international relations. He said: 'Once you know the interior situation of a country, you will be able to gauge its credibility and influence abroad.' One has to admit that when one applies this adage to Russia, its inherent irony becomes evident. Nevertheless, it seems unlikely that Mr Martens intended it . . ." Ho-ho. The last thing I need is such a revealing barb coming through the English pipe-smoke curtain – either now, or after I'm gone. Despite the obviousness of their arrogance, such remarks are insidious and serve to incite the dogs already growling at me in my homeland. And after I'm gone – Kati! Where are you? No matter, I know you understand me: even after my death that kind of qualified praise, be it in the columns of *The Times*, would still seem stingy and merciless . . .

Come to think of it, I haven't really thought about what and how they *should* write, for the result to meet with my approval and satisfaction.

One of the most eminent internationalists of our time . . . Yes, of course. Perhaps *the most eminent* . . . No, no; objectively speaking, that would be an exaggeration. Subjectively, well . . . Considering the social advantages enjoyed by practically all my competitors, and the difficulty of the course on which I had to run my race . . . While my Swiss colleagues, for instance, enjoyed a pleasant collective run on the well-tended turf of an ancient internationalist tradition, I was compelled to struggle through the mud of absolutism, and all alone, at least as far as theoretical work is concerned. While I had many well-born colleagues who were capable of making small talk in French (too many, to tell the truth), there were only a few genuinely civilized European spirits among them. Thus, all things considered, it might not be such an exaggeration to call me the most eminent internationalist of our time . . . But when have historical judgments ever been based on such considerations? Not that one could call it an injustice – how could eminence be measured according to such outwardly invisible criteria? To see those criteria, one would have to get very close to them; one would practically have to enter the human being in question.

Good God, Kati, why should I help them write my own obituaries? The world never remembers who or what we were, it only remembers what it needs – if, indeed, it needs us at all. Or else it may need us in different places, at different times, in different ways, and then paint our portrait in whatever way it chooses. There is no way we can protect ourselves from that arbitrariness, and no point in worrying about it.

138

Choo-choo – choo-choo – choo-choo – choo-choo . . .

Kati, my love, I've made an astounding discovery: whether I feel closer to you or more distant – whether I think you're receding or approaching – somehow seems to depend on the content of my thoughts, and on the moods they induce in me. The more confident I feel about myself, the further away you seem to go. The closer I come to despair, the stronger your presence seems. Right now you're here again, next to me, I can feel it! And I'm able to move my right hand again. I put it round your waist . . . Kati, you're still gazing out through the window (now, *that* river surely is the Gulbene) – you're still averting your eyes, but your ear is right in front of my mouth. A pretty white ear, half-covered by dark curls. The conch of your ear: an orifice that still excites me – as do all your other orifices. Please don't be offended by that remark, don't disappear . . . Good, you're still here. Because you know that even wiser minds than mine have come up with such associations. Otherwise, dear old Rabelais wouldn't have let Gargantua be born out of Gargamelle's ear. The idea is even older than that. Rabelais was, in fact, poking fun at an ancient hymn:

Gaude, virgo, mater Christi
Quae per aurem concepisti . . .

As you know, I am not a believer. Nevertheless, a trace of naïve religious sentiment has stayed with me, from the evening prayers I used to say with my parents and Aunt Krööt – so that my recollection of that hymn in such a frivolous context (I know you won't laugh at me, Kati) feels a little sacrilegious. I can atone for that sacrilege only by confessing everything to you. Kati, I know where I am; at this moment, I'm on my way to St Petersburg on this train, and you are with me only in my thoughts. But believe me, I'm no more accustomed to total candour than you are; so, indulge my rehearsal, before we put total candour into practice tomorrow, at Sestroretsk, on our white dowel-backed bench by the shore.

Kati, you have been faithful to me for thirty years. Both my experience and my intuition assure me of it. Faithful for many different reasons, but also for love. During our thirty years together, there have been times when we've truly loved each other. No doubt

139

about it. Our love may not have matched our own, or the world's, expectations, but it has been real enough. Then, there have been times when you've been my faithful wife out of habit, pride, weariness, forgiveness, revenge – and, I would like to add, because it is a part of your upbringing. Faithful in any case, and also wise, formidably wise. You have never questioned my fidelity.

I went on more than half of my many journeys abroad without you. When I returned from those trips, your sensitive nostrils may have guessed at some suspicious foreign scents, but you kept your suspicions to yourself, and you never bothered me with them. But I have not been faithful to you. My liaison with Mary – about which we haven't exchanged a word, although your female intuition must have made you aware of it – is not my only infidelity. This is not to say that I've been an inveterate womanizer, far from it. But first, I have to tell you another story. Not about Mrs Christiansen and my intimacy with her (which came as a complete surprise even to myself), nor about a couple of brief episodes in Paris or Berlin. I will tell you about those, even those, in the name of candour. But first I want to tell you about Yvette.

Let me take a moment to review that memory. I don't want to hurt you with unnecessary details . . .

17

Lapshin was supposed to arrive in Brussels that afternoon, from Namours, and I was walking from the embassy, where I was staying, down Waterloo Boulevard to meet him at the Quartier Léopold station. I could have taken a hackney, but I have always liked to walk.

I had been in Brussels for a week, preparing for the congress against slavery. The weather was cool, it was October, and the chestnut trees of the Parc Central and the boulevards were already grey and had lost some of their leaves. I walked along the Wavre embankment in the direction of the train station, then realized I had come too far east, almost to the railway tracks; so I turned at Godescharle Street and followed a tree-lined avenue all the way to the station. The train from Namours was due in eight minutes. On a parallel track, a row of grey wagons was approaching the station, pushed by a huffing locomotive. To the right, by the crossing, an old man was working the chains that lowered the barrier. I noticed his big white moustache, then heard him shout:

"Mademoiselle! Mademoiselle! The train is coming! The train is coming!"

Fifteen paces away, a woman stood between the rails in the middle of the crossing. She hadn't stumbled or fallen, she wasn't calling for help. She just stood there, exerting herself in some curious way, but did not step aside. The train approached, slowly but certainly. I rushed over to her and saw that the heel of one of her yellow lace boots was caught between a rail and a paving stone. She was unable to pull the heel out of the crack, or her foot out of the shoe. Without even looking at her, I said *Pardon!*, bent down, grabbed her right ankle with both hands, and pulled. My bowler hat fell off my head and landed between the rails, but the boot-heel broke, and she was able to move. At almost the last possible moment, we jumped out of the way. I held her and noticed that she was trembling. I also noticed how slender she was. I said: "Don't be afraid. Everything is all right now." The train rumbled past. I picked up my hat and looked at her. She was quite young. When she spoke, there wasn't a trace of embarrassment in her voice (and it may have been her amazing forthrightness that impressed me so):

"Thank you so much, sir. Without you, I might no longer be among the living . . ."

I laughed and said: "Oh, no . . . At the last moment, you would have managed to pull yourself loose . . ."

We returned to the boulevard. I noticed that she was limping, then realized that she was limping because she had lost that boot-heel. I felt that this was, to some extent, my fault – so I said:

"Allow me to assist you. And, let's find a shoemaker. I think I saw a sign back there, a couple of houses down on the left." I walked beside her, holding her left elbow, and saw her face close up. It was a Walloon woman's face, narrow, clean, light-skinned, framed by brown hair so dark it was almost black. Her delicate lips were still blue from fright, her eyes large and dark grey, with long, now slightly tremulous lashes. With my left hand, I raised my hat and said:

"Allow me to introduce myself. My name is Martens. Frédéric Martens. I am a professor."

At the same time, I was saying to myself: "Strange – instead of being at the station to welcome a distinguished official of the Ministry of Foreign Affairs – who is bringing me my latest instructions from the Minister, Nikolai Karlovich de Giers – I am doing something entirely different! I am a councillor sent to this conference by the Emperor of Russia, at the request of the King of Belgium and the Queen of England. I am forty-four years old, a full professor, happily married to a senator's daughter, the father of an eight-year-old son and two little daughters – but here I am, looking for a shoemaker with this apparently quite ordinary, probably quite poor, and in any case, quite unknown young woman, holding her elbow; through the sleeve of her thin jacket, it feels like a bird's wing . . . Strange."

She turned her pale face – Kati, in profile her face resembled yours – to me and said:

"My name is Yvette Arlon. I am a student. Of the arts."

I remember how shamelessly pleased I was. Pleased because she wasn't just a milliner or a waitress in a beer hall – she was more distinguished than that. We didn't have to worry about class distinctions. Besides, she was involved in one of the traditionally more light-hearted disciplines . . .

We had reached what turned out to be quite a large shoe shop – with, I noted, a café next door. We proceeded to the ladies' shoe department, and the sales assistant led us to the master shoemaker (they always have one in these shops). Yvette retired behind a curtain and took off her boot. When the master told her that the repair would take at least fifteen minutes, I suggested to Yvette that she take off the other boot, and asked the assistant to lend Yvette another pair of shoes, so that we could go to the café next door. Yvette found this agreeable.

We walked through a short vaulted passage to the café, and soon two cups of coffee were steaming before us on a lace tablecloth. I asked Yvette:

"And what discipline are you studying? Ballet?"

The fluidity of her movements had given me that idea.

"No," she said. "Painting."

I glanced at her hands. Painters' fingertips always show traces of their medium, but I couldn't see hers because they were covered by dark blue lace gloves that more or less matched her sea-green jacket and skirt.

"At an academy?"

She mentioned a private atelier. In January, she told me, she would apply to the Academy of Art at Antwerp, to study with Verlat. Her favourite subjects were flowers and animals, and she was particularly interested in African art. She said: "Maybe I got bitten by our Congo bug." Africa provided us with a conversational topic. I told her about our congress and its objective, the abolition of slavery. She told me she had read about it in the newspapers and was very interested in it. I told her that I lived in St Petersburg ("But surely, French was your first language?") and came to Brussels almost every summer. She told me about herself, in a reserved, laconic, but completely unaffected manner. She was twenty-two years old. Her father, who had died a few years ago, had been a glass-blower at Hainaut. After his death, her mother had moved back to her native La Panne, by the sea, the last Belgian village before the French border, where she kept a flower garden and sold flowers to the vacationing gentry. She, Yvette, lived close by, near the Parc Léopold behind the Wiertz Museum, in a large house on a quiet and pleasant street. Her apartment was in the attic, the rent was cheap, and it had a big skylight. She did not make this description sound like an invitation, and I didn't take it that way. The assistant appeared to tell us that her boot was ready. Yvette let me pay for her coffee but insisted on paying the three francs for the repair. As we left the shop, it occurred to me that it was time for me to go back to the embassy to meet Lapshin. I said to Yvette:

"But now you must take a hackney home." I hailed one that was just passing. "Because I know that you're still feeling the after-effects of what happened back there."

She protested. "No, no, no. I'll walk."

I said: "In that case, I'll walk you home."

"Oh, Professor Martens, that won't be necessary!"

"Oh yes, it will, Mademoiselle Arlon."

"All right, then. I'll take the coach."

I thanked her for her sensible decision, helped her into the coach, and slipped the coachman five francs. I couldn't be sure that she had enough money on her. And then – Yvette had already taken her seat, and I was holding her hand to say goodbye – I (or another "I") suddenly said:

"Mademoiselle Arlon, may I expect you tomorrow – at that same café? What would be a good time for you?" And my first "I" immediately thought: Tomorrow I have a preliminary meeting with the Englishmen at eleven, and at three I have a discussion with some members of the State Council on the Congo, probably followed by dinner with the same gentlemen . . .

Yvette looked at me for a surprisingly long while with her large dark grey eyes. Then the left corner of her mouth twitched in an almost imperceptible smile. She said, gently:

"Shall we say six o'clock?"

And six o'clock it was.

The small café next to the shoe shop, near the Quartier Léopold station, became our base of operations. We met the next day and the days that followed, in the evenings, after my long sessions at the African congress. I obtained tickets for us to hear the violin

144

virtuoso Hauman at the conservatoire. We went to the opera, two or three times. I was familiar with the city's museums, and Yvette didn't insist that we visit them. But when I asked her what we could do on the one day off that delegates were given each week, she said something unexpected:

"Would you like to go to the seaside?"

No one in Brussels goes to the seaside in October. The bathing and excursion season ends in September. Then it occurred to me that Yvette perhaps wanted to visit her mother in La Panne; I had no interest in turning our acquaintance into a family affair. So I said:

"To the seaside? In October? Is there anything worth seeing there? And what place do you have in mind?"

"It's just this pleasant little village by the sea. There are sand dunes; there is the sound of the sea. About ten kilometres from the Dutch border."

So it wasn't La Panne. It was practically at the other end of this tiny country.

"And what are your connections to the place?" (I'm afraid there was a touch of jealousy in my question.)

"None, really. I've gone there to paint pictures of sheep. But *you* might have some connections . . ."

"Me?"

"Well – I'm sure you're really Belgian, descended from some ancestor who ended up in Russia or Livonia. The Martenses are Belgians. There are some Martenses in that village. They're peasants. I paint their sheep."

I can't say what my motives were – a desire for adventure, a playful impulse, an urge to test myself, a need to relax, a sense of curiosity – but I agreed to her suggestion with an astonishing degree of enthusiasm. We made arrangements to meet on Saturday morning by the ticket windows at the Gare du Nord. And only a little later, as I found myself making a few purchases for our trip, it struck me: over the years, I had spent time in Brussels on at least ten different occasions, often in the summer, yet I had never found an opportunity to go on the three-hour train ride to the shores of the North Sea . . . But that morning of a windy but fortunately dry day, at the half-dark crack of dawn, a certain serious Councillor of State,

145

feeling quite frivolous and excited, put on his informal attire, picked up his travelling bag, walked down the steps of the embassy, and took a cab to the station. At a quarter to six in the morning, because the express train to Ghent and Bruges left at six. The gentleman told the coachman to let him off by the pond at the Botanical Gardens; for some reason, he felt it might be embarrassing to arrive in a hackney coach. Yvette might already be there, and she would, of course, have taken the tram . . .

But she wasn't there yet. I bought two first-class tickets to Bruges, where we would change to another train that would take us to the seaside.

Yvette arrived five minutes later. She was wearing her modest sea-green suit, her rather worn yellow boots, and a blue cape in case of rain. I felt still a little deranged by the early hour and a mild feeling of embarrassment, but she looked charmingly fresh and pleased. She was carrying a woven picnic basket.

"What's that for?"

"So we won't have to buy lunch at a tavern."

Then we were on our way, in a first-class carriage whose few passengers mostly looked prosperous, elegant, and distinguished. As they passed by the glass door to our compartment, they glanced at us with indifference. Who did they think we were – man and wife, father and daughter, businessman and secretary, man and mistress? Who cares; all those assumptions were wrong. We sat facing each other across the small table attached to the window, and never stopped talking during the whole trip – the way old acquaintances would never do, yet again, the way only old acquaintances could. God knows what about. Yvette told me about one of their artists, Vincent Van Gogh, a strange painter (as I was listening to her, I remembered a few of his works). She said the heavy outlines of his paintings were powerful enough to haunt people even in their dreams. Only a few months ago, he had succumbed to an incurable mental illness. Then I told her about Nietzsche:

"Have you heard of him?"

"Yes, I have. I've even read his *Zarathustra*. But I don't like it. It's too foamy and bathetic. Too German for my taste."

I responded with a polite laugh and went on to say that Nietzsche, too, had become incurably mentally ill only a few months ago. I probably went on to say that we seemed to be living in a time of many such breakdowns; even Maupassant seemed to have lost his mind, or so I had overheard in the hallways of our congress. Then I told Yvette that if I could manage to detach myself from the affairs of that congress, if only for a week, I would like to invite her to come with me to Paris, where we could ascend to the top of the tower M. Eiffel had just finished building, a sensational edifice – I said:

"Imagine what the view must be like! Paris, from a height of three hundred metres!"

She smiled and said: "I haven't even seen Paris on the street level."

I asked, feeling a little frightened now, but completely charmed: "So you'll come, if I can manage it?"

Yvette shook her head: "No. I can afford a trip to Knokke, but not one to Paris."

I exclaimed: "But, listen (thinking, I can't believe I am saying this!) – I'm *inviting* you –"

Yvette said: "I'm sure you are a Belgian. I can feel it. But you have lived in Russia for too long. When generosity becomes too great, it is no longer generosity."

All right, then. I abandoned the idea of a trip to Paris, and we talked about what we saw through the compartment window. Yvette told me the names of the villages we passed on the grey autumnal plains of Flanders. They looked less like villages than small towns joined by straight roads, so that they all seemed to be holding hands in a long chain. There were rivers that looked like canals, and canals that looked like tree-lined boulevards covered in water. I described a bear hunt in the forest of Tahkuranna – I have no idea why, since I have never taken part in one . . . Then we arrived in Ghent, at its Gare du Sud, and rumbled on ten minutes later. I observed myself and my surroundings and felt amazed: this town where I had stayed so often, on the business of our Institute of International Law and on missions of arbitration, with all its familiar red brick and yellow stucco buildings and towers, or what I could see of them from the train window – it suddenly seemed like a distant, strange, almost dreamlike stage set. What was real and genuine and alive was this play for two characters, with its unforeseeable conclusion;

147

and in that play, the most real character was the one who sat right across from me.

I remember leaning back in my seat and looking at her, and I must admit that I don't think I have ever, before or since, been so completely aware of another person's existence as her own spiritual and physical world. I had discovered this world by accident, as a "life-saver", and now, looking back, that seemed almost a little ridiculous. Here she was, this light-skinned, dark-haired, delicate girl-world: different, distant, feminine, childlike, in a word, utterly alien – a world that aroused a little sympathy and pity, a world I really did not need, had no business even visiting – yet a world I found irresistibly attractive. "Independent and interesting," I thought, "just like a strange country." And maybe I even thought (oh, I hope I did!): "Just like a small independent nation – and in one's dealings with it, one should respect its human rights."

In Bruges we changed to a local train, and after three-quarters of an hour we got off at Heyst. It was windy, and the sky was overcast.

The strong wind made us pleasantly short of breath as we walked through the village and down to the shore. Like many others in these parts, the village had ambitions to become a resort, rather like the main village at our Kuressaare. We stopped by the perfectly straight and vacant shoreline, then turned northwest to walk on the damp sand that looked the way it does before the tide comes in, mauve, green, and brown. To our right were the sand dunes, to our left was the sea, striped with foam and dark grey, with a thin dark line on the horizon that Yvette told me was the island of Walcheren.

We weren't able to continue our chat as easily, once we proceeded along the surprisingly deserted beach. Yvette walked ahead of me and turned once in a while to say something, but the sea wind pushing us onward blew her words away. Every time that happened, I caught up with her and made her repeat what she had said, and her hair, flying in the wind, almost touched, then touched my cheek.

She walked at a fast and seemingly effortless pace, and I walked behind and next to her, taking in all that enormous space and wondering what I had come here for. What had *she* come here for? Why does one go on journeys like these? And what was the relationship between my reasons and her reasons, and between our reasons and ordinary and general reasons? These were not so much thoughts as tattered shreds of questions, and the wind that scattered everything made it impossible to arrive at any kind of fixed answer. I told Yvette, my lips close to her ear, that this beach reminded me curiously of my own beach at Pärnu – except that the sand on my beach was much lighter, and the sea even darker in this kind of weather.

After we had been walking for a quarter of an hour, she stopped:

"Please wait for me a moment. I'm a little cold. I'll put on a sweater."

She took off her cape and was about to drop it on the sand. I took it from her. It was obvious that she wasn't used to the attentions of gentlemen. She opened her basket, which I had been carrying, and took out a bright blue lamb's-wool sweater wrapped in a sheet of paper, handed it to me, a little hesitantly, and then took off her jacket. Through the thin, tight-fitting blouse her breasts looked small, trusting, fearless. After she had put on the sweater, I held her jacket for her. Her windblown hair and her slightly pensive face were a hand's-breadth away from my own. I'd already raised my hands to grasp her shoulders, to turn her towards me, to kiss her. But I didn't do it. I really don't know why; after twenty years, it is quite impossible to say why. Because I was concerned about my dignity? Her dignity? Because I was a Puritan? Because I was afraid to appear ridiculous? In any case, because one of my "I's" kept resisting any attempt to guide events in the direction the other "I" longed for. We continued our walk.

An hour later, another village appeared from behind the sand dunes and green sheep pastures to our right. The cottages were built of the local light-coloured stone; among them stood a few larger two-storey buildings. There was a small church with a flat-topped tower, and up on a ridge there were wooden windmills just like at Pärnu, the only difference being that these were huge. We didn't turn towards the village but walked on and let its houses disappear behind the sand dunes again. And then, on a green spit of pasture between the dunes, pulled back from the waterline, there stood a yellow box on four wheels – a beach hut.

"Let's go in there," Yvette said, "and have our picnic. We'll be out of the wind. I'm sure you must be hungry."

We sat down on the two wooden benches of the beach hut, at the little table attached to the wall. Yvette opened her basket, laid the table with a white napkin, small plates, knives and forks, a small glass bowl of shrimp salad, and some sandwiches with red cheese. I took a bottle of hard cider out of my travelling bag. Yvette said "Aha" and took two tiny ceramic cups out of her basket. To see this doe-like girl act like such a perfect hostess was unexpected, amusing, touching. After we had eaten, she put the utensils back in the basket, took them down to the water's edge, rinsed them, and brought them back. Then she said:

"Professor Martens, now I must leave you for a short while. I'm going to the village to pick up my paints and brushes, and my models. Then I'll do a little bit of painting. But you can tell me things while I'm working – about St Petersburg, or Paris, or that hometown of yours, what is it called again?"

"Pärnu."

"And about Pärnu."

After a quarter of an hour, she returned, carrying a paintbox and followed by a flock of some twenty sheep and their shepherd. He was a sturdy fifteen- or sixteen-year-old Flemish country boy named Dolf, rather tongue-tied out of shyness or respect. He was carrying a small easel. He and I helped Yvette push the beach hut where she wanted it, turning it so that its door and front steps faced inland. Yvette selected two white sheep and a black one. The boy tethered them on a patch of grass at the edge of the sand and left again, taking the rest of the flock with him. Yvette called after him:

"Dolf, come and get your sheep around three o'clock. I'll be finished by then."

She put up the easel in front of the beach hut steps, where it was sheltered from the wind, and went to work. I went into the hut, picked up a deckchair, took it outside, unfolded it and stretched myself out close to Yvette, taking care to position myself so that I could watch her work but couldn't see the canvas. I didn't want to make her self-conscious. In the village, she had put on an old paint-stained smock and tied a blue silk scarf round her head. I offered her some chocolates I had brought along, but she fed most of them to the sheep in order to bribe them to assume the poses

150

she wanted. Whenever they attempted to escape as far as the tethers would let them, I tried to bring them back; I pulled their tethers and their surprisingly soft woolly coats, fed them some more chocolates, and let them lick my hands with their rough tongues. I don't remember exactly what Yvette and I talked about that afternoon. About everything, I suppose, as she had suggested – about St Petersburg, Paris, Pärnu. I do remember that I did most of the talking, although Yvette by no means assumed the role of a passive listener. And I remember how, from time to time, I caught myself observing our strange little tableau in a detached manner. Suddenly, the sound of the sea grew louder behind us, and the spacious emptiness of this entirely unfamiliar place became a little frightening. In that turbulent void, the beautiful girl whose fingers were now quite clearly stained with paint, who was concentrating on her canvas three steps away from me, seemed close to me in a way that moved me. A couple of times, emboldened by that feeling of familiarity – and justified by the cold wind – I invited her into the beach hut and filled our cups with cider. But I refrained from kissing her, refrained from making any advances; suddenly, even the possibility felt cheap, although I kept asking myself on yet another, a third level: *How far do we want to go?*

It turned out she didn't mind my seeing her unfinished canvas:

"But of course you can take a look! I don't think that'll put a jinx on it."

Those slowly emerging sheep in Yvette's painting, on a greyish green pasture rippling in the wind under a grey sky, weren't drawn with as heavy an outline as the shapes in Vincent's work, nevertheless they have come back to me innumerable times to haunt me in my dreams. But I don't want to dwell on those anguished moments; I would like to be able to recall what we said that afternoon, there, by the sea, in and out of the wind – but all I come up with is the way those hours *felt*. I noticed that I was no longer bothered by the strange environment, that my words seemed more inspired, soaring to unaccustomed heights of wit, gaining colour and texture. That feeling encouraged me to double my efforts, and I remember Yvette's sincere and concrete interest in what I was saying. I remember how neatly and honestly she divided her interest between the canvas and myself. Her glances. Her questions. Her perceptive responses. Her laughter. Very similar, by the way, to Kati's little laugh . . .

(Kati, in case you have been following my thoughts, and it would be better for you if you hadn't – I know what you would say: "Oh, Fred," you would say, with that little laugh of yours, "Oh, Fred, now you have painted such an image for me of that girl that I have no choice but to admit that she was *inevitable* . . . To think that she was so erudite. Me, I've never even opened a copy of *Zarathustra*. And she was so talented. Maybe not a Van Gogh, but still very gifted. And in an art form for which I've never had the least little bit of talent. Besides, her profile was so much like mine. And we resembled one another in the way we laughed. And her intuitive intelligence resembled mine. Was perhaps even more acute than mine. So that I *have* to be understanding, simply because she reminded you so much of me, the main woman in your life – isn't that so? Besides, she wasn't a senator's daughter like me, whom you have always treated with impeccable manners, not your own, it is true, but those you have assumed; me, whom you have loved from time to time, and sometimes for long stretches, I won't deny it. But you have always, in your heart, in your *inmost* heart, felt socially inferior and estranged from me . . . I don't have to tell you that. There was no need to feel estranged from her. She happened to be the daughter of a glass-blower and a countrywoman. So it was liberating for you to descend to her level, and ennobling to raise her up to yours . . .")

At half-past two, Yvette stopped painting. She scrubbed her fingers with a rag soaked in turpentine, then washed her hands with sea water and sand. By then, the water's edge had receded a hundred paces, and to reach it she had to walk along a stone jetty that had been invisible at high tide. At exactly three o'clock, Dolf arrived to take his sheep back. We followed him into the village where we handed him Yvette's easel, smock, and paintbox to take back home, and went on to have a meal at Spander's inn on Pepperstraat – I still remember those names. I told her about the Congo until they brought us bowls full of mussels, salad, bread, and some anaemic but passable wine. She asked me:

"When were you there?"

152

I laughed and admitted that I had never set foot in the place. I explained that all I knew about it came from the books, travelogues, official reports and private letters I had read in preparation for our congress.

Yvette gave me an incredulous look. "But if that's so, how can you know – for instance – that the river mud smells like – what did you say – 'like the droppings of birds that have been fed poppy-seed'?"

"Did I say that?" I laughed. "Oh, I suppose I got that from some journal written by someone with a weakness for literature."

Maybe that is what I said, maybe I didn't put it quite that way. After twenty years, one can't be too sure of anything.

When we had finished our meal and I was about to order coffee, Yvette told me that we had been invited to coffee and gin at the house of my namesakes whom she visited every time she came here. We went there. Among the generally modest houses of this coastal district, this one appeared quite large. The sturdy Flemish lady of the house poured us some fragrant Dutch coffee, and her husband, a fellow with large hands and a ruddy face, poured us small glasses of the juniper-flavoured liquor whose aroma filled the large room for a moment. We raised and drained our glasses, then sipped coffee from large earthenware cups. Speaking with strong Flemish accents, the couple told me that since last spring, Mademoiselle Yvette had come here three times to paint. "The sea and the sand dunes, but mostly just cows and sheep. And sometimes, when the weather's been sunny, she's been able to catch them even better than she did today." Each time, she had paid them a visit, and now she was practically family, even though she was a young lady from Brussels and they were just simple country folk, and Flemish, to boot. Yvette told them briefly who I was and talked a little about the congress, saying that it concerned the Congo and was, therefore, of interest to Belgians. Then we discussed whether it would be possible to find out if I was related to the local Martenses. The sons of the family, twenty-year-old Pieter who would inherit the farm, and his younger brother Dolf whom I had already met, sat at the other end of the table and listened to our conversation. Dolf had put on a clean shirt, and I noticed that he had placed Yvette's painting to dry on top of the sideboard, up against the wall, and was now studying it so

153

intently that it was obvious he was simply afraid to look at Yvette herself . . .

At four o'clock, Pieter's father told him to take us to Heyst station in a little cart, and we arrived there with time to spare before the departure of the train from Bruges. It was evening when we got back to Brussels. I hired a hackney coach, and we rode through the lantern-lit streets to Yvette's apartment near the Parc Léopold, still engaged in animated conversation. Only when we were just a couple of hundred metres from our destination, I noticed that Yvette hadn't said anything for a while, and my own discourse on the extraordinary carvings of certain Bantu tribes had come to a sudden halt. For a moment, we listened to the noise the wheels made on the paving stones, and to the first raindrops falling on the top of the coach. Then we came to a halt in front of her house. Yvette thanked me, and I thanked her for the agreeable company and an interesting day. I stepped down from the coach, and as I extended my hand to her to help her down, she said:

"I really should invite you up, but my place is in such terrible Bohemian disarray . . . How long will you be staying here?"

"Another week."

"Well then, we'll do it before you leave."

Simply. As if it had been the most natural thing in the world.

After that, we went to one more concert at the conservatoire, where we heard César Franck's *Le chasseur maudit* and *Psyche*. When I escorted her home, she asked me how I had liked the music. I told her:

"I don't know if you noticed, but those self-styled critics from Paris who were sitting right in front of us were complaining about its German solemnity – while those from Munich, behind us, thought it was too frivolous, too French . . . And so, I thought it was really excellent music."

"So you noticed, too, that it was your kind of music? How interesting . . . And tomorrow is the last day of your congress?"

"Yes, our last session is tomorrow morning. At noon, we go to Laeken, to pay our respects to the king . . ."

"My, my," Yvette exclaimed, a little ironic tinkle in her voice.

"Then we dine at the Palace of Justice. But after that, in the evening, I'm free – and I hope we can . . ."

154

"Yes, you must come and see me in my dovecote. At seven o'clock, if that suits you."

Perhaps it wasn't "suitable", but it suited me just fine. I confess: on the evening of the day King Léopold handed me the gold watch in the presence of all the other delegates, in the castle at Laeken, and also gave me that other present I couldn't remember before – a scroll declaring me a member of the State Council of the Congo – that same evening, I climbed the stairs leading to Yvette's attic.

(Kati, if you're following my thoughts, and I know that you are, you'll realize into what kind of a hole I have managed to talk myself. I wanted to spare you, but since I have decided – or both of us have decided – to be completely candid, what can I do? I beg you, please stay with these reminiscences of mine only for as long as you can stand it. Don't come with me so far that you end up hating me. Or do! Come with me to the end! Hate me! And be magnanimous, and forgive me. Because that will be my only shield against death . . .)

18

I climbed the stairs – stone for the first couple of flights, then wood – up to the attic of the building. There was some kind of pharmacist's shop on the ground floor, and the fresh and spicy fragrances of all kinds of herbs permeated the air of the staircase all the way up to the large metal doorbell I had been told to ring.

Yvette came to the door without delay, wearing a cream-coloured housedress, her thick, dark hair braided and piled on top of her head. She looked as alert and delicate as ever, but there was a trace of anxiety in her expression. I put the cardboard box I had brought on a dresser and kissed both her hands. They smelled of lilac-scented soap, and once again I became keenly aware of her independent and sovereign existence – and of the fact that I really shouldn't have come here. Yet it was more exciting to be here than *anything* had been for a long time.

I picked up the box – it was tied with a ribbon and decorated with a bow – and handed it to her.

"What's this?"

"A little repast for two. So you won't have to . . ."

"But why? I've already made supper."

A small low table in front of a couch had been set for two. I thought (yes, indeed, that's what I thought), well, maybe we can have those things in the box for breakfast . . .

Her dovecote was larger than I had imagined, but otherwise it matched my expectations. It was the attic studio of a poor art student, elevated by the art it served to a realm beyond social hierarchies, up into the air, to become a space fit for kings and outlaws. Its walls were covered with pictures, and rows of stacked canvases leaned against the walls. Oil paintings, most of them unframed, some in cheap wooden frames, watercolours, pastels, crayons, drawings in charcoal and ink. Horses, dogs, cows, sheep, daisies, violets, children. The coloured works were mostly in greys and browns with areas of startling yellow and dark purple. Offhand,

I couldn't make any critical judgments, but there was a surprising amount of finished work, and this in itself was evidence of a serious commitment. All of it had a pleasing quality of freshness, gave the impression of a firm and resolute hand. Two low tables were covered with small African wood carvings and brass artifacts. The easel, retired to a corner, was surrounded by an array of paint tins and brushes. I took her hands in mine again and told her what I felt:

"Talent is a divine thing. It frees a person from the shackles of society – I mean, shackles imposed by social standing."

Yvette's reply surprised me by its worldly wisdom: "That may be true. But as I'm sure you know, it can also put a person beyond the pale."

"Oh? Have you experienced that?"

"Oh, yes . . ."

Perhaps this was an invitation to be asked about her experiences – but this possibility only occurred to me later . . . I said, and I meant every word:

"Yvette, what I see here on the walls of your dovecote is proof of such solid talent, such strong wings, that you'll fly right over such experiences!"

"Golden words, Mister International Expert," she said with friendly sarcasm. "Shall we dine? I skipped lunch today, since I was expecting you."

We sat down on the couch. Strangely enough, I can't remember what we ate. It was plain student fare, but after the elaborate farewell luncheon at the Palace of Justice, its improvisational character struck me as delightful. No wine was served, only a small bottle of dark beer – for me, none for her.

Then – well, it happened. Once again, I took her hands in mine and covered them with kisses, and she let me carry on, did not mock me or say: "But my dear professor, wouldn't you like to tell me about your wife and your children?" She knew that I was married, and a father; I had mentioned it in passing. But she didn't mock me, didn't resist my hands and lips. Nor did I tell her, as is customary in such situations, that it was fate, that I had fallen in love with her, that I could not live without her. Lord, no – I was leaving the next day, not committing suicide . . . No, I really tried to tell her the truth. I said that if God was our creator (I put it in

157

these conditional terms so as not to appear more solemn or religious than I am, even though she had told me that she went to confession once a year), then He must have created her in a moment of inspiration. As I heard myself saying this, it occurred to me that this was taking the Lord's name in vain, but in too harmless a manner for Him, *if* He existed, to take serious offence, especially since my words really corresponded with what I thought and felt . . . So I continued:

"And you carry that inspired moment of creation within yourself, and radiate it outward. Anyone who is near you – whom you allow to approach you – receives a part of it. That is how I feel, right now."

She did not disagree, but gave me a searching look and whispered:

"You are a strange man, Monsieur Frédéric . . . The day we met, you hadn't even seen my face. You had no idea that I was someone you could take to the theatre, someone with whom you could talk about art – and yet you almost risked your life for me."

I said, in a fit of that sweetly magnanimous feeling of humility that comes to us only in the presence of people we love:

"Dearest Yvette, I am not a hero. That was merely a reflex action – a result of that notion of chivalry that may be stronger in former cowherds than it is in high-born knights . . . Simply a reflex. And by sheer coincidence, I discovered a treasure."

Even though my words were more or less sincere, they still struck me as so pretty, so well-chosen with the skill of a person who is used to choosing his words with care, that I felt ashamed for them, and for myself. But Yvette did not take them too seriously. Instead, she raised her hand and ruffled my hair with a mischievous and girlish gesture – and I picked her up and carried her to her bed, a narrow bed in an alcove separated from the rest of the studio by a cheap curtain.

And why shouldn't I remember what she was like in that bed? In all honesty, I have to admit that I haven't forgotten. Let me say it once again – I have not been a Don Juan. It has not been my ambition to sleep with a great number of women; from the very beginning, my ambition was directed towards other goals. But I am old enough to have encountered a considerable variety of responses in bed. Mostly routine or simulated, if those can be distinguished from each other. Practised kindness, as well, in the best of cases, but only rarely a response of authentic intensity. Analysing Yvette's behaviour twenty years after the event, I would say that I encountered three things: first of all, a surprising readiness, of the kind men tend to find initially exciting but a little tawdry in retrospect. Then, a strange, perhaps French lack of inhibition, expressed in completely unembarrassed whispers: "A little higher . . . Slow down . . ." Until then, I would have considered such instructions indecorous, unless they came from my own wife. Nevertheless, as I later realized, they weren't so much indications of experience as expressions of her courage to be open to her own desire. Another thing that surprised me was that she did not turn off the light and didn't ask me to do so. The thin alcove curtain softened the gaslight, and in that penumbra she must have seen me just as clearly as I was able to see her and watch her face as it assumed a multiplicity of expressions, all of which had one thing in common: a completely untheatrical, pure, childlike – yes, now, after twenty years I am not ashamed to say it – *paradisiacal joy*! She was radiant with it, she wore a halo of joy and inspiration, and just as I had told her, it affected anyone who came close to her. It certainly affected me.

At nine o'clock the next morning, we had breakfast out of the box of titbits I had brought. We had put on our clothes and were sitting at the table, both of us (yes, me, too – I have to admit it) still rather stunned by what had transpired between us. The doorbell rang. It was Yvette's friend, a small brunette, also an art student, who lived in the attic room next door. When she saw me, she looked surprised and was about to leave again – which would have been quite all right by me – but Yvette asked her in, not with any great degree of insistence but in a sufficiently welcoming manner to encourage her curiosity. To my dismay, this Philippine Meunier, a woman in her late thirties (I only learned her last name much later), proceeded to make sprightly conversation with us for a whole hour. Once again, Yvette's behaviour surprised me. While not bragging about me, she nevertheless destroyed the *incognito* I wouldn't have minded preserving:

"Philippine, this is Professor Martens, from Russia. He is a jurist, and he has been attending an international congress here in Brussels."

159

"Oh, how interesting!"

Hmm. What would be so interesting about it, to a pair of young female artists?

"And surprising, too – to meet a foreign professor in our humble garrets . . ."

"Life in general is a game full of surprises, dear mademoiselle. I have experienced that here, in a most surprising way."

I was impeccably dressed and groomed, but Yvette's loose hair and generally informal appearance and the mere fact of this early morning tête-à-tête couldn't leave any doubt in the mind of an observant third party as to what was going on. After our visitor had left, Yvette said:

"I've never kept any secrets from her . . ."

And she wouldn't keep any from Philippine in the future, either. A fortunate circumstance – or was it? God alone knows.

I stayed in Brussels for another week, a week of complete, school-boyish self-forgetfulness. Nothing like it ever happened to me before or since. Not that I didn't remain conscious of my responsibilities to my profession and my family; not for a moment did I lose sight of my tasks, duties, attachments, and people – but I was separated from them by a wall of glass. I didn't seriously consider taking any revolutionary steps in my personal life, but there were many times when I fantasized about them. I would move away from St Petersburg to, let us say, Ghent. Yes, Ghent would be ideal – our Institute of International Law would provide a plausible pretext. It wouldn't take me long to find a professorial appointment in international law, in Belgium or in France. If not in Paris, then at least in Lille, at their new university, where they would be pleased to have me. And that would be close enough to Ghent. I would help Yvette to gain admission to the Academy of Art at Antwerp. I'd find out about the proper channels. We would live in Ghent, that orderly and peaceful town, perhaps somewhere in the vicinity of its lovely flower market. Or even in the suburb of Sankt Amandsberg. And we would be happy together, as they say. Mmm. For how long? No, no, no. It was out of the question, I told myself, considering my familial and social obligations, not to mention my duty to my government. Was I cut out to be a scandalous person? And *what a scandal* it would be! Of course, there had been others, even worse ones. But in order to commit such follies, one would have had to be far more deranged than I was at that time – far more, indeed, than my character would ever have allowed.

In any case, it was absolutely impossible for me to stay on for more than a week. The personnel department of the Ministry of Education (which kept track of professorial appointments and missions, even those ordered by the Emperor) was an extremely pedantic office.

On the morning of my last day in Brussels, after I had left Yvette, I looked up an old acquaintance, the attorney Charles Robet, a discreet and competent man who had for years taken care of various civil affairs of our Institute of International Law. I was confident that he was the right man to take care of my particular personal matter. I gave him a banker's cheque to the amount of five hundred gold roubles, or circa two thousand gold francs, and asked him to make sure that his office would post one hundred francs on the first of every month to Mademoiselle Yvette Arlon. I told him that it wouldn't be necessary to send any notifications of these payments to me at St Petersburg. Then I gave him a sealed envelope with a note to Yvette and asked him to send it to her with the first payment. The note read: "*Dearest Yvette, I think of you with love and grati-tude. May this ease your everyday circumstances a little. Au revoir. Your F.*" During the past two weeks, I had understood that Yvette found it hard to make ends meet. Once in a great while, her mother would send her small amounts of money from La Panne. The income provided by occasional and unpredictable sales of her paintings was equally minimal and irregular.

A week before my departure I had left the embassy and taken a room at the Pension Etterbeek, not far from Yvette's studio. I had made absolutely sure that no one from the embassy would come to see me off; otherwise Yvette couldn't have come to the platform at the Gare du Nord that evening, to kiss me goodbye in front of other people, to wave at the rain-splattered train window as it pulled away . . . But she did come. Here she was, in her perennial sea-green tailor-made and her yellow boots, a pale, fragile, black-haired young woman, a stranger yet mine, mine yet a stranger – and I thought: Now it all depends on me, whether she will be mine, or a stranger. Under the tin awning of the platform, in the bright light of the gas lanterns, she embraced and kissed me long but without a trace of theatricality, just as if she had been my wife. And since she wasn't, I was doubly grateful to her.

We had already agreed that we would write to each other only if it was absolutely necessary. In such cases, I would write to her home address, and she would send her letter to the address of young Baron von Nolde, a friend and colleague on whose discretion I could count. It had not been too hard to agree on this, since I had been able to assure Yvette that I would be back in Brussels the following June. Yes, she kissed me for a long time. I remember that her eyes were closed at first, but halfway through the kiss she opened them and looked at me, so close that her dark blue-grey eyes with the light of the lanterns reflected in them completely filled my field of vision. Then we waved to each other, and the compartment window, wet with rain, soon took us out of each other's sight . . .

Choo-choo – choo-choo – choo-choo – choo-choo . . .

Marshy woods with overgrown paths on both sides of the tracks, which means that we'll soon arrive at Pikksaare. But I would like to finish this story before we get there. This story which in my mind really doesn't have an end, even though all departures are, in some sense, final.

I did not go to Brussels the following summer. It simply proved impossible for me to do so. All my time between the beginning of June to the beginning of the autumn term was spent on Imperial missions to Vienna, Rome, and Athens, from where, at the end of August, I sent Yvette a letter in which I told her I would come the following year. When I returned to St Petersburg and found out that Boris Emmanuilevich did not have a single letter for me, I felt relieved, because I thought it meant that all was well with Yvette . . . My state of mind when I recalled the moments we had spent together – the way those memories would fade in a reassuring way, then surface again with startling and joyful intensity – all that is too broad and diffuse a subject for me to deal with, at present. But I have to admit: even the following summer, the summer of '91, I was unable to go to Brussels, even though I travelled to places not too distant from it. I spent June and July with Kati and the children in Baden-Baden, as we had been doing from time to time, in the Villa Thur, an old if somewhat dilapidated structure overlooking the valley of the Oos river. Kati's father had bought the villa, rather improvidently to my mind, and tried to keep it up as a place where the family or some members of it could spend a few weeks in the summer at Germany's most distinguished spa in the most illustrious company of summer guests. I had visited there on several occasions. Our Edit had been born there. Personally, I had always regarded these visits as working holidays. Upstairs, in my study with an oval window from which I had a magnificent view of the mountainsides, I was able to concentrate on my work. Once I finished the draft of a whole new consular plan there, in just a week. But that summer of '91, my rheumatism took a painful turn for the worse – ironically enough in Baden-Baden – and it was your suggestion, Kati, that I should try the mineral baths at Bad Nauheim for a change. And that was two hundred versts closer to Yvette . . . I agreed to go there, but I asked you, Kati – do you remember? – perhaps just for form's sake, perhaps just in passing, I asked you to come with me. I still don't know whether this was sheer politeness on my part, in the hope that you'd prefer to stay in Baden-Baden and I could visit Yvette in Brussels. Or whether I hoped that you would come with me, and thus make it impossible to go to Brussels . . . In any case, you did come with me.

It would not have been impossible for me to arrange things so that Kati would have stayed at Bad Nauheim by herself for a couple of days, and I could have visited Brussels on some pretext. I didn't do that. Why not? I could still feel the attraction Yvette had for me, but its intensity had diminished to some degree. Perhaps I felt jealous (on purpose, as it were), afraid of rejection – I couldn't deny the fact that I might find myself in some ridiculous situation when I showed up to see Yvette after two years. There was that, and then, God knows, I seem to have felt that I really needed to be faithful to Kati, despite my previous infidelity. I must have needed that the way I needed my loyalty to authority; in spite of my critical perceptions, I had managed to remain loyal to three emperors.

I did go to Brussels in the late summer of 1892, on my way back from Ireland, where I had attended the tricentennial of the University of Dublin.

I set down my suitcase in the same room at the Pension Etterbeek I had inhabited three years ago, and the mere fact that the same room was available struck me as a tantalizing and seductive omen. Looking across the buildings on the other side of the street I could see the same green tops of lime trees in the Parc Léopold that I had contemplated standing by this same window three years ago, hands in pockets, shifting my weight from one foot to the other, and whispering (and it really doesn't matter whether it was in jest or earnest): *To be or not to be – to stay or not to stay?* And so, I set my suitcase down on the floor, went outside, bought a bouquet of roses in the street, and hurried over to Yvette's. I remember how the pharmacy's scents in the stairwell – in themselves, not at all heady and suggestive of the boudoir, but fresh and hygienic whiffs of mint and lavender – brought back a surprisingly powerful surge of memory, the half-forgotten memory of our intimacy up there in the attic . . .

The doorbell's slightly squeaky sound was more than familiar, but the face that peered out into the staircase was not. It belonged to a sixty-year-old Jew in a paint-stained black calico smock.

"Mademoiselle Yvette Arlon? She moved away. A long time ago."

"How long ago?"

"Well, my dear sir, what do we mean by a long time? If we're talking about fire, a minute is a long time; about a drop of water, an hour; about a rock, ten thousand years . . . But Mademoiselle Arlon – it has been a while. I've been here for two months. Before that, a German fellow lived here for two months . . ."

"What about next door – Mademoiselle Meunier – is she still here?" I asked, getting impatient with him.

"She's here, she's here, for sure. And she knows where Mademoiselle Arlon has gone."

There was a note, scribbled with a piece of charcoal, pinned to Mademoiselle Meunier's door. It said: "Back at 11."

It was half-past nine. I handed the roses to the Jewish gentleman and asked him to give them to Mademoiselle Meunier. Then I took a hackney coach and went to M. Robet's on Boulevard Anspach. Luckily, I found the soft-spoken and elegantly moustachioed lawyer in his mahogany-panelled office.

"What an honour, Professor Martens! But of course . . . I seem to remember we had some difficulty acting upon your instructions. Just a moment – we'll find out what it was."

He asked his clerk to bring him the appropriate ledger. The

entries showed that on the first of every month, Mademoiselle Arlon had been sent one hundred francs net. In each case, the postage had been deducted from the remaining sum. And in each case, the recipient had sent the money back to this office.

"Since we did not have specific instructions for such an eventuality," said the lawyer, "we interpreted these returns as occasional, and repeated the remittance on the first of every month, regardless of the returns. As you can see – the first remittance was made on the first of December, 1889, and was returned to us on the fourth. And so on . . ."

It occurred to me that M. Robet, nevertheless, should have tried to find out more – whether the recipient had moved away or something else had happened. But before I was able to voice that opinion, he turned the page and said:

"But then, suddenly, see here – the remittance of September, 1890, was *not* returned to us. And from then on, for a period of thirteen months, the remittances were accepted. After that, they started coming back again, and this February the post office informed us that the recipient had moved away without leaving a forwarding address. So, Professor Martens, we are obliged to ask you for new instructions."

I told him to stop the remittances until further notice and went back to see Mademoiselle Meunier. The note had been removed, and Philippine herself came to the door. She seemed even more frail than when I had last seen her, and there was not a trace of friendliness in her expression.

"Mademoiselle Meunier – I am Frédéric Martens, the professor – perhaps you remember . . ."

"Of course I do. Come in. I'm a portrait painter, so . . . Of course, your face isn't all that memorable, except for those slightly Mongol eyes. But your posture, your way of dressing, your stature – well, you've got something. How can I be of assistance?"

As if she hadn't known. We were standing in a studio similar to Yvette's, with the difference that no one had cleaned this one up in anticipation of my arrival, and that its natural state of chaos was, in any case, somewhat greater.

"I would like to know how Mademoiselle Arlon is doing. What has happened to her? Where is she?"

Philippine leaned over a table and picked a cigarette out of a welter of tins of paint, books, and dirty coffee-cups. I lit it for her with a match from a box I managed to find in the same mess.

"Please sit down."

We sat down on rattan chairs with tattered cushions.

"What you're interested in should have interested you three years ago."

She puffed nervously on her cigarette and looked at me like a stern schoolmistress. I suppose I just smiled, trying to hide behind a false air of superiority while also attempting to appear concerned – a combination that probably made a far from assured impression.

"You may be right, Mademoiselle Meunier. But my tardiness makes it all the more imperative for me to know."

Philippine took another puff on her cigarette and looked straight at me.

"All right, then. Yvette did not tell me to keep this a secret from any third party, or from you. She had a child."

That was, of course, a blow. Even though I knew that I really had no right to feel hurt, I did. At the same time, I felt slightly relieved. To know that Yvette was alive somewhere, and, God willing, not unhappy. But if someone tells you, speaking of a single woman, not that she got married, but merely that she has had a child, that does not bode well . . .

"So – you mean – she got married?"

"Yes."

"I see . . . And when?"

"Two months ago."

"But the child – when was it born?"

"*Mon Dieu*, Professor, you should know that better than anyone."

Yes, indeed. Yvette's son had been born on the twenty-seventh of July, 1890. I didn't go so far as to start counting weeks on my fingers, even if I have done so since. Philippine admitted that she herself had established the date of conception to the week, if not to the day, by going to the library's newspaper morgue to find out when the congress ended and I first appeared on Yvette's doorstep. Yvette had refused to accept my money, but the following summer, when I hadn't returned, and when Frédéric (Frédéric!) was born and both mother and son were practically starving, Philippine had managed to persuade her to accept my money for a few months.

"And for that, her gratitude is exactly as great as it should be," Philippine added, with a touch of irony.

Then, oh Lord, then Yvette had gone up there, to that seaside village, to the people she had visited when she went there to paint, and there, she had married a farmer who had been madly in love with her for a long time. For love, the young man had kept his mouth shut when the parish priest reproached him for having fathered a child on his bride before marriage.

At that time, I had given up smoking, but I suddenly noticed that I must have asked Philippine for a cigarette and smoked it down so far that it burned my fingers. I asked her:

"Well, the boy did that for love of her. But why did Yvette do it?"

"Yvette told me why," Philippine said. "Not that you couldn't work that out for yourself . . . First of all, she did it because she wanted to be with a good-hearted and generous soul who would help her to get away from here, as far as possible."

"Where have they gone?"

"Wait. Secondly, she did it because she wanted her son to have the legal right to use his true father's name. The young man she married is a Martens."

I didn't say anything for a while. Then I asked her again:

"But where did they go? To Holland? France? America? I have a right to know."

"I don't know if you do or don't," Philippine said. "They went to the Congo. Immediately after the wedding. At Zeebrugge, they embarked on a small steamship bound directly for Boma at the estuary of the Congo River. I went to the wedding, and I saw them off at the pier."

"And where are they now?"

"Yvette hasn't sent me an address yet."

"But will you send me her address, to St Petersburg? As soon as you know?"

"No, I won't."

"Why not?"

"I'll have to write to her first, and get her permission to pass it on to you."

"All right," I said. "I understand. But tell me – whose idea was it to go there? Yvette's or her husband's?"

"Yvette's, of course. The idea never would have occurred to him. But he does everything she wants him to do."

"But why the Congo? Such an uncivilized country, and with such a terrible climate . . . With a two-year-old child? That's madness!"

Philippine picked up another cigarette and looked sarcastic.

"I can't help saying it again, Professor Martens – but your concern for the child is rather belated."

I took that like a man, without comment. I lit her cigarette. She crossed her arms inside the sleeves of her smock as if she were cold. After a drag on her cigarette, she continued:

"As far as the Congo's concerned – I told Yvette the same thing. I told her I understood her desire to get away, to leave things behind. But why not rather go to America or just about anywhere else? I talked to her about it, several times. But no, it had to be the Congo. She seemed spellbound by the idea . . ."

"Did she explain it to you at all?"

"No, I never got a sensible explanation, only some silly talk. Once she told me that she'd heard that the river mud of the Congo smelled exactly like bird-droppings would smell after the birds had been fed poppy-seed for three years . . . And she claimed she wanted to smell that odour."

I never received an address for Yvette. I have never done anything to obtain it, and I haven't heard a word about her since then. I don't even know if this is a sorrow or a relief to me. Frédéric should now be eighteen, soon nineteen years old. I don't know what and who he has become, but one way or another I'm often reminded of his existence, and of the fact that I don't know anything about it. There are times when thinking of him engenders a wave of secret pride that raises me off the ground, but at other times (and I don't know what causes the difference) the thought of him feels like a blow, not too vicious, not too soft, but rather like a blow struck by a heavy and weary arm . . .

Choo-choo – choo-choo – choo-choo – choo-choo . . .

At times, it seems to me that none of this happened to me in my present life as Friedrich Fromhold (or, for many years now, Fyodor Fyodorovich) Martens, but in that previous incarnation, as Georg Friedrich Martens. If, in a case like mine, it is even possible to figure out exactly what happened in either life . . .

In my life as Georg Friedrich, I was born with ties to Denmark, through my father and the municipal councillors of Hamburg. They were strong enough to encourage me to learn Danish, which wasn't hard, since Hamburg's *Plattdeutsch* dialect has many related elements. It was no accident that the Congress of Vienna later, in 1814, sent me to Denmark on a mission for the allied powers, to persuade Prince Christian Frederik to relinquish all his claims to the Norwegian crown – which I managed to do, quite successfully. They probably wouldn't have sent me there at a time when my alleged ties to Napoleon might have disqualified me from such a mission, if my old Danish connections hadn't been considered as valuable as my general reputation as a diplomat. I had been to Denmark several times before – but why? Let's see if I can remember . . . Well, I was there to advise the Danes when they re-established the law school of the University of Copenhagen. It was only natural that they turned to Göttingen for advice. There were similar reasons in later years. So – what if the whole story first happened to me there, let's say in 1799 or thereabouts? In Copenhagen, a professor from Göttingen, approaching middle age, meets young Stina who plays the violin – who later, with their son and a young fisherman named Martens, leaves Isefjord for Saint Croix, an island regularly ravaged by hurricanes, or some similar place . . .

There have been times when I've asked myself: What if neither story is true – what if both Stina and Yvette are just mirages, characters from novels I never wrote? Now and again, the idea of fictional invention has really attracted and then again repulsed me by its enervating boundlessness, by the anguish-laden freedom it offers – compared to the egocentricity of autocrats, the utilitarian thinking of governments, the strict limitations of the language of the law.

Of the romance between Georg Friedrich Martens and Stina of Kronoborg I have only a dim memory. Very dim, compared to the romance of Fyodor Fyodorovich and Yvette, which has the bright glow of embers buried beneath a layer of ashes. I have to admit that the young women of these stories embody my longing to escape from convention. While I have based my life on a masterful command of every imaginable convention, I admire, and always have admired, others who were able to ignore those rules, at least within acceptable limits. Kati, can you hear me – I have also admired that quality in women. Yes, in women too, even though there is very little of it in you, due to your excessively good breeding.

And here we are, at Pikksaare station . . .

19

Pikksaare it is.

We stop here for five minutes in front of the low yellowish station building. The engine keeps puffing. People get off, others get on. Lettish and Estonian peasants are milling about; the men have weather-beaten faces and blond moustaches, the women, whether old or young, look older than they are, wearing their white or black Sunday scarves tied around their heads in that way that always reminds me of church windows with Gothic arches.

The horse and buggy standing in the shade near one end of the station building must have arrived there on a road that winds down from the north. The horse is a well-fed sorrel, its harness has brass decorations, and the buggy looks quite elegant. And these must be the people who have driven it here, a young woman and an old man emerging from the station building onto the platform. Blessed with a penetrating gaze, I also congratulate myself for having lived a long and various life that has enabled me to encounter a great number of people: this has given me the advantage of being able to define a person's class, background, and type without much of a margin of error, at least within the relatively simple categories found here in the governments of Livonia and Estonia.

The woman is twenty-five years old, perhaps even younger, considering how small, round, and childlike her face is; on the other hand, she has a great deal of presence. She is almost imposing. Her gestures are supple and graceful, and her features have a healthy glow. A typical young wife. She is wearing a suit of beige and maroon checks, rather loud, and a large hat with lace trim. Even though she strikes me as a slightly surprising variation of my image of a Baltic noblewoman from Livonia, there is no doubt in my mind that that's what she is. At a border station like Pikksaare, I can't say with any certainty whether she comes from the Estonian side, from one of the estates of Umpalu or Holdre, or from God knows where on the Lettish side.

The man is my age or a little younger, Estonian, Lett, German, hard to tell, but not of the land-owning class. His half urban, half rural appearance, and the way he behaves towards the young lady, make him easy to place: he is the manager of the young lady's estate. After a closer look, I decide that he is Estonian – a bit of a peasant, but not unschooled, a bit deferential, a bit clumsy, a bit sly. He must have driven her to the station. There is no sign of a coachman, and besides, that buggy wouldn't accommodate three people. They are talking. I can't hear what they're saying, but I'm sure they're speaking German. The young lady is giving him instructions, he responds, then hurries to lift her foreign-made leather suitcase into the first-class carriage, my carriage, and says goodbye. She must be standing on the carriage steps. In any case, their parting takes place so close to the carriage door that I can't see it from my window. These days, she may even let him hold her fingertips for a moment.

Then the train starts rolling again. The stationmaster must have held it up just long enough to allow this local celebrity to get on board, exactly the way Mr Huik would have delayed the departure of my train from Pärnu if this had been necessary. Now the lady and her suitcase must be standing in the corridor. Her suitcase looked quite heavy; even that sturdy old fellow had to exert himself as he heaved it into the carriage. Unless she decides to travel in the first compartment which offers the bumpiest ride, being right above the wheels – or if she finds it already occupied – she will have to drag the suitcase behind her down the narrow corridor. There simply isn't room enough to carry it, even if she didn't find it too heavy . . . Come, come, I tell myself, this young lady hasn't jammed her boot-heel into a crevice right in front of an approaching train. It would be easier to repress this gallant impulse if I hadn't caught a tantalizing glimpse of her – now I can't be sure whether I saw the face of a guileless, curious, egocentric child, or that of a proud porcelain doll . . . Besides, I am tired of sitting so long in the same spot, and I'm beginning to feel a little oppressed by the aggressive and uninhibited flood of thoughts and memories that sometimes assails me when I'm alone, and that is doing so now – so I step out of my compartment into the corridor, and there she is.

I think: This is really quite unnecessary. Then I say:

"*Gnädige Frau, gestatten . . .*"

I take a step forward and put my hand next to hers (she is wearing more than one ring) on the suitcase handle. The fragrance from her glossy brown hair rises into my nostrils. My goodness, it is *Brise de Paris* – quite a rarity here, even among ladies of noble birth. I pick up the suitcase.

"*Wohin darf ich?*"

"*O, vielen Dank! Ja, es ist einerlei. Bloßirgendwohin . . .*"

"In that case, madam," I say (smiling at myself for the assurance and ease and deep voice I still manage to assume), "how about right here – if it's all right with you?"

I open the door to my compartment, set the suitcase on the floor, move my briefcase and the basket from Möisaküla to the backward-facing seat, and point to the seat I have cleared for her.

"But we'll put your suitcase over here, so it won't be in your way."

I lift it onto my seat, next to the briefcase, because it would take up too much of the narrow floor space between the seats, and is far too large to fit into the luggage rack. The lady enters the compartment, smiles, sits down facing me. Before I take my seat, I bow, a little foppishly, I have to admit, and say: "Professor Martens". She nods, smiles again, and says her name. The train is making so much noise that all I can make out is something like "*Frau Soundso*".

"If you don't mind my asking, madam – are you from this region?"

"Yes, I am."

"From the north or from the south? What I mean is, from the Estonian or the Lettish side?"

"I see – yes, of course, in these parts that really makes a difference, doesn't it? From the Estonian side."

"So – from Holdre? Or Pupsi? Or – well, what are the other estates in that direction?"

"I can see that you really know your local geography, Professor Martens. I'm from Taagepera."

Hmm. In other words, she's not *aus Hollershof* nor *aus Pupsi* but *aus Wagenküll*, to give these localities the names we're using in our German conversation. Now, as far as I know, Taagepera (Wagenküll) belongs to the von Strycks. A name that doesn't sound at all like *Soundso* . . . But they may, of course, have relatives

173

bearing other names. And it would be absolutely incorrect on my part to ask her for her name again. I say:

"Well, as far as the geography goes, that's only natural. I'm from Pärnu, and I've been travelling along this line ever since it was opened. Before that, I took the coach . . . It's been sixty years."

The young lady does not lodge a protest against that statement. She doesn't say that sixty years is impossible, considering my youthful appearance. No, she doesn't utter any of the banalities I would expect from a lady of her class. Who is she, anyway? I don't know why I suddenly feel so critical of a young woman who only a moment ago inspired me to gallantry. It must be said, however, that the actual standard of education among the ladies of our landed gentry leaves much to be desired. A nanny, a couple of governesses, a little bit of Schwab, a little bit of *Werther*, a couple of dozen memorized lines of Schiller's "The Song of the Bell", a little French, piano, ballet, pastel drawing. And manners of infinite assurance. Now her foot, a surprisingly small foot clad in a brown half-boot of foreign manufacture, rises off the floor, and she crosses her legs quite nonchalantly – a posture certainly frowned upon by arbiters of provincial manners. She asks me:

"Excuse me, but are you a professor at St Petersburg – or at Tartu?"

"St Petersburg."

"I see. I hardly know any of the faculty at St Petersburg. But I know most of the professors at Tartu."

"Really?"

Interesting. Where does she know them from? Well, if she does, she does. Why shouldn't she?

"So perhaps one of the professors at Tartu has the good fortune to be your husband?"

As far as I know, there aren't too many Germans left at that university. In order to ensure and strengthen the university's loyalty towards the government, most of them have been retired or removed by intrigue, or else they have left of their own accord. I suppose there still are a few there who have married into the local nobility. I don't know their wives, but I do know at least a few by name – unless they've left quite recently: Bergmann, Bulmering, Hahn.

174

To my surprise, the young lady laughs heartily, then says, in her bright, high-pitched voice:

"Oh no! No, that is not the case. But I went to the *gymnasium* in Tartu. And it's not a very large town."

"So you went to the German high school for girls?"

I know that they have one of those in Tartu.

"No, I went to the Pushkin School."

Now that is interesting. If, in Livonia, a noble family of German stock sends a daughter to the Pushkin School, which is a Russian school, that is a sign of the family's Russification. The school also has many Estonian students, daughters of civil servants or prosperous farmers. In their case, it is not a question of their families' desire to become good Russians, but rather an expression of the Estonian population's desire to become educated. There is now an Estonian high school for girls, though it was only opened three years ago. But speaking of the Russification of certain German Balts – it is strange to see how this splinter group that has proudly maintained its character for six hundred years, suddenly starts rusting and disintegrating, like iron in a bog . . . Still I won't bother this doll-faced lady with that question. Perhaps that disintegration is merely a sign of the extreme adaptability of the German Balt? If we applied to them what Grenzstein has been preaching to the Estonians, then, of course . . . So that even suicide, by merely refraining from any kind of resistance, might be regarded as adaptation. Which is nonsense, if you ask me. In this particular region, such signs of Russification have been very rare among the Baltic nobility. They are much more visible in St Petersburg. For a moment, I entertain an amusing notion: perhaps the law of gravity does not only apply to mass, but also to *power*. Perhaps we could reformulate it to make it more applicable to these trends. When, in regard to mass, we speak of distance, we could speak of "proximity" in regard to power: the attraction stands in an inverse ratio to proximity squared . . .

So much for that. She mentioned that she did have some academic acquaintances in St Petersburg.

"Once again, if you don't mind me asking – tell me, whom do you know among my colleagues at the University of St Petersburg? Just so I'll know – so I can feel jealous of them, because they've met you before I did . . ."

"Oh, you're so gallant! Well, actually, I know quite a few professors: Pachmann, Petrushevski, Inostrantsev, Bauer, Miller. And Sänger, Grigori Eduardovich. If you can count him as a professor. I met him when he was the Minister of Education, in the spring of 1904. Now, of course, he has stepped down, and I don't know if they've allowed him to return to his chair."

I look outside. We're travelling across the plain of Grotemuizha. Green fields of young rye stretch into the distance on both sides of the track. To our right, I can see the brick buildings of the estate and the white puffs of smoke from the train floating above the sunlit fields. Everything seems to be in its place. But when I turn back to look at my travelling companion, I feel a little queasy and ask myself if I have heard her right. Because if I have, this smiling, porcelain-faced girl must be a truly important lady . . . Or an incredible swindler. Or is it just that I'm not used to the young generation's cheeky sense of humour . . . ? I conceal my astonishment and confusion with a sweet smile:

"And how, if I may ask, did you get to meet all these gentlemen?"

"Of course you may," she says, without the least trace of affectation in her voice. "All of them were either members of the first Douma of the Empire, in the spring of 1906, or else they frequented the hallways of the Tauria Palace."

"I see, I see. And did you frequent them, too? There weren't too many ladies among them . . ."

"I was there as a journalist."

Voilà – she is one of those fashionable Baltic German bluestockings. Or a suffragette. There seem to be quite a few of those, these days. Let's see, what was it I heard not too long ago . . . Oh yes, about von zur Mühlen, of Voisiku estate: he was having trouble with his young wife, an Austrian countess, because of her excessive insistence on freedom of speech and pen – Hermynia is her name, if I'm not mistaken.

"I see. And you also met Sänger, when he was Minister of Education, in your capacity as a journalist?"

"No. I went to see him to ask him for permission to matriculate at the university. It was quite a complicated affair . . ."

"And – did you receive permission?"

"Yes, I did."

This so-called journalist is so naïve she thinks she can pull the wool over a university professor's eyes with such balderdash. As if that professor wouldn't know that in Russia no minister has the authority to admit women to the university. Bestuzheva's college is a different matter, but that's not a university. And you don't need a minister's permission to attend there.

"To tell the truth," she says, a little coquettishly, "if it hadn't been for the Minister's Saint Bernard, I might not have received that permission . . ."

This is getting better and better.

"And what university did he admit you to?"

"I asked him for a recommendation to the president of Bestuzheva. You see, I was only seventeen at the time. I had graduated from the *lycée* with a gold medal, but that wasn't enough, because I was too young."

"And then – did you go to Bestuzheva College?"

"No, I didn't. It never was my intention. I only wanted to be enrolled there as a student."

Well, I knew it. That's completely in character. She is a coquette who likes to play merciless games.

"But why were you in such a hurry to enrol there that you went to see the Minister?"

I ask this out of curiosity, but also out of sheer courtesy. I sincerely doubt that she ever went to see Sänger. Not that it would have been impossible for an arrogant young lady of noble birth, and imperious habits, and with connections and patrons in high places. But she had already blown too much transparent smoke into my eyes for me to give her credence at this point.

Now she gets animated and explains:

"I was in such a hurry, because otherwise I would have lost a whole year. I wanted to be enrolled as a student in Russia, and use that to gain admission to the University of Helsinki. As you know, women in Finland have been admitted to universities for thirty years. I don't know why Russia considers her own women inferior, but that is still the case."

Well, ahem. I am, when all is said and done, a rather competent product and part of the Russian system of education. I should fill in the gaps of her knowledge. I could give her a lecture, several

177

lectures, on the history of women's higher education in Russia. Nevertheless, I won't be able to give her a straight answer to the question *why*, even after many other things were set in motion after 1905, women still don't have full and equal admission rights to our universities. I can't tell her that the reason is the stupidity of those who have the power to decide, and the indecision of those who have the power to implement things. The Czar's debility and his Ministers' cowardice and inertia. Certain quarters would immediately decry such liberal innovation as an example of revolutionary contagion . . . But this little flibbertigibbet who was so eager to enrol at a university – I'll put her in her place with a little paternal irony:

"And so, armed with a certificate of enrolment at Bestuzheva, you were able to enrol at the University of Helsinki?"

"That's right."

"And after that, you made some lucky man very happy?"

"Not until I had finished my studies at the University of Helsinki."

"Oh, really?"

I may have to start believing her, after all . . .

"I received my Master's degree from them."

"A Master's degree! In what discipline, if I may ask?"

"In philology. My particular field of study was folk poetry, especially that of Estonia. Well, you're a jurist, you may not know that the University of Helsinki is the home of Doctor Hurt's collection, the most amazing collection of folk poetry in the world. I compiled a scholarly index for it, under the direction of Professor Krohn. I modified his method considerably."

No matter how incredible that sounds, she can't be making it all up.

"But, dear madam – a *German* lady goes from a *Russian* school to a *Finnish* university to study *Estonian* folk poetry – that is truly extraordinary . . ."

She raises her eyebrows, looks at me with wide open eyes.

"What do you mean, a *German* lady? I'm not a German lady. I'm an *Estonian* lady!"

No matter how I look at that definition, it still seems like an oxymoron. However, many other phenomena of this sort already have prepared my sensibilities to the extent that such a statement no longer disconcerts me. Eminent Estonians, of whom there aren't all that many, usually have a spouse who declares herself a German lady, no matter how flimsy the grounds for that declaration may be. But I have heard that there are some among the youngest generation who don't hesitate to think of themselves as Estonian ladies. Aino Tammi, Mari Raamot, others of their ilk. But right here, and from this young lady's lips, that phrase, that exclamation still seems shocking. True, I've had some big surprises in my life, for better and for worse. They're inevitable in any diplomat's career. Hence, I'm a little jaded in regard to surprises, and find it quite easy to receive her mildly impudent and slightly naïve announcement with a benevolent smile. I also swallow my pride, since my diagnostic powers have proved so weak. But then I fall into another trap, because I want to redress the balance somehow – I want to surprise this Estonian lady. I have no idea what I'm letting myself in for when I suddenly address her in Estonian:

"*Armuline proua on siis, tuleb välja, eesti soost?*"

She looks at me, her eyes full of enthusiasm:

"But of course, Professor Martens. Just as you are. I know, my father told me. That we have among our number a Professor Martens, a world-famous authority, whose texts are used by half the students in the world. And who went to America to make peace between Russia and Japan!"

Now I ask her, my interest aroused to some degree, who her father is. God knows that there aren't too many Estonians whose daughters have a master's degree from a foreign university. From what she tells me, I still don't get a complete picture. He is, of course, a freeholding farmer, and a parish elder, I'm not sure whether in Viljandi or Valga province. A lawyer – without a diploma, it seems, but I refrain from asking embarrassing questions. Also, I gather, the owner of a building and a bookshop in the town of Valga. Well, all right. Although it seems like a lot of different hats for one man to wear.

"So that was your father who saw you off at Pikksaare?"

"Oh, you saw him? Yes, it was."

"But, listen –" I'm dropping the "madam" and adopting a tone more familiar and appropriate in her case. "You said something really intriguing when you told me about your audience with Sänger.

179

You said that if it hadn't been for the minister's Saint Bernard, you wouldn't have received his recommendation? I would love to hear more about that."

She tells me the story with all the gusto and enjoyment of a born teller of tales, and in such colourful detail that I get the picture immediately. While her story is almost too perfect, too literary, to be entirely believable, it is also too detailed to be dismissed as sheer fabrication.

20

She is seventeen. Someone has written a letter of recommendation and arranged an audience for her with Sänger, the Minister of Education. That someone must have been fairly influential; the Minister doesn't receive high-school graduates every day. If his official duties leave him with any spare moments at all, which is unlikely in the turbulent year 1904, he prefers to spend those relaxing with the poems of his beloved Horace. But she has been granted an audience, and she arrives at his office at the appointed time. I ask a question to see if she really knows the location of the Ministry of Education. She does: it is on the Fontanka, down a little from the Alexander Theatre, on the left-hand corner, an enormously large building. She arrives at four o'clock in the afternoon. It turns out that the Minister is still tied up in a very important meeting, in another room of the same building, just across the grey marble floor of the entrance hall. It is a meeting of all the deans of students in the Empire's institutions of higher learning. The young lady will have to wait. The Minister's secretary is aware of the young lady's appointment and invites her to wait in the Minister's office. "Red carpet treatment," I say to myself. I really would like to know who wrote that letter of recommendation. Then she sits there, alone, in a big leather armchair. It occurs to me that I must have occupied that chair several times, and in a lower stratum of my brain I derive from that fact a feeling of some sort of remote yet indecent intimacy with the young woman facing me.

She sits there, and waits, and is, of course, quite nervous. She watches the flames in the fireplace, then notices something glinting in a dark corner – and sees a pair of eyes and their owner, a dog. A gigantic black-and-white dog. Rigid with fright, she considers whether she ought to shout for help or run out of the room, but her intuition tells her to stay put. Her meeting with the Minister is so important to her that she may well be guided by some primeval sense of things; besides, she is reminded of many literary examples

– maybe not there, in the ministerial office, but certainly here on the train, as she describes the scene to me: "And, you know, I had just read *Little Lord Fauntleroy* – I don't know if you remember . . ." She overcomes her fright and starts talking to the dog, in a gentle, friendly, and calm manner. This girl has a great deal of self-confidence, more than one would assume at first sight. Slowly, the huge creature rises and pads over to her. The scent of one of the bitches she owns, back home in Valga province, lingers in the hem of her skirt which the Minister's majestic dog now sniffs with great interest. She gathers enough courage to raise her hand, slowly and gently, to scratch the Saint Bernard behind his ears and under his chin, while talking to him in a quiet, soothing voice, in the impeccable Russian she has acquired at the Pushkin School.

Only when she hears someone behind her clearing his throat, does she realize that the Minister has entered and has – good God – perhaps stood there observing the scene for some time. She jumps up and introduces herself. The Minister offers her a chair and sits down to listen to her plea, which she presents (I'm sure) clearly, persuasively, and succinctly. But the Minister seems inattentive. He is probably saying to himself that this young woman is either naïve or impertinent; he finds the former alternative less taxing, and decides to deal with her request in the way one deals with the unreasonable demands of children. I have no trouble understanding him. He must be worn out, to the point of despair, by the continuous unrest among the nation's students. He is, after all, a minister who takes these matters seriously. In the spring of 1901, after one Karpovich, a former student of the universities of Moscow and Tartu, had murdered the then Minister of Education, Bogolepov (who had tried to repress student unrest by drafting malcontents into the army), the government-appointed successor was a former Minister of War, General Vannovski. The General, who had previously distinguished himself by building new barracks and modernizing the Russian artillery, appointed two assistants: Meshchanov, the director of the imperial prison system, and Sänger, who was a professor of Latin literature at the University of St Petersburg. When Vannovski died a year later, with no end to student unrest in sight, it turned out to be the Latinist, not the director of prisons, who succeeded him as Minister of Education.

So, at the time of the story, it is Sänger who has to deal with the red-hot witches' brew boiling over in our universities and other schools. He would much rather be back at the university, giving his rather boring but decent lectures, complaining about the stupidity and merciless parsimony of the government's educational policy, spending comfortable evenings at home, translating Pushkin into Latin . . . Instead, here he is, exhausted by the deans' muted cries of distress, listening to this rather touching slip of a girl who is talking about her upstart ambitions as if they were the greatest problem in the empire and the whole world. He opens his tired and smarting eyes and looks at her:

"My dear young lady, I regret that I'm unable to help you. It is not in my power to order the president of Bestuzheva College to accept or reject anybody. Please understand my position. At this time, when all of our academic institutions are clamouring for more autonomy, you are asking the Minister of Education to interfere with the autonomy of Bestuzheva. I am very sorry, but I can't do it."

The Minister stands up, giving her no choice but to do the same. She is on the verge of tears. Then she looks at the dog. During her entire conversation with his master, he has rested his warm and heavy chin on her knee, and is now gazing back at her with big moist eyes. She kneels down in front of the dog, presses her cheek against one hairy ear, using it to wipe off a tear that has managed to escape, and says, not in a whisper but only just loud enough for the Minister to hear (and with, I suspect, a measure of premeditation):

"Oh, dear dog, you understood me so much better than your master . . ."

Suddenly, the exhausted Minister bursts into wheezy laughter and says:

"One moment, young lady. Please sit down again."

She obeys, weak from the shock of renewed hope. The Minister sits down at his desk again, says: "Well, let's see what I can do for you," and writes the necessary note.

21

Choo-choo – choo-choo – choo-choo – choo-choo . . . We are crossing the northern reaches of Latvia. It must be really windy outside – the clouds of engine smoke are being blown into tatters. One hopes that this weather is not too hard on the two emperors and their vessels, up there in the archipelago. But in here, in this compartment, sits a smiling young woman, childlike, confident, physical, concrete – fragrant with a whiff of "breeze of Paris" . . . I should be talking with her about timely matters, about today, and tomorrow. I should express interest in what she's engaged in, where she lives, who her husband is.

"Will you be going on from Valga to St Petersburg, like me?"

"Yes. And from St Petersburg to Helsinki."

In that case, we still have a lot of time. And I can keep on talking about things of the past – not that her past is all that long . . .

"Please forgive my curiosity, but who was it who arranged your audience with Sänger? It is quite unusual to take such a personal matter (I refrain from calling it *trivial*) all the way up to the ministerial level."

"Please, don't apologize. It's no secret. My audience was arranged by Mr Tönisson, through his own contacts. I'm sure you know him."

What does "know" mean, in this instance? In the spring of '04, after the Douma had been convened, Tönisson came to see me. He wanted to invite, to my home on Panteleimonovskaya Street, about half the members of the Autonomist faction of the Constitutional Democratic Party – Estonians, Letts, and at least half of them Poles – so that I could give them a private lecture on the international legal aspects of the autonomy principle. I ask you . . . This Tönisson is not a revolutionary firebrand, far from it. But there was no way that a lecture of this sort could have been kept secret, and as soon as word got out, certain quarters would have spread the rumour that Martens had been "advocating separatism" to members of the Douma – never mind what I actually would have told them. Well,

184

I listened to what Mr Tönisson had to say and took a good look at him. Then still in his thirties, a tall, bony man with a Vandyke beard, he looked more like a Baltic baron than a descendant of Estonian peasants. I knew, however, that he was engaged in a vociferous campaign against the Germans in Estonia. He obviously thought of himself as a great orator and relied, even in private conversation, on dogmatic statements, powerful gestures, and a booming voice. In his own circles, at least, he was and is still regarded as an incorruptible and honest man – a rarity, in our time. And I repeat: he was and is not a revolutionary. But he did seem to pursue the cause of his Estonian bourgeoisie with tiresome insistence, and I could not, and really did not want to, become involved in these provincial politics. I felt even more reluctant about participating in coalition-building of that sort. That was not for me. So I arranged my features in a friendly smile and told to him, in Estonian, the language he had been using so demonstratively: "Certainly. By all means – in principle. But as I see it, the question of autonomy is strictly a matter of *constitutional* law, and there is really no way one could apply *international* law to it in any effective manner. So there really wouldn't be much point in my lecturing about it. I do regret," I added, to forestall any objections, "that I really wouldn't have the time to present my views to you and your friends in any case, because I have to go to Paris to attend a board meeting of the Institute of International Law." (I carefully avoided calling this entirely imaginary meeting a "congress" – had it been one, it would have been mentioned in the newspapers.)

"I see," said Mr Tönisson, in an unpleasantly stentorian voice. "Well, then we'll have to see how your colleague, Baron Taube, responds to our request. I had thought that an *Estonian* expert in international law might give us a more favourable answer than some baron. But maybe the baron is a little more *courageous* and will deign to speak to us."

I let that pass, still smiling, pretending that I hadn't really heard that remark. I said, noncommittally:

"Mr Tönisson, Baron Taube is an excellent specialist. Even though he is fifteen years my junior, he is just as *experienced*."

Tönisson left, with a toss of his head and that pointy beard. So – can I say that I know him?

"No, I can't say I do. I know *of* him, to some extent. I do, of course, hear about developments in Estonia, at least once in a while. I even met him once, but I really don't know him at all."

"But I assume that you *respect* him?"

Hmm . . . Is there a little more ardour in that question than mere political sympathy would warrant? Is there not, in those round grey eyes, a little too much aggressive hopefulness? And am I – it's hard to believe – but am I suddenly *jealous* of Mr Tönisson? Well, let's see . . .

"Please forgive me for taking an objective view – but from a St Petersburg perspective, and even more from a European perspective, Mr Tönisson's endeavours seem rather insignificant. However, his *way* of pursuing them is certainly laudable. By all accounts, he is a man of rare integrity . . ."

I can tell, from the way the young woman's eyes light up, and from the faint blush that spreads from her rosy face to her white neck, that my words have pleased her. Then, of course, I feel a need to assert my objectivity, to cool off her enthusiasm by adding:

"An integrity that may be out of place in today's political life. Many people even regard his politics as completely quixotic." To prevent her from contesting that view, should she find it offensive, I ask her:

"But you also told me that you observed the sessions of our first Douma, as a journalist. Were you there as a representative of Mr Tönisson's paper? The *Postimees*?"

She nods, looking pleased.

"Yes. I had just finished my second year at the University of Helsinki. That April, Mr Tönisson left Tartu to go to the Douma in St Petersburg, and he invited me to come along – to observe the proceedings for his paper, at least to the extent that journalists were permitted to do so."

Her expression tells me that she is reviewing her memories of those eventful weeks. Now I understand her completely – her childishly lively and naïvely enthusiastic demeanour, the way she combines a self-conscious touch of extravagance with a miniature internationalism. These qualities indicate her social coordinates. She is not a descendant of the German barons – I admit my mistake; she is, however, a member of the Estonian country elite in the

186

fertile southern regions of Mulgimaa. I add a gloss in the margin of my memory: lately, some of the latter have produced individuals who could easily be mistaken for the former. She is obviously infatuated with the leader of the liberal conservatives of Mulgimaa province. I would be willing to bet on it – but I'm not a gambling man, and besides, there's no one here to take my bet . . .

"And what, may I ask, was your most memorable impression of the Douma?"

Will she start praising Alyadin's uncouth tirades? No, this female *magistr* from Mulgimaa is too sophisticated to applaud that provincial ham's grotesquely theatrical Russian imitations of Mirabeau, even though they made the capital's liberal ladies bombard him with red carnations. Her tastes are too serious for that. Besides, she is in love with the vice-chairman of the Peripheral Nations Faction of the Constitutional Democratic Party . . . No, I know: with her Finnish education, she is going to praise the English style of Struve's and Nabokov's speeches.

"Let me think . . . Well, perhaps this wasn't my most memorable, but it certainly was my most lasting impression: the fact that the space allotted to the press was *tiny*! I managed to get a seat, just because there were only two women present. Most of the men had to stand. The entire domestic and international press corps was crammed into that gallery like sardines in a tin! Obviously, Stolypin had decided that the fewer journalists there were in attendance, the better this was for the interests of the Russian state. But if you ask me for my most memorable impression – it was simply that it was all a charade, a completely staged event."

Good Lord! That's exactly what I had felt as I sat there in the observers' box, even though I had never managed to tell that to anyone quite so bluntly.

"It felt unreal, right from the start – from the very fact that the sessions were held in Potemkin's old palace."

I had noticed that too, and found it amusing; without, of course, ever mentioning it out loud.

"Then there was the inhuman scale of the meeting rooms. You couldn't recognize persons at the other end; you probably couldn't recognize anyone even from the speaker's lectern. And then," she goes on, "the most important thing was that out of those four or

187

five hundred representatives, only the supporters of Purishkevich seemed to be in control of the situation. In spite of all those speeches by Alyadin, and all the electricity in the air, everybody else seemed jumpy and anxious. All the doors had guards posted at them, and the place was teeming with secret police in plain clothes . . ."

With this woman, I have not concluded a treaty of candour. That treaty exists only between Kati and myself. But I have to admit that the thought this young woman has just expressed has also occurred to me. Whenever I find myself in imperial institutions, I am amazed by the ubiquity of *uniforms*, worn by gendarmes and others – and by my awareness of how many more there must be whose uniforms are of the invisible kind . . . Every time I notice this I tell myself, all right, very well, the more of uniforms there are here, the safer I am – yet this does not seem *so* self-evident that I won't have to remind myself again, each and every time . . .

"Every so often, up there in the press gallery, I shivered a bit when it occurred to me that the whole palace was simply a gigantic gilded trap, with the mice squeaking inside and the cats yawning by the doors. Until the big black Master Tomcat gives a sign – a twitch of his tail – and all the cats rush in, and the doors slam shut behind them. And the horrible feast begins . . ."

I close my eyes, not really knowing if I do this in order to see the young lady's impudent and coarse image from a Grimms' fairy tale more clearly, or in order to escape from its excessive clarity. I hear the engine huffing, feel the train's jerky progress, and think, my eyes still closed: "But while the cats are devouring the mice, the red wolves may already be on their way – and not just anybody, but my own blond nephew Johannes with his red pack – and they'll gnaw and *file* the golden trap to pieces, and proceed to make a meal of both cats and mice."

I open my eyes. The learned young lady has produced a notepad and an elegant silver pencil from her roomy brown leather purse. She covers a page with a fast and fluid hand, then explains:

"You know, Professor, that image – of the Tauria Palace as a great big mousetrap, with the Douma as a crowd of mice and the gendarmes as black cats – it came to me a moment ago as I was telling you about it. So I want to jot it down. Maybe I'll use it on some other occasion."

Why shouldn't I tell her my further development of that theme? It seems to me that if there is anything disloyal about the parable, it is *her* part of it. My sequel would redress the balance, tilt it back to the loyal side – even though I didn't invent it to that end. I made it up because I think it is politically possible. Besides, it is quite clever, so my vanity comes into play. Let her see that even jurists are capable of metaphorical thought:

"But, my dear lady, what if, while those black cats are devouring the mice, a pack of wolves arrives on the scene – *red* wolves – and they break down the doors and make short shrift of both cats and mice . . ."

"But why do you call them *wolves*?" she exclaims in a surprisingly shrill voice. She stares at me with round eyes, silver pencil in hand. "They aren't *wolves*, they are *workers – revolutionaries – socialists*! And that 'short shrift', if that's what you want to call it – it is coming, Professor, it is coming anyway, and sooner rather than later!"

We are rumbling through the forests between Purgailis and Eglis, on our way to Stalenhof station.

"I see," I say, very quietly, and with a very sweet smile. "You sympathize with the revolutionaries. Or perhaps you are even a socialist?"

Now this strong young woman leans forward, in her childlike excitement, and instinctively lowers her voice, the way every subject of the Russian Empire lowers his voice when speaking of matters such as these:

"Yes, I am. I'm not afraid to tell you that. Despite everything . . . You know, Mr Tönisson told me about the time he went to see you in the spring of 1906. And he said about you the same thing you said about him – almost word for word: he told me that when all is said and done, Professor Martens is an honest man. So – yes, I am a socialist. *Of course* I am."

I listen to her surprising outburst, to this confession that probably has an element of personal defiance in it, and ponder her incredibly serious and yet somehow playful enthusiasm, all the while retaining an "understanding" smile on my face. What else can I do? I say:

"I see. It doesn't really surprise me. In these days of so many gross injustices." And I say to myself – what a fatal mistake! What an astounding aberration! *What am I saying?* What has come over me? Yet I find this young woman so likeable – both in her pugnaciousness and in her touching vulnerability – despite the fact that she seems to belong to the category of young ladies who consider it natural and self-evident that every man within a radius of five hundred versts is hopelessly enamoured of them.

"Nevertheless, your confession does surprise me a little. You told me that Senator Genetz has been helpful to you – but he is one of the most respected Finns in the Governor General's ken! And you have told me, several times, how fond you are of Mr Tönisson – who really has no use at all for socialists. At the Douma, you were a correspondent of *his* paper, the *Postimees*. You are the daughter of a wealthy man –"

"But, Professor Martens – after everything I saw and experienced in Finland, after the events of 1905, it would be impossible for me to remain an honest person, if I . . ."

Hmm. What could this little scatterbrain have seen and experienced *there*? Compared to what I've heard about events in Moscow and Tallinn and Estonia, and to what I saw with my own eyes in St Petersburg, first of all on the unfortunate day that became known as Bloody Sunday.

(That morning, I sat down at my desk at eight o'clock, my usual time, ready to go to work. I was in the middle of an article on the origin of treaties. Then I realized that I had inadvertently left some materials for it at the office when I came home on Friday. I put on a fur coat, hailed a hackney sleigh, and went to the university. I arrived there around nine o'clock. It was just getting light. I told the driver to wait for me, but there were complications: the building was closed on Sundays, and the caretaker, who had the keys, had gone to church. So I let the driver go and waited for the caretaker to come back. After I had retrieved my dossier, I was unable to find a sleigh and set out for home on foot, a prospect I didn't find daunting at all. But just as I set foot on the Palace Bridge, I heard shots from the direction of the Winter Palace – several long volleys of rifle fire. My heart started pounding. I remembered that the day before, in the midst of my preoccupation with the origin of treaties, I had heard about Gapon's plans for this Sunday morning. I was tempted to return to the university and wait for further developments, safely within its walls, but then I decided that this was

190

cowardly and kept on walking, although my knees were shaking and my insides were gripped by a burning sensation of anguish. I heard further volleys and the deep-throated roar of a large crowd. I broke into a run and was halfway across the bridge when several hundred people, fleeing from the Winter Palace, charged towards me from the other direction. I backed up against the iron railing. I knew that I would never forget the faces of the people running past me: faces distorted by panic, fear, rage, and desperation – bulging eyes, dishevelled hair . . . The poor wretches had unbuttoned their Sunday overcoats in order to run faster, and many among them were wounded, staggering and falling, being dragged along or trodden underfoot. The snow was littered with trampled icons. Someone was still carrying a huge dark brown and gilded Saint George, perforated by bullet holes, the white sky showing through, and I saw it sway and fall to the ground on its face and shatter under the pounding feet of the runners . . .)

A thousand lost their lives on the square in front of the Winter Palace. Then, everything that followed – in people's expressions, words, deeds, dreams, nightmares . . . What could this young woman have experienced in Finland that was so remarkable? No turn of events has ever been able to budge me to the left of the Constitutional Democratic Party's position, not then, not now. I have given a great deal of thought to our internal political life, but I have never advertised that fact. Why not? I remember how embarrassed I felt when four years ago, on my sixtieth birthday, some young man from the *Guardian* interviewed me in the United States and asked me: "Mr Martens, right now your country is going through a period of many problems and tensions. Could you tell me if such internal problems are of any interest to you?" That's what he asked me, and I was so flustered that I told him: "They both are and they aren't. Take your pick. In either case, my interest is only that of an observer." He did not pursue the matter, did not ask me to define the "interest of an observer", or to tell him whether or not it might evolve into the interest of a thinker or a searcher for solutions. And whether, if no such evolution took place, one might even call it any sort of interest at all.

I say, in a moderate and even voice, with an appropriately serious mien but inwardly amused by both of us:

"Very interesting . . . Could you perhaps tell me what were your most significant experiences – leading to your, shall we say, *conversion*?"

It seems obvious to me that only *emotional* reasons can sway a young woman to become a socialist. People like her never become converted only by their reading of Marx and Kautsky and whoever else there may be. Things must affect them personally. Then she starts telling me, and I listen and look at her, closing my eyes once in a while. From time to time, her lively descriptions, given in a somewhat muted voice, metamorphose into images of my own, and I begin to feel that she is indeed describing events unfolding in my own imagination . . .

The Great Strike – she pronounces the words with both defiance and respect, those splendidly theatrical yet mortally dangerous and terrifying words, referring to the general strike that began in Helsinki one day after Witte had issued his manifesto in St Petersburg. Suddenly there were huge crowds in the streets and gathering in front of the Students' Building . . . I have visited her Helsinki, I can imagine the scene. On its modest thoroughfares, as well as on the suburban hills with their red wooden houses, unprecedented harangues and slogans are heard: *How long will we let the gendarmes go on ruling this country? How long will we let the Governor General sit in his palace? "Kuinka kauan vielä tässä maassa . . ."* That is all the Finnish I know, but I can see the dark autumn night and the mysterious, practically silent crowds moving in the streets and along the rocky shores. The Governor General takes refuge on a battleship, and the crowds storm and occupy the city's Police Headquarters . . . The gloomy corridors and rooms are packed with people. Industrial workers, carrying rifles on their shoulders, come and go to and from their guard posts . . . Young women of the Socialist Student Union spend days and nights at office desks copying documents, drawing up lists – when she says "drawing up lists", I manage not to ask her what kinds of lists, because it occurs to me that they could have been lists of members of the bourgeoisie to be arrested (which was certainly not the case). I can see the young women hard at work copying documents on large tables covered with ink-stained green blotters . . . And making sandwiches and tea for the riflemen departing for and returning from their sentry duties . . . And in the office of the Chief of Police, Captain Kock (who has now, if I'm not mistaken, fled to America), around his table, under the gaslight, bent over maps of the city, faces of a new generation of the likes of Camille Desmoulins, as in a painting by Latour . . . Night after night, day after day, but it is all merely one great Sunday of liberty! And in the coarse jokes, the solemn determination, the firm handshakes of the workers – *a brand new,* the young lady says, *a brand new and unprecedented feeling of strength and solidarity.* Until the moment when the strike collapsed and everything was suddenly lost again, in some inexplicable way. The bourgeoisie regained its power and declared that the new Diet would be a great magic mill to grind the flour of justice for all . . .

"And then," she continues with muted yet almost religious fervour, "after I had thus witnessed, at the closest possible range, how divided the Finnish people really were among themselves – then came the summer of 1906 when the first wave of Estonian revolutionary refugees arrived in Helsinki. As soon as I established close contacts with them, I understood immediately that my own notion of a united and unified Estonian people – that it, too, had been a childish mistake. Now do you understand me?"

I reply, perhaps a little condescendingly, since I see no reason to pretend that I am not in a position of authority, but nevertheless in a friendly, paternal manner:

"Of course, of course. You know, you just told me that you experienced the discord among the Finnish people *at the closest possible range.* And you said that you saw the discord of Estonia when you established *close contacts* with the refugees. But don't you see that that's the crux of the matter? The quality of any image always depends on one thing – the *distance* from which you view your subject."

I see the young lady open her little mouth and draw a deep breath to refute my relativism. However, she doesn't say anything, and it seems to me that she is smiling indulgently and thinking: "All right, let the old fellow deliver his lecture; that's all he is good for, anyway. Although I think I've had my fill of such lectures, from Mr Tönisson, for instance . . ."

And I do give her a lecture. "Dear madam, let's imagine that we're observing all of humanity from a certain distance. Humanity, or an ant-heap. All the ants, all the people really look the same to us. We can't make any distinctions between individuals. This is true as long as we observe them from far away. Let's step closer, take a closer look. Well, the ants still appear more or less undifferentiated, because we're not used to recognizing what distinguishes one from another. But among the people we notice the first difference. We notice, I think, that some of them are men and some of them are women. As we get even closer, we see that some are young and some are old, some are middle-aged, some are at death's door. If we go on observing them for a while at close range – their activities, dwellings, customs, clothing, manners, and so forth – we can say: Some of them are aristocrats, some are intellectuals, some are bourgeois, some are proletarians. All right. Now let's get *even* closer to them! Please notice that the closer we get, the greater will be the number of details that permit us to make possible distinctions between them. I know that you, with your education, are familiar with scholarly and scientific methods. You are, in fact, a –"

Here, I pause for a fraction of a second to make sure that there won't be a trace of irony in the way I utter the next word:

"– *scholar*, yourself, so I'm sure you won't find my reasoning hard to follow."

At the same time, I ask myself: What is going on here? Why am I so taken by my own improvised train of thought? Why do I feel almost intoxicated by my desire to reach my foregone conclusion? When I can see, very clearly, that this conclusion amounts to intellectual suicide? That it makes a mockery of the scholarly principle of classification? Nevertheless, I go on:

"What I'm driving at is this. As soon as we get close enough to humanity and humans, we notice that each individual differs so radically from all the others, in so many distinctive ways, that it becomes futile to attempt any kind of classification. Now, with your permission, I would like to ask you: Why do you choose, among hundreds of possible distances, *one in particular* from which to conduct your examination of humanity, or Russians, or Finns, or Estonians – the one distance that allows you to distinguish those, shall we say, *socialist* markings? From a little further away, they wouldn't be visible. Closer up, they disappear. Don't you think that it is a little, shall we say, *biased* to consider one possibility in a hundred the only true one? Pray tell."

And I think, feeling ravaged by a bittersweet self-irony: but what is it *you* do, yourself?

Then she says it, out loud:

"But Professor Martens, you're guilty of that yourself! And you can't help being guilty of it, as a scholar. Because the *states* whose relationships you study –"

She looks straight at me with her round, slightly reproachful, slightly coquettish eyes:

"No, don't smile, let me pursue this line of thought. Seen from somewhere in outer space, those states might just look like witches'-broom or clumps of grass, not like empires at all! And closer up, closer than necessary for your specialized studies, they would be – I don't know, merely teeming herds of people, men and women like you said, and even closer up, merely a man and a woman – and so on. Only from a particular, well-chosen distance can you see them the way you need to see them – as ant-heaps, just like you said, and the ant-trails between them as some kind of system! And we *socialists* –" (oh, goodness, now this elegant young lady, whose physical opulence is almost too seductive, spreads her bejewelled hands for emphasis) " – we proceed in exactly the same way. Because we find that the distance we have chosen enables us to construct the best explanation of the evolution and character of modern society. It may be crude, but it is irrefutable."

I could, of course, argue with her. I could start out by joining her train of thought, then I could skate past her and pull her along onto truly slippery ice! "But of course, madam. Every distance we choose will, in fact, show us a different subject – will correspond to a different discipline, even *create* a different discipline. From astronomy to microbiology – from Mädler to Mechnikov, it you wish . . ." She would probably agree with me on the spot, and then I would ask my paternally superior question: "Now tell me, why are you claiming that a *single* distance and the discipline that corresponds to it – I see no problem with calling your socialism a kind of scientific discipline – why are you making a claim of *universality* for it?"

But she pre-empts that by a sudden turn. She leans forward and fires another intense salvo.

"You asked me for the deepest and most enduring impression I received during those revolutionary days in Finland. I'll tell you what it was. Because, believe it or not, that particular experience involved *you* personally. Well, if not personally, it did involve a relative of yours . . ."

A light tremor runs through me, and I think: What on earth does that mean? My only familial connection to the revolution is that nephew of mine, Johannes, but as far as I know, he has never been in Finland. Although, God knows . . .

"Really," I say, smiling. "How very interesting."

And she tells me the following:

"I'm sure you've heard of the Viapori rebellion? Pretty much everybody has. In my opinion, it was the most heroic event I've ever seen, and I saw it at close range. No, I didn't manage to get out to the island, not before nor during the rebellion. But for a whole week I was in touch with the representatives, the spokesmen the rebels at the fortress sent to the city. I took part in their meetings and gatherings. Such summer nights . . . With the thunder of cannon rolling across the clear sky. Among the Viapori rebels, there were only a few officers. One of them was a friend of mine, Lieutenant Yemelyanov. It all started on a Monday . . . The last meeting was held in a house on Mariankatu, in the early hours of Saturday. They already knew what was going to happen. They all knew that the Navy had left Kronstadt – not to come to their aid, but to crush them. I didn't know, I was still hoping against hope . . . But I knew that some other officers had managed to leave the island. We had helped them go underground. I remember saying goodbye to the lieutenant at Katajanokka, next to the boat that was taking him back to the fortress. The waves were lapping against the sides of the boat and the rocks of the shore. I asked him if he wouldn't rather stay in the city – because if the rebellion failed, he, as an officer, would inevitably . . . He shook his head and took my hand. "No, I can't desert my boys. Goodbye." He said that quite calmly, in the full knowledge of what awaited him. That was three years ago, and his decision, the look in his eyes, his handshake – those are the things I will remember forever. Two days later, after a horrendous naval bombardment and the explosion of the ammunition store, the fortress surrendered."

The young lady is silent. She is watching the fields and pine woods float past the window. I say to myself, well, it's exactly as I thought. I give her a moment before I ask:

"And – this Lieutenant Yemelyanov?"

"He was court-martialled and executed by firing squad. At the fortress."

But where does my mysterious relative come into all this, I wonder, and she gives me an answer before I ask the question. She turns away from the window and leans forward so that I can feel her breath and smell the scent of *Brise de Paris*, and then she does something completely unexpected and unnerving: she reaches out and takes my hand. We have obviously left the sphere of good manners. It is the impulsive gesture of a young woman whom life has liberated from the timidity of a country girl. She says:

"A week or two ago, before I came back to Estonia, I sought out that relative of yours – Doctor Martens, the military surgeon of Viapori fortress. I asked him to tell me about the executions. He had witnessed them. He didn't want to talk about them, but I begged him, and he told me . . ."

But of course! Of course! Friedrich. Julius' son. A navy surgeon. After a long time with the Tallinn Squadron he was posted to Helsinki, several years ago. I've even visited him there. But he never told me anything about this . . .

"He admitted that it had been his regrettable duty to attend the executions, and he remembered Lieutenant Yemelyanov instantly. He remembered, because the other rebels had done this, that, or the other during their last moments – some stared at the ground in silence, some gazed into the distance, some tried to pray. But Lieutenant Yemelyanov had tried to *say* something. Before the fusillade rang out, he managed to speak just one word. Doctor Martens said to me: 'Imagine – he turned to the soldiers who stood next to him up against the wall, and he didn't say *Bratsyi* – brothers – which would have been the normal thing to say. No, even then, at the last moment of his life, he said *Tovarishchi – comrades!*' And Doctor Martens, a decent man, your kinsman, simply couldn't understand that. Tell me, do you?" She squeezes my hand, shakes it, urging me to respond, then asks again, in a voice shrill with emotion: "Professor Martens, do you understand that?"

"Oh, of course, yes," I say, "of course I do . . ." What else can

I say? And I do understand that lieutenant. First of all, any man of character who was facing death *would* insist on proclaiming his belief, even if it has proved fatal, simply as a matter of pride . . . God knows, I might even understand him if his last word *wasn't* motivated by pride, but was simply a true believer's calm reiteration of his faith. I ask her, and I notice that I'm almost whispering:

"Did Doctor Martens tell you *how* the lieutenant said that word?"

"Yes. I asked him, and he told me. He said that Lieutenant Yemelyanov had said it very, very quietly. With a calm that was terrifying. *Tovarishchi.* And then, the fusillade . . ."

She says no more. I am suddenly much more aware of the loudness and vibration of the train's progress.

No, Friedrich didn't tell me that his duties required his presence at executions. It doesn't surprise me that they do. Whatever else our professional obligations may be in this era of oppression, all of us (not me, thank God for that, at least) – or many of us – have been made accomplices in the violence oppression requires . . . Pärnu's stationmaster Huik, that decent fellow, has been put in charge of prisoner transports, and so have his colleagues up and down the line. The engine drivers are carting prisoners from one town to the next. Instead of investigating the crimes of which those prisoners are accused, the judges are obliged to hand down blanket death-sentences. Young recruits may find themselves ordered to act as executioners. And Friedrich, as a surgeon in the service of the state, has to watch the executions and to confirm that the bullets have done their work . . . To be honest, I can't deny my own part in all this. I'm an accomplice too, perhaps the most culpable one, at least compared to the Huiks and the engine drivers and Friedrich and the recruits. Because I am in a position really to see the big picture. In fact, am I not the one who renders the most important services to the machinery of the state – even if I don't directly serve the machinery of slaughter – God, no, not that . . . One might even say that I'm the one who has helped that machinery of the state to survive, that I have generated a rather essential portion of the energy it has needed to go on functioning during these years of massacres! I won't say the *decisive* portion, but an essential one, nevertheless.

By that, I don't mean our treaties regarding Central Asia, or the

Treaty of Portsmouth. Not that they haven't kept the machine going too, but I'm thinking of something much more concrete: the *loans* the Russian government has managed to arrange in recent years, especially those it received in 1906. A hundred million roubles, two and a quarter billion francs, most of it from French banks. We really needed that money to go on breathing. Our own funds were so utterly depleted that Shipov wanted to invalidate all Russian banknotes in December, 1905. Then, as we know, the French said all right, let's give Russia the loan – provided that she clearly sides with us against Germany at the Conference of Algeciras. We didn't hesitate to do so. However, in the meantime, the legal foundations had been laid for the election and establishment of the Russian Douma. Then it occurred to the French, who are always respectful of constitutional law, and especially to Poincaré, to question the Russian government's authority to seek and receive such an international loan in these changed constitutional circumstances, *without the assent of the Douma*. And then – not too many people know this – Poincaré proposed yet another, final condition: France will lend Russia two and a quarter billion francs *if* Professor Martens proves to the French government, by means of convincing arguments, that the Russian government is competent to seek and accept the loan. Well, Poincaré didn't specifically name *me* in his official letter. He said that the *Russian government* had to present those arguments, that proof. But he let it be known through an intermediary, the Director of the Banque Franco-Hollandaise, that the most expedient way to effect a favourable decision would be to have Professor Martens write this clarification of the Russian government's authority.

I wrote it post haste and without hesitation. That is to say, I had misgivings at every turn. From the juridical point of view, the question was whether, and to what degree, the October Manifesto had introduced parliamentary democracy into Russia's autocratic system. The manifesto and the legislation it had engendered could be interpreted in ten different ways. The main problem was to decide which interpretation was the best in terms of logic and honesty – which interpretation was *right* in that sense. From a political or shall we say patriotic point of view, however, there was no time for delay or hesitation. We were on the brink of a catastrophe. So

199

I wrote my paper as fast as I could, and Witte sent it on to Poincaré. I stated that in matters concerning foreign loans, the Russian government's legal authority had not been curtailed in any way by recent constitutional reforms. Thus, its application for a loan was still entirely valid. We received our two and a quarter billion francs. Soon enough, certain circles claimed that this was, in fact, the money the government had needed – and used – to put down the revolution. But that was not the case! Or, at least, that wasn't *all* it was used for. The government also used it to avert a great famine. Nothing in this world is unequivocally black or white . . . As for the rounds of ammunition that killed Lieutenant Yemelyanov, they had been paid for before I helped the government get the loan. But the loan may have paid for the handcuffs Johannes was wearing that time I handed him a file in the men's room at Pärnu station . . .

Thank heaven she can't read my thoughts, this poor ridiculous beautiful young woman with whom I'm sharing this train ride.

22

But you, Kati – you can read my thoughts, can't you? It is to you that I'm addressing them, and I have yet another confession to make.

For years, I have been haunted by a certain dream. Not every night, of course, but I have seen it dozens of times, dozens of nights. Now and again, images from it rise into my consciousness in broad daylight. I realize it may well be nothing but a reflection of Rozhdestvenski's fateful expedition, yet it seems to me that it pre-dates that event – that it has been with me since my childhood, perhaps even my first childhood in Hamburg and the ships I saw in the harbours along the Elbe.

I am travelling on a ship – I'm never sure what kind of a ship it is, sail or steam; I suppose it can be either, at different times. I don't know why and how I find myself on board, but there I am, in an elevated place. When it is a sailing vessel, I find myself up on the quarter-deck, when it is a steamship, somewhere on the command bridge. Parts of the sea are as black as ink, others a milky white – the former lying in the shade of lead-grey clouds, the latter touched by bright sunbeams breaking through those clouds. Everywhere around us, all the way to the horizon, there are similar vessels (sometimes under sail, sometimes powered by steam), and it looks like they're all moving in the same direction. I don't know their destination. Now and again I notice other people, sailors or passengers, either on my own ship or on others close by. I could ask my fellow passengers about our destination. I could use the megaphone I'm holding in my hand to ask the people on the other ships where we are headed, but I don't, and my suppression of the question makes me feel anxious in a curious way that feels both exasperating and pleasurable – because I know, with a sleepwalker's certainty, that none of them have the answer, not even the captains studying their charts and setting the course. Hence, it would be rather odd, even crazy, and certainly inappropriate to ask anybody. Besides, I don't have time do so. I am holding this megaphone, and I have a task to accomplish. I hold the megaphone to my lips and look past its funnel at the large dream flotilla. This is what I see: from time to time, flashes of fire and clouds of smoke emanate from the decks or gun ports of those vessels, and holes appear in the sides of other vessels; masts break, smokestacks are pulverized. Sometimes all this seems to be happening without a sound, but then the booming of the cannon and the crash of explosions reaches my ears, rolling across the sea. At some level, I'm aware that this is simply a composite image based on tales I've heard about Tsushima and Port Arthur and Viapori (didn't someone just say: "Such summer nights . . . With the thunder of cannon rolling across the clear sky"?) – and then I feel the deck trembling under my feet, and I realize it is the narrow-gauge train between Härgmäe and Valga, perhaps even the mailcoach on the road to Frankfurt, or the world at large. I feel it vibrate under my feet as the guns down below fire a broadside. I hear their thunder rolling over me. I'm holding the megaphone, with the sour taste of its brass on my lips, and I'm talking into it: "Ships of the Navy of Civilized Nations! Listen to me! I, the son of a man who was a parish clerk at Audru and a tailor at Pärnu; I, who was the brightest student of the Lutheran Paupers' School at St Petersburg; I, who am the plenipotentiary of the most world's most pacifist emperor Alexander II, or III, or IV – what's the difference – I want to tell you this: If, indeed, we must shoot and kill and drown one another, let us do these things only with the strictest observance of the provisions of maritime law!" A law, I say to myself, in large part composed by yours truly, in precise and flexible language, proposed by those most pacifist emperors of mine as the law governing warfare at sea, received with great acclaim by all civilized nations at The Hague and Geneva and Brussels, and violated by all of them, daily, in every latitude and longitude . . . "But if, in battle, we do not kill all our adversaries . . ." I'm still speaking into the megaphone. It still has that repugnant brassy taste. I can feel my lips and facial muscles move as I speak, but I can't hear a word I am saying for the din of the guns, the roar of the sea, the howling of the wind. Besides, I am speaking quietly – the contents of my words would make roaring seem inappropriate – and even a roar would be drowned out by this pandemonium. Nevertheless, I can't simply whisper or fall completely silent, since I am obliged to give this speech. "If we do not kill all our adversaries," I continue in my inaudible megaphone voice, "if we take prisoners of war – let us treat them humanely! Let us at least allow them to see their relatives – or those among them who have relatives willing to support them in their distress – because, from a humane point of view, such support is incredibly important to those prisoners! I am keenly aware of this from my own years as a prisoner of war – from my imprisonment at the paupers' school, at the gymnasium, and at the university, and from my seemingly interminable struggle against poverty – all the years in all those institutions – when I had to apply for exemptions from tuition fees, when I could honestly write: *because I am without means and do not have any relatives who are able to pay the fees on my behalf* – nor any professors who would sponsor me . . ."

Of course I never wrote *that*, but it was true. I never had any sponsors. I might have found some if my pride hadn't kept me from applying to anyone, Ivanovski for example, the way poor students have turned to me for help over the years. Kati, you know that I haven't been a great benefactor of poor students. We are relatively wealthy; I should have been more generous. (Kati, you understand, and I don't negate, at least not in front of you, the fact that this sudden self-critical spirit is nothing but a version of the early Christians' childlike belief – engendered in me by *fear* – that honesty will somehow protect us from death.) Of course I should have been more willing to sacrifice. But I did, after all, support a few young men, especially when I perceived traits in them that somehow reminded me of my own younger self. Like that boy at the Military Academy of Medicine, what was his name again, whose father had been a shoemaker at Rakvere and Kiev . . . Ah, as soon as I think of him as a tradesman's son, his name pops into my head: *Puusepp* was his name. Do you remember, Kati – he first appeared on our doorstep twelve years ago, wearing the uniform of the academy, a slight blond fellow, rather nondescript at first sight. But he turned out to have an iron will and great ambition, and he was quite clever in his dealings with people. I remember the time he entered my study and handed me his letter of recommendation. When I saw that it was signed by Hirsch, I looked up to offer him a seat – after all, this boy had a letter from the Emperor's personal physician – and saw that he had proceeded to the window and was waving to someone in the street. Just look at that little cockerel, I thought. His sweetheart must be waiting for him down there; here he is flirting with her while I am reading his recommendation.

"Who is the lucky lady?" I asked, with exactly the right amount of sarcasm in my voice.

"Oh – I'm sorry, Professor Martens!" But he didn't look embarrassed in the least. "That's my friend Tolya. He has just arrived from Zurich. He has been studying at the University of Zurich for two years, and I met him on my way to see you. He will be going on to Kiev. We were classmates at the *gymnasium* in Kiev. He is a philosopher."

Before I knew it, I was standing next to him by the window, looking down into the street where a pale, bespectacled boy in a black coat paced back and forth, glancing at his watch.

"He studies the creations of the human brain. I want to study the brain itself. And that is why I came to see you, Professor Martens. Doctor Hirsch assured me that you could help me. You see, during the summer vacation I would like to travel – I wish it could be to Charcot, in Paris – but this would simply be a study trip to Vienna, to see how far they have advanced *there* in their research into brain surgery. But the department responsible for such matters at the Ministry of Foreign Affairs has to approve my application. And I don't have the necessary funds, either."

I remember that I tried to do something for him, but nothing came of it, as far as I know. He remembered, however, that I had been well-disposed, and asked me for assistance on many later occasions. Several times, I was able to help. Now he is about to become a full professor at the University of St Petersburg. I am told that his friend Tolya – Tolya Lunacharski – lives in Paris or London and has become a ferocious revolutionary, and a talented writer, as well. There were other boys from Estonia, over the years; one named Ruttoff who was quite insistent that I take a more active interest in Estonian circles, and who, I am told, has written a few plays. There was another young fellow, only last year, a first-year student of law who managed to seek me out. Piip is his name, and he is an almost comically serious young man. He's only in his first year but has already decided that he wants to study international law. And is, of course, poor as a church mouse. I told him that every time he won an award for one of his academic papers, I would match that award out of my own pocket; if he really was as serious about his ambition as he seemed, this would help him achieve it.

All along, I have importuned my influential acquaintances on behalf of other people's little affairs so many times that some of the former have ridiculed me for it behind my back. You know all about that.

Nevertheless, dear Kati, I should have been more generous . . .

23

This rosy oval face, like a cameo against the purple velvet of the headrest – but it isn't you, Kati – oh, now I understand: Once again, everything has turned eighty-nine degrees – eighty-nine years . . . Frau Professor Martens: Your Friedrich, your *Georg* Friedrich really wasn't as generous to needy students as he might have been. On the other hand, dear Mrs Magdalena, he did support – I did support – the five children of his late brother until they came of age. And when rumours reached our ears (long before the French invasion) that Professor Martens was worth eleven thousand thalers, that he was the wealthiest of all the professors in Göttingen, that he always found time to dance the minuet at the rich students' parties but hardly ever extended a helping hand to the poor ones – I was, of course, indignant, *profondément offensé*, but only for half an hour or so. I did not consider the students at Göttingen (or anywhere else, for that matter) such paragons that I could feel resentful about that kind of gossip-mongering, at least not for long. Besides, being offended was not one of my favoured states – I really couldn't *afford* to sulk in a world ruled by princes. In that world, a scholar's functions were strictly limited to three possibilities: one, he could be a tutor of princelings; two, he could act as a guide for bored old princes when they decided to learn something about their private collections; three, he could hold their hand when it was time to sign treaties . . . No, in a world and time as difficult as the one in which I lived, there really was no room to stand on dignity. Early on, I adopted a simple philosophy in regard to insults: if an insult was justified, it affected me – if it wasn't, it didn't. If it was justified, there was no need to feel insulted, only a need to correct my course of action. If it was unjustified, and thus did not affect me – why should I then pretend to be offended?

No, the low points in my life, in Georg Friedrich Martens' life – if they are worth considering, and at the moment I feel like considering them – occurred at a far more concrete level. I can imagine or remember – and doesn't that amount to the same thing? – one evening in particular. An evening in Kassel at the end of October 1813.

The kingdom of Westphalia had collapsed. King Jérôme, brave, stupid, greedy, generous Jérôme, had fled Kassel the previous day. Jérôme Bonaparte, Napoleon's younger brother, to whom the Emperor himself had recommended me when I visited Fontainebleau in 1807 to solicit protection for Göttingen. At that time, the kingdom of Westphalia was only three weeks old. It had been created by the Tilsit peace treaty and Napoleon's decree, the way kingdoms were created and destroyed in those days, with a stroke of his quill. I remember – or imagine, what's the difference – how he received me in his study, a splendid octagonal room with, curiously enough, a canopied bed in one corner. He was sitting at a small table, and next to him stood King Jérôme of Westphalia. (Later, I visited that room twice; once by myself, once with Kati.) As I straightened my back after my ceremonial bow, the Emperor asked me:

"What does Göttingen wish for?"

I was holding the city's letter of petition in my hand. I replied:

"Your imperial benevolence, Sire. Only that. To be exercised in three regards: the granting of our liberties, the granting of aid, and the granting of protection, particularly against billeting." Crystal clear and to the point, in the Roman style the big-headed genius himself liked to affect. It went over surprisingly well. (Perhaps the Martenses' powers of suggestion have not really grown stronger from one incarnation to the next?) The Emperor stretched out his small, feminine hand, and I, Court Councillor Martens, handed him the letter of petition, with another bow. He said, in his typically brusque and almost comically self-important manner:

"I grant Göttingen its wishes." Then he turned to his brother: "Your Majesty, I suggest you have a chat with Professor Martens. You may find it useful for your kingdom."

The imperial audience was over. Instead of backing out of the room, I followed Jérôme, my gaze fixed on the back of his dark and curly head, to a door between two mirrors and through a passage to a small side room, and on the way there I thought – I imagine thinking: now they can all address each other as Your Majesty. The whole clan, from Joseph to Jérôme. Except for the one whom all the others have to call *Mon Empereur*. It would be interesting to know if the Bonapartes observe such formality even in private. They certainly didn't back in Ajaccio, not so very long ago, when they chased and pelted each other with dry goat-turds in the alleys of that town . . . Come, come! Unless I'm very much mistaken, Court Councillor Martens did not think anything of that sort. Whatever the case may be with the Martenses' powers of suggestion, the Martenses' *powers of irony* surely are an evolving trait. And since, even now, I restrict the use of those powers to my private thoughts, they surely couldn't have been as highly developed eighty-nine years ago . . . Or could they?

In any case, the curse of the Emperor's favour already cast its shadow over me. My conversation in that small room with the King of Westphalia marked the beginning of my meteoric and perilous rise. I have often asked myself: Was I perhaps too forthcoming, too enterprising, in my replies to the king's questions? But what else could I have done? I was merely trying to make my answers as clear and comprehensive as possible. Jérôme obviously found them more than satisfactory, since he really knew very little about his new kingdom – while I knew the country, its estates, its moods, and its problems like a tailor knows his pincushion. The consequences of this exchange manifested themselves quite soon, and I let them take over my life. I kept on smiling my understanding, patient, forgiving, hedonistic, enterprising smile . . . Immediately after my return to Göttingen, I was invited to Jérôme's coronation in Kassel. Then to a grand reception. Then to swear a loyalty oath. Then to a private audience. Then to become a Councillor of State. Then to preside over the kingdom's exchequer. I had to move to the capital, into an official apartment on Königsplatz – which had already been renamed Napoleonplatz . . . Lord, those were strange years! No one who didn't live through them can imagine what they were like.

The clatter of hooves on paving stones, then the drumbeat of hooves and rumbling of wheels on the highway . . . Let me try to remember. This is the coach with the State Council's crest on the door, the coach that once in a while takes me to my beloved Göttingen, then back again to the capital to perform important tasks I have accepted as mine, God alone knows why. The Emperor's incredible and inhuman victories continue all over Europe and along its borders – Pamplona and Madrid, Wagram and Vienna, on and on. After each victory, I go to the palace in Kassel to express my official congratulations to King Jérôme; at my familial dinner-table, I only mention those victories with a noncommittal smile, because I have no way of telling who among my servants is a French or German spy. While the apocalyptic, thunderous victories continue, I try to give my naïve, even irritatingly credulous Magdalena the impression that I'm in complete control of our Westphalian home-land's destiny, and that it is child's play for me to deal with any outside developments in an unflappable fashion. But later, when I sit in my study examining documents that propose to finance the French victories by yet another tax on the Westphalian peasant population, I feel miserable. Particularly when I look down at the square and see soldiers in French uniforms guarding the statue of Napoleon that has replaced the old fountain. They have been posted there to prevent the townspeople from throwing rotten eggs at the Emperor's marble visage. We are encircled by the horizon of his apocalyptic victories, and closer in we are surrounded by the threat of rotten eggs, by resistance and riots in the towns, and open rebellions in the countryside. God only knows the ideas the people in my immediate vicinity are pursuing, the decisions they are making. The commander of King Jérôme's Westphalian Guard, Colonel Dörnberg, an intelligent man, with whom I've had many conversations at royal banquets, has suddenly left Kassel to become the leader of a peasant uprising, and has been condemned to death *in absentia* by a royal tribunal! A sentence tacitly approved by me, since I haven't protested against it to anyone . . . But what can I do? I am caught between the terrifying thunder rolling across the continent on the one hand, and the increasingly vocal grounds-well of resistance among my own German countrymen on the other – caught between sledgehammer and anvil. I can survive only by remaining completely neutral, *unbeteiligt*, towards both parties . . .

Then, suddenly, the triumphant drums no longer sound quite so triumphant: there are pauses, hesitations, missed beats . . . In Spain, first of all. At the very moment when the subjects of the Kingdom of Westphalia (in certain circles, at least) are slowly beginning to comprehend the essential principles of the French form of government – the moment when the rather unscrupulous application of those principles begins to seem tolerable (to a large extent because I have miraculously managed to balance the kingdom's budget) – the Treaty of Tilsit is broken. In addition to everything else I have done in my life, I've had an abiding and profound interest in treaties. By now, the eleven volumes of my compilation *Recueil des Traités et Conventions* – no, I mean my eleven-volume *Recueil des Traités d'Alliance et de Paix* – has made me the recognized expert in the field. I have worked on so many treaties that a broken one should leave me cold, completely *unbeteiligt*, but I can see the shape of things to come . . . The Grand Army marches into Russia. Many think that this campaign will lead to the army's greatest and final victory – but I know better . . . At the head of twenty-four thousand sons of Westphalia, King Jérôme hastens to join his brother, but is brusquely ordered back to Kassel with the remark that "hussar-style bravery isn't enough – a military commander needs some brains!" He returns, but his twenty-four thousand men stay with the Emperor's army. Only some fifteen hundred return, invalids, their frozen limbs wrapped in rags. The apocalypse reaches its climax in 1813. All lines of communication are interrupted. The Emperor is presumed lost. Then he reappears in Paris, just as General Malet is about to proclaim France a republic again. General Malet is shot, but merely out of a sense of duty, not out of any enthusiasm for the Emperor, because everyone knows that Napoleon's Europe is falling apart. The Prussians stage an uprising. The Russians march into Germany. The French retreat to this side of the Elbe. At night, those citizens of Kassel who have been openly supportive of the French throw their imperial cockades into the Fulda river's waters flowing high and fast in the spring flood. I move my Cross of the Knights of the Westphalian Royal Crown into a lower desk drawer. Once again, Napoleon manages to gather a hundred and twenty thousand men under his banners. He defeats the Allied forces at Grossgörschen and Bautzen. There are many who ask, some in dismay, a few (in Germany, very few) with a glimmer of hope: *Will there really be a miracle?*

I know there won't be. One by one, Napoleon's field marshals lose their battles: Macdonald at Katzbach, Vandamme at Kulm, Ney at Lützen. Certain gentlemen of Kassel's German party already ask me, with amicably ironic smiles:

"Dear *Monsieur Conseiller d'Etat* – you will, no doubt, soon leave us for your beloved France, *n'est-ce pas?* Since you have such close ties to the *dynasty*. And have served the state so well . . ." (All those gentlemen have been paying King Jérôme only three quarters of the tax levies that he wanted to impose on them. Who persuaded His Majesty to temper his demands? I did. They know it too, but here they are, nevertheless, not yet threatening, but mocking me for my service to the state.) "Yes, that's what you'll have to do, because you can't expect much sympathy from either the Russians or the Prussians – particularly not from the Prussians. Whereas, in imperial France . . . True, it's a sinking ship. But as clever as you are, we're sure you'll manage. Besides, you have written most of your books in French, and your wife is a Frenchwoman, isn't she?"

The army corps of General Chernychev reaches Kassel. For a few hours, he bombards the town with his artillery, while I hold Magdalena's cold and trembling hand and give her a calming mixture of valerian and Moselle wine to drink. Whenever the barrage grows louder, she starts shaking all over, and whispers that we should try to get away. Some of the town's buildings are destroyed. The windows of my library are shattered. Are these true memories, or am I merely fantasizing? I can't tell, and it really doesn't matter . . . King Jérôme leaves, the Russians enter the town, at their head the same General Chernychev – a hero to the Russians, an abomination to the French – who was Russia's ambassador to Paris, and in 1811 bribed someone to give him the French master plan for the conquest of Russia. I stay in my apartment and console Magdalena. We stay away from the windows, but I catch a glimpse of the square: now the marble emperor is lying on the ground. Then the Russians leave, King Jérôme returns to Bellevue Castle, and the emperor's statue returns to its plinth. I am summoned to the royal presence, but excuse myself because of illness. Word has reached us that the Battle of the Nations has been joined at Leipzig. Then comes the night or rather early morning, the crack of dawn, whose memory – or imagined memory – I cannot and, for some reason, do not want to forget.

Jérôme has fled again, taking with him the art treasures of Kassel and what was left in the state's coffers. I don't know whether he took to his heels before or after he heard of his brother's crushing defeat at Leipzig.

A chilly October wind blows through the broken library windows. The sky is a gloomy steel-grey turning a faint brassy yellow at its eastern edge. A few buildings are burning in the southern part of town, near the Orangerie Palace. Shouts and rifle-shots can be heard in the streets of our quarter. Rumour has it that the retreating French have reached Eisenach, and that they may be here soon, marauding and pillaging, with Russians and Prussians in hot pursuit. I sit at my desk in the dark library, still in my nightclothes, and try to collect my thoughts. How old is State Councillor Martens at that moment – how old am I? Fifty-seven years old. All my life, in all situations until now, I have known what to do. I have even known what others had to do. Suddenly, this morning, I have no idea what I should do. I sit in the dark, afraid of the day that is about to break. A rain shower has just passed over our house, and there is a puddle on the parquet floor below the broken windows. I stare at it without a thought in my head. It is cold; I am shivering. Magdalena is asleep in the next room, thanks to the pill I persuaded her to take. The windows in her room are still intact. Next to her, I would be warm, and since she is asleep, I wouldn't even have to console her. But I can't get out of my chair. There are logs in the fireplace, but it seems impossible to go through the motions required to light a fire. The broken windows would render it useless in any case, and everything else seems just as futile. I can't pinpoint the cause of my inertia. I don't think it is due to Napoleon's final defeat – although I do regret, from an objective point of view, the demise of the French system of government. It was, admittedly, an odiously Francocentric system, but in many respects it was also a basically intelligent and exemplary system, a more equitable system than those that are now bound to re-establish themselves. Napoleon came as a liberator. But that was not why I joined him; like everybody else, I joined him because I had no choice in the matter. But I knew that he had been a liberator before he became a tyrant, as liberators always do when they remain in the territory they have liberated and start imposing their will on it – in person, or by delegating authority to their younger brothers. Now there are more liberators on the way.

They will liberate us from the liberator. Who are they? Metternich, the Prussians, and Alexander . . . Well, maybe – maybe one could – try to adjust – to these new circumstances . . . But would it be worth it?

Slowly, I turn my head to the right, surprised that I have actually managed to do that. I can see myself in the mirror above the fireplace – a bent, grey shadow outlined against a yellowing sky. Suddenly my mirror image strikes me as repugnant. Those grey side whiskers, that prematurely bald pate, that pointy nose, those lively but now so anxious eyes – I detest them! As I detest this world in its merciless collapse. And I don't doubt that I'll detest the new world that will be erected, even more mercilessly, on top of the old one. The inevitable return of the old aristocracy will be an odious thing; all those coarse, arrogant, ignorant faces whom I served, outwardly a law-abiding bourgeois, inwardly feeling superior to them, until they were deposed by the French – I can't stand the thought of their impending return to power. Not that I think anyone is going to put me in front of a firing squad, or to throw me in jail as a spy left behind by Jérôme. No, nothing like that will happen to me, but I'm bound to suffer ostracism, sarcasm, rebuffs. I don't relish the prospect, and I find the idea of starting a new career – which just might be possible – even more odious . . .

This surprisingly cold, clear, and bitter feeling of repugnance propels me into action. I get up, very quietly, without hesitating or looking round, and go next door where enough dim light filters through the drawn curtains to allow me to find and pick up a small cut-glass bottle. I take the stopper out and shake the small saffron-coloured pea-shaped pills onto my palm – one, two, three, four, five, six. An hour ago, I gave Magdalena one of these. Her glass of water, still three-quarters full, stands on the table. One pill guarantees ten hours of uninterrupted sleep. Six pills – dreamless sleep forever! Well, I'll leave something behind. My syllabus for a course in international law, my *Recueil des Traités*. They won't be swept off the earth's surface. That's all I ask; everything else seems secondary. My mind is made up. One motion, a couple of sips of water . . . and the curtain falls. Standing there in the half-dark room, I see a pale shape on the grey pillow. It has to be Magdalena's face. I must say goodbye to Magdalena. I return the pills to the bottle,

213

taking care not to drop any on the floor, set the bottle on the table next to the glass of water, and walk over to the bed. I must say goodbye. I stand there, and it seems to me that I am, in those moments, reliving my marriage to this woman, one heartbeat per year. It is still too dark for me to see her clearly, and I feel both strangely close to her and oddly distant from her. It is as if our closeness also had been a kind of darkness, as if it had kept me from truly seeing her. This stranger is my wife. My beloved, tolerated, taken-for-granted, barren wife. Whose barrenness has been disappointing at times, a relief at others, but, ultimately, a disappointment. I bend down, touch her forehead with my cold lips. Her forehead is cool and sleepy, yet I can sense the warmth of her life. I inhale the fragrance of her hair. (It's *Brise de Paris*! But that's impossible . . .)

I tell myself that as soon as I've straightened my back, I'll put the pills in my mouth, wash them down with a drink of water, walk round the end of the bed and stretch out next to Magdalena to wait for sleep to come. It should only take ten minutes, and I hope there won't be any pain or anguish, although those minutes may still be hard to endure in the knowledge of the irrevocability of my decision. But after that, I'll be free of everything. Magdalena, do you understand – when you wake up, I'll be *free*! But . . . you? God, what a gut-wrenching thought: Magdalena, how will you manage without me? No, no, I'm not merely thinking about my own funeral in the midst of the chaos caused by the Frenchmen and Prussians and Russians that will soon sweep through this town. I'm thinking of your utterly vulnerable existence as a suicide's widow . . . Magdalena, will you forgive me? You'll be homeless! Although you'll inherit houses in Göttingen, you will no longer have a *home* there. Besides, I'm sure those properties will embroil you in prolonged litigation with my brothers. Who will represent you in court? Göttingen will once again become a part of Hanover, thus subject to the English crown. After I'm gone, it'll be so easy to denounce me as a French spy – who poisoned himself for fear of being caught . . . So you may never be able to take possession of what I leave you.

And tomorrow morning, this morning – even if I were able to disregard the grief and disarray caused by my death – Magdalena, you don't even know where the glazier lives, whom I summoned here a week ago to repair our windows, and who still hasn't come. He may have been impressed into the town militia. You don't know where to look for another one. When the defeated French come trudging through, followed by the victors, the Prussians, the Austrians, the Russians – how will you protect yourself from them? From robbery, theft, billeting, all the violence of war? Your fear, your troubles, your lack of funds? Your situation will be desperate. Later, you'll have to travel back and forth between here and Göttingen, you'll have to pack, and move, and arrange matters . . . Ever since we became man and wife, I have taken care of such things, with an ease that both surprised you and made you a little contemptuous of me. But I found it amusing to make such arrangements, to take advantage of all the merchants and entrepreneurs whose sons were my students at the university, of lawyers who were my friends from student days, even of university personnel, since I was a professor and a dean and a vice-president. Here in Kassel I used my connections to the court and the government. No, Magdalena, you won't know how to deal with all that, especially not in the middle of the collapse that is bound to come – all alone, the widow of a suspected suicide . . . Oh Lord, forgive me, Magdalena. I can't do it . . . but I can't do anything else, either . . . Yes, I can. Please forgive me for even thinking of leaving you this way. The weakness that overwhelmed me a moment ago now seems incomprehensible even to myself. I can still feel it trying to gain the upper hand – but now I know what to do.

I'm standing next to the bed. I take Magdalena's hands, soft with sleep, and place them on her chest. I go to the table and drop the pills back into the bottle – one, two, three, four, five. The sixth one I put in my mouth and wash down with a sip of water. I walk round the end of the bed, stretch out next to Magdalena, and wait for my ten hours of sleep to begin . . . Memory or fantasy, it doesn't matter. It seems to me that at the moment I begin to sink into the dark cradle of sleep, I already know what the future will bring. At noon, when I wake up, I find out that the French have turned south at Eisenach, towards Hünfeld and Fulda, and that no one seems to be pursuing them. So that by the time the Prussians and the Russians finally reach Kassel, a few weeks later, our windows have been repaired, Magdalena is attending to her affairs as energetically as

215

ever, and I have picked my winning card with unerring skill: *Count Münster*.

That lucky fellow, both a student and a colleague from my Göttingen days, managed to extricate himself from the disintegration of Germany by securing an appointment as the Ambassador of Hanover, first to St Petersburg, then to London. Now he has returned to Germany as the plenipotentiary of the King of England and Hanover. What is it I have been lecturing about for decades? About the skills of negotiation, about diplomatic discourse, about the persistence and elegance and impudence it takes to reach one's goals, to bend others to one's will . . . Count Münster will soon receive my letter. Memory or fantasy? It doesn't matter. I can't remember that I felt any moral scruples writing that letter, but I do remember that I felt exhilarated by this first new move in the great game. (It seems that the Martenses' moral fibre also has grown stronger with time.) ". . . *So that, my esteemed Münster, I want to apprise you of my ardent desire to devote myself once again to the service of our lawful and deeply revered Sovereign.*" (I didn't specify whether I was referring to George III who had gone mad and was now locked up in Windsor Castle, or to his son the Prince Regent, whose scandalous debts and prodigality have for years given rise to many painful debates in Parliament.) Count Münster does not ignore my letter. On the contrary. He summons me immediately, practically swoons into my arms: "Dear Professor Martens! How wonderful! You are a godsend, you'll be absolutely indispensable to us . . ."

As history records, he then sends me to the Crown Prince of Denmark as an emissary of the Allies. A few months later, I attend the Congress of Vienna and participate in high-level negotiations. With Magdalena, I waltz across the floor of the Apollo Ballroom at the Imperial Palace. Among the other dancers we see, over there to our left, the dull and ruddy visage of the Emperor of Russia, smiling his perennial angelic smile while leading yet another lady of the court around the floor; to our right, Metternich with his Mephistophelean grin . . . Threading his way with a limp through the crowd of dancers comes the Prince of Benevento (by the grace of Napoleon), the restored French monarchy's Minister of Foreign Affairs – Talleyrand, a dry crust of a man with a pale and angular face and the melancholy of omniscience in his eyes. I take a good look at him across the shiny curls of Magdalena's ballroom wig (such relics from Marie Antoinette's days have come back into fashion) and admire his princely and dazzling white stockings and culottes; he has kept them quite clean and dry, leaping with such skill from Napoleon's sinking ship into the frail vessel of the Bourbons . . .

Tomorrow I'll join them again, to sit next to Count Münster at the negotiating table, to help them parcel out a Europe whose clock they are trying to turn back by a quarter of a century. Not that this bothers me overmuch. What else can I do but remain *im Innersten unbeteiligt*?

Magdalena . . . This rosy oval face, like a cameo against the purple velvet of the headrest – it isn't you, is it? Is it Kati? But no, it is someone I don't know . . . Who is it?

"Forgive me, Professor Martens, for interrupting your nap. But we'll be arriving in Valga very soon, and we have to change trains there."

24

I wake up. I recognize the young lady facing me. I return to time and space and feel quite embarrassed to have dozed off like some senile old creature in the presence of a lady. I'm so mortified I don't even offer an apology, but accept hers instead.

"That's quite all right, madam. It's a good thing you woke me up. We really don't have far to go."

I look outside. I must have slept through our stop at Härgmäe, but that must have been only a short while ago. I know this stretch from the distant bends of the Pedel river beyond the hay fields. We're still at least half an hour from Valga where we'll have to wait an hour for the arrival of the Riga train, and another seven or eight minutes before it departs for the long haul to St Petersburg.

"Please excuse an old scholar's eccentric desire to classify everything – give flowers their Latin names, give international ladies their social co-ordinates . . . Tell me about your husband."

She looks out at the shadows of clouds moving across the fields along the Pedel, and she tells me about him, without reticence, but also without the degree of enthusiasm one might expect from a recently married woman. I notice that this pleases me a little; then I find that pleasure contemptible.

Her husband is a Finn. There you are. She has been talking about Estonian folk poetry and the Estonian cause with far greater enthusiasm than she talks about her own family, but she, too, will be lost to the Estonian cause. Or maybe she won't – what do I care? But perhaps I do. Her husband is the son of a wealthy, conservative, stubborn owner of a large estate. I can well imagine what such gentlemen must be like, over there in the fertile southern regions of Finland, and what problems they may present to young daughters-in-law, even though she does not mention them. And even though I'm not really interested in any of that . . . But her husband is a socialist. Ah-ha. He even represents his party in the Finnish Diet. That piece of information does irritate and alienate me, but once again, it is none of my business. I can well imagine the family conflicts. The old man has told his son: "I own a few things, and I support those who also own something. You don't own anything – so, go ahead, support those who have nothing." Still gazing out of the window, the young wife tells me this in a noncommittal, conversational manner, with a proud and apologetic smile. She returns her silver pen into a silver case she takes out of her expensive crocodile-skin purse, so casually that it seems the categories of haves and have-nots only exist far below her level. But it's all a matter of total indifference to me. Kati – you must believe me when I tell you that . . .

You're here again, Kati! In that faintly glowing outline of a face whose details I can't make out. Yet I know. Those curved, a little foreign, slightly Byzantine eyebrows, the steady gaze of a pair of icon-like eyes. The small mouth with its attentive expression – my wife, whom I have deceived a dozen times, abandoned a dozen times, yet found again, and again . . . Come here. Sit down beside me. Move that pretty basket from Möisaküla. I admit I wasn't thinking of you when I got it – but to whom else can I give it? Only to you. Or would that be the kind of deception that would cause you to abandon me? To protect me no longer against – you know what . . . The basket will be yours, to keep skeins of yarn in. On our verandah in Pärnu, on the floor decorated with painted flowers, in the corner with the purple stained-glass windowpanes. You'll sit in the rocking chair we brought from Töstamaa, remember? And knit some knee-high socks for Edit's little boy. I'll read the boring, dishonest, warmongering, traitorous newspapers of Russia and Germany and England and France until I've had enough, and push them aside, and we look into each other's eyes and feel joined by a bridge of complete trust . . .

Have you noticed, Kati, I can't manage to turn towards you. Once again, I am paralysed by sleep. But I know you're there. And we have half an hour. Listen: *choo-choo – choo-choo – choo-choo – choo-choo* . . . Half an hour. And we're heading in another direction. I have to confess to you: I am afraid. Not of what I was talking about, although that worries me as well. There is another fear in me now. Kati, I am afraid of what I have been thinking and trying to imagine, and I am afraid that if I had to start my life over again

. . . I'm sure you understand how inevitably my thoughts drift that way, towards the idea of some kind of reincarnation. But even if I had to start at the beginning again, I wouldn't know how to do any of it differently. I would do everything the same as this time around, and I would feel that I did right. Or at least, some things would be right, others inevitable. And only very late in the game – yes, it is very late this time, as well – I would begin to have doubts that I might have done many things wrong, that I might have done everything wrong, not only objectively or idealistically speaking, but wrong even from a subjective standpoint. So many things could have been avoided. But if I had to start over from where I did start, or thereabouts – what *could* I do differently? My memory works a little better than it does for others of my kind. I'm a little quicker on the uptake; a little more capable of using my imagination, of making generalizations; I am spurred on by the knowledge of my low estate. Should I sacrifice my advantages, refrain from testing them, just because the very idea of competition is odious in itself? Because the Creator has not given all the runners legs of equal length? No – once again, I would believe that the right was on my side. All of my competitors, or almost all of them, would have a tremendous social headstart, and again I would do my best, because I would like to win, because I would enjoy the competition. And I would do it simply because I wouldn't know what else to do.

Should I really believe that in a bad country, even good deeds are evil, because they do not make the country better but only reinforce its badness? No – because (for instance) even the insensate behaviour of the Black Hundred becomes less repugnant to the rest of the world when the world notices the extent and effects of the actions of my kind of imperial subject . . . Should I pull back and retire from it all? Should I give up – should I have given up – the senator's daughter I fell in love with? Should I renounce the esteem in which I am held – as well- or ill-deserved as it may be? My reputation as a conscientious peacemaker, gained by years of hard work? Give it all up, because it is, in the final analysis, a lie? But there are no monasteries for Lutherans . . . Should I become a convert of the Orthodox church – something I've managed to avoid despite all the pressures to do so; I really don't know why, it certainly hasn't been due to religious scruples. Kati, if I had to start my life all over again, should I embrace the Orthodox faith, and retire to a monastery to grow flowers, and to meditate on a God of whose existence I am not at all certain? Inevitably, I would start reading their books, and then I would express opinions on what I had read, if on nothing else then at least on how well or poorly written it was; sooner or later, my superiors would summon me, and talk to me, and ask me to work in the monastery library. I know that they would keep on discussing things with me while I worked there. Should I then lay my cards on the table and tell them my doubts? And follow their advice, and mortify my flesh by fasting, and solitude, and perhaps even heavy chains, as do the most zealous wrestlers with Satan? Good Lord – given who I am, I would once again live exactly the way I have lived, hiding my doubts about God's existence, about the value of monasteries, about the godliness of the holy fathers. Or I would express them, nevertheless, but in such a carefully edited manner that except for myself, only a few of the most liberal brethren would understand . . . Naturally, that wouldn't prevent them from asking me to compile a bibliography of sources for, let us say, the biography of Constantine the Church Father – and I would be back in the scholar's seat . . .

Tell me, Kati, what should I do, if I had to live my life over again? But you're right: this is not a time for us to be speaking of beginnings . . .

25

And yet, that is where I want to go. Back to the beginning.

Last Monday, I sent Kaarel to the livery stable to rent a horse and cart, no driver, for that same day. Then I drove back to the beginning, and even past it, all the way to Audru, to see, once again, the church where my father had rung the bells and played the organ, and the rectory, and the parish clerk's house where I would have been born if my father hadn't been dismissed from his post as parish clerk and schoolteacher – for what reason, I don't know. Years later, I heard Aunt Krööt disdainfully mention a name in that connection. As I understood later, her disdain may not have been well-founded, but the name she uttered, pursing her thin lips in an odd way, has stuck in my mind: "Old Saebelmann". He had replaced my father as clerk and schoolteacher in Audru parish after my father's dismissal and our family's move to Pärnu, about a year before I was born.

In the cart that is taking me to Audru, past the pine barrens of Pappsaare, I wonder, once again: what would I have become if my father hadn't lost his position? And if he hadn't died before I was five years old? And mother hadn't died before I was ten? If, instead of being an unwanted nine-year-old orphan, the youngest of a poor tailor's brood, I had been the son of the parish clerk and school-master, growing up in his parents' care and under their roof – what would I have become?

My father would have insisted that I learn to play the organ. I still remember, very clearly, the times when he would sit me down at the harmonium in the sunny room facing the garden of our house in Pärnu; I remember how he would get up from his sewing, spitting needles onto the floor, to scold and impatiently show me where to place my fingers on the keys. Later on, of course, the parish clerk's son would have been sent to Valga to study at Zimse's school, just as old Saebelmann's son was sent there. I would have become the schoolmaster of the parish. Perhaps something else, as well?

Another Carl Robert Jakobson?* No, no. For that, I would have needed a different temper – more dynamic, more egotistical, more uncompromising. Different, in any case. At Zimse's school, I would have concentrated on developing my musical talent, as did Saebel-mann's boy. I still am enchanted by the world of music, even though some types similar to Vodovozov have sneered at my regular attendance at concerts and attributed it to sheer snobbishness. My private box at the Marie Theatre has called forth similar jibes. But my loyal old friend Platon Lvovich has told me more than once that I could have achieved something in the field of music. For more than forty years, he has been an inspiration and support in many things, but also a cautionary example. He is a serious musicologist and a creditable musician, but a dilettante nevertheless. He also has a doctorate in international law. Even in that field, he is a minor light – Chief Secretary of the Ministry of Foreign Affairs. An important administrative position, but that's all. He is interested in too many things at once. This may be due to his multinational background – he's a Russo-Germano-Franco-Swede. Vaxel is his last name. A comfort-loving and unambitious man.

Well, descendants of officers, diplomats, and scholars can indulge in that view of life, and pleasant musical soirées in their homes with the likes of Rubinstein and Nalbandyan, and good French wine. I had no time for such things until I was forty-five, and precious little after that. For him, they've been part of his life since he was a student, as were his long summer holidays on the island of Madeira where his family owned a villa. It was, in fact, Madeira (the island, not the wine) that transformed our casual classroom acquaintance into a friendship. Curiously enough, I too had connections to that island, since my brother August had moved there after he'd received his medical doctorate, to minister to the Madeirans, and to cure his own tuberculosis. Madeiran air was considered to be particularly beneficial to persons with afflicted lungs. August and I exchanged four letters every year, but I hadn't seen him since our father's funeral, when I was four and he was eighteen. After he graduated from the *gymnasium* in Riga, he had been admitted to the University of Königsberg, on the recommendation of old Baer. By the time he

* (See Notes – Translator)

got his diploma, his lungs were afflicted, after years of living in cold garrets and being unable to afford enough food and warm winter clothes, years of incredible hardship and effort. Evidently, he did not spare himself on Madeira either. In any case, I hadn't seen him for twenty years, when suddenly – I think it was before the first lecture of the autumn term of our last year at the university – Platon Lvovich Vaxel, tanned to a mulattoish hue (at that moment I didn't know where he had acquired that tan), sat down next to me and said:

"Martens, I met your brother this summer. An excellent doctor. And a wonderful man."

He proceeded to give me a description of my brother's life that was far more complete than what I had been able to glean from those four letters a year. Platon Lvovich was a rare teller of tales. I realized that he was very fond of August. So fond that it was, in fact, he who inspired the workers in the sugar-cane plantations and vineyards around Funchal, whom August had treated gratis, and the wealthy tubercular Englishmen in their villas, whom he had not charged overmuch, to find a common cause and to erect a small statue to August in the town of Funchal. A couple of months later, the disease killed him. A freshly minted *magistr* on my first foreign mission to Paris, I had been tempted to go to Bordeaux, find a ship, spend four or five days at sea, and see my brother. Of course I didn't do it. The Ministry wasn't paying me fifteen hundred roubles a year for pleasure trips to see relatives, and the faculty would not have approved Madeira as an acceptable location for postgraduate studies. Thus, I never saw my brother August again, but Platon Lvovich transferred his affection for him to me. While August didn't leave me a single *real* – he never had made any money – he left me Platon Vaxel's friendship, and it has been worth a fortune.

Choo-choo – choo-choo – choo-choo – choo-choo – chee-chee – chee-chee – khee-khee – khee-khee – ka-bump – ka-bump – ka-bump – ka-bump . . .

Yes, last Monday I drove to Audru in my rented cart, holding the reins of an old grey mare. I hadn't been there for – God, fifty years. I drove past the church and the parish clerk's cottage, turned onto the Töstamaa road. When I reached the entrance of the birch-lined drive to the rectory, I suddenly felt embarrassed – surprisingly enough – at the thought of entering the office of Pastor Oebius and allowing him, surely a man younger than myself, to jump up and greet me and chat with me for a moment . . . At the thought of then driving back to the parish clerk's cottage, where seventy-five-year-old Tarkpea would perform an even more agile obeisance to the Privy Councillor, and invite him to take a seat on the old thread-bare sofa . . . At the thought of then pointing at the low ceiling with its flaking paint, at the little windows with their calico curtains, and saying, yes, this is the room where by rights I should have first seen the light of day – or something to that effect. How embarrassing. It occurred to me that everything would be much easier if I visited the church first. After many decades, I would once again see Bierbaum's crucifixion altarpiece, spend a moment breathing in the forlorn and reproachfully sour smell of the old floorboards and pews, then climb the creaking stairs up to the organ loft, and sit down for a moment under that high whitewashed ceiling to search for traces of my father's fingers on the yellowed keys of the ancient instrument built by old Thal. Resolutely, I drove past the rectory for a short distance, then turned round and drove back to the church. I tied the reins to the hitching post next to the gate and walked up the gravel path that led to the door.

It was locked. Yes, indeed. The hundred-year-old door, decorated with long, branching, hand-forged iron hinges, its yellow paint flaking away to grey, was locked. A gust of wind raised a whirl of dust off the gravel by the stone wall. A hand's-breadth from my face, the wind rippled through strips of flaking pale yellow paint, and it was as if this seemingly dead wood, in collusion with the wind, had been trying to signal to me that it was still alive . . .

Of course, I could have gone to the parish clerk's cottage and asked Tarkpea to unlock the door for me. He would have been eager to comply. But I didn't go there. I understood that I was not meant to enter that church again, and since I decided that this would have been my only reason to see Tarkpea, I didn't go to his cottage either. But I wasn't giving up altogether. I got into the cart, drove to the Lihula road, and turned left to travel another fifteen or sixteen versts, past the beginning of my beginning.

I drove all the way to Völla without stopping, on a road that led to a high ridge and followed the northern boundary of the park. To my left, I caught glimpses, through the thicket of hazel bushes that had grown up under the old lime trees, of the dilapidated stucco on the old estate building's walls. From the looks of the building, it seemed unlikely that the leaseholders, the Fischer family, were in residence. Not that I cared; I didn't know them, had never met them, and at that particular moment didn't feel like meeting anyone at all. I turned onto a deeply rutted road that ran around the northeast corner of the park, and there it was – exactly the same as fifty years ago: a grey stone ruin on a hilltop, at the edge of a field of rye that had spread all the way up here – the ground floor of an old Dutch-style windmill. I tied the horse to a tree at the edge of the park and climbed up to the ruin. It was the highest point of the estate, and on a clear, windy spring day, one could see far. Beyond the estate lands lay the small village parcels; beyond them was a stretch of grassland, and beyond that, almost all the way to the horizon, the huge Völla marsh, many versts wide, a brownish-grey, completely flat expanse dotted with ponds and clumps of light green marsh-grass, a lake slowly turning into dry land, with an island in the middle. The island was wooded, and one could see the buildings of two farms. On the near shore, scattered among the small fields, stood a few low houses with thatched roofs. There, in one of those sunken houses – I didn't know which one, and it probably wasn't there any more – my great-grandfather had been born. And my grandfather, and my father as well.

Grandpa Otto Reinhold started out as a shoemaker in Völla. Later he became a customs guard at Pärnu, assigned to foot patrol along the coast between Pärnu and Töstamaa, his task to make sure that salt and other contraband wasn't smuggled past customs. Later, when he had worn out his rheumatic legs, he repaired the other guards' boots in a shop on the outskirts of Pärnu.

I stayed up there on the old windmill's foundation for a while, braving the wind, waiting for a sign – a cow-parsley stalk waving in some special way, the surprise appearance of some animal, a lark suddenly soaring up into the sky – that would tell me in which house my grandfather had seen the light of day, or which overgrown hillock marked the spot where it had stood. However, it seemed that animals, birds, and plants considered me too much of a stranger to grant me such a sign. Once again, the exact location of my father's and grandfather's birthplace remained as unknown to me as it had fifty years earlier when I had stopped there with Aunt Krööt and stood on the stone ruin that was still a little taller then. And I'm sure Aunt Krööt couldn't have told me even if I had bothered to ask – but fifteen-year-old boys are not interested in such things.

I climbed down, got into my cart, drove back to the Lihula road and followed it to the inn at Ellamaa where a cousin and namesake of my grandfather's had been the innkeeper, ages ago. I drove past it a little way, then stopped and looked northwest, down the road that wound its way towards the elk meadows. This was the road on which grandfather Otto had brought his bride to Völla: Ann, the daughter of an emancipated artisan from Tuudi estate.

According to Aunt Krööt, Priit, my grandmother's father, had been a weaver in Lihula township where he lived with his wife and daughters. Their names were Liso, Leno, Ann, Mari, and Viio. His place was known as *Katko saun*, "the cabin in the marsh". Even though Priit's letter of emancipation had been lost in a fire at Lihula, no one had questioned his status as a free man. But when German officials at Lihula assigned him, as was the custom, a family name based on the name of his domicile, they gave him the name Pest, even though it really should have been Pfütze or Sümpfchen or something along those lines. After Ann had been working for a while as a housemaid at Karuse rectory, Pastor Middendorff had noticed that Pest was not a pleasant name. He added Stein to it, a name that occurred in his own family, and came up with the name Steinpest. The pastor's wife had noticed that Ann was too plebeian a name for a rectory housemaid and had started calling her Anna, adding Sophia for good measure. In this manner, Priit the Weaver's daughter Ann became Anna Sophia Steinpest, who would later become Anna Sophia Martens – a shoemaker's bride, a customs guard's wife. Over the years, their union was blessed with three sons and three daughters. The eldest, Friedrich Willem, my father, was born in Völla on the eighteenth of August 1795. Being the youngest of my parents' nine children, I never met my grandparents. I know that Otto died in 1822, Anna in 1840. My maternal grandparents had also passed away long before I was born, so I never found out much about them. I did hear that my mother's father was known in Pärnu as Friedrich Knast – according to some

227

a German translation of Koorukese Priit, according to others, of Viri-Vidrik. Be that as it may, for thirty years Friedrich Knast served as a bailiff of the Land Court. Every kopeck he was given as a bribe – for losing certain papers, confusing certain addresses, finding himself unable to deliver certain summonses – he would deposit on the desk of the Land Court judge, and when the judge asked him where the money came from, he would always reply: *"Auhv täär Strasse jehvunden."* So the story went. Nevertheless, he proved a loyal and devoted husband to his wraith-like and rarely smiling wife Olli. By the way: if any of my ancestors were of German origin, as has been claimed now and again, the most likely candidate is this maternal grandmother Olli, whose documented maiden name was Olympia Frisch. However, even her background was one of deprivation: she was the daughter of a shoemaker who had died in the poorhouse.

I remember my mother better than I remember my father, which is natural, since I was only four when my father died. When my mother died, I was nine. But what do I really remember, even of her? At the time, she seemed to be everything I expected a mother to be. She was slender and straight-backed; her blonde hair was braided and piled on top of her head under a small black cap such as widows wore; she was always in motion, striding about, always busy, looking after her children, mending the boys' trousers or the girls' skirts, making porridge, tending the potato patch, running off to do the gentlefolk's laundry, always humming a tune. Thinking back, it occurs to me that she must not have felt as cheerful as she seemed, that she put on that merry front for her children's sake. I remember that her hands were red from all the laundry she had to do, and that her palm felt rough when she stroked my neck or cheek. I remember that very clearly. She had four sons and two daughters to clothe and feed. Of the sons, only Julius and August had already flown the coop, one to St Petersburg, the other to Riga, and both the daughters still lived at home. Alide got married a couple of months before Mother's death, Emilie a year after Aunt Krööt had sent me off to St Petersburg. Later I understood that my mother's humming must have reflected her moods – it was quieter and more subdued on days when she managed to make ends meet, but grew louder and clearer whenever the wolf was at the door.

I've also realized that when the cholera epidemic ended her brief and truly harsh life at the age of forty-four, she was still almost a young woman.

Choo-choo – choo-choo – choo-choo – choo-choo . . .

And so, Kati – it is you, there on the opposite seat, isn't it? – I can barely see the outline of your face, through eyelids that have grown curiously heavy . . . So now you already know what I'm going to tell you tomorrow, in the last rays of the setting sun, on our white garden bench by the shore: the complete truth about my origins, as far as I know it. It replaces the vague and unfounded pretence that I am really of German stock, one of those Livonian Germans whose bloodlines have a little Estonian admixture . . . As you know, that version has gained currency in your circles without any active promotion on my part, but with my passive permission. I have rarely hastened to champion the truth when people in high society – including your own family – have kindly classified me as a German or "almost" German. Now and again, in certain situations, I have corrected that assumption. But to be completely frank with you: it has always been a careful and conscious *decision* on my part, to agree or disagree, to deny or to assert my Estonianness. I have deliberately chosen to be either German or Estonian depending on which allegiance seemed most advantageous. And I'm not proud of that.

Certain people connected to our imperial court would not have found me socially acceptable unless they could assume that I was German. Whenever one of them has made that assumption, I have not contradicted him or her. There have been a few exceptions. Prince Yusupov, Yevgeni Andreyevich, was one of them; to him, I denied my Germanness and admitted my Estonianness – out of a kind of sportive vanity, no doubt, since everybody knew that *he* was a Tartar. Besides, I had heard rumours that his family tree also included a certain Estonian barber, a fellow from Pärnu, no less . . . True, the prince is a rather insignificant figure, but I'm glad I let him into my confidence. It has made him treat me as a comradely spirit. But generally I have never advertised my Estonian origins among people of that ilk. It started when I allowed Prince Gorchakov and his circle to believe that I was a Baltic German, from an im-poverished but nevertheless *German* bourgeois family. I never disabused him, and he took his belief to the grave. To his way of thinking, my being Estonian would have been too unprecedented and simply incomprehensible.

But to my own headstrong students, to young Russian revolutionaries, militant populists, those wearing threadbare coats reeking of tobacco and the barracks, those who saw their country as a "prison of peoples" (a phrase later used in Majoritarian tracts) – to such young Russians, Poles, Jews, Letts, and Caucasians, I often revealed my Estonian origins, either directly or indirectly. Not because I tried to manifest some cheap solidarity with them – that would have been below my dignity as a professor – nor to evoke any easy sympathy. At least, I don't think so. I did it to make it easier for us to discuss matters with one another. Tell me, Kati – do you understand me? Do you believe me? Or do you assume, nevertheless, that my fits of candour before the students (my references to my brother Heinrich, the shoemaker, and to the fact that most of my ancestors had been millers and innkeepers and blacksmiths with roots in the peasantry) – Kati, in the name of our pact of complete candour, do you believe, in view of the student unrest of the Nineties and the heated atmosphere of 1905, that they were simply a cheap attempt to gain popularity?

I don't know. I really don't know. You be my judge. Because I do know one thing: Even your "guilty" verdict will protect me.

26

Puff-puff-puff – puff-puff-puff – puff-puff-puff . . .

Listen, Kati – this isn't our narrow-gauge train leaving the last station before Valga. No – this is a steamship.

It is a vessel of the American navy that has brought us from New York to Portsmouth and is approaching the pier, its engines running in reverse. I know why it has come to mind; I have something else to confess.

My participation in the negotiations at Portsmouth is, of course, my greatest triumph apart from those aborted Nobel Prizes. Not in the eyes of those who know something about international law; *they* still admire me for my role in the peace conferences at The Hague. But to the Russian mind, the peace treaty with Japan seems more important, and many Russians regard my efforts to achieve it as the most important thing I've ever done – again, provided that they have an inkling of such matters. Even our own son, our Nicol with his pomaded moustache . . . Every day in his life he takes his revenge on me with a superior air that reflects nothing but a sense of inferiority. Let us assume that I know the reason for this. It may well be that he considers me a first-class specialist who is also a boring pedant and sophist, and whose only positive achievement in these fateful years has been that Treaty of Portsmouth. And I confess that my own, shall we say, impatience with him, an impatience that verges on intolerance, is aggravated by his ignorant opinion of me.

I'm sure you remember, Kati, it was Muravyev who was first appointed to lead our delegation. Using Lamsdorf as his intermediary, he asked me to join his team. As you know, I wanted to decline the offer. First of all, I didn't want to leave you alone for two months during that explosive time. Secondly, the prospects for those negotiations looked dim: Why should victorious Japan accept our intransigence? Thirdly, Muravyev had included Rosen in his team. I knew that this Baltic baron had a pathological aversion to me; being our ambassador to President Roosevelt, he would remain a member of the delegation. So, as you know, I declined. Only after Lamsdorf interviewed me personally and appealed to my patriotic sense of duty did I decide to go, but only on the condition that I would participate in the negotiations as a fully empowered delegate. I told him I refused to go as a mere expert who has to sit in the courthouse corridor, and wait until he is called to testify, and then be sent away again. Why did I make this demand? I was concerned that without me and my experience, our delegation might end up agreeing to less favourable terms. But I must confess that this was not my only reason. My main reason for the demand may well have been a desire to be treated as Rosen's equal. In this major political endeavour, I wanted to be formally acknowledged as the peer of a German baron, a descendant of generals and admirals, who regarded his diplomatic career as a birthright. In terms of knowledge and experience, he was no match for me, and as a full-fledged delegate I would have no trouble holding my own against him. You know, Kati, it is obvious that I can be – at certain times, in certain situations – a rather small-minded person. As in this case, when my recognition as Rosen's peer became a decisive factor. I see you smile ironically, indulgently. I hear you whisper: "But Fred, it really wouldn't have made that much of a difference . . ." Lamsdorf immediately agreed to my demand:

"But of course, Fyodor Fyodorovich. We'll instruct Muravyev accordingly."

Whereupon I said, small-minded or not: "Count Lamsdorf, in that case I'll go, and I'll do my best."

Then Muravyev announced that he was ill. He went to Nicky and tearfully begged him to be relieved of his charge. His nerves, his stomach, his heart, his gout were all acting up, both separately and together . . . In reality, he simply got cold feet, and a frightened man obviously wasn't fit to engage in a trial of strength with the Japanese. Lamsdorf persuaded Nicky to appoint Witte in Muravyev's stead. Whatever my opinion of Witte may be, in this case he was the best possible choice. Muravyev's abdominal pains (or whatever they were) proved a timely blessing for Mother Russia. Witte's motivation for assuming this heavy responsibility was the same as mine – a patriotic sense of duty. He assumed it in an unemotional and stoic manner, indicating that he had no great hopes. He probably felt a little flattered to have been asked, but mainly he agreed to become the head of our delegation out of a sense of patriotic obligation. While we shared that sense, it expressed itself differently, and the difference reflected our respective temperaments. I regarded our enterprise more as an adventure and a gamble, while he undertook it in a manner so solemn and serious that he reminded me – and I don't mean this pejoratively – of a sacrificial bull led to the altar.

Witte accepted Muravyev's choices for delegates without making any changes, and we left St Petersburg for Paris, Cherbourg, and New York. I've told you about that journey in great detail – except for one event, the most humiliating one . . . A navy ship took us to Oyster Bay, where the President received us on his own yacht. There, in his presence and at his table, we met Komura and the Japanese delegation for the first time. I have told you how I watched the stony-faced Japanese during Roosevelt's speech, how I reflected upon the enormous difficulties that lay ahead of us. But Witte (who, behind my back, has called *me* a person of limited horizons!) whispered to me: "I only hope Roosevelt won't toast the Mikado before he toasts the Czar . . ." What nonsense! Roosevelt simply saluted *both Emperors whose ambassadors of peace are now meeting, to the great relief of all mankind,* and so forth. Then two navy vessels – one for the Japanese, one for us – transported the delegations to Portsmouth. Only Witte, who can't stand travelling by sea, took the train – I found this slightly embarrassing, but didn't lose any sleep over it. We disembarked at the dull little town of Portsmouth and made our way through swarms of journalists and a throng of curious spectators to the automobiles that were waiting for us. Counting our secretaries and foreign service assistants, there were about a dozen of us. Planson, Shipov, Yermolov, and the rest. Rosen had already joined us in New York, and I have no complaints about the way he treated me. During the two or three years he had spent in Washington, he had managed to cover his baronial stolidity with a solid veneer of American bonhomie; enhanced by his equine face and his silvery side whiskers, the effect was startling in its duality – one moment he was the Baltic German baron dropping staccato phrases like *"bäi uns in dem Zimny"*, the next he sounded like Uncle Sam himself with his "how do you do?" Despite his amiability, I

233

treated him with reserve, because I knew his opinion of me as expressed to a member of his own circle of friends:

"Martens? The so-called living encyclopedia? He's merely a gatherer of facts, an entomologist of jurisprudence . . . He does know how to spin an endless silken thread of arguments. Son of a shoemaker or tailor. Just an itinerant tailor on the international scene. Der weltberühmte Konflikthosenflicker. Ha-ha-ha-ha. He's managed to ingratiate himself enough to receive every third-class medal in Europe, and now he thinks he's an authority . . ."

Smiling at each other, Baron Rosen and I strode through the crowd and traded sarcastic remarks about the swarm of journalists that immediately descended upon us. Nowhere else are these gentlemen as aggressive as in that country. I had discovered that on my previous trip to America, a few years earlier, when I represented the University of St Petersburg at the one-hundred-and-fiftieth anniversary of Yale. This time, of course, they were even more tiresome. Pencils and notepads in their hands, on their knees, between their teeth, cameras slung over their shoulders or mounted on tripods that people stumbled over, they pursued us all the way to the automobiles. I said to Rosen:

"Robert Robertovich, doesn't it just look like every Colonel Diver in the country has come here to hound us?"

From the baron's vague nod and smile I could tell that he had never read *Martin Chuzzlewit.*

We drove to the Wentworth Hotel and settled in. In its boring New England way, it was quite a luxurious establishment – grey marble, red plush, oak beams, cut glass. All of it sweltering in the summer heat, despite the proximity of the ocean.

In the evening, we went to the dinner at the officers' club where the speaker made that strange reference to my imaginary Nobel Prize, an incident both flattering and humiliating. The Japanese had arrived on the same day, and the Americans wined and dined them in a similar manner. The following day, the negotiations were to begin, in quarters provided by the United States Navy. We were chauffeured there in large convertibles. Rosen and I rode in the same car. "Good morning, Robert Robertovich. Did you get a good night's rest?" "Ah, good morning, Fyodor Fyodorovich. Well, not bad. What about you? Is your powder dry?" "I hope so, I hope so.

234

Although I must say it's hard to keep *oneself* dry in this weather."
We arrived, got out of the cars. By the entrance to the building
stood a row of schoolchildren waving small flags. American flags,
Russian, even Japanese flags. We entered the building, Witte,
Rosen, myself, all the others, and proceeded to the double doors
of the conference room, where the Americans welcomed us. We
stopped, shook hands, chatted. Through the open doors of the conference room, we could see an identical set of open doors on the
other side framing Komura and his entourage. Then, just as we
were about to enter, there was some commotion. A few Americans
came from the Japanese side and hurried across the room to speak
to Witte. Something was amiss.

Immediately, I had a sense of foreboding. I don't know how
spontaneous it was, but it wasn't totally unexpected. Thinking
back, it seems to me that this moment on the threshold to the
conference room in Portsmouth was one of those rare yet typical
moments in my life in which no one, or nothing, has given me an
indication of the fateful nature of the situation, and yet I know,
sometimes days, sometimes only seconds before the event, that
there is something threatening in the air, and that it concerns
me directly.

And so it did, in the most ridiculous and direct way. Fate had
chosen me from among all these important and busy gentlemen
carrying briefcases and wearing starched collars that made the heat
seem even worse.

Witte, who had been the first to enter the room, turned back
and came over to me. He looked straight at me, then averted his
eyes. His large, normally pallid face was mottled with agitation.

"Fyodor Fyodorovich, I'm sorry, but there has been a misunder-
standing. The Japanese say that your name is not on the list of
delegates they've been given! I was just shown that list, and it looks
authentic. Your name really does not appear on it. I can't imagine
how that happened, but now they refuse to let you participate in
the negotiations. I don't know what I should do . . ."

As I replied to him I could hear the dismay in my voice. I was
thunderstruck, but his explanation had given me time to gather my
wits, more or less, and I said:

"Sergei Yuliyevich – you are the head of our delegation. You must decide what kind of response is appropriate to the dignity of Russia. That, I think, is the sole criterion in this case."

I admit that I wasn't sure at that moment (nor am I now) to what extent I included my own dignity in that of Russia. But I did know that it was a question of both.

Nevertheless, I wasn't able to tell him: "Sergei Yuliyevich, you say you don't know what you should do? You should tell them that Russia chooses its own delegates. You should say that if the Japanese insist, we can present them with a new list of names that includes mine just as it should have been included from the beginning. You should say that the delegation's composition is not determined by some typist – or forger! – but by the Emperor of Russia, who has appointed the person in question to be his delegate."

However, since the dispute concerned me personally, it was impossible for me to tell him that. If it had been a question of someone else, I wouldn't have hesitated to do so, even if – yes, yes! – even if it had been Rosen. But of course. (Kati! Kati! Come here, come to me, tell me – you do believe, don't you, that I would have said that if the dispute had concerned someone else? Even Rosen, right? Kati?)

But it was Rosen, smelling of Havana cigars and smiling like a horse, who came up to us and said:

"Gentlemen – Sergei Yuliyevich, Fyodor Fyodorovich – it might be extremely risky to ask for a postponement of the negotiations, merely to allow us to reinstate Fyodor Fyodorovich as a delegate. We know how hard it has been to get the Japanese to come here at all. It's an extremely sensitive situation. No one knows this better than Fyodor Fyodorovich . . ." He looked at me, smiled: "Fyodor Fyodorovich, considering your insight and your patriotism . . ."

Can you believe it, Kati? The blue-blooded swine was trying to convince Witte that he should simply sacrifice me to this stupid situation! And trying to persuade me to agree to that sacrifice, in the name of patriotism . . . At the same time, and from the very beginning, I suspected that it was he, Rosen, who had engineered the whole thing – I still don't know how! What could I do? From the looks on their faces I could tell that all of them, Shipov, Yermolov, Planson, and the rest, realized that the danger Rosen had mentioned was real enough. I was aware of it myself – and probably understood its significance better than any of them. But was that a reason for not speaking up for a fellow delegate? I looked at each one of them in turn, then at Witte. I said:

"Sergei Yuliyevich is the head of our delegation, and he must decide what will best serve Russia's interests . . ." I added: ". . . to take a certain risk and preserve our dignity, or to . . ."

"Fyodor Fyodorovich," said Witte, looking straight at me, then down at the floor, *"I thank you . . ."*

I didn't understand what he was thanking me for until he went on:

". . . for your readiness to put Russia's interests above a personal slight."

He had sacrificed me.

"Now I have to ask you to withdraw from today's opening session. Believe me, this is a painful decision. After this session, today or tomorrow, I'll find out how this happened. Don't worry, we'll re-establish your right to participate. And we will, of course, consult you. You are our most experienced negotiator. Once again, I thank you. And now we must go. Vasilchenko (his assistant secretary) – make arrangements for Fyodor Fyodorovich to be driven back to the hotel."

I have always told you, Kati, and everybody else, that Witte is favourably disposed towards me. I have to admit that this is a lie. True, he has always treated me with impeccable courtesy – but his fundamental attitude towards me is one of suspicious intolerance. It is a rough-hewn politician's, a mediocre and uncultured man of action's intolerance of a specialist whose knowledge intimidates him, and whose loyalty implies a superiority that he finds incomprehensible. By claiming that I enjoyed his favour, I was only – Kati, I'm telling you this under the sign of our complete and mutual candour – I was only making yet another pitiful and servile attempt to exculpate our highest authorities by blaming underlings for their offences. This is a common pattern. It allows us to despise the lower ranks of power for their transgressions while we retain our belief in the nobility and fairness of their superiors; at least it gives us an opportunity to pretend that we still retain that belief.

Back at the hotel, I went to my room and put my head under the tap of the marble washbasin, almost wishing I could simply leave it there in the cold rushing water, but I couldn't rinse the odious event out of my mind. I dried my hair with a towel, stood in the middle of the room, and felt those questions battering me like a merciless steam hammer, at the pace of a rapid heartbeat: What had happened? How did it happen? What should I do?

The fact was that I had been scandalously excluded from the negotiations. More bluntly: I had been thrown out of them. This, Kati, is the one aspect of my trip to Portsmouth which I have never discussed with anyone until now. Due to certain events (and I'll tell you about those too) it was easy enough for me to keep it under my hat. I still believe that Witte had no part in my eviction, but whoever engineered it took advantage of Witte's passivity. To this day, I don't know who caused it, and I doubt that I ever will. Perhaps Lamsdorf had deceived me from the start. Perhaps the noble Minister of Foreign Affairs had simply lied to me when he told me I'd be a full-fledged delegate, and had gone on to list me as just another adviser to the delegation. This sort of aristocratic duplicity is an essential ingredient of the dear fatherland's management style. Perhaps the incident merely arose from a typist's oversight and Witte's negligence in putting his signature to an incomplete list of names. When has anyone ever been attentive and meticulous in this land? If that was the case, the Japanese simply used our carelessness to get rid of me, because they had reason to believe that they'd find it easier to press their demands without me at the negotiating table. After all, my reputation was greater in Japan than in many other countries. My *International Law Among Civilized Nations* had been translated into Japanese as early as 1889, and their middle-aged generation of jurists had gained their basic knowledge of the subject from that book. Then Rosen jumped at the chance to use the Japanese protest against me – with his appeals to Russia's interests and my patriotic spirit. And Witte let him get away with it.

Kati, I've never told you this before, but I was desperate. I blush to think how desperate I was. Because I can imagine – I can see you smile and hear you consoling me, with an invisible shake of your head: "But Fred, was that really something to feel desperate about? With all your experience of the intrigues of this world?" Of course you're right, I can understand it now, and I can say that I blush to think about it. Then, my desperation was real enough. I

238

knew the tenacity of the Japanese, I knew the muddleheaded ways of our own side. With a perverse pleasure in plunging deeper into despair I convinced myself that Witte's promise to clear up the matter and to reinstate me was merely vain talk, or that it would prove impossible for him to keep it in any case, and that I would have to spend the duration of the conference in my hotel room. The best I could hope for were a couple of sessions with Witte, if, after long and exhausting days of negotiations, he should happen to remember my existence and deign to invite me to his suite to ask for my advice . . .

That was, indeed, the idiotic situation in which I found myself for two extraordinarily depressing weeks. It was aggravated by a circumstance I hadn't been able to foresee – by my fateful notoriety in this small town teeming with journalists for the duration of the conference.

After my return to the hotel, it took me a couple of hours to recover from my initial anguish over the incident. While still deeply doubtful, I began to nurture a glimmer of hope that Witte would be able to resolve my ridiculous situation. I went down to the bar and ordered a cup of coffee and a glass of ice water. A moment later, four or five Colonel Divers descended upon me, reporters from whatever scandal sheets they had in New York or Washington or Portsmouth:

"Mr Martens, do you have a moment? Haven't the negotiations started yet? They have? But why aren't you there? We heard that the Japanese ousted you? (It hadn't taken long for that rumour to spread!) But that's unheard-of! Please explain why your Mr Witte allowed that to happen? And what do you yourself have to say about it? No comment? All right, what have you found most remarkable about our country? Nothing? Very well – oh, you say there is something that you *would* find truly remarkable if you could find it here? What would that be? A discreet journalist? Ho-ho-ho-ho! A really marvellous answer! But, as a Russian – oh, you're not a Russian? Well, as a German, you – oh, you're not a German either? Well what are you? An Eskimo? No? An *Estonian*? Where is that?"

I abandoned my coffee and fled outside to take a walk in the incredibly hot and sunny streets of the port. Four or five times I was accosted by journalists. I told them that I had absolutely nothing to say to them and fled back to the hotel, my shirt sticking to my back, my coat collar soaking wet. My eyes were hurting, I felt dizzy, probably close to a heatstroke. In the entrance hall of the hotel, five or six press photographers stood waiting for me. I told the receptionist I wasn't receiving visitors, fled upstairs, and locked the door of my room behind me.

This went on for over a week. As I had feared, Witte completely forgot my plight in the heat of the negotiations, about which I knew no more than what I read in the newspapers. This may seem incredible, but it is true. The newspapers contained a great number of conflicting reports. Naturally, the negotiations were being conducted behind closed doors, and, as always, the press heard from its "well-informed sources" exactly what it wanted to hear. Republican papers wrote that the negotiations were proceeding most successfully thanks to the personal moral support provided by Republican President Roosevelt. Democrat papers claimed that pressures exerted by the President had doomed the negotiations from the start, and that they were indeed going nowhere at all. Personally, I didn't know much more, even though I was, or should have been, a member of one of the delegations . . . You can believe me, Kati, when I say that the other members of my delegation had suddenly stopped telling me anything of consequence, and their collective betrayal of me was the most depressing aspect of my situation.

It goes without saying that they were too busy to engage in prolonged conversations with me. Everyone had breakfast in his room. At nine o'clock, my colleagues assembled in front of the hotel and got into the cars that were waiting for them. My pride didn't permit me to run downstairs to ask them for the latest news, especially not after I had run into Planson and that little fellow Vasilchenko on the stairs and found them extremely reserved:

"Gentlemen – what will you be discussing today?"

"Oh, Fyodor Fyodorovich, all sorts of things, most probably . . . But, sorry, we really have to run – I'm sure you understand . . ."

They did, indeed, have to run to be whisked away in their cars. Nevertheless, it was obvious that they enjoyed their status of zealous initiates, and that they took care not to reveal anything to an outcast. After that, I steered clear of them in the mornings. In the evenings, the delegation ate in a small dining room at the hotel. Only Witte, who was said to suffer from chronic migraine, had supper brought to his suite. Sometimes he invited Rosen to join him there, probably in order to discuss some questions with him. I considered following his example, to avoid the strain of those shared meals, but decided against it, and pretended that everything was exactly as it should be. I spoke freely, mentioning my exclusion in passing as a clever and dirty little Japanese trick that might only please Japanese sympathizers – not that there were any among us, I said, smiling at Baron Rosen in a perfectly light-hearted manner. I abstained from asking questions, but not entirely, just enough to make it impossible to decide whether I *was* being reticent or not . . . Kati, I must admit that it wasn't easy to strike and sustain the right note. I had two main motives for attending these gatherings, and to this day I don't know which one was the most powerful: on the one hand, I felt that my calm and nonchalant demeanour would prove my imperturbable democratic superiority; on the other, I was consumed by a childish, intense, and feverish curiosity, hoping to hear something about the progress of the negotiations just by listening to my fellow delegates' conversations, without having to ask humiliating questions.

The avoidance of such questions seemed most important, because I had noticed from the very beginning that my dear colleagues had joined in a kind of conspiracy of silence against me. It wasn't complete, but it was quite conscious and selective; in my presence, they studiously avoided any talk about essential matters. It was scandalous, but it was true. A week later, some Americans I met at the bar reported to me the rumour that my colleagues claimed a telegram had arrived from St Petersburg with orders to keep me in the dark about details of the negotiations . . . I don't know who had come up with that piece of impertinence; it may have been the brainchild of Japanophile Americans. In any case, some, quite a few of my colleagues seemed to behave as if such orders had been issued and they had to obey them. They would fall silent or smile in that obedient manner of loyal civil servants that I understood and accepted only too well.

Kati, I have never in my life experienced anything as trying as those weeks! Witte invited me to see him on two of those evenings. He offered me a cigar. I remember pondering whether I should accept it, as a sign of my good intentions and willingness to collaborate, or refuse (I had given up smoking long ago). I said no thanks. He closed the cigar box and spoke wearily and apathetically about the extreme inflexibility of the Japanese negotiators. Then he asked me for arguments – political, legal, historical arguments we could use to justify our rejection of Japan's demand that a peace treaty should include the surrender of all the Russian Navy vessels that had managed to seek refuge in neutral ports.

Although I hadn't accepted his cigar, I was willing to collaborate, and I gave him a loyal and closely reasoned answer. First of all, I gave him ten minutes' worth of my own views on general tactics in dealing with the Japanese. He listened to me, snuffling and sniffling and casting the occasional quick glance of approval in my direction. Then I gave him a review of all the possible arguments, including the rules of maritime law, which might be invoked to justify our refusal to surrender the ships, the weaknesses of opposing interpretations, the opinions of theoreticians, and the precedents to be found in individual treaties and decisions handed down by the International Court at The Hague. While he took notes, I discussed everything that was pertinent to the question and laid it all out for him in a plain and comprehensive pattern. After I had finished, he stuck out his lower lip, looked pensive – and said (I was waiting to hear something about my ridiculous position):

"Fyodor Fyodorovich, your overview gives me a glimmer of hope. Thank you. I won't keep you any longer."

As I'm sure you understand, Kati, my pride didn't allow me to raise my personal problem. Compared to the problem he had to deal with, it even seemed insignificant, at least at that moment. I wished him a good night and took my leave.

After another seemingly endless, murderously hot and humiliating week, Witte summoned me again. This time he wanted to hear arguments against Japan's demands for war reparations, and I gave them to him. When he had finished taking notes, he remarked that there had been some softening in the Japanese position on the navy ships, thanked me for my time, and once again wished me a good night. Once again, I wasn't able to overcome my inhibition to bring up my own situation. Once again, I excused his inexplicable and inhumane silence by his fatigue and the stress he was under while dealing with extremely important questions. But I was getting close to the limits of my endurance, and the following day brought a crisis.

In the morning I had watched, once again, the delegation depart in a cloud of exhaust fumes. I had spent another day suffering from the horrible heat and dodging journalists whose interest in me hadn't abated at all in the course of that week. All of them knew that I was *the outcast*, and for that very reason they tried to extort sensational revelations from me. Suddenly, all the pain I had endured so far, feeling disappointed, weary, ridiculous, and absurdly useless, coagulated inside me into such a nauseating lump that I had to do something about it. Perhaps I was really hoping (keeping this hope secret even from myself) to shock Witte into remembering my absurd position – who knows. But when the delegation returned to the hotel at five o'clock that afternoon, I marched to his suite and told him:

"Sergei Yuliyevich, it seems to me that I can no longer render any service to Russia by staying here. I request your permission to leave. To go home."

He looked at me absent-mindedly.

"Hmm. I suppose you're right. Go ahead."

Kati, I won't deny that this was the final straw. I tossed my things into the suitcase – for the first time in my life, I simply tossed them in – and told the receptionist to get me a train ticket to New York and to make a reservation for passage from there to Cherbourg. Then I sat down at the desk and wrote a letter to Platon Lvovich. Yes, Kati – not to you, but to him. I had written to you from Portsmouth, I'm sure you remember, telling you that we had a lot of work to do, that we hoped to succeed in our task, and that I was feeling hale and hearty despite the incredible heat. Not a word about the humiliation I had suffered. I did not want to burden you with it. But while that is true enough, I mainly kept this secret from you because I was too embarrassed to tell you about it. To Platon Lvovich I poured out my heart. I purged myself of all my bitterness. At the present moment, I feel embarrassed by the memory of that bitterness. In a fury, I tossed my shoes in a corner, tore off my shirt, wrapped a damp towel around my bare shoulders and wrote to Platon Lvovich. In that stifling room at the Wentworth Hotel, I told him everything. I told him that I found myself in a situation that was both ridiculous and horrifying; that my situation had been both ridiculous and horrifying for a long time, perhaps even *all* the time, and that I felt suffocated by the permanent suspicions, the ingratitude, and the callousness that were my lot. While I didn't wallow in Dostoyevskian excesses of suicidal self-pity, I still wrote with a degree of self-loathing that I had never managed to express before that evening. I told him that I had had enough. I wrote: "Now I shall return to St Petersburg to wind up my affairs. I intend to leave for good before the first of January. Any country in Europe will provide me with a more dignified existence than Russia."

But, dear Kati, I wasn't even allowed to enjoy my humiliation to the full. The following evening I went to say goodbye to Witte.

"What? What are you saying, Fyodor Fyodorovich? No, no, no! You can't leave. That's out of the question. Tomorrow we tackle the war reparations, and you absolutely *have to* be there. Oh, yes, of course – I compelled the Japanese to accept your participation."

What could I have done? Perhaps I should have refused, in the name of my personal liberty. But I didn't. I surrendered. I don't know if I was pleased or displeased to hear that reasons of state compelled my resurrection from the gutter. Or, I do know – Lord, yes, I do. I won't deny that this chance to fight for Russia at a critical moment made me feel good. I participated in the two sessions dealing with Japan's demands for war reparations. Quite contrary to expectations, the Japanese made concessions. I certainly don't delude myself into believing that their retreat from previous positions was all my doing. In equal (or even greater) measure it may have been due to Rosen's efforts. Kati, it makes me so happy and relieved to be capable of this admission, first to myself, right now, and tomorrow, to you, on our white spindle-backed bench at Sestroretsk: the admission that it may have been Rosen's, our ambassador's, reports to Roosevelt on Japan's intransigence that turned the tide – when Roosevelt, after hearing those reports, pressured Komura to comply with his wishes. Maybe so. Witte, by the way, still suspected Roosevelt of pro-Japanese sympathies; to my mind, his suspicions were myopic and unfounded. Witte identified with the imperial grandeur of Russia to such a degree that it bothered him to see official and neutral America treat us and the Japanese as equals. In his heart, if not in his rational mind, he would have liked to see a protocol in which we would have been given precedence at every turn. This attitude even distorted his view of Roosevelt. In reality, Roosevelt was too worried about Japan's expanding influence in the Pacific to sympathize with the Japanese in any way that would have an adverse effect on us.

By the way: as soon as Witte took me to the meetings, all the delegates shed the reserve with which they had been treating me. They reverted to normal in a way that was both laudable and ridiculous. Rosen immediately asked me to review the minutes of all the previous sessions with him. Should I have told him I wasn't interested?

A couple of days later, Witte said it was time to compose the definitive text of the peace treaty. On the Japanese side, Komura himself was undertaking this task, but on our side I should be the one to accomplish it. Should I have told him I didn't want to do it?

Of course, I understood why they needed me. They needed me for the same reason they had always needed me. They had decided what they wanted, and now it was my task to express their decisions in words that were unambiguous and terms that could not be misinterpreted. I had to put these words in their mouths, in their pens, in their printing presses. I did not refuse. Kati, I wouldn't refuse even now, after gaining a deeper insight into these things. But I have to admit that my reasons for not refusing, four years ago, were essentially different from those on which I would base my decision today. Then, I did Witte's bidding mainly out of a sense of triumphant vindication. Now, after our agreement on candour, after I have felt that strange fear, caught that glimpse of my interior being, through a window, as it were – now I would simply do my job because I know that a refusal would merely be a show of small-minded pride. I would understand that someone had to do that job, and that whoever did it assumed enormous responsibility. That it was necessary to make the treaty maximally favourable to Russia's interests (as I understand them). Back there in Portsmouth, the assignment also represented a personal triumph over the rest of the delegation, and over Rosen in particular. After Witte had charged me with the final version of the treaty, Rosen suddenly became quite un-baronially obsequious towards this itinerant international village tailor. Or perhaps it was baronial obsequiousness, who knows. The way a person is treated by our aristocrats, or by the haute-bourgeoisie that imitates them, depends entirely on the imperial favour or disfavour that person may expect – and thus varies according to the prevailing wind. Thus, the reason my colleagues began to shun me like a leper in Portsmouth was simply the fact that my name had been left out of the list of delegates by mistake. That was all it took to activate those social reflexes.

Just as with Pavlov's dogs.

So much for kudos . . .

27

Kudos – kunos – kunis – kuni . . .

What is this curious, possibly senile, tic that has started to affect my brain in recent times? Some meaningless syllable, or an almost meaningless word, enters my consciousness and suddenly gets stuck there, starts repeating itself mindlessly, mechanically, like a broken gramophone record. After a while, I find myself compelled to say it out loud: *kuni – kuni – kuni – kuni* . . . Sometimes I catch up with what I'm after, or rather, what seems to be after me. But not always. It may simply be some vague assonance with something that has been on my mind. So, what am I to do with this *kuni – kuni – kuni*? What does it mean? What does it try to evoke? *Cuneiform*? Nonsense. *Kunigund*? *Fräulein Kunigund*? *Den Dank, Dame, begehr ich nicht* . . .? My feelings about Portsmouth? My feelings about everything? Maybe. *Kuningasaare*? Where is that? It must be a village somewhere near Audru.

Kunileid.

What's that? Who was that? Ah, of course.

A while ago, I wanted to return to the beginning, to move forward from there . . . Saebelmann! We are, or were, sons of parish clerks of Audru. Young Saebelmann and I. Frankly, I never thought that *Kunileid* was a well-chosen pseudonym. Of course it wasn't his fault that Jakobson started calling him that, but I regret that he accepted it, and used it to sign his musical compositions. Never mind how accomplished and important those pieces may be . . . But why am I carping about his chosen name? *Kunileid – Lunileid – Unileid –* what do I care?

Yes, both our fathers were parish clerks at Audru. Although we are of the same generation, he a year younger than me, we never met when we were young. I was still in nappies in Pärnu when he first saw the light in the parish clerk's cottage, a small but handsome house that sported a manor-like porch with carved wooden pillars. Out of which his father had – God alone knows, perhaps he really *had* ousted my father, by some mysterious machinations. But even his father had to leave quite soon, and again, I don't know why. The Saebelmanns had moved away from Audru to Suure-Jaani in Viljandi province. For a quarter of a century, I didn't hear much about Alexander, except for the occasional remark when I visited my sisters and brothers in Pärnu on summer vacations from the *gymnasium* or from the university.

In 1869, the year I finished my course work at the university, the first Estonian choral song festival took place in Tartu, and that was when I saw his name in a St Petersburg newspaper. It said that he and Jannsen had been the principal conductors at the festival, and that the choirs had sung his songs with great enthusiasm. Already using his bizarre new name, he had become a local celebrity, for what that was worth – at the time, it struck me as a little pathetic, although I was aware that he had been called a *genius* by Doctor Bertram, either in speech or print. I remember Bertram, an owlish little fellow – God knows where I ran into him, probably in St Petersburg. The good doctor was just the man to heap that kind of sentimental praise on Saebelmann; he bestowed it on many young Estonians of his day. They were all geniuses – Weizenberg, Köler, and Mrs Michelson, whom Jakobson had given the (rather more felicitous) pseudonym Koidula. So, why shouldn't our Kunileid also be one?

Soon I had forgotten him and his hypothetical genius again. The choral song festival was over, and I was busy writing my master's thesis and already preparing an outline for my doctoral dissertation. That autumn, I was also invited to serve at the Ministry of Foreign Affairs. Then, a couple of years later – I don't know if it was before my first trip abroad or soon after it – in any case, I already lived on Ofitserskaya Street – he suddenly sought me out.

Rang the doorbell and entered. A bow-legged, swarthy young man, with a huge angular chest and a slightly curved spine. He spoke in a soft bass voice:

"My name is Alexander Saebelmann. That's what it says in my passport. But I sign my compositions with the name Kunileid. I don't suppose that either name means anything to you."

He spoke elegant and impeccable Estonian and was awkward in an impeccably provincial fashion. It didn't take him long to get to the point. For two years or so, he had been working as a teacher in St Petersburg, I can't remember at which school. Now he was moving away from St Petersburg and going to Poltava. I asked him why he wanted to leave the capital, considering the opportunities it provided for his talent. I don't exactly know why I decided to be so friendly – perhaps because I had a suspicion that Aunt Krööt and the rest of the Martenses might have condemned his father unjustly. Or maybe it was the other way round – maybe I enjoyed pretending that there was no grudge between our families.

"Why am I going to Poltava? You're right, it is a provincial place, as far as music goes. But it is warm and dry there. My lungs are afflicted."

Then he stared at me with his sad poet's eyes and explained:

"You see, I can't be sure when and if I'll ever be able to return from there. So I've been trying to take care of my outstanding debts . . ."

I thought: Ah-ha, he needs money. I'll lend it to him, I'm sure he won't be asking for much. If he has any sense at all. I've been earning a very decent salary, the last couple of years. Why shouldn't I lend him some money? Yes, I wanted to be generous to him. Because of his slightly threadbare coat. Because of his childlike musician's bow tie, a narrow black velvet ribbon. Because of the effort that it had obviously been to come to see me. I could see drops of perspiration on his angular forehead framed by a shock of unruly hair. Did he have a fever? He said:

"And I owe you a debt. Or rather, I owe one to my father's memory. You see, I know that your family has always thought that your father lost his position as the parish clerk at Audru because of some slander my father had spread about him, in order to inherit his post. But I know that my father was an entirely honourable man. In that affair and in all others. And I want to assure you . . ."

That certainly took me by surprise, but I interrupted him:

"My dear Mr Saebelmann, you referred to my family. I must tell you that *I* am completely unaware of any such allegation . . ." (Kati – I don't know if it was a good thing or a bad that I didn't have a candour treaty with that young man; I didn't have one even with myself.) I said: "I don't know anything about it. My parents passed away many decades ago. I don't have the slightest reason to doubt that your late father was a perfectly honourable man."

Kunileid wiped his face with a blue-checked handkerchief. He looked at me with feverish eyes:

"I want you to know that I've been suffering from that story ever since I first heard of it. It does not do him justice. It came about – forgive me, but I must tell you this – because of your aunt's youthful infatuation with my father. An infatuation which he did not reciprocate. And she never forgave him for it . . ."

I suppressed my curiosity (something I don't always manage to do) and told him:

"Please, Mr Saebelmann, let's not dwell on that any longer. If you would like me to tell my aunt about your visit, and your firm conviction that your father never did anything dishonourable – I guarantee that she is the only person alive who might still be interested in this matter – I'll be glad to talk to her when I have the opportunity to do so."

He looked a little disconcerted. "As you wish. The main thing is that you, yourself . . . Who can do anything about the rancour of old ladies . . ."

I struck a playful note. "Who, indeed? It may be incurable. But please don't burden yourself with this any longer. Now, could we perhaps talk about music? You, of course, are a true professional, a well-known composer, and I'm simply a music lover, but nevertheless . . ."

He grunted, looked almost embarrassed. "Oh, I've just written a couple of songs . . ."

I said: "Now, now, please don't be too modest. I haven't heard your songs, nor have I seen your scores, but I know . . ."

I knew hardly anything, but I wanted to be kind to him. I'm afraid that my kindness was a little disingenuous. Looking back at that conversation, and applying my theory of "comparativism" to it, it seems to me that my words reflected a deplorable degree of benevolent condescension.

"Yes, I have heard the opinions of real experts. Tell me, what have you been writing lately? Have you composed larger works, apart from your choral songs? Any symphonic works?"

"Oh, yes . . . I've made some attempts. Unfortunately, I lost all my unpublished music manuscripts this spring. In a fire. Caused by a defective flue in my room. The fire didn't destroy the whole building, thank God, but when I came home from school, I found the walls of my room charred, and my papers were just a pile of ashes. I have rewritten most of it, but now that I'm moving south . . ."

"Well, as soon as you've settled in there, in Poltava . . . Did you say you'll be the organist of the Lutheran church there?"

"That's right. And yes, as soon as I get settled, I'll get back to work."

"If I may be so bold as to ask: when you compose your music, do you envisage some further-reaching, shall we say fundamental, goals?"

I'm afraid there was a touch of irony in my question. In my own work, at least then, I did have one such goal. I wanted to prove the special position occupied in international law by the so-called civilized nations vis-à-vis the half-civilized ones. International law, in itself, was a labour towards universal goals. But what would such an objective be to a graduate of Zimse's school, a composer?

"Well – since you're asking me so directly, I'll admit that I do have such a goal."

"And it is?"

"To free Estonian music from the German influence that has plagued it until now."

"You don't say! That's really ambitious . . . Hmm."

It was a grandiose project, and he had described it with economy and ease. My reply was more light-hearted and frivolous:

"That really is a radical ambition. But will you be able to come up with something that will take the place of that influence?"

"If I couldn't, there would be no point in composing Estonian music. It simply wouldn't exist."

"And where do you think you'll find the ingredients for your *Estonian* music?"

"In Estonian folk songs, first of all. And Finnish folk songs, as well."

"I see. But why should Finnish songs be better than German ones? To my mind, Finnish music can't be mentioned in the same breath as German music."

251

"You know, it's the same way with our languages. If you compare German and Finnish, you'll find that they reflect two entirely different worlds. But compared to Estonian, German is entirely foreign, whereas Finnish seems entirely familiar, like a relative one had forgotten about but recognizes immediately."

"And how do you propose to develop this Estonian music? You must have big plans?"

Again, I hoped I didn't sound too ironic, but he gave me a belligerent look and said:

"Yes, one must have plans, mustn't one? I intend to write an Estonian opera."

"My goodness!" I exclaimed. "And what will its subject be?"

I thought: This young man doesn't know what he is talking about. He proposes to build a great edifice out of nothing, on a practically non-existent foundation. Where will he find his material? Where will he find his style? But come to think of it, Kreutzwald did write his Estonian epic in equally unpromising circumstances . . . I said:

"I can't for the life of me think of a suitable subject. Unless it would be the *Kalevipoeg*."

Kunileid stared grimly out the window, then turned back to me:

"Sir – I'd rather not talk about it, at this juncture. I feel superstitious about it . . . You've already encouraged me to say too much."

"All right, all right," I said. "I understand. Artists tend to be superstitious. But I would like to get to know your work." I surprised myself with my enthusiasm. "I have friends in musical circles here in St Petersburg. Mr Vaxel, for instance, Platon Lvovich, you may have heard of him. He knows everybody – Stasov, Jürgenson, Kross, Nalbandyan. Even Rubinstein. People that could prove helpful to you. So that if . . ."

He shook his head. "I haven't written anything that would attract notice in St Petersburg. It may be that I'm not capable of writing anything like that, not that I've really tried. As for the few things Jakobson has published in Estonia, they are available here – if nowhere else, at least in our landsman Jürgenson's music shop on Nevski Prospekt . . ."

I promised to obtain his songs, and he took his leave. While he was putting on his galoshes in the entrance hall, I asked him to

252

write to me whenever he needed anything, or when he had finished a new work. I can't remember if he promised to do so or simply muttered some vague remark. I never saw him again, and I have never heard a performance of his songs, even though I did see his scores later. My expertise is not great enough to allow me to reach definitive conclusions, but the ones he composed to words by Koidula, the former Mrs Michelson, struck me as quite original. A couple of years later (and before I had looked at his songs – he never wrote me a word) I heard that he had succumbed to tuberculosis in Poltava. And I understood, all of a sudden, a strange feeling that had haunted me for many weeks after his visit and our conversation, and that revived with the news of his death. It had a strong component of regret, naturally, but it was also a curious mix of nostalgia and envy.

And then, quite recently, only two weeks ago, forty years after our only meeting in the flesh, I had another memorable encounter with him.

Kati, you had gone to visit Edit at Petrodvorets, and I had our home to myself. For a whole week, I had been working from seven in the morning until ten at night, taking only short breaks for meals, on the second chapter of my theory on treaties. And then, one evening, I laid down my pen: it was done! I felt relieved and pleased and still energetic in a way I hadn't experienced for a long time. First of all, the chapter added something new to my theory. In it, I classified all legal documents according to their authors: individual documents, collective documents, documents produced by one author, documents produced by two or more authors. Both internal and international contracts and treaties belong to the last-mentioned category, and should be considered as such. That was my first point. Secondly, I realized that a review of the two-thousand-year-old history of civil law contracts, an analysis of all their refinements from the Romans on down, would help me to formulate and analyse the theoretical concept of the international treaty. I also realized that I could easily complete such a review within the next couple of months, and that knowledge gave me a good warm feeling. Thirdly, it was a pleasant, still rather cool but crisp May evening, and the view from my windows had a particular clarity.

I put the last pages of my manuscript on top of the pile, aligning them carefully. So many inspired, elegant, fast-moving sentences that began with tall and vigorous capitals and continued in a flow of lower-case letters. Perhaps they were a trifle too smooth, perhaps even a little irritating in their practised fluidity . . . But they proved my continued ability to work in a concentrated fashion, and they also proved that I was still in excellent shape even though I was a professor emeritus, as they say in the West, or an old nag put out to pasture, as they say here. I was aware that this book on the theory of treaties, after the completion of two additional chapters, would be seen as the crown of my creative theoretical work. At least until I finish the large monograph on tribunals of arbitration. I expect to start working on that in October. My theory of treaties is a work that in the next few years will be studied in all the leading universities of the world . . . I decided to ask Taube to include a translation of it into French in his work plans for next year. I could of course translate it myself, but I feel that I have better things to do, and Taube is so much younger that he has time to do it. Of course I could have written it in French to begin with, but I did write it in Russian, probably because I was still thinking in terms of lectures to students. Within a few years, it will be translated into the major European languages. My work does not belong to only one nation; seen in the light of that work, I am an entirely international phenomenon.

I got up from my desk, stretched. Still animated by my intellectual exertions, I stepped over to the window. In the evening light, the pink, grey, and beige façades of the buildings along Panteleimonovskaya looked bright and detailed. Then I walked through the entrance hall and the living room to the dining room, stood by the moiré curtains and looked at the buildings on Mohovaya, and then admired the room itself: the massive dining table, its legs protected by brass fittings, the high-backed chairs around it, and the gigantic sideboard with cut-glass doors – all of it made out of dark oak by the court's cabinet-maker Wiltmann, a fellow from Tallinn, the year before last. Most of his commissions came from various grand dukes who wanted more ostentatious stuff, but he had based this dining-room set on the most austere English designs.

I returned to my study, picked up the earpiece of the telephone (a handy innovation), turned the crank, and asked the operator for Vaxel's number.

"Platon Lvovich – I'm lucky to catch you at home! Do you know, I just finished a chapter. Of my book on treaties, I've told you about it. And now I feel a little like a student after an exam. Yekaterina Nikolayevna is at Petrodvorets. And I have a few bottles of red Mignal here. Yes, the very same you obtained for me through the Ministry. So I was thinking, if you don't have anything better to do, why don't you walk over here? We can sit and talk. If you don't find my treaties all that interesting, we can talk about music."

Platon Lvovich accepted my invitation, as I had expected him to, and he did so with surprising enthusiasm:

"Fyodor Fyodorovich! You have the most amazing – amazing antennae! We've been discussing the possibility of finding a hackney and coming over to your place. Yes, yes . . . A bottle of that same Mignal . . . My two guests and myself. Who are they? Oh, they're excellent company. One is Yokim Viktorovich. Yes, Tartakov himself. We are, in fact, celebrating his promotion. You didn't know? He has been informed that he'll be the principal director at the Maria Theatre, starting this autumn. We have drunk a few toasts to that, but he hasn't sung anything for us yet. Now he can sing at your place . . ." Platon Lvovich turned away from the telephone, but I could hear him ask: "You will sing for us there, won't you? Well, maybe some romances by Tchaikovsky. And whatever you like. And finish up with that great aria from Rubinstein's *Demon* . . ."

I couldn't hear Yokim Viktorovich's reply. I said:

"Wonderful. But who is your other guest?"

"Well, Fyodor Fyodorovich – let that be a surprise. All right? Excuse me? A hint? Oh, I know, you're such an inquisitive fellow. All right, then: it's a relative of yours. No, that's all I'll tell you for now. A surprise is a surprise. We thank you kindly for your invitation, and we'll be there within the hour."

I asked Elli to set out some wineglasses, took a couple of bottles of Mignal out of the Wiltmann sideboard, uncorked them, and placed them next to a cut-glass bowl of salted almonds and a box of cigars. While making these preparations, I kept wondering what sort of "relative" was coming over. Considering the fact that the person was spending time with two gentlemen over bottles of wine, the person had to be a male . . . Perhaps one of the sons of my brother Julius? But as far as I knew, they were dispersed all over the world. And what kind of "surprise" would that be to me? I have hardly any contact with my relatives. I don't even know why this is the case . . . I thought: Well, let's hope that it won't be an unpleasant surprise. And let us hope that even if their surprise should contain a seed of unpleasantness that Platon Lvovich isn't aware of, we'll manage to deal with it in a smooth and elegant fashion. And there they were at my door – three slightly tipsy gentlemen.

I hadn't seen Platon Lvovich since Easter, and I couldn't resist pointing out to him that his girth had made remarkable progress in the intervening two months. He merely laughed, as always, showing his startlingly white teeth. He introduced me to my unknown kinsman – truly unknown, because I had never set eyes on him before that moment. He was in his thirties, sturdy, bespectacled, and sported a bristly blond head of hair. But before I spoke to him (he was introduced to me as Arthur Yosifovich Kapp, a composer), and even before we sat down, I made a brief congratulatory speech to Tartakov. I expressed our delight at the fact that the Maria Theatre now would be under the aegis of a spirit as eclectic and as experienced in matters of the stage as himself. I said we hoped that Yokim Viktorovich would not be so burdened by his important position as principal director that he couldn't go on enchanting the public with his interpretations of great operatic roles. Since I didn't know which of these were his present favourites, I didn't mention any by name. (In questions that aren't of prime importance to myself, I mostly don't proffer my personal preferences.) I also avoided the slightest reference to the fact that some connoisseurs thought his once so incomparably velvety baritone voice was now past its prime. Not being intimately involved with the music world, I could pretend not to have noticed any such thing, and appear entirely sincere when speaking of his great performances. We were about to drink a toast to Yokim Viktorovich and had just raised our glasses when Mr Kapp spoke up:

"I would like to propose another toast to Yokim Viktorovich. Living in Astrakhan, I've had very few opportunities to visit the Maria Theatre in recent years. On those visits, I have often found myself infernally bored, but I trust and hope that Tartarean boredom will now be banished from the stage! Goodbye, Tartarus! Long live Tartakov!"

We drained our glasses, shook Tartakov's hand, and sat down. I looked at my mysterious kinsman and thought: Well, well . . . I said:

"Mr Kapp, my friends tell me that you are a composer. Forgive me, but I'm sadly ignorant of your work. They also say that you're a relative of mine. Could you tell me a little about yourself, to give me an idea – ?"

He refused the cigar I offered him, but lit a straight-stemmed pipe he took out of his pocket. Then he told me about himself, in a slightly brusque and defensive manner that was obviously habitual. He was an Estonian from Viljandi province, a graduate of the conservatory at St Petersburg, a student of Rimsky-Korsakov and the late Gomelius. For five years, he had been the director of the Imperial Academy of Music at Astrakhan. At the moment, he was holidaying in St Petersburg, and would soon be leaving for Tartu, where Mr Tönisson had invited him to conduct the symphonic programme of the music festival. As far as our kinship went, all he knew was that his mother's maiden name was Martens. Her father had been a merchant in Viljandi.

Our putative kinship didn't seem to interest him in the least. I can't say that this offended me, but I found it a little surprising. And yet, who was I to reproach him for a lack of family feeling? We drank some more wine. I said:

"Yes, indeed, God alone knows. Martens is a pretty common name. I am from Pärnu, and I have no idea whether the Martenses of Viljandi are related to me . . ."

"If they were, that would be a great honour, obviously," Mr Kapp said with what seemed to me a touch of irony, and then went on to participate vehemently in Platon's and Tartakov's discussion of the future repertoire of the Maria Theatre.

No, this gentleman surely wasn't close kin to me. Apart from that, I instantly classified him as a provincial celebrity. However, considering that he had been appointed director of an imperial academy of music despite his rudeness and poor command of Russian, he had to be a first-rate musician. After he had energetically defended Wagner against Meyerbeer, and we had imbibed a little more, I asked him:

"But tell me, Mr Kapp – back in Astrakhan, you must feel pretty

257

isolated from the real music world. Do you ever get to hear any celebrities there?"

"Lord, no!" Mr Kapp exclaimed. He almost sounded offended. "Only Chaliapin – when he happens to be passing through, he always comes to visit me."

Then he got up and started pacing back and forth along the other side of the table with the perfect posture of an athlete, his pipe in one hand, a half-full glass of wine in the other – and in his deep, imperious voice and awkward Russian, but with absolute and incontrovertible authority, began a lecture on European music from Bach to Bruckner. He discussed the creators and the imitators, true talent and fashion, classicism and boredom, modernism and nonsense . . . Platon listened with obvious fascination, Tartakov with a quiet smile. We drank some more wine. I opened a few more bottles. Then Tartakov got up and stood next to my Schröder. I'm not good enough to dare to play it even in the presence of friends. When there is no one around, I sometimes pick out one of Chopin's preludes. I've never had time to study and practise enough, but I do own an excellent grand piano. Tartakov stood next to it, Mr Kapp sat down to accompany him, and we heard a rendition of Tchaikovsky's "I bless you, forests" followed by the great aria from Rubinstein's opera *The Demon* which had made its composer famous a quarter of a century ago. I listened and watched. Tartakov, a youthful fifty-year-old, was obviously still someone to be reckoned with, despite all the pampering and all the wear and tear – still a first-class singer. He was a notorious womanizer, rather true to type in that respect. Recently I had heard one lady whisper to another: "*Die dicke Selig ist jetzt seine letzte Seligkeit . . .*" It appeared that the lady in question was the wife of some Muscovite textile manufacturer. I said to myself: God help them. Then there were those who held the entirely unjustified and absurdly malicious view that he was not, in fact, an exceptional artist, and that his career had been based merely on the fact that he was Rubinstein's bastard son . . . It was true that Rubinstein had been said to bear an amazing resemblance to Beethoven, and as I looked at Tartakov, it struck me that he might indeed be such a father's son . . .

The "sad Demon, spirit of exile" poured out his despair for us, not at full operatic volume – which might have endangered the glass doors of my sideboard – but toned down to the appropriate chamber-music level, without losing any of the aria's power to move us. Platon and I expressed our sincere appreciation with applause. Tartakov and Kapp sat down at the table again, and I filled everybody's glass. Then I asked:

"And your father's side of the family, Mr Kapp – who were they?"

He relit his pipe. "My father was the parish clerk at Suure-Jaani."

"At Suure-Jaani? " I exclaimed. "But wasn't *Kunileid* the son of the parish clerk there?"

"I'm impressed, Professor Martens, by your familiarity with the lives of our musicians. Yes, Kunileid was born there, and so was I. My father was old Saebelmann's successor."

Platon had lit a fire in the dining-room fireplace. As I watched the wavering reflections of the flames in the glass doors of the sideboard, and on the array of bottles on the table, my mind wandering in a way somewhat affected by the wine, I marvelled at the way fate, or coincidence, or whatever it is, manages to draw these dotted lines between people, whether they are related or not . . . Then Platon declared, with a degree of enthusiasm I wouldn't have expected from him:

"But now Mr Kapp must improvise something for us on the piano! I wish you had an organ – Fyodor Fyodorovich, you can't imagine what he can do on the organ! But I know, from our conservatory days, that he can perform miracles on the piano as well – particularly after he's had a drop to drink! Please, Mr Kapp!"

Kapp sat down at the piano. He started out in a lyrical, even sentimental mode. I thought I recognized an allusion to the theme of Tchaikovsky's *Souvenir de Hapsal*, but after a moment, his music became unfamiliar, assumed tremendously temperamental rhythms in variations that undulated, gained volume, broke, started out in an entirely different flow and crescendo, calmed down again, produced angular, hermetic boulders of musical ore that crashed, boomed, tinkled, melted, disintegrated, and finally faded away into a sunny calm . . . But the improviser didn't leave it at that. He immediately transposed that sunshine into a dark whirlwind, then let the music swell and boom in a rising spiral that descended back into the depths, rose and fell, rose and fell, until a high, dissonant tremolo – like the knife peasants will throw at a whirlwind, hoping to strike the witch inside it – broke the turbulence into a multitude of radiant light-beams that began to arrange themselves towards a finale . . .

Kapp left it at that, jumped up, slammed the piano lid shut, and returned to our table, sitting down so hard that the chair made a cracking sound. We applauded. Tartakov shouted "Bravo!" Platon shouted "Bravissimo! Well, Fyodor Fyodorovich – what do you think? Isn't he amazing?"

"Magnificent," I said, and I meant it too. "Genius" was what I thought, but I felt it might sound like a superficial platitude. We clinked glasses. Mr Kapp looked sweaty and pleased. I said:

"Mr Kapp, we mentioned Kunileid, a moment ago. I remember that someone wrote – while he was still alive, I believe – that he was a genius. Is that true?"

I remember asking that question in the fervent hope that Kapp's answer would be affirmative, never mind that it might seem improbable. And I know why I was hoping for that. It was because I felt a kind of remorse, a sense of having betrayed that young man who had been connected to me by another one of those impalpable dotted lines. If this Mr Kapp, clearly a connoisseur, were to admit that the boy had been a genius, this would relieve me from at least some of that remorse, because true genius does not need trivial support or sentimental charity. Genius makes its own way. Yes, I was hoping that Kapp would admit that Kunileid was a genius. At the same time, I had a parallel urge to hear him laugh in the sonorous manner of the superior professional, to hear him exclaim: "Kunileid? A genius? God, no!" Because if he did *not* react that way, I wouldn't be able to rid myself of the inevitable and ridiculous envy I felt towards that pale, long-forgotten boy . . .

But Mr Kapp's response was more equivocal. He waved his pipe so that small sparks flew out of its bowl, and shouted:

"What does 'genius' mean? Maybe God is a genius! But when you apply that word to a man, you're indulging in sentimental nonsense. A man is either talented or untalented, productive or lazy, honest or dishonest. And either lucky or unlucky. Of course Kunileid was talented, of course he was honest. But he had no time to create a life's work. He was cut down right at the start. He wasn't a lucky man. But he was granted one rare piece of luck . . ."

"Which was?" I asked, with a degree of curiosity that surprised me.

"He had the rare good fortune," Kapp said, removing the pipe from his mouth, "to be the first national composer of his own people."

I don't remember much of the rest of our conversation that evening. But I do recall that after my guests had left in the small hours, I sat in the dining room by myself, stared at the chair Mr Kapp had vacated, and thought: Any moment now, Kunileid will materialize in it, a pale, bushy-haired boy with beads of sweat on his forehead, and he will ask me what it is I really want from him. And I won't know what to tell him. But he didn't come. After a while, after I had poured myself yet another glass of wine and sipped it slowly, I was able to smile at that moment of anxiety. Instead of waiting for Kunileid's ghost, I tried to remember if anyone had ever referred to me as a genius, and if so, who that had been. I reviewed a long list of words of praise – *an incredible polymath, vastly erudite, exceptionally tactful, indefatigably industrious, a true humanist, a cultured man in the best sense of the word* . . . I must be ridiculously vain to remember all those epithets. But there was only one person I could remember who had applied the word "genius" to me, and that was Vodovozov. And even so, he had applied the word, twenty years ago, only to a certain train of thought of mine – my hidden comparison between Russia and the barbaric nations ruled by tyrants. A comparison I had not addressed to readers of his ilk; it had not been my intention to provide them with a handy quote out of context. And so, even that praise sounded like mockery to me. Yes, only Vodovozov came to mind that evening, and I was still unaware of the Judas kiss he had already bestowed upon me . . .

28

Kati – where are you? Why do I no longer feel your presence? There's not a trace left of you, nor of that woman who wasn't you at all, but who was here for a while – in this compartment of the dream train? There is no compartment, either. This is an entirely different space. No more purple velvet, no more polished brown wood. Dark purple, light brown. A rather repulsive combination. No, now everything is a uniform, dark grey, and that is even worse. This is a uniformly grey, swaying, shaking prison carriage, and I am rooted to my seat in it. Nowadays, these cars are commonplace on our trains. Maybe the door isn't locked at all, but I am unable to check that. Even if I could move my hand and discover that the door was locked, I still couldn't get up, and even if I could regain the use of my limbs, I still couldn't jump off without breaking my neck, because we are going much too fast.

I am alone in this shaking prison cell on wheels. All alone. With no one to help me in my struggle against Vodovozov. No matter how well-secured these prison cars may be, they're always open to those who wish to enter. But Mr Vodovozov doesn't come in through the door. He comes directly through the wall, just as Kati did some time ago, when this was a regular compartment. First his arms, then his beard, then his glasses, then his black shock of hair, and his head, and the rest of his spindly body. And I know, and then see, that he isn't alone. He is, after all, a lawyer, and he brings a witness, a strange, faceless figure that now stands behind and beside him, a creature covered in some kind of grey gauze from head to toe. Beside Vodovozov in his formal black frock coat, the figure looks like his negative, his bright shadow . . .

Vodovozov is standing right in front of me. In reality, he isn't very tall, but now he looms oppressively large, because he is standing, and I am sitting on a low bench. He is like a huge black tree, its branches full of witches'-broom, threatening to topple onto me.

He hasn't said a word yet, but there's no point in trying to postpone the inevitable, so I open the conversation by saying:

"Vasili Vasilyevich! Did you consider your own parents, even for a moment, when you wrote that slanderous article about me for the encyclopedia? Of course you didn't. Your parents were the founders of modern Russian pedagogy. Just think about what that means! Your father's primer is worth its weight in gold. Your mother's writings about Fröbel's kindergartens, and her *Book for Educators*, are perhaps even more valuable . . ." (My God, I sound as if I were trying to flatter this infamous slanderer. As I realize that, I can sense my tongue turning heavy and clumsy, and it takes a tremendous effort to overcome that feeling and to continue, with jaw-clenching sincerity.) "But you, Vasili Vasilyevich, you are the most ill-bred brute I have met in the course of a long life. Tell me who, in your opinion, will learn anything from your satirical piece about me? To whom will it provide guidance? What is its intention? What constructive benefits does the world gain from it? Why are you glaring at me through those blue spectacles that prevent me from seeing your eyes? What are you smiling at? Are you trying to say that a destructive commentary may be just as valuable as a constructive one? Well, I agree. Everybody knows that. But it is valuable only on one condition: if it is uttered or written *for the sake of some true value*. For the sake of something more universal and elevated than mere personal vanity! You reveal your desire to ridicule an old man, to dismiss him with a couple of sentences – inert, poorly constructed sentences, by the way. What do you gain from that? Well-informed people will respond to your remarks with a shrug. Some of your cohorts will hoot with joy. And you may gain a few votes within your little splinter party. That's all. Nevertheless, you've managed to sow seeds of mistrust in the minds of many, and for a long time, in regard to that old man. But what do you care? No, Mr Vodovozov . . ." (Now my jaw has gone rigid. I struggle against its paralysis, and against the heaviness of my tongue, and try to enunciate my words with the utmost clarity, but it seems to me that all I'm saying is just meaningless babble.) "Mr Vodovozov, I'm not asking for your compassion. On the contrary, let me assure you, categorically and emphatically, that I consider you to be a morally despicable individual. Because you understand perfectly well why I wrote that article that you use to ridicule me before the eyes of the world. You understand perfectly well what the word . . . 'loyalty' . . . means. And what it may . . . demand . . . from a person. You know that there are times when loyalty . . . takes . . . precedence . . . over logic. Stop sneering at me. You know very well that my article really isn't the reason for your indecent attack on me. The article is just a handy pretext. The real reason is simply my attitude. My tolerance in regard to things you don't approve of. My *apparent* tolerance – you're incapable of seeing beyond it, and you don't even want to see beyond it. It is my tolerance for . . . institutions you wish to destroy. I know you've been imprisoned and exiled, and imprisoned and exiled again. I'll admit that there is something authentic about your destructive ardour. Do you hear me? I'm willing to admit that. But your primary motive, in your article, is simply a miserable itch to create a sensation! A vulgar vanity. And your favoured strategy is the ambush! I suggest we let history decide which has served justice better – my steadfastness, or your agitation."

He smiles and stares at me with his empty blue spectacles. Then he says – I don't really hear it, but I know that he is saying this, in his deep, arrogant, well-modulated voice:

"Why get so excited? Indeed . . . Let history decide."

At that moment, The Witness steps forward, and I assume that he is coming to speak on my behalf.

Now he is no longer half-hidden behind Vodovozov's back, and I must confess that he strikes fear into my heart. All I can see is his fuzzy grey outline, and he is more bizarre, by several degrees, than the rest of this scene. He pushes Vodovozov aside, up against the wall, and out of the room – simply pushes him through the wall, and I ask myself: Will that idiot Vodovozov break his neck the way I would if I fell off the train, or won't he? I decide that he won't. His kind never do.

Now I am confronting The Witness. I'm still sitting on the low wooden bench of this prison cell, and I feel as if I had become part of it, just a chunk of wood. Or maybe it isn't a wooden bench, maybe it is just a pile of dirt, and in that case, that is all I am too. The Witness stands right in front of me, but I can't recognize his face. There are moments when he looks like a gigantic baby, swaddled

in peasant fashion; then he takes on the appearance of a huge cater-
pillar, or a cloud shaped like a human being. Now he begins to peel
off his swaddling clothes, to step out of the cloud, both slowly and
very rapidly. He holds out his hand. He is showing me something
– something ridiculous. It is a file. He stabs me in the chest with
it, at the level of my heart, and the pain takes my breath away. I
lose consciousness in one world and regain it in another. As I wake
up, I hear myself cry out:

"Johannes . . ."

29

I have returned to my spot, in time and space, to the dark purple velvet and polished light brown wood of the train compartment. Through the window I see the blue sky with its tattered windblown clouds, the spruce hedge beside the tracks, catch glimpses of fields and grey cottages. Next to me on the seat stands a yellow briefcase. It is familiar. And there, next to the briefcase, is that incongruous basket woven out of pine-roots. I remember it too. No sign of Kati, but that's understandable. No sign of that young lady, either, who got on at Pikksaare station. Well, that's not surprising. She must have left the compartment after I fell asleep in this extremely impolite, extremely ridiculous fashion. She's still on the train, though; her suitcase is right there. She must have watched the old codger fall asleep, must have smiled a little, and left ("Why should I sit here and put up with the snoring of this old professor?"). This is truly embarrassing. And it happened only because I had so little sleep yesterday, just a couple of hours with the help of a soporific. Well, I'm glad she's still on the train . . .

A conductor with a face like a wrinkled apple comes limping down the corridor, knocks on the glass windows of the compartment doors, and announces, in three languages (butchering two of them):

"*Kospodaa passassiri – Väreerte Passassire – Austatut reisijat – Walk – Valk – Valga – Valka!* All change for Tartu, Tallinn, Narva, St Petersburg!"

To our left, the first houses of Valga with their vegetable patches glide towards us and past the train windows. I run a comb through my hair, check the knot of my tie, adjust it, and step out into the corridor, where I find my travelling companion. She is standing there in a relaxed pose, leaning on the safety bar attached to the window frame. She is balancing on her left foot, the tip of her other shoe barely touching the carpeted corridor floor, and looking out of the window, her nose right up against the pane in a quite unladylike fashion. A superstitious premonition tells me it would be better if she weren't there. Yet, at the same time, it curiously pleases me that she is. Then again, I sense that it would be wiser to let her go. We really don't have much in common. On the train to St Petersburg, I should try to find a compartment to myself and try to – try to sleep or meditate, it doesn't matter. Meditate on how, tomorrow morning at eleven o'clock, at the Baltic station, I'll take Kati's hand, and how I'll tell her, still holding her hand in the carriage:

"Dearest – I made a decision yesterday, on the train, as I passed a certain village – Punaparg, but it doesn't really matter. It's a decision that will make our life, at least our life together, and that's what is really important, isn't it? – it'll make our life easy, light, and transparent, as long as we manage to hold on to it . . ."

But instead of contemplating how I'll tell Kati this tomorrow morning, or contemplating whether I really have made such a great and childish decision or whether it is only a figment of a dream – instead of all that, I approach the young lady with a smile, and she notices me, and says, before I've had a chance to say anything:

"See, Professor Martens, we've arrived."

She says those words spontaneously, unaffectedly, as if nothing had happened, with no allusion to my stupid somnolence. For a moment I wonder if she isn't simply feeling sorry for me, but find myself in a surprisingly good mood, nevertheless.

"So we have," I say. "And here in Valga, we'll have a whole hour before the train to St Petersburg leaves." I speak with an enthusiasm that makes me smile at myself (and to shrug and shake my head, at some lower level of thought). "A whole hour. Madam, may I suggest that we spend that hour in the station restaurant? It's a pleasant enough establishment – quiet, clean, and even the service is reasonable." I gaze as persuasively as I can into her round blue eyes. She smiles, looks hesitant. We are riding along a high embankment, passing board fences, gardens, houses, the tower of St John's church, the domes of St Isidore's, the flat roof of the Catholic church (we were granted our freedom of religion by decree on the seventeenth of April, 1905, but only two years ago, the Catholics still didn't have permission to build a clock tower). I look into her blue eyes. "So, we can spend a pleasant hour there, and I would very much like to talk to you again. You see, I've never met an Estonian-born lady *magistr* who is also a fiery socialist. And I find that fascinating. And when the train to St Petersburg arrives – it stops here for ten minutes, so we'll have plenty of time – we'll find a nice compartment in the first-class carriage . . . Listening to you a while ago, I realized that you are a wonderful storyteller. We'll have hundreds of interesting subjects to discuss . . ."

My own fervour makes me smile. I am surprised by it, despise it a little, and enjoy it at the same time.

"But Professor Martens – I'm not going on to St Petersburg . . ."

"Oh? But – you said you were."

"Well, yes, I will be going there. But not until tomorrow, or the day after. First I have a few things to take care of here in Valga, in our town house."

I won't say that this very moment, as our narrow-gauge train is slowing down and the daylight in the corridor is turning red because the seemingly endless brick wall of the station building is flowing past the windows – I won't say that this is the moment of the deepest disappointment in my life. By no means – but it is a disappointment, and of a magnitude that seems completely disproportionate.

I touch her elbow to steady her as we come to a stop with a light jolt.

"Just a moment, madam." I return to the compartment and lift her suitcase onto the other bench. I put the newspapers into my briefcase next to the volume of the encyclopedia. I pick up her suitcase and my briefcase. There is still that basket I bought in Möisaküla. It seems as pointless to leave it on the train as it does to take it along. I grab its handle with the hand holding the briefcase and return to the corridor. We are the only passengers getting off from this carriage.

"Is someone coming to meet you?"

"No, it isn't far. I'll take a hackney."

She walks ahead of me into the building, on her way to the entrance facing the square.

"Just a moment."

She stops in the middle of the waiting room, next to a palm tree twice the height of a man planted in a patch of dirt in the middle of the stone floor. It is a symbol of this little town's pride in being a railway junction. She turns, gives me a questioning look. A handsome woman, full of life and curiosity. And a woman who excites one's curiosity. As she turns her round blue-grey eyes towards me, the broad brim of her soft brown hat decorated with lace touches one of the palm tree's leaves; both woman and tree look rather incongruous in the middle of this otherwise rather bare and functional waiting room . . .

"Did you say something, Professor Martens?"

"Well, yes . . . But that's all right. It can't be helped. Go ahead, take a hackney. I'll help you with your suitcase. But not yet. Not immediately. In an hour."

I'm adopting the tone of an old charmer – a tone I haven't used for a long time; maybe once or twice with Mrs Christiansen. But in my day, I've adopted it in conversations with more than one woman, and even with Kati before our marriage, and during the first years of that marriage, until it was gradually replaced by a more quotidian and less self-conscious tone. I go on, puzzled by my own strange intensity and ridiculously sonorous voice:

"Dear madam – let us sit down for a moment. In the restaurant. Let's have a cup of coffee and perhaps a glass of liqueur. Let's get to know one another, even if only for a short while." As though there wouldn't have been time for that on the train, if I hadn't fallen asleep in her presence like an old fool; but I have spent much of my life persuading others, even in very precarious situations, and I've developed a theory of persuasion based on my experience. First of all, one must address people in their national manner. With Germans, one should speak in sentences that sound complicated and scientific but end with a snap and pull things as tight as the belt round an academic Prussian beer-belly. With the French, one should strive for smoothness and charm, be a little risqué, and, depending on the interlocutor, quote from either Voltaire or La Rochefoucauld. The English are best addressed in a clear-cut, dry, and athletic manner, with some recourse to historical anecdote. But that's not enough; one must also consider the personality of one's interlocutor, pay attention to the individual, particularly in the case of women. This is all the more imperative now, since I really don't have much experience in persuasive conversation with Estonians . . . As all that flashes through my mind in a rather comical manner, I realize how useless my theory and practice are in regard to this young woman. I also realize that I don't really know how to speak to her as an individual, and that I am sounding repulsively insistent and imploring:

"You see, madam, I have never met a lady – an Estonian lady like yourself . . ."

"That may be true," she says, smiling. I can't tell whether she is pleased or a little bored with me. In any case, she is entirely self-possessed, in a way that strikes me as enjoyable, pitiful, and quite delightful at the same time. "But, Professor –"

I interrupt her:

"No, please, don't deny me this hour. You see, I have this feeling that if we got to know one another even just a little better, some good might come of it. For a long time, I have felt the need . . ." Listening to my own enthusiastic and persuasive utterances with a feeling of doubtful surprise, I'm no longer certain of the exact boundary line between lies and truth. While much of what I'm saying is flirtatious improvisation, some things that have led a shadowy existence at the back of my mind are surfacing and blending into my words. If she notices that, I think, it will really make me look like an old fool. "Yes, for a long time I've felt the need to establish contact with Estonia's young intellectuals. I've had an inkling that there are these new people, new horizons, new aspirations. And now I run into – you. Just a country girl, pardon the expression, who has grown up to be a charming university-educated lady. A *magistr*. And is completely at home in the culture of Finland. And who is a scholar of the fascinating field of folk poetry. You see, I had thought that we'd have hours to talk on the train to St Petersburg. I was going to put you in touch with my own connections in Finland. I know that you're acquainted with some of the senators there – you mentioned Genetz – but I know a few other ladies and gentlemen who might prove useful to you. And I was hoping that you would tell me about the views of young Estonian and Finnish scholars, and a little more about your, well, your road to socialism. Not because (I say with a rather cheaply coquettish smile, trying to look apologetic and forgiving at the same time), not because you want to turn this old bourgeois liberal – yes, a liberal, after all – into a flag-waving socialist, but to give me an idea of your generation. Something tells me that we might well stay in touch. From what you've told me, I realize that you are far to the left of Tönisson, perhaps a world apart, and yet you seem to agree with him on many things. So I'm sure *we* could find common ground. I think I know the folk poetry of Estonia almost as well as Mr Tönisson . . . ." I smile again: "Of course I may be mistaken about all this. In any case, you, dear madam, could give me some ideas how I might support the Estonian community's endeavours, the cultural ones in particular. And perhaps even *some* political endeavours." I ask myself, for a moment, if I should tell her about Johannes, but decide against it. Instead, I say: "As you must know, there was, about fifty years ago, a group of so-called St Petersburg patriots – a circle of Estonian-born people living in the capital, among them persons close to the court. You might be interested in the re-establishment of a new circle of that kind, and I could . . . But now I find out that you're not going on to St Petersburg. So, please, let us sit down and talk!"

I'm embarrassed by my own loquaciousness. I've made a fool of myself, and she'll refuse. I can tell by looking at her that she hesitates, or pretends to hesitate, but she'll say no. Her hesitation doesn't console me at all. She says, with a smile:

"Dear Professor Martens . . ." (She says "*dear* Professor", but that doesn't console me either. The old man has made a complete fool of himself . . .) "I am sorry, but I can't. My mother is waiting for me. The last few years, she's had to wait for me a great deal. And I'll only have a couple of days at home . . . I have to meet my mother as soon as possible, and then we'll both take the train to Antsla. But the next time you come to Finland – and you do visit there, don't you? – your kinsman Doctor Martens will make sure we meet again. I'll contact him as soon as I get back to Helsinki, and I'll ask him to let me know immediately when you get there. All right? And now I thank you so much for everything. If you could just be so kind to help me put the suitcase in the luggage rack . . ."

She sees my plea as more flirtatious than it really was, and considers my "programme" more frivolous than it is . . . It seems to me that if I now made a total fool of myself, if I took her hand, and implored her, she might give in and spend an hour with me in the station restaurant. But I can't bring myself to plead with her more openly than I already have. To do that, I would have to be, I don't

know, younger, more frivolous, less self-absorbed, altogether someone else. I say:

"Very well, dear madam. But I regret it. I regret it very much."

I have no trouble imagining our reunion in Helsinki. Why not,
indeed? At the Kappeli café, for instance, on the Esplanade, over
the steaming cups of coffee we won't be having now. Or at the
university, at the folklore collection of the recently deceased Hurt,
in a room where the air has that sweet and comforting smell of dust
and printer's ink. For a fleeting moment, I can see it all in my
mind's eye. But I know it won't happen.

She turns away, and we leave the palm tree, and walk across the
chequered Vermeer floor of the waiting room to the door opening
onto the square. A few steps away stands a hackney coach, and the
sturdy red-moustachioed coachman leans down from his seat, eager
to serve. She steps onto the running board, turns, smiles, has
already seated herself. I lift her elegant suitcase and place it next
to her on the worn leather seat. I take her hand. I'm reminded of
another adieu, long ago, one that was merely a beginning, and it
becomes a background for this one that won't lead to anything . . .
Once again I think, and I'm glad she can't read my thoughts: An
old fool is the greatest fool . . . I hold the young woman's hand; I
can sense her restlessness and impatience to get going, but I'm
consoled by the way she lets her hand rest in mine. I say:

"Please tell me your name again."

"My name is Hella Murrik . . . Or, since my marriage a year
ago, Hella Wuolijoki."*

"Thank you. And forgive me for not really hearing it the first
time. Now I'll remember."

I let her hand go. Then I notice the basket woven out of pine-roots
standing on the pavement next to my yellow briefcase. I pick it up
and place it on top of her suitcase.

"Please take this basket, Mrs Wuolijoki. I doubt that you do much
knitting" – she shakes her head and smiles – "so you probably won't
use it for that, and it won't do for keeping note cards in either. I
don't know what you could do with it. Perhaps you could just keep
it as a memento of our meeting. Until next time . . ." I seem to

* (See Notes – Translator)

have run out of things to say to her. "Until next time, then."

I feel a little treacherous giving her the basket – treacherous in regard to Kati. But why shouldn't I give it away – or am I not *obliged* to give it away, since I first bought it with Mrs Christiansen in mind?

"Oh, thank you so much, Professor Martens!"

They drive off. She turns and smiles at me, I wave, she waves back through the dancing shadows of the tree-lined avenue. The wind has picked up, it agitates the branches of the lime trees and makes the wrinkled sleeves of my silk suit flutter.

With a start, I remember: that same wind is now rocking the emperors' ships up there among the islands . . .

30

I'm still standing on the pavement, facing the spot left vacant by
the coach. I close my eyes and ask myself what I should do now. I
can feel the wind blowing through the thin fabric of my suit; I'm
cold. Should I take a walk? No. I can't understand why I feel so
tired. I pick up my unpleasantly heavy briefcase and go back into
the station building.

The small restaurant is by no means a first-class establishment,
but it will do. Better to sit there than to walk in the dazzling sun
and the gusty wind that blows grains of sand between one's teeth
and raises cold shivers on one's sweaty skin.

There are about a dozen tables covered with more or less clean
white tablecloths and surrounded by cheap Viennese-style
bentwood chairs. Each table has an ashtray, small bowls for salt and
mustard, a toothpick container, all made out of cheap china decorated with blue flowers, and a vase with buttercups in it. Each vase
is decorated with a small oval cityscape in brown and blue – probably
German manufacture. Three Valgaites sit at a table enjoying their
steins of beer and their pipes. All the other tables are vacant.

I pick one in the corner furthest away from the windows and
the beer drinkers, next to a potted palm that'll protect me from
their stares; it also reminds me of its more imposing relative in
whose shade I invited Mrs Wuolijoki to join me here. In whose
shade I was, for a moment, almost close to her – only a cubit
between us.

I sit down and notice that my knees are a little shaky, for some
reason, and that it is a great relief to be seated. I put my briefcase
on the next chair (although there really is no need to discourage
people from joining me) and fall into a reverie. It seems to me that
because of the kinship of those two trees, and because of my decision
to choose this table because of that kinship, everything I'll be thinking or deciding here about my candour towards Kati – the candour
I want to achieve, the candour that will protect me (why should I

make any bones about it?) against death – will nevertheless be tainted by secrets; that my efforts to achieve honesty are half-hearted and insincere . . . Nonsense, of course . . .

Then the waiter arrives, thank God, and I order a cup of strong coffee and a double cognac – Napoleon if they have it, and they do – and a cigar, the best one they can provide.

Then I just sit there and close my eyes.

She declined my invitation to join me for this hour. But what difference does that make? Objectively speaking, none whatsoever. If I'm interested in gathering the kind of information I mentioned to Mrs Wuolijoki under the palm tree in the waiting room, I can always obtain it from far more solid sources. Subjectively, it seems ridiculous to consider it a loss – to an old man who has experienced so many losses . . . True, my life can be seen from another point of view, as a succession of completely unexpected gifts, from the very beginning. But that would only be the pretty side of the coin. I really don't want to indulge in regrets, but between the thin rungs of those gifts and achievements on my life's ladder, there has also been an infinite series of bottomless losses. I have fallen into them time and again, and have had to fight my way back onto the ladder. With implacable efforts masked by a smile . . . Yes, indeed, one loss after another. Even before I was born, I was deprived of the slight social edge the honour to be born in a schoolmaster's home would have given me. Then I lost my father. Then the miserable home we had been living in while he worked as a tailor. Then my mother. Then the corner of a room in which the widow washer-woman had lived – thus, any semblance of a home. Then I lost even my nationality. At St Peter's School I was a non-German, at the university and the ministry I was a non-Russian. In Pärnu, I almost became a non-Estonian . . . When I ask myself what language I think in, I find it hard to answer. Sometimes I think in German, sometimes in Russian, sometimes in French, sometimes in Estonian. Now and again in English or Italian, occasionally in Latin. And most of the time in a mélange of all these languages. I used to tell myself that I did so for the sake of practising them, and it has become a habit of long standing. Nevertheless, everybody to whom I speak in his or her native tongue tells me that I have an extraordinary, brilliant, first-class command of it, but also that it obviously

275

isn't my mother tongue. That is what they all say, the Estonians, the Germans, the Russians, and the French.

So what does that make me? Am I *ein unabhängiger Weltbürger von Format*, as some have claimed? Or merely a cosmopolitan loyal to the Czar, able to think in eight languages, as I assume Mr Vodovozov would say? I was also deprived of any genuine advancement within the Ministry of Foreign Affairs – year after year, and now my career is over. A member of the collegium, for almost forty years – that's what I was, no more, no less. I lost a woman I loved. Every time I think of Yvette, my heart aches. As it does right now, in a bittersweet, but also frightening and powerful manner. And I was deprived of our son, Frédéric. If he's still alive, God knows where, he probably is a brilliant, lively, intelligent, active young man, but for me he is just a thought that makes me wince with pain. As recently as two years ago, I was denied the post of ambassador to Holland. Due to the disapproval and intrigues of the Black Hundred. A cosmopolitan who speaks eight languages may teach at the university as long as he wants, but a Russian ambassador is another matter – in their opinion, an ambassador is the incarnation of Holy Russia, and someone like me must never be allowed to become that. Then, there is the Nobel Prize I never received. I've been denied it for eight years running, even though some very influential people have supported me, including Björnstierne Björnson. And finally, I have been stripped of my honour, my elementary human dignity. I have been denied the right to be discussed calmly and impartially in my homeland's encyclopedia; instead, that vicious caricature . . . I notice that I'm swinging my leg towards the yellow briefcase on the chair. As if I were able to reach it and kick it . . .

Kati, please, why don't you come and join me at this table, behind these palm leaves that will hide you from the beer drinkers? Thank heaven, I can sense your approach, I know you're here. You see, I want to confess something to you. What Vodovozov says about me in the Jefron-Brockhaus had been said and written long before he did. I've known that for some time. Until now, it could be seen only in the confidential papers of the Norwegian Nobel Committee, and it remained hidden from the eyes of the general public. That is the reason (well, there were a few others) they never gave me their Peace Prize. Count Prozor, at the moment our consul at

Geneva, caught a glimpse of the committee's "reasons against" and told me about it a couple of years ago. I haven't mentioned it to you until now. But now, today, tomorrow – I want you to know. Some adviser to the committee, I don't know who, and Prozor didn't know either, all he could tell me was that the person's initials were N.G., some unknown and disembodied figure, had catalogued all my so-called inconsistencies, along with all my so-called unethical concessions to my government. Naturally, he also listed my merits, achievements, honours and awards, mentioning that the English and the Americans were said to have called me *The Chief Justice of the World.* And more of that sort of thing. Then, however, he noted that I have not condemned war in any of my theoretical works – that I consider it an inevitable human phenomenon, and only strive to make it more humane. Tell me, Kati, how is it possible for a presumably intelligent person to come up with such a childish conclusion? It is as inane as it would be to accuse a physician for not "condemning" diseases, but only wanting to heal people!

The upshot is that I am, supposedly, nothing but the mouthpiece of a great expansionist power. My sovereign irony towards the autocracy of Russia, a dangerous irony often noticed by more observant persons at home and abroad, was something that little moralist was too myopic to recognize, despite the fact that the confidential papers of his committee would be the only appropriate document in which this could be pointed out . . . Besides, what about war? If we didn't admit the inevitability of war, we'd be complete imbeciles! I did write that war is a human phenomenon, partly rooted in the nature of society, partly in the nature of the human animal. And that is the truth! Or perhaps a serious moralist shouldn't – dear God, the question makes me shiver, but I swear that this is the first time it has occurred to me – perhaps a serious moralist should not, after all, admit the inevitability of war in such a calm and formal, almost triumphant fashion? Perhaps there is, in that admission, a touch of cynicism, hidden from myself up to this very moment? But I am *not* a moralist! I'm a scholar, I'm a politician, I live in the real world . . .

Once again I thank the deity for the arrival of the waiter. He is wearing a white summer jacket and black trousers; his narrow face reminds me of a fox. His professional experience must tell him that I'm someone important despite my modest appearance and the shabbiness of my old briefcase. He appears attentive to the point of obsequiousness, and clearly enjoys the almost exaggerated precision of his gestures.

With a white napkin, he sweeps some non-existent crumbs off the tablecloth.

"Your cognac – sir. Your coffee – sir. Your cigar – sir."

After paying and tipping him, I say:

"Excuse me, waiter . . ."

He stops, looks expectant. He thinks that this gentleman of expensive tastes who already has tipped him a rouble wants to see the menu and order lunch, which means another tip. I ask him:

"Tell me what you think: could the people in this world manage to live without fighting wars?"

He doesn't register surprise. Why should he, in his profession he must be used to people asking silly questions. He purses his thin, bloodless lips a little under the thin black moustache, closes his right eye, and says, not stopping to reflect for more than a moment:

"Sir, I believe people could live without it. But not states."

This thin fox in his fifties is almost a philosopher. I laugh. I ask him:

"But could people manage without the State?"

He opens his right eye and closes the left one.

"Sir, that question is too complicated for a mere waiter. These days. But if I may hazard a guess – no, I don't think they could."

"And that means they can't avoid war – doesn't it?"

"Right you are, sir. That's what it means."

He confirms my opinion. I laugh, triumphantly, even though I'm shivering. He smiles conspiratorially, waits. Suddenly – suddenly, Kati, I feel ashamed. Because it occurs to me that this quick-witted waiter has second-guessed me – thanks to his intuition, his experience with all kinds of customers and their expectations. He has told me what I wanted to hear. He has pleased the important gentleman. He deserves another tip. *And I have done the same thing, all my life*. Right, Kati? Isn't that the truth? That's the way I've been acting all my life. Or are you about to tell me that – Kati, where are you?

The waiter has left. My coffee cup is steaming. I knock back my cognac, quite unceremoniously, in order to get warm again, to get rid of these shivers. A warm wave runs through my body, makes me feel strong again, and the coffee will rinse this bitter taste of emptiness out of my mouth . . . How did I get into this conversation with the waiter? Oh yes, I was listing all the losses in my life . . . But why was I doing that? I remember: I was using them to convince myself how insignificant young Mrs Wuolijoki's absence at this table really is. Of course it's insignificant, but it is also regrettable. As I told her. But now, after all that, I still feel as if I had been deprived of something else, something possibly important – what was it? It escapes me. Maybe it didn't exist, after all. Just as there are times when some situation, memory, thought fragment *seems* real but somehow submerged and impossible to drag up to the surface. Enough of that.

I pick up the cigar, and just as I'm about to apply a lit match to it, it occurs to me that I don't even feel like smoking. Nevertheless, I light the long dark Havana and inhale a dense mouthful of fragrant smoke. I try to decide if it is pleasant, refreshing, calming – or suffocating and repugnant. I'm also trying to recall what my last deprivation might have been. When I get on the train, I'll think about Kati again, about our new relationship, our paradisiacal, delightful, confidential relationship. But now I'm trying to recall what my most recent loss has been. Suddenly, through a grey veil of smoke, I notice something under the bouquet of buttercups, on the side of the vase: a small, oval cityscape, and above it, in Gothic lettering, the words "Frankfurt am Main".

From far, incredibly far away inside myself, a feeling wells up, at first almost imperceptible because of the great distance, but actually powerful and becoming more so, a feeling of malaise. I pick up the vase, regretfully push aside the buttercups from its edge, and study the picture.

It is Frankfurt, all right. Not the way it looks now, not the city I've visited several times in the last couple of decades and studied with some interest, for obvious reasons. Not the pompous and boring modern city created by Koch and his cohorts. This is the old Frankfurt of the turn of the last century. In the foreground, I can see the narrow and tortuous streets lined by the dark high-gabled buildings of Sachsenhausen, and behind them, the bright blue Main river. To the left, a small paddle-wheel steamer with a tall smoke-stack, a marvel in those days (yes, eighty-nine years ago), heading out of the picture, but curiously fixed in place forever. In the centre of the view, its surfaces outlined by sun and shade, there is a stone bridge that connects this bank of the river with the island in the middle and its enormous mill building and old towers, and then continues on to the far side. The bridge is teeming with gentlemen wearing tall hats and ladies in billowing gowns, some solitary, some in pairs or small groups. I find it hard to believe that I can see all of that so clearly in this hastily painted view. So clearly that I join the people on the bridge with the greatest of ease; the image sucks me in, and I am walking across the bridge with the rest of the crowd . . .

31

I make my way across the bridge, in the slightly rowdy, anonymous crowd. Professor Martens crosses the river . . . He or I, I or he, what does it matter in the end? Even N.G., I was told, wrote to the Nobel committee that Professor Martens came from a family whose members had long made their mark in the field of international law! From a family, or a series of reincarnations . . . He or I, who cares . . .

I cross the incredibly long bridge with its fourteen arches. When I first set foot on it, I still feel warm from the cognac and coffee, but once I'm on the bridge I realize that a cold northerly wind is blowing, and by the time I reach the walls of the great mill on the island in the river, the icy gusts are penetrating my thin jacket. I also notice that what I thought were pools of reflected sunlight on the surface of the bridge are, in fact, patches of powdery, slippery snow. The wind is whirling snowflakes into my eyes, and I can feel my cheeks freezing. I ask myself why an elderly and dignified gentleman like myself is out in this kind of weather without his overcoat? My question runs into a curious wall of ignorance, and this ignorance frightens me. I'll be sixty-five tomorrow, and here I am outdoors in the winter in a thin silk jacket – what does this mean?

I manage to get across and keep walking, ever faster, it seems to me, against the wind, past the cathedral and the tall merchants' houses along the Fahrgasse. I turn right onto Schnurgasse. Now the wind strikes me whenever I pass a gap between buildings or an arched entryway. It strikes my left side, and now and again it feels as if I were struck through the heart with a sharp blade. I turn onto Neue Kräme, follow Liebfrauengasse across the Zeil, a tree-lined street that runs along the ramparts of the old town, and finally reach Gross-Eschenheimer Strasse. I have reached my destination, the Thurn-und-Taxis Palace. I hurry inside. The palace, formerly the home of an exceptionally wealthy family of imperial postmasters, has been the meeting place of the German Diet.

Having spent four years here as a delegate of Hanover, and as a member of four different commissions, I know this place like my own pocket. I know the centenary gloss of these shiny floors and stairs and chandeliers, these meeting rooms, large and small, these small Biedermeier chairs for the delegates, these thrones with swan's-neck armrests for the monarchs; in fact, the latter are less comfortable, since they don't have backrests ("nothing to fall back on," I've sometimes thought) . . . These statues of Justice, Unanimity, Wisdom and who knows what else, half-naked marble women in the classical style, cold between the snowy windows of the great rooms. And the forty-one little monarchs of Germany who may put in a personal appearance on important occasions, but are otherwise represented by their delegates.

The opening of the Diet was an orgy of grandiloquent proclamations of mutual trust, candour, and true German spirit – all the things that would earn us the deep respect and admiration of our most distant descendants. At first, each and every decision was made public, and even printed, and made available to all, but only too soon came a return to what the Hessians called *government by the Seven Sleepers*: a restoration of the old regime and all its worst bureaucratic excesses. Here in Hesse, all things were "regulated", all the way down to the exact length of soldiers' pigtails. The light breeze of genuine parliamentarianism that had wafted here all the way from England, through my Hanover, was soon dissipated and lost among the perfumes of the Austrian court and the smell of Prussian saddle soap. Until the odious Carlsbad Decrees put an end to it all. But what choices did the governments have, after young Mr Sand stabbed and killed Kotzebue in broad daylight, on a public thoroughfare in Mannheim – Kotzebue, the famous playwright who had become a spy for the Czar? And after the students proclaimed that this noble youth was, in fact, a new Wilhelm Tell? What choice did the governments have but to institute strict censorship throughout Germany – ironically enough, on Goethe's seventieth birthday . . . And what choice did *I* have but to accept it?

I accepted, and kept on working to this day in the four commissions: Financial Affairs, Highways, Borders, and Foreign

Treaties. Professor Martens hither, Professor Martens thither – Frankfurt, Hanover, London. While our illustrious Governor General, Adolph Duke of Cambridge, spends a great deal of time in London, he wants to stay informed of the activities of his delegates at the German Diet. He prefers to have them reported by his old professor of diplomacy, rather than by Count Münster himself . . .

And so, when I'm in Frankfurt, I'm either here at the palace or at home. Home – probably some rented apartment, with a view of the lime trees on the Zeil . . . Strange, right now I can't see what it looks like. With Magdalena. I help her water the flowers, and in the evenings we have a glass of champagne. I stroke her wrinkled and powdered cheek. Stranger still, I can't even remember her face too well. I don't know what causes this amnesia; it frightens me and makes me hurry up the steps of the palace. Most of the time I work in the offices reserved for the delegates of Hanover, or in the central office of the Diet, and in the offices of the various commissions. I use black ink for my explications, interpretations, plans, and drafts, and red ink for addenda, emendations, and reservations. As I've said before, I am in constant demand, in the lecture halls, corridors, staircases, in the winter garden, and even in the restaurant, where the delegates take their meals.

At this moment, I'm hurrying along a habitual route across the familiar Vermeer floor of the entrance hall. On my left, through the tall glass doors, I catch a glimpse of the palm tree in the winter garden. I can't remember where I'm coming from, and I try to forget that I can't remember, but I do know that I'm on my way to the office of the commission on financial affairs. Lord, yes, all my life I've been regarded not only as an expert on international law but also as a specialist in financial affairs – and nobody knows how little I understand about those things, and how repugnant they are to me. Not that I have anything against money, but I detest financial affairs. Now the Diet has declared that Germany is teeming with orphans, with the children of casualties of war and cholera epidemics, and wants to ask the governments of the German states to make available funds to help these orphans.

I don't quite understand how the Diet has gained authority and interest in such matters, and my own government, that of Hanover, is lodging a protest that I am to present to the Diet. If, out of pity

for Germany's orphans, I should refuse to do so, I would be regarded
as a sentimental idiot. It is my duty to present this protest. I must
obey orders, and I have to remain *im Innersten unbeteiligt*. If I
can't manage that, I won't be myself any more . . . Fortunately or
unfortunately, I won't reach the office of the commission for financial
affairs. I already know this, and it is a great relief. I have reached
the door to the office. I see it and all its details with astounding
precision. It is a wooden door, painted a cream colour, with decorative white rococo carvings and a shiny brass door-handle. Suddenly
I feel incredibly weak. My legs tremble, my knees lose their
strength. I stagger. I am falling – and the door opens, and two
gentlemen (two complete strangers – they must be secretaries of
the commission) rush towards me. They too know exactly what will
happen. In some miraculous, horrifying, but also liberating way,
there is always someone who knows exactly what will happen. These
two strangers rush towards me and catch me as I fall. They support
me from both sides and take me to a side room, some sort of office
space I've never seen before.

Then I'm lying on a chaise longue upholstered in grey silk, facing
a tall cold white tiled stove. Up on the cornice of the stove sits a
small porcelain boy blowing a porcelain trumpet. Boy, angel, orphan
child, who knows. And I am *im Innersten unbeteiligt*. The grey silk
of the chaise longue is the same material my wife wore on the
day we first met. The gentlemen, these secretaries, these know-alls
whose names I can't remember, bend over me. Their shockingly
large and wide faces smile apologetically at me, and I try to respond
with a similar smile. Then I feel pierced by a sudden pain. It is
sudden, but not as intense as I would have thought, because I realize
that one of these apologetically smiling gentlemen has stabbed me
in the chest. Since I am lying down, I can't quite see with what,
but one end of the object is piercing my heart, the other end sticks
out straight from my fine white linen shirt, and the more I stare
and try to guess what it is, the less clear its outlines become. Finally
I realize that it is a file. Indignant, I want to ask the smiling face
hovering above me why I've been stabbed with a *file*, but I can't
get the words out. Even so, he understands, smiles some more,
shakes his head, and motions to his companion to come closer. That
one is holding a pair of scissors. He cuts through the object I thought

was a file, and I realize to my embarrassment that it is, in fact, a quill. A goose quill. A writing implement. The gentleman with the scissors tosses it up into the air, and it flies away. Nevertheless, two transparent inches still protrude from my shirt front. I look at it and see red ink bubbling up and down inside it, appearing and disappearing in a strangely irregular rhythm. Now it rises higher – keeps bubbling up – *poof-poof, poof-poof* – now it overflows, and I want to shout, you're ruining my shirt beyond repair! You're covering me in this red – in this – perhaps it is blood? – but I'm unable to make a sound, and I lose consciousness . . .

32

And wake up with a start.

Thank God. Everything is in its place. Everything is completely clear. I: Professor Emeritus Friedrich Fromhold Martens. Valga Station. July seventh, 1909. The emperors are meeting in the Finnish Archipelago. On Tuesday, a consultation at the Ministry. On the negotiations with Japan. Tomorrow at eleven o'clock, Kati, at the Baltic Station.

Poof-poof – poof-poof – poof-poof . . .

That's the train to St Petersburg. It has arrived. I can see it through the restaurant windows. We'll be leaving in eight minutes.

With a bored, proud, resolute expression I pick up my briefcase (with its odious contents), get up, and head for the door. The waiter smiles and bows. Although the palm tree obscures my view of the beer drinkers, I can tell they're still there.

I walk along the platform next to the train. My nap has refreshed me considerably. My stride is firm and lively. The train keeps blowing steam. It smells of coal, oil, dust, and energy.

The grey gravel of the platform crunches under my shoes. Now I'll find an empty compartment in the first-class carriage. That should be easy; there won't be very many passengers. Who would return from Europe to Russia at the beginning of June? At this time of the year, only the westbound trains are crowded. I know it won't be hard to find a vacant compartment, and as soon as I've found it, I'll put this damned briefcase down and get comfortable. And as soon as the train starts heading towards Tartu, or even before that, I'll lean my head against a cool blue-and-white-striped seat cover, close my eyes, and think: *Kati . . .*

I'm striding down the platform, the gravel crunching under my shoes, towards the first-class carriage.

No, it doesn't mean anything at all that I had this experience of Georg Friedrich's demise, back there in the restaurant, while I was napping. First of all, I've experienced it several times before, in similar or only slightly different ways. Secondly, Georg Friedrich died one day before his sixty-fifth birthday. I still have a year and seventy days to go to mine. Thus, my critical day will be August fourteenth, 1910. I've known this for forty-five years, and on that day, next year, I don't intend to stay in bed and wait to see if the old story will come true in my case . . . The story of the man who has been told that he'll be killed by a lion on his birthday. Every year, the night before his birthday, the man goes to a certain hotel and locks himself into a certain mansard room that no lion escaped from the zoo could possibly reach. He stays there for twenty-four hours. Then, one day, he is found dead in that room. A heavily framed painting, a flower piece, has fallen off the wall and on his head while he lay sleeping. And on the backside of the canvas is a picture of a lion cub. A naïve, superstitious tale, familiar enough. I'm not superstitious, and no one has made any predictions to me. I haven't needed a fortune-teller to point out the similarities between my life and Georg Friedrich's life, and I haven't been the only one to notice them. Certain close acquaintances, students of international law with a taste for encyclopedias, have noticed them, from the late Ivanovski to less reliable adherents of occultism, not to mention spiritualism. Princess Dvoryanskaya once invited me to a séance in which she wanted to invoke Georg Friedrich's spirit. She took both my hands and pleaded with me, her heavily mascara'ed eyes wide open: "Fyodor Fyodorovich, you *must* come! It will be an incredibly interesting *scientific* experiment! Because you know what will happen? When the spirit appears, you'll lose consciousness, and you'll remain unconscious as long as he is there. And this will be absolute scientific *proof* that you *are* the reincarnation of Georg Friedrich Martens!"

I thanked her for the invitation, but I didn't go. Those people are too silly. The princess told me later that the spirit had materialized, and she wanted to know what I had been doing at that hour of the night. I told her that I had been fast asleep in my bed. She clapped her hands with delight. "There you are, now we have scientific proof! While you were asleep, you couldn't be aware that you had lost consciousness!" I refrained from asking what Georg Friedrich had told her. I was sure that the answer would have been too idiotic.

Nevertheless, it is impossible to ignore the similarities of our lives. When I was younger, I felt uneasy when I was reminded of them, yet they also gave me a certain amount of self-confidence by provoking me to attempt things that seemed to fit the parallels. There were times when I imagined that I was reliving Georg Friedrich's life, that I really was identical with him, but on a different plane which enabled me to realize myself in a new and more creative way. Later on, I simply became used to the similarities, and so I don't really know to what extent our double nature has been, let us say, the deity's doing, and to what extent my own . . . There hasn't been any exact, cast-iron, calendarial congruence between us, only a few general rhythms and approximations of the sort materialists could easily explain away as mere coincidences. A series of coincidences, in itself a coincidence. And therefore, superstitious or not, I don't intend to take to my bed on the fourteenth of August next year, and to lie there waiting for the lion cub to descend.

Here we are. I climb the steps of the first-class carriage. Mr Huik has made a reservation for me in compartment number seven. He knows that it is in the middle and thus least subject to vibration. It is a two-person compartment, and there is no one else in it. Three compartments down the corridor, two small boys in starched sailor suits are satisfying their curiosity about the newcomer, until their bony French governess pulls them back inside: *"Allons, rentrez, je vous dis. Cela n'est pas poli, comprenez-vous . . ."* The whole carriage is practically empty, just as I had thought.

I put the briefcase down and take my seat, facing in the direction we'll be going – my preference. I sit there and look at the briefcase and think that I am, curiously enough, rid of even that burden. If I want to be, I am rid of it. Then I do exactly what I've been planning to do: I lean my head against the cool blue-and-white-striped seat cover, close my eyes, and whisper:

"Kati . . ."

Yes, I know, you're here, sitting there across from me, on the striped seat. I won't open my eyes. Why should I? I can see you better with my eyes closed. Your little face, framed by smooth black hair turning grey at the temples in a touching way. Your dear little face, still pale after last winter's long bout with bronchitis. The high arches of your eyebrows, a little like those on icons, as I have noted before, and your large, observant, dark-grey eyes. Your small mouth. Elegant lady that you are, you rarely use lipstick, but always freshen your lips with a colourless flower-scented balm. Even now, a yard away, I can smell its light fragrance of wildflowers. Your lips are half-open, ready to frame a question, and your upper lip trembles in readiness for a sudden message of grief.

Don't worry, Kati. In the name of the complete candour we'll inaugurate tomorrow, I must confess that there really is something that frightens me. But the closer you are to me, the further away it recedes. It is true that the thought of death has occurred to me with some frequency in recent times. I've surprised myself thinking about it. I suppose that is quite natural at my age. But at this moment . . . No, no. Let me tell you something. Some time ago, I wrote an autobiography, one hundred single-spaced typewritten pages. I made four copies and gave them to my four closest friends, *for their eyes only*. Not long after, I had to ask for the return of all four copies, and they now rest in the left-hand drawer of my desk on Panteleimonovskaya Street. A locked drawer. The reason? One of those four friends didn't heed my instruction, wasn't content to read it by himself. No tragedy. I won't say that he broke his word, but he did abuse my confidence. Never mind who it was, I won't tell you his name. Or is that a breach of our pact of complete candour? Are you saying it is? All right, tomorrow, when we'll be talking about this in Sestroretsk by the sea, I'll ask you again. But I don't think you'll feel that way about it. In any case, one of those four was Platon. In the letter I wrote to him, asking him to return his copy, I explained what had happened. I told him I didn't doubt his discretion in the matter, not for a moment. I reminded him that he was the only one of those four who told me, after he had read it, that such a candid memoir could prove dangerous if it fell into unreliable hands. In conclusion, I said: "Dear Platon Lvovich. It is truly not your fault that I have to ask even you to return my typescript. If you wish, the executors of my estate will return it to you after my death, and you can deal with it then as your conscience dictates. Now – don't imagine for a moment, dear Platon Lvovich, that I am getting ready to die, because that is not the case at all." And – Kati – I think I'm remembering this because I want to ask myself, and to ask you: Every time we claim that something is *not* the case, aren't we also admitting that it just could be?

You don't have an answer. Instead, you're asking me if I won't let you read that autobiography. Of course I will. As soon as I can. Tomorrow. We can drive past Panteleimonovskaya, and I'll bring along a copy for you. It'll be the first step towards our candour, if only a preliminary, preparatory one. You see, I didn't write it for you. And I wrote it before our pact. Before I passed that village, this morning – the village of Punaparg, and decided . . . Thus, it is still far from complete candour, from the candour I now want to achieve. No, no, don't worry, I don't mean a puerile, pathological candour, the kind that digs around in the debris of the psyche, a sado-masochistic, absolutist candour . . . Although I have some-times pondered the idea that if a person became *absolute* in some respect, that person would also become immortal. It is probably false, and I'm unable to pursue it to any kind of conclusion. It does, however, seem to contain some measure of truth. Does it? You don't think it does? But if tomorrow, when we drive to Pantelei-monovskaya, we should find Johannes there . . . It occurred to me earlier today that he may be there: he is sitting in front of our apartment door, on the stone steps covered with red carpeting, his prisoner's knapsack under one elbow, leaning against the stuccoed wall of the staircase, and looks at me with his bright eyes. Kati, if he really is there (and I think he will be), we'll take him with us in the car, all the way to Sestroretsk, and I'll help him across the border to Finland. I should have asked Mrs Wuolijoki for her address. She would be a most suitable person to help Johannes on his way. But I know her name, and I know where she works. At the department of folkloric studies at the University of Helsinki. That'll be enough for Johannes to seek her out, and then he'll be able to make his way to Sweden, or Switzerland, anywhere beyond the reach of our police. Until times change for the better . . .

Oh, Lord, Kati – "better times" . . . The candour I aspire to will be the only "better time" we'll ever see. In our country, in our position, with our attachments, at our age, we really can't start to change anything except for ourselves. Perhaps you could free your-self from all those attachments. Women seem to be more capable of doing that. But I couldn't do it. Not me. As I've told you, I don't

290

want any kind of strenuous, painful, Freudian candour; all I want is a natural human frankness, the kind that would free people, in private at least, from the great social lie – the kind that calls a lie a lie, and a truth a truth. Do you see? At least this kind of *island* sanctuary. You know, Kati – I won't go to the meeting with Lamsdorf on Tuesday. I'll send word that I'm ill. For truth's sake, I'll tell a lie . . .

My dear little Kati. Your waist is still as slender as a young girl's. So I'll forgive you your robust derrière, with a secret chuckle. You are (see, there is no greater fool than an old fool), you are the silver jam-spoon of my life. A spoon for blackcurrant jam. With a supple and slender stem, a gilded bowl, and that sweet tart homey taste of blackcurrants.

Kati – how is it that you're wearing that grey silk gown again? The one you wore at the tea table in Nikolai Andreyevich's house, your father's house? A grey silk gown, with a pattern of small light-grey and white ovals? Elongated circles, like minuscule galaxies?

Two more minutes, Kati. No, no, I feel just fine. I feel marvellous. Because you are here with me. All my fatigue has evaporated. So I think I'll step outside for a moment, just to take a deep breath. Of that air of, shall we say, my native land. You wait for me here.

33

I open my eyes. Kati must be hiding. (This is really comical – the old man is really going round the bend. Well, let him. Who cares.)

I walk down the empty corridor and step out onto the platform.

I take a deep breath.

The long brick wall of the station building. Behind it, to the left, the green treetops of the cemetery. Sun. Wind. The emperors' ships on the waves of the archipelago. A stationmaster, another Huik, is standing ten steps away from me and getting ready to raise his red and white semaphore stick to send the train on its way.

A whole minute to go.

I turn back towards the carriage steps. I stop. Suddenly I have this thought: *If I fall down now, my face is going to smash into the small light-grey galaxies of the gravel on the platform . . .*

Mr Huik, the son of my father's friend, a self-made man like myself, comes running towards me for some reason, waving his red semaphore stick.

No need! No need! Kati is already here. The hem of her grey gown flies into my face, soft, caressing, saving me. Lord, how good I –

NOTES

293

dynasty / We do not have a care in the world / And can shout without pause / The Czar is dead, long live the Czar!

39 *tertianus* (Latin): pupil in fourth/fifth year of European secondary school

42 *gymnasium* (L, G): equivalent of British grammar school

44 *Membre du Conseil supérieur de l'Etat de Congo* (F): Member of the Supreme Council of the State of Congo

45 *Vostotshnaya Voyna* (R): The Eastern War

51 Douma (R): the Russian parliament, created by imperial edict in 1905

55 *homunculus novus* (L): literally, "new little man" = upstart

71 *"Prenez place"* (F): "Have a seat"

75 *Recueil des Traités et Conventions conclus par la Russie* . . . (F): Compendium of treaties and agreements entered into by Russia with foreign powers, published by order of the Ministry of Foreign Affairs, by F. Martens

75 *Recueil des Traités d'Alliance, de Paix* . . . (F): Compendium of treaties of alliance, of peace . . .

75 *Tome premier* . . . (F): First volume

78 *ausgeschlossen* (G): out of the question, impossible

78 *corriger la fortune* (F): to correct fortune (= cheat)

93 "Lurich and Lasker": Georg Lurich (1876–1920), Estonian world champion in wrestling; Emmanuel Lasker (1868–1941), Grand Master and world champion of chess 1894–1941

95 *skoptshy* (R): the "Castrati", a Russian sect

104 *Haug? Siik? Latikas?* (Estonian): Pike? Whitefish? Bream?

105 *Lammas, Oinas, Härg, Karusitt* (Est): Sheep, Ram, Ox, Bear-Shit

106 *Vanaperse* (Est): Old Arse

109 *Il faut une science politique nouvelle à un monde tout nouveau* (F): We need a new political science for an entirely new world . . .

112 *sans aucune cérémonie, comme un simple chien* (F): without any ceremony, like a common dog

121 *Die Waffen nieder!* (G): Down with (the) weapons!

122 *"Si de l'Antiquité à nos jours on a répété l'adage romain* Inter arma silent leges *nous avons proclamé hautement* Inter arma vivant leges. *C'est le plus grand triomphe du droit et de la justice sur la force brutale et sur les nécessités de la guerre* . . ." (F, L): "From the days of antiquity to our own, we have been repeating the Roman adage 'when arms clash, the laws are silenced,' but now we have proclaimed loudly that the laws are alive even in war. This is the greatest triumph of right and justice over brute force and the necessities of war . . ."

124 *Oberhofmeister* (G): Head Tutor

125 *Mundus vult decipi ergo decipiatur* (L): The world wants to be deceived, so let us deceive it.

139 *Gaude, virgo, mater Christi / Quae per aurem concepisti* . . . (L): Rejoice, virgin, mother of Christ / Who conceived through her ear

173 *"Gnädige Frau, gestatten* . . ." (G): "Permit me, madam . . ."

173 *"Wohin darf ich?" "O, vielen Dank! Ja, es ist einerlei. Bloß irgendwohin* . . ." (G): "Where may I – ?" "Oh, many thanks. Well, it doesn't matter. Anywhere, really . . ."

173 *"Frau Soundso"* (G): "Mrs So-and-so"

179 *"Armuline proua on siis, tuleb välja, eesti soost?"* (Est): "So madam is really Estonian?"

186 *Postimees* (Est): Postman

191 *"Kuinka kauan vielä tässä maassa . . ."* (Finnish): "How much longer in this land . . ."

203 *Puusepp* (Est): Carpenter

206 *profondément offensé* (F): profoundly offended

211 *Monsieur Conseiller d'Etat . . . n'est-ce pas?* (F): Councillor of State, sir . . . is that not so?

217 *im Innersten unbeteiligt* (G): fundamentally detached

223 "Another Carl Robert Jakobson?": Carl Robert Jakobson (1841–1882), writer, journalist, pedagogue and liberal Estonian politician

227 *katk* (Est): 1) plague, 2) marsh, swamp, bog

227 *Pest* (G): plague

227 *Pfütze* (G): puddle

227 *Sümpfchen* (G): marsh(let)

228 *"Auhv täär Strasse jehvunden"* (German with a heavy Estonian accent): "Found in the street" (*"Auf der Strasse gefunden"*)

233 *"bäi uns in dem Zimny"* (German with a Baltic accent): "back home in the Winter Palace" (*"Bei uns in dem Zimny"*)

234 *"Der weltberühmte Konflikthosenflicker"* (G): "the world-famous mender of the trousers of conflict"

247 *Kunigund? Fräulein Kunigund?* (G): "Cunegond? Miss Cunegond?"

247 *Den Dank, Dame, begehr ich nicht* (G): "Thanks, my lady, I do not desire" – a line from a ballad by Schiller, in which the above Cunegond appears

247 *Lunileid* (Est): literally, "dream find"

258 *"Die dicke Selig ist jetzt seine letzte Seligkeit . . ."* (G): "Fat Selig is his latest bliss . . ." [*selig* (G) = blissful]

266 *"Kospodaa passassiri – Väreerte Passassire – Austatut reisijat – Walk – Valk – Valga – Valka!"*: "Ladies and gentlemen passengers – Valga!" [The conductor repeats these words in Russian, German, and Estonian, and also gives the Latvian name for Valga]

272 Hella Wuolijoki (1886–1954) published her early work in Estonian, but became one of Finland's leading playwrights in the Thirties (*The Women of Niskavuori*, 1936). It was at her home, and after a concept provided by her, that Bertolt Brecht wrote his play *Mr Puntila and His Servant* (1940). She published her own version of that play seven years later.

274 cubit: a measure of length = about eighteen inches

276 *ein unabhängiger Weltbürger von Format* (G): an independent citizen of the world of great stature

288 *"Allons, rentrez, je vous dis. Cela n'est pas poli, comprenez-vous . . ."* (F): "Come back in, do you hear me? Don't you see that's impolite?"